A Regency Romance

Elisabeth and the Marquis
Book One of the House Party Series

Ann Snyder

PenZen Productions

Elisabeth and the Marquis,
Book One of the House Party Series

Copyright @ 2012 by: Ann Snyder

Published by: PenZen Productions
(www.penzenproductions.com)

First paperback printing: October 2012

Paperback book ISBN: 978-0-9857718-1-2

Edited by: Ann Snyder, Phillip Spiegel, and Margaret Cross

Cover designed by: Becki Trachsel Hesedahl
(www.redwallstudioarts.net)

Book formatted by: PenZen Productions

For more information, visit www.penzenproductions.com.

To Phil, my poet,

for your constant love and support

England
1817

One

Lady Elisabeth, middle offspring of the Earl of Chadwick, was having a bad day.

First, she'd been roused to another unseasonably warm morning by the sounds of an energetic brawl outside her bedroom door. She'd thought somewhat hazily for a moment that she still might be dreaming, but the crash of a crystal vase brought her fully awake.

Struggling out of her tangled sheets, she'd made her way to the door and opened it to see Jacks and Barton, the manor's two footmen, engaged in a heated exchange of fists and curses. From what she could understand of their curses, they'd just discovered they were both walking out with the same maid from the nearby Marquis of Edmonton's estate. Like maid like master, apparently, based on what she'd heard about the Marquis's amorous adventures.

She'd stared at the angry combatants until it became obvious they had no intention of interrupting their spirited debate just because the lady of the house was standing there in her nightgown glaring at them. So she'd walked back into her room, picked up the water pitcher on the night stand, calmly carried it back to the hallway, and flung a gallon of water on them.

After all, she thought, it usually worked on dogs in heat.

An hour later, Elisabeth entered the breakfast room. She was dressed for a day of readying the house for a visit two days hence from her father's less-than-charming Aunt Lister. She was just preparing to enjoy her breakfast when a series of shrieks emerged from the general vicinity of the linen closet.

Which turned out to be caused by a mouse nest. Which meant all the linens had to be turned out, examined for holes, patched, cleaned, pressed and returned to a scrubbed-down closet by tomorrow evening before Great-Aunt Lister arrived on the following day. And before that could happen, Elisabeth had to soothe the shredded nerves of Mrs. Mavis, a worthy if occasionally overwrought woman, who was an excellent housekeeper as long as mice weren't involved.

"Dear Mrs. Mavis," Elisabeth had said in the crooning tones she usually reserved for nervous dogs, "the footmen will have all the mouse holes patched within a few hours, and they'll set out traps. We'll be rid of mice by morning, mark my words."

"Not if those two idiots keep beating each other half to death," the housekeeper replied brusquely, not mincing words. "What am I to do with the staff in this house?"

"I think they're done with that for the moment," Elisabeth smiled. "After getting their attention with a pitcher of water I was able to convince them that any maiden who would step out with two men at once was beneath their notice."

"Hah! Beneath something is right, I've no doubt. No better than she should be, that one." Mrs. Mavis sniffed. "And how they can see to do any patching is beyond me. Their faces are so swollen their eyes are nearly slits."

"Perhaps it would be better to use some of the stable boys," Elisabeth suggested. "Actually, they probably have more experience trapping mice anyway."

"Bring those smelly lads into my clean house?" said the housekeeper in disbelief at such an outrageous idea. "Never!"

Restraining her irritation, Elisabeth had laid a hand lightly on Mrs. Mavis's shoulder and suggested vaguely that all would work out, then had beaten a hasty retreat back to the breakfast room, where she finished a quick meal before heading out to the kennels.

And now, just after noon, Charles was sitting on her chest and preventing her from breathing.

"Get off my chest, Charles," she said irritably.

Charles looked down at her where she lay in the yellowed summer grass, his dark brown eyes soulful, as her eyes narrowed to angry green slits.

"Charles!"

He licked her nose.

Elisabeth shifted uncomfortably as the dry, prickly blades of grass scratched the back of her neck and arms. Just dandy, she thought, she would be sporting a nice rash with which to entertain Great-Aunt Lister. Elisabeth would have sighed in exasperation, but her chest and stomach were being squashed by 120 pounds of Scottish deerhound.

She whomped Charles on his left shoulder with the heel of her right hand. He retaliated by licking her nose again. Then he started shifting position, sighing in pleasure as he prepared to take a nap, with her playing the role of the bed.

"Charles! You will not – oof – lie down on me, you – erk – lazy hound! It's too dratted hot, and you're too – umph – heavy!" She twisted and turned, trying to throw him off balance.

Charles, his comfort disturbed, grumped and groaned, but gave up the argument. He wasn't sure what the problem was, but he deferred, as always, to the light of his life, the human who had rescued him from a situation best forgotten.

As he moved aside, panting in the heat, Elisabeth rolled over and struggled to her feet. She shook bits of grass and brown leaves off her dress and arms. Running her fingers through her wheat-gold hair, she dislodged more debris. She was sure she looked a right mess.

"Charles, you are going to have to learn to stop jumping on people. You're setting a bad example for the others." She frowned at him as she tugged a twig out of her hair. He sat down and licked his left front paw.

"Hmph. If you're going to ignore me, there's no point in having obedience lessons today. Let's get you back into the kennels, and I had better go in the back door, I think. I need to brush off before anyone sees what a disaster I am."

Charles signaled his agreement by standing up and amiably nuzzling her waist. He knew the word 'kennels,' the place he lived now with the others. It was a nice, open area with cover from the weather, fresh well water, good food and lots of interesting companions. He was looking forward to taking a nice long nap in the shade.

Trying to look more like the lady she was supposed to be rather than the hoyden she liked to be, Elisabeth sedately made her way across the large front lawn of the family estate. The lawns, so lush and moist and green earlier in the year, had withered to a brownish yellow as an unusually hot and arid summer had worn on, week after week. Crops were dying and cattle were finding watering holes turned to dust.

Just yesterday she'd listened to her father and several neighbors negotiating use of the local creek by several estates' and farms' dairy cows and pigs. The stream still had a goodly amount of water in it, but there was no question it was lower than normal. Times would become very hard if the dry spell lasted much longer.

The peaceful walk across the front grounds was interrupted by the sounds of a carriage arriving up the gravel drive off to her right. She could see the dust billowing up behind the trees that lined the near side of the drive. No water could be spared to wet down the gravel this summer.

Charles perked up. Carriages sometimes brought people who liked to pet him and feed him treats. But as it rounded the curve of the drive and cleared the trees, he lost interest. He knew this carriage.

Elisabeth, on the other hand, came to abrupt attention. She suddenly felt hotter and grimier as she realized Great-Aunt Lister was coming to call two days earlier than expected. Of course. It was just like her father's irascible aunt to stage an early arrival to see how well Elisabeth and her father were keeping house.

She sighed. "Come along, Charles, let's see if we can slip you into the kennels." She veered to the left, heading toward the stables and kennels that lay to the left and slightly behind the manor house.

The carriage pulled to a stop at the manor's entry just as Elisabeth and Charles crossed the drive where it passed in front of the manor and turned toward the working buildings. She took Charles firmly by the collar and paused briefly to watch as the carriage drew up under the large, covered portico and the rear coachman leaped to the ground to let down the carriage steps. This was followed by the manor's two footmen, their purple faces clashing nicely with the estate's blue and gray livery, running from the manor to open the carriage door. Other servants flowed from the house, ready to assist as needed.

The young woman and her canine companion started moving again just as Great-Aunt Lister, more correctly known as Lady Lister Burton, the Dowager Countess of Cwmhaven, was helped down by a small mob of footmen, maids and coach drivers. Elisabeth's hope was to pass unnoticed and get Charles to the kennels, then slip inside the house. She would need to fix her disheveled appearance before greeting her great-aunt.

But, alas, the best laid plans gang aft agley. The Dowager glanced in Elisabeth's direction and stiffened in disapproval. Her aging eyes were still well able to see and recognize Elisabeth and notice her disarray even halfway across the front grounds. And then Elisabeth discovered the hard way that the latch on the door of the kennels, which she had noticed last week needed replacing, now needed immediate replacing.

The other dogs, hearing the exciting sounds of a carriage's arrival, had flung themselves with great gusto at the kennel building's door, and the lock had obligingly broken. She heard the crash and turned to see twelve Scottish Deerhounds racing her way, covering the distance from kennels to drive in a matter of seconds. They landed on her with joyful exuberance.

Yes, she thought from the ground, as the melee of dogs tried their best to trample her with loving affection and the servants abandoned Great-Aunt Lister to race to Elisabeth's rescue, she definitely was having a very bad day.

But at least she had learned some new and quite inventive curses this morning from the two footmen.

John Loveland, the Marquis of Edmonton, was having a bad day.

First, he'd awakened to another stifling morning of this unrelenting heat. If it didn't rain soon and cool off the land, he fully expected to see the estate's rose bushes begin to spontaneously combust.

Then his dour steward has sent up a message while the Marquis was being shaved, and the footman's knock on the door had startled his valet into nicking his Lordship's cheek quite nicely. Wonderful. It was a good thing his mother wasn't here yet; she would fall into a tizzy over the breakfast table at the sight of a cut on her precious son's face.

But although his mother hadn't been at the table, neither had any food. Something had upset the entire kitchen staff, all of whom apparently were engaged in a fit of mass madness.

"Mice," his steward, Meerson, had intoned gloomily when the Marquis had descended into the kitchens, following the sounds of the shrieks and curses. "That's what I wanted to talk with you about."

His Lordship had taken a long look at the melee, which seemed to involve his entire indoor staff as well as an astonishingly large number of brooms.

Then, without uttering a word, he'd turned around and made his way up the stairs. He'd grabbed his hat and gloves and headed for the stables. If he were going to be besieged by mice, it might as well be in a location where he expected them. And that would be the local inn.

Situated in the middle of the village's single street across from a row of shops, The Red Clown was a popular resting spot for travelers passing through the area and for the local men. It was known for its excellent food and ale, and for the surliness of its owner, who maintained a high-quality establishment, but did so begrudgingly.

When he entered The Red Clown three-quarters of an hour later, after tipping the ostler to brush and water Crosspurposes, it seemed half the village was there. Certainly most of the men. Not much field work to be done when everything was withering to dust in this heat.

He walked into the taproom and found a small, unoccupied table. He nodded to the Earl of Chadwick, whom he knew from London, and who owned a neighboring estate. The Earl returned a salute, then went back to his conversation with several of the locals about the problems the dry spell was causing for the region's dairy herds.

The Marquis sat in the dimly lit taproom, listening to the worries and complaints of his neighbors while he drank several glasses of the inn's hearty ale and ate fresh bread and cheese. He enjoyed the ale's mellowing effect as he thought about the mouse invasion and his servants armed with brooms. Where on earth had they gotten all those brooms, he wondered. Just how many damned brooms did an estate need? Was this the sort of housekeeping detail a wife would know? Did women talk about brooms over tea?

The door from the inn yard banged open and heavy footsteps made their way to the taproom bar. He looked up to see a large man accepting a pint of ale from the innkeeper. As the man turned around to face the room, he spied the Marquis.

"Monton!" he boomed, striding over. The Marquis grimaced in irritation as the bellow was followed by a hard clap on his shoulder.

"Mills," the Marquis nodded coolly to the Squire. He noticed the Earl of Chadwick, two tables over, look up with a quick frown at Squire Mills before returning his attention to the increasingly loud discussion about the weather.

"Finally decided to take a look-in at Loveland Manor, Monton?" the Squire asked loudly as he wedged into the other chair at the small table. "Been a year since old Lord Loveland passed on. Was wondering if we'd ever see you in the West County. In fact, I haven't clapped eyes on you since Wiltshire's hunting party."

The Squire made himself comfortable as he rambled on. "Not much entertainment for a sportsman like you in these parts. No real hunting to be had hereabouts. All the foxes likely have died of thirst." He laughed loudly at his joke and swigged down some ale. "So what's brought you so far south?"

The conversations in the room stilled as the village folk waited for the answer. The Marquis suddenly felt as though he were on stage. He was here to look over the estate his father's uncle had left him a year ago, but that was no one else's business.

He picked up a new pint of ale that had appeared before him and wondered a little hazily if he'd had too much to drink. He knew he'd downed several pints already, accompanied by too little food. Which he wouldn't have done if his staff hadn't been too distracted by mice in the larder to feed him a proper breakfast this morning.

"Mice," the Marquis said irritably as the barkeep brought yet another round of ale to the table. He was certain he'd had too many pints when it came out sounding more like "mieesch," but it was close enough to draw everyone's attention.

"Damn mice!" Farmer Appleton growled from the next table. He slopped his glass on the table in agitation.

"It's an infestation," said another farmer. "Got 'em everywhere. Found some in the grain bin just yesterday."

"Looking for any source of food," the Earl of Chadwick commented.

"Well I'd rather they not find it in my damn kitchen," the Marquis retorted.

"Hah! That what brought you to Loveland Manor?" the Squire asked. "You got word about all the mice overrunning the countryside? Seems like something old Meerson could have handled for you."

"Not Loveland Manor, The Red Clown," the Marquis said, although he noticed that most everyone looked confused. "Sshwhy I'm here. Sshcreaming," he clarified.

The other men in the room continued to stare at him. A few began to look slightly alarmed.

"Mice in the kitchen," the Marquis explained, enunciating his words carefully. "Everyone screaming. No food on the table."

"Not much food here, either," another patron commented, to the group's general laughter. "I'm for home."

"Aye," Farmer Appleton said, struggling to his feet. "I'll head off with ye, Marks. Might need yer arm to help me down the road." He laughed as Marks, the village butcher, tottered into another customer. "Or mayhap ye'll need me help."

A few other men stood, leading a general exodus. After a few noisy minutes, just six men were left – the Earl of Chadwick, Squire Mills, the Marquis and three others. Chadwick dragged a chair over to the table where the Marquis and the Squire sat, although the Marquis noted Chadwick was rather pointedly ignoring the Squire.

"Monton," the Earl said politely. "Haven't seen you at Loveland Manor since you were a lad. In fact, you and your brothers were all still in short coats the last time you were here."

"Well, Great-Uncle Reggie wasn't known for his sociability and love of family visits," the Marquis said with a slight smile.

"No, I'd say he was a downright recluse," the Earl laughed. "But you picked a poor time to visit this part of the island. It's been a deuced hot, dry summer."

"To be shooor," the Marquis agreed. He shook his head and tried speaking more carefully. "Meerson wanted me to inspect the tenant housing and discuss some new crop ideas. Seems rather pointless now to talk crops, though." He paused uncertainly. Had he said "talk crops" or "caulk trops"? The ale had been stronger than he'd realized.

Chadwick grinned briefly. "Yes, this is a bad summer. Hope you'll be around a while. Have you over for dinner one of these evenings."

"M'mother's due to arrive next week," the Marquis said suddenly. "Wonder if she knows how many brooms we have."

"Brooms?" the Squire repeated.

"To be sure," the Marquis nodded owlishly. "Need to get home. Need food. Got mice." He stood up carefully, resting his hands on the table while he gained his balance. It occurred to him that he might want to avoid the inn's ale in the future.

The Marquis saluted his table companions, then made his way out the door. He tacked across the stable yard to where the ostler was seeing off the last of the departing company, waited while Crosspurposes was saddled, then mounted the big grey stallion and let the horse amble back to Loveland Manor while he lightly dozed along the way.

He'd just handed off Crosspurposes to the head groom and entered the side door of the house when the sounds of loud voices erupted in the entryway. He walked through a series of rooms until he'd gained the front hall. There he found his mother, arrived a week early, clad all in black and weeping with abandon.

His heart clenched in his chest. Had someone died?

"John!" she cried out at the sight of him, then flung herself into his arms.

He staggered slightly under the attack. He might stand six feet four inches and be well muscled from an active life, but his mother, albeit short, was no lightweight. She clutched at him, weeping inconsolably.

He looked over her shoulder at her dresser. That worthy stared at him stone-faced, giving away nothing. No help there.

"Mother, what's happened?" he asked as he held her up.

"Lady Marybell has accepted Carrington's offer of marriage!" she wailed. "It is official! There's no turning back! I pleaded with her to wait for you! Her mother and I begged her, but she refused! What am I to do? What will happen to you now?"

Edmonton knew himself to be well to grass, so maybe he hadn't heard correctly?

"I'm sorry, Mother. Are you telling me you're wearing widow's weeds because your friend's daughter is getting married? As in wed, not dead?" Either option was acceptable to him, actually, since escaping the snares of Lady Marybell Wister and her mother was the chief reason he'd traveled here from his primary estate in Leicestershire. He'd never understood why his mother had so desired he shackle himself to that giggling henwit.

Suddenly she froze in his arms. Her tears stopped and her nose twitched. "John! You smell like a brewery! Oh my lord, you've turned into a drunk! And your face is cut! Have you been in a brawl? I knew I should never have let you come here alone!" Her weeping resumed with renewed vigor.

And then, while he tried to conjure up a good reason for being in such a state so early in the day, she gave a pitiful hiccough and smiled up at him tremulously. "Oh, my poor dear, you must have received word of Lady Marybell's betrayal, and your heart is broken. Oh my poor, poor dear!"

"My heart is entirely whole," he said calmly. "I'm sure she shall be much happier with Carrington." He knew he'd be much happier now that she was with Carrington.

But his mother was having none of it. "John, there's no need to pretend for my sake that all is well. I'm sure you are just devastated by what Lady Marybell has done. Why, she was almost your fiancée! But I know just the thing to keep your thoughts occupied. Yes, and to help me endure the loss of my future daughter-in-law as well. We must have a house party."

He stared at his mother as her tears magically dried up. She stepped away from him and clapped her hands, smiling beatifically. And she then proceeded to launch a battery of ideas for a house party.

Yes, he thought, as he nursed a growing headache and listened to his mother happily lay out her plans to destroy his quiet summer at one of his lesser estates, he definitely was having a very bad day.

But at least he wasn't engaged to Lady Marybell Wister.

Three

"Are you out of your mind?!" Great-Aunt Lister demanded of Elisabeth as the young lady made her way into the drawing room after having replaced her ruined gown and straightened her hair.

The Dowager's companion, a small birdlike creature named Mrs. Doty, fluttered nervously around her ladyship, waving a feathered fan and uttering little tut-tut sounds.

The Dowager Countess, every bit as petite as her companion, but made of much sterner stuff, ignored Mrs. Doty and sat bolt upright in the least comfortable chair in the room. Her spine stiff and her face furious, she leveled her attack at one of the few relatives she still had not cowed into submission.

"I am so delighted to see you, too," Elisabeth replied sweetly as she made her way to her great-aunt's chair and bent down to offer a kiss to one of the woman's powdered cheeks.

"Faugh," the Dowager said in disgust. "You still reek of the kennels. I cannot for the life of me understand why you insist on engaging in such unladylike pursuits, or why your papa allows it!"

Elisabeth smiled demurely and settled herself in a nearby chair. She was well aware that Great-Aunt Lister deplored her interest in breeding and training dogs. Especially dogs the size of small horses, as the Dowager had complained more than once.

"I find it quite an enjoyable pursuit," Elisabeth said calmly. She knew better than to rise to the bait her great-aunt dangled before her. "And I am delighted to see you looking so well, ma'am. You had quite alarmed us with your letter about the influenza in your neighborhood."

"Faugh," the Dowager said again. "I am not one of those niminy-piminy women who find it interesting to be ill. You won't be rid of me any time soon, missy."

"I'm sure Papa and I have no wish to be rid of you," Elisabeth said obediently. "Indeed, I am quite delighted to see you betimes. And so will Papa be when he returns."

"And exactly where is my nephew, missy? I should have expected him to be here to greet me."

"Well, you must remember, ma'am, that we had been informed to expect you two days hence. Had we known you meant to arrive today we certainly would have been awaiting you."

The Dowager sat forward in her chair, her back still stiff as a poker, and leveled a frown at Elisabeth. "I should expect you to always be prepared for the possible early arrival of family when you know a visit is intended. This is no way to conduct a household."

"Yes, ma'am."

"And that reminds me," the Dowager said, jumping to another matter. "What is the meaning of sending those two horrible-looking footmen to greet me? Are you deliberately trying to scare off visitors? They look like pugilists! I nearly fainted in alarm at the sight!"

Behind her, Mrs. Doty apparently felt compelled to mime the threat. She clutched briefly at her chest, widened her eyes and gave a little gasp, before returning to her job of fanning the Dowager.

Elisabeth enjoyed a momentary vision of her great-aunt falling to the ground in a dead faint, but controlled the laugh that threatened to break out. No, it was more likely the Dowager had wanted to chase after the two footmen with her parasol. Great-Aunt Lister was fearless.

Feeling what she was sure was the onset of a headache, Elisabeth gamely kept on trying to do the pretty with her father's terrible aunt. "Indeed, ma'am, you must have been gravely shocked. Perhaps you would prefer to rest a while after such an experience?"

The Dowager leveled a narrow-eyed look at her great-niece. "Impertinent miss. What I want is some hot tea. Where is your parlor maid? I ordered tea quite ten minutes ago." She checked the watch pinned to her sleeve. "This is no way to run an establishment."

"I shall just check on your tea, ma'am," Elisabeth said, nearly jumping up at the opportunity to quit the room.

"Nonsense. Ring the bell. Or don't your servants respond to a normal summons?"

Elisabeth sighed and walked over to the bell pull. She hoped the housekeeper had righted herself enough after the morning's mouse fright to be adequately overseeing the rest of the staff.

The underbutler appeared in the doorway. Not a good sign, Elisabeth realized. If Applewood weren't at his post when the likes of the Dowager Countess of Cwmhaven was visiting, some sort of emergency was taking his attention.

Elisabeth, still standing near the bell pull, took the opportunity to turn away from her great-aunt as she spoke to the underbutler. "Dorn, please check on the tea and dainties for our guests," Elisabeth said. "I assume all is well in the kitchens?" She gave him a wide-eyed questioning look followed by a severe frown.

He nodded uncertainly and began to back out of the room.

"Dorn," she said again, trying to keep her voice casual as she glared pointedly at him, "is Applewood helping Mrs. Mavis see to the departure of our morning visitors?"

Dorn stared at her blankly. She sighed. Applewood would have had no trouble interpreting her coded question.

"Visitors, m'Lady?"

"What visitors?" the Dowager demanded from behind Elisabeth.

"Ah, just some … er … small … neighborhood urchins," she said with a glance over her shoulder at her great-aunt. She turned back to the confused underbutler and frowned heavily at him while saying lightly, "The tea and dainties, Dorn. Now, if you please."

He gave her a baffled look, but nodded again and backed out of the room, shutting the doors behind him. Which reopened immediately as Elisabeth's father made his belated appearance. He'd obviously just arrived home, as he was still clutching his gloves, riding crop, and hat.

"Robert!" exclaimed the Dowager angrily. "Are you in the habit of receiving guests in your riding clothes?"

"Aunt Lister," he replied with a twinkle in his eye. "Given the choice between offending you by my dress or by being even later in greeting you, I chose the former crime, and hope the punishment will be lightened by my haste in welcoming you to Chadwick Manor."

In a lesser personage, the sound the Dowager made would have been a snort. "And I hope you understand I know fustian when I hear it. You are far too casual in your concern for appearances. And your daughter takes after you."

"Thank you," the Earl and Elisabeth said at the same time, and then burst out laughing. The Dowager's frown grew more severe. Mrs. Doty scrunched up her face for a moment, apparently her version of a frown.

Elisabeth returned to her seat, relieved to have the burden of entertaining shared.

"Well, Aunt," the Earl said after he'd made his bow and seated himself, "what brings you with such haste to our household? I had thought we had two days. I mean, I thought I understood you would be here Thursday."

"I am here when I want to be," his aunt said shortly. "Which is more than I can say for the refreshments I should expect to be offered in a well-run household."

The Earl turned to his daughter with a raised eyebrow. "Elsbet?"

"Apparently there is some delay in serving tea," she said. "I shall go inquire."

She stood again, just as a commotion arose outside the door.

"Good heavens," said the Dowager. "Is that the tea service? Is someone shouting? Are all your servants so noisy?"

The door burst open and a young maid ran full-tilt into the room, pushing the heavy tea service cart ahead of her. From behind her in the hallway came shouts and banging. The kitchen boy ran past the doorway, wielding a rolling pin. The Earl leapt to his feet, prepared to do battle with some kind of intruder.

The tea cart's high-speed entrance ended abruptly when the front wheels of the cart caught on the thick carpet under the seating area. The cart rocked to a halt, but the tea and dainties continued their momentum. And so did the maid, running right past the cart and jumping onto a footstool by the fire, where she appeared to dance some sort of jig.

The teapot somersaulted off the cart and crashed to the carpet, pouring its contents onto the Earl's boots. The dainties arced through the air and landed dead center on the Dowager's lap.

The Dowager shrieked in anger. Mrs. Doty fainted. The parlor maid continued her dance on the footstool. The Earl's astonished gaze swiveled back and forth between his aunt and the maid and Elisabeth. The sounds of the hallway melee continued unabated.

"Well," Elisabeth said after a few moments, "it looks as though tea is served."

"Well," the Dowager Marchioness of Edmonton said at the dinner table that evening, "it looks as though we'll have quite an amusing group of guests at our house party."

The Marquis regarded his mother gloomily. "I fear to ask."

She glanced up at him over a spoonful of soup. "Is that sarcasm? Well, I assure you there is no cause to speak that way. I am inviting the Benson-Smythes, the Childers, the Griegsons, your friends Sir Clapham and Lord Ringwood and Lord Wentworth, and of course…."

She continued to list names as the Marquis mentally tallied up the count. Nearly twenty guests including a bevy of eligible daughters and a few single gentlemen.

The Marquis's thoughts drifted off as he looked around the dining room. His mother, as usual, had reduced her sense of consequence not one bit despite their being in the country at one of their lesser estates. She had held to Town hours, so they were eating at eight of the clock, with no thought to the disruption caused to servants accustomed to a five o'clock service schedule.

And she had rather ridiculously, he thought, insisted on the two of them sitting in state at opposite ends of the long dining table, forcing them to nearly shout at each other across its length, and causing extra dashing about on the part of the servants.

"I am so glad you have set aside your wild ways and are ready to look to the succession," she said.

"What?" he asked, jolted out of his reverie.

"Your interest in Marybell, that was when I knew."

"What?" he asked again, feeling suddenly at sea.

"When you began seeing Marybell, and you stopped spending all your time in the clubs and running about with all those… women… that's when I knew you were ready to take a serious look at marriage."

"Well, as to that," he began, stopping suddenly when he realized his mother knew about his string of mistresses.

"After all, you're nearly forty. Well past time to start settling down."

"I am nowhere near forty," he said irritably.

"Thirty-four is much closer to forty than it is to twenty," she said firmly. "You have a duty to ensure the succession and future management of your estates. Matthew has been gone for several years now."

The Marquis watched his mother carefully. This was the first time he'd seen her mention his older brother without tears. She had worn blacks for fully two years after the death of her oldest son and his wife. His grief, on the other hand, had taken the form of unrestrained debauchery.

He'd never been much for drinking and gambling, but he'd always enjoyed the favors of bored wives, young widows, and exquisite opera dancers, who were attracted in equal parts to his looks and his wealth. As the second son he hadn't had to worry about marrying and begetting an heir. He'd been able to enjoy life, and enjoy it he had.

When his older brother and his bride had died within days of their marriage, he'd thrown himself fully into an excess of sensuality, trying to bury the pain of losing Matthew and seeking to avoid the sudden onslaught of responsibilities that had come with the unanticipated title. His rakish ways had never involved eligible young ladies, though, and, in fact, had served as a convenient shield against matchmaking mothers who'd frowned at his wildness.

But sometime in the past few months, he'd come to terms with the loss of Matthew, and had grown bored with mindless wenching. Without even realizing what he was doing, he'd begun setting his affairs in order. He'd given parting gifts to the various mistresses he'd enjoyed, and had begun meeting regularly with his man of affairs in London.

And now here was his mother, speaking calmly about Matthew. Maybe, finally, they were both healing.

"I'll never forgive his wife," she said coldly.

Or maybe they both still had some healing to do, he thought.

"And, of course," his mother said, reverting to the topic of the house party, "we must invite the local gentry to a few entertainments. I was quite delighted to learn that my dear friend Lister Burton is planning to visit her nephew the Earl of Chadwick for a few weeks. We must invite both of them to one or two gatherings, and I believe he has a spinster daughter who raises pugs or some such thing. Lady Elisabeth."

"I wouldn't know," the Marquis replied helpfully.

"Is there anyone else of note hereabouts I should invite?" she asked. "It's been at least twenty years since I've been here, and your father and I never stayed too long. Reggie was never one to encourage visitors. I know the Earl of Chadwick lives next door, but I don't recall who else lives in the neighborhood. I don't want to inadvertently offend any of our neighbors who would expect to be acknowledged."

He considered the question, but didn't have an answer. "I don't know, Mother. The last time I was here I was five or six years old. I was planning on paying Chadwick a call tomorrow morning after my ride, just to do the polite. I can let him know about your plans and ask him for the names of the local gentry."

"Excellent," she nodded briskly. "I'll write a note this evening and you can take it round in the morning."

She took another spoonful of soup, then raised her eyes to him questioningly. "Now, would you please tell me why every servant in this house is carrying a broom?"

Elisabeth woke early the next morning with a deep desire to leave the premises as quickly as possible, and certainly before Great-Aunt Lister made an appearance. Yesterday had been horrible beyond belief.

Her great-aunt, rigid with anger, had first demanded that the parlor maid and several other servants be sacked upon the spot. Once the Earl had flatly refused to allow the Dowager to dismiss any servant, she then had demanded all the servants in the house be summoned immediately.

This the Earl had agreed to do. Once the line-up of servants was assembled in the hallway, Elisabeth and her father had regarded them with astonishment. Two bruised footmen were the least of it. Several looked as though they had been rolling in dust, two had tattered clothing, and most were panting heavily.

That was when her great-aunt had made the discovery there was a mouse infestation. She had turned in rage upon her nephew and great-niece, and dressed them down with terrible anger, after which she had stormed up the stairs. Mrs. Doty, now back on her feet, had bobbed after the Dowager like flotsam in a boat's wake.

At that point the Earl had pithily informed his servants they were all idiots, ordered them to clean themselves up, and instructed the male servants to meet him in the stables in half an hour to make plans for ridding the house of mice.

Now, before sunrise, Elisabeth stood and stretched, then quickly washed and dressed. It was another warm, close morning, so she donned a lightweight flowing, pearl gray dress that would allow her to walk freely across the grounds. She tied her long wheat-colored hair back in a ribbon, decided she could do without a hat, and hurried down the back stairs, out the kitchen door, and to the hound kennels.

The thirteen occupants stood hopefully as she arrived at the door, waiting patiently to see what she did next. They appeared to be restored to their usual calm, placid behavior after yesterday's brief romp all over her person.

"You will be good for me today, won't you?" she asked the deerhounds as she opened the door and stepped inside.

They gazed somberly back at her, which she took to signal agreement.

She opened the building's door wider, and the dogs trotted outside. She followed them out and closed the door behind her, noting its new latch with satisfaction. The dogs formed a half circle as they gazed at her. Most were various shades of gray, but a few brindles and one red completed the pack.

"We're going for a walk," she said.

At the magic word, the dogs turned as one and began to amble with her toward the rear of the property, over a rise and down into a dell where a line of trees bordered a creek. Despite the lack of rain, enough water still ran in it that Elisabeth knew she would find a cool early morning mist over the streambed and among the trees.

As the group approached the edge of the property, a few of the dogs took turns leaving the circle and dashing after various small game lured to the area by the water source, but quickly returned at a whistle from their mistress. She would smile and stroke each dog's neck upon its return, watching as they tucked back their small ears in contentment.

A slight breeze wafted over the hillock behind the group, but not enough to yet disturb the mist that hung over the stream and nearby trees. Elisabeth led her hounds into the trees, where the mist closed around them as a cool, refreshing presence, separating them from the rest of the world.

This must be what it felt like to live in the clouds, thought Elisabeth as she and the dogs made their silent way to the stream's edge and then walked alongside it. The dogs happily caught scents, lapped up some water, and looked about them for more game, but in general they were content to bide their time by their mistress's side.

"Shall we just stay here all morning?" she asked her companions. Thirteen sets of alert eyes raised themselves to her, working to divine the meaning of her words.

It was a nice thought, but soon the mist would rise and the day would turn to heat, even in the stands of trees that lined the water. But at least she would enjoy the moment.

She rambled along the stream's edge, looking for rising trout and enjoying the peacefulness of the mist-shrouded world. Every few minutes a dog would sidle up next to her seeking a bit of affection. Elisabeth smiled at them and absently stroked each dog as it wandered near her.

Most of these hounds she had raised from puppies, continuing a long tradition her mother's family had started in Scotland many generations ago. They had been granted the original four dogs by a king grateful for service to the crown, and had become known as breeders of some of the country's finest deerhounds.

Other dogs had joined the pack in different ways. Charles had come to her after being rescued by her father from a life of toil and abuse. The dog had been tied to a turnstile attached to a butter churn, and spent his days walking in a circle in a small fenced area near the side of the farmhouse. Her father had been riding home from a visit to his brother when he had come upon Charles being beaten by his owner for trying to sit down.

Money had gone into one set of hands and Charles had gone into the other. From a frightened, stand-offish animal, Charles had grown into a loving and trusting dog, but he could be shy of strangers. Two other dogs, another gray and one of the brindles, also had come to her from situations where they had been mistreated.

"What do people want dogs for if they cannot treat them well?" Elisabeth asked Cork, the rescued brindle.

Cork raised his head and gazed at her with quiet affection. He was the smallest of the deerhounds, but since his withers still rose nearly to her waist, he wasn't by any means a small dog. Had he been fed adequately as a puppy he no doubt would be as large as most of the others.

Elisabeth found some berries still on the bushes, but left them for any enterprising animals that might find them, and that certainly needed them more than she did.

Dogs came and went from her as she walked along the bank. She watched them disappearing and emerging from the fog, until she glanced at the fob watch she wore suspended from her waist.

"Goodness! It's past time for breakfast, friends! Let's head home." As she turned to walk up the slope from the stream, every dog swiveled its head and perked its ears at a distant sound. A moment later she heard it, too – the soft clip clop of horse hooves approaching from the nearby field.

A few of the dogs at the front of the circle surrounding her led the way up from the stream as she and the others followed. Emerging from the mist she encountered the transfixed gaze of a rider on a large, grey stallion.

Elisabeth and the rider stared silently at each other for several long moments until his horse moved restlessly and began to shy at the sight of the thirteen large hounds. She gave her dogs the command to stand still, and then waited while the man quickly and effectively controlled the nervous stallion.

When he had stilled the horse and turned his attention to her again, she put one hand on Turk, a brindle and the largest of the hounds, and asked calmly, "Who are you and what are you doing on my land?"

The Marquis had set out early in the morning on his favorite hack, Crosspurposes. The large grey stallion covered ground with a combination of distance-chewing speed and smooth strength. Obliging in the country, but skittish in town, Crosspurposes was not unlike his owner, the Marquis thought with a smile.

He'd planned on riding over his property for an hour or two, then seeing if the Earl of Chadwick was about, when he would do his mother the service of gathering information about the local gentry. Man and horse ranged about the fields for a while, enjoying the opportunity to get some exercise before the heat of the day made being outdoors a misery.

"Blasted weather," he groused. "Come on, Cross, let's have a run."

The stallion came to attention at the light snick of reins on his neck and the pressure of knees against his sides, and surged forward. Horse and rider flew across fields, down lanes, and along meadows until the Marquis gradually pulled back on the reins, encouraging the horse to slow to an easy walk.

The Marquis judged it soon would be a reasonable time to drop off the invitation and possibly catch the Earl at home after breakfast, but first his mount needed some water. He knew the bank of fog he'd glimpsed at different points during the ride hid a stream that ran through several estates in the area, including his, so he turned Crosspurposes toward it, allowing the horse to take his time and cool down.

As they ambled toward the water, the Marquis admired the old oaks that appeared at the edge of the mist. He brought the stallion to a standstill while he took a few moments to enjoy the scene. He dearly loved the country. And it had been far too long since he'd been in this part of England.

The mist hung still and silent. But then, just as he was about to motion his horse forward, the fog seemed to come to life. He watched as it began to roil and churn, almost with intent. The hairs on his arms and neck rose as eerie, dark shapes began to emerge. He fought the urge to cross himself.

What was he seeing? He stared as the shapes gradually resolved themselves into a large gray animal, followed by another, then several more. More of the creatures silently padded out of the mist, forming a circle as they moved toward him. He felt Crosspurposes tense.

And then, amid the animals, appeared a woman. She wore a flowing dress the color of the mist, almost as if she had been created from the mixture of air and water. He stared transfixed as she stepped forward – willowy, impossibly lovely, with long wheat-colored hair flowing behind her in the light breeze stirred up by the moving fog. Her eyes, the color of green leaves, gazed at him unblinkingly.

The Marquis and the young woman stared silently at each other for several long moments. But Crosspurposes had had enough. The horse was close to taking fright, and the Marquis didn't blame him. Was this real? He could almost believe the woman and the animals were a vision. Then the horse shied and the Marquis wrenched his attention from the young woman and her animals while he settled his mount.

Once he had the stallion under control, he turned again to the sight before him. At which point the spell was broken as the young woman asked calmly, "Who are you and what are you doing on my land?"

Seven

Elisabeth watched as the rider made a brief, automatic bow from his saddle. "I'm the Marquis of Edmonton," he replied. I'm not certain whose land I'm on, but I'm bound for the Earl of Chadwick's home."

He saw her eyebrows rise in surprise. "To what purpose?" she asked.

Now it was his turn to raise his eyebrows. "I'm not sure what business it is of yours, but I'm making a social call. And you are…?" He let the question hang in the air.

She eyed him a moment before replying. "I am Lady Elisabeth, daughter of the Earl of Chadwick, so it is a bit of my business, I think," she said, gazing steadily at him.

"You're the Earl's daughter?" His eyes skimmed over her person. Surely, he thought, this flaxen-haired beauty with the leaf-green eyes couldn't be the spinster daughter his mother had mentioned who raised pugs. He nearly laughed aloud at the incongruity of the description.

She scowled slightly as he clearly bit back a laugh. He was just as she'd imagined – an arrogant rake, above being pleased by others, and with no concern for any but himself. Riding on her family's land without a by-your-leave, she thought irritably, ignoring the fact that everyone in the area made free with each other's fields.

"You find that amusing?" she asked. She lightly stroked one of the dogs as it grew restive at the pause in their stroll. Rude man, she thought. Handsome, but rude.

"Are you his only daughter?" he asked in reply, then immediately wanted to kick himself. Lord, he thought, what had come over him, to ask such an inane question? But surely this wasn't the daughter his mother had described.

She narrowed her green eyes at the question. "Why is that any concern of yours? And I don't believe my father is expecting you, because he has mentioned nothing to me, so I suggest you turn about and ride that big beast back over your own fields. Or are you in the area too infrequently to know which lands are yours?"

He narrowed his blue eyes right back. Perhaps there was a good reason she was a spinster after all, he thought, irritated by her attitude. There was no reason he couldn't ride wherever he wanted without being questioned by a rude little country cousin. He'd never seen her in town. Maybe the Earl was ashamed of her manners.

"Are you suggesting your father must clear his visitors with you, miss?" he asked, throwing all his arrogance into the words.

"If you really are on the way to see my father and you won't turn back, then I suggest you proceed," she said coolly. "No doubt he will be much delighted at your neighborly condescension." She turned away with the obvious intent of starting off across the field. He watched as the dogs, almost in unison, turned and began pacing with her, still flowing around her in a protective circle. "I'm heading back to the house now," she said, glancing back at him, "if you would care to follow me."

He smiled grimly. Rarely had he heard such disinterest in a young woman's voice. And he'd be damned if he'd trail behind her like a lackey in her train.

"Much as I am honored by your welcoming offer, Lady Elisabeth, I need to let Cross get a drink of water." He motioned the horse forward toward the trees and stream. "You may tell your father I hope to see him in a little while," he said dismissively.

Elisabeth stopped abruptly and turned back toward him. He watched in fascination as the dogs swiveled with her, all now facing him. Not hostilely, he thought, but he wasn't entirely sure.

"Don't worry," she said drily, seeing his uncertain glance, "I won't sic them on you. Unless you deserve it."

"And would letting my horse rest a while and drink some water be deserving?"

"Of course not. I have no reason to wish him harm."

"Charming," he said softly, but she was certain he'd meant for her to hear the word.

She crossed her arms and tsked. She had half a mind to sic the dogs on him just to teach him a lesson, but that wouldn't be fair to the magnificent beast he was riding.

"I would wait while you water your horse," she said, "but it's time to return the dogs to their kennels. The house is just over that rise," she pointed. Then she turned and, still surrounded by her pack, made her way home.

The Marquis dismounted and led Crosspurposes through the strip of trees bordering the stream and toward the water he could hear babbling through the rising mist. It seemed like the perfect spot to relax for an hour or so. After meeting the Earl's daughter he wasn't exactly in a hurry to finish the ride to Chadwick Manor.

"Well, Cross, that's one neighbor I don't have to worry about chasing me," he said as the stallion bent to take some long laps of water. "Unless, of course, she and her hounds take after me for the crime of being male. Do you suppose there actually is another sister who raises pugs? Perhaps several sisters, each with a favored breed."

Crosspurposes snorted in reply and returned his attention to the fresh water.

The Marquis glanced behind him, thinking about those magnificent green eyes. An astoundingly beautiful woman. Beautiful and shrewish. A dangerous combination, he thought, one that could ensnare a man into a life of misery.

Up the rise, Elisabeth was sharing similarly critical thoughts with her companions.

"And how rude he was," she complained. "Laughing at me. Treating me like a country servant. Horrid man. I hope he plans only a short stay in these parts." Oh, but what beautiful deep blue eyes he had. And she had felt the insane urge to reach up and run her fingers through his thick black hair. He wore it a little long, and it had become tousled during his ride. She had wanted to straighten it for him.

It was just like a man to be so good looking and so uncivil. He was the kind of man whose looks could seduce you into falling head over heels for him, and then subject you to casually delivered insults the rest of your life.

"Terrible man," she said, as she topped the rise and paused for a moment to view the estate grounds before turning toward the kennels.

The Marquis and Crosspurposes paused at the crest of the rise that separated Chadwick Manor's main grounds from the woods near the stream. From this point, the Marquis could look down on the manor house and the nearer outbuildings, which included the stables, kennels, and other structures.

The view was impressive. The fields in the distance were well-tended, and the nearer grounds and gardens were laid out to take advantage of the views afforded by the manor's many large windows. The house and other buildings were constructed of the local stone, and no signs of neglect appeared anywhere.

A well-run property and an affluent landowner, the Marquis decided. He knew the Earl from London, but they were not close friends. The generational difference led to different party invitations and interests, but he'd always found Chadwick an interesting conversationalist and he'd heard nothing but positive comments about the Earl from mutual acquaintances.

Prodding Crosspurposes forward, the Marquis rode up to the entry, which was protected from the elements by a large portico. From his vantage point on the rise he'd seen that the manor was shaped like a cross, with the top of the cross consisting of the front entry and portico that projected out into the drive. On each side of the entry, the arms of the cross held two large bow windows that gave sweeping views of the front lawn.

The two side wings also featured long lengths of French doors along the sides, leading to terraces on the first floor and balconies on the second floor. The fourth wing, the stem of the cross and the longest section, obviously contained the main living and working areas of the house. It stretched out toward the back of the estate and rose to three stories, with the top level no doubt reserved for the servants' quarters.

The stables and kennels sat on this side of the manor, just below the rise where he and Crosspurposes had stopped. Farther off, behind the house, he could see a cluster of buildings that included a large glass structure, which no doubt functioned as a hothouse to grow fresh produce during the winter.

As the Marquis brought Crosspurposes to a halt under the portico, the manor's entry doors swung open and a footman ran forward to help hold the horse as the Marquis dismounted. He stared at the servant's battered face, unsure whether to release his stallion to the man's care. But the footman seemed to know horses, and promised the animal would receive a rubdown and oats as he led Crosspurposes toward the stable.

The Marquis strode up the steps to where a butler held open the door. He pulled out a card and handed it to the man, announcing his hopes of finding the Earl in and available to see him.

"Yes, my Lord. Lady Elisabeth informed us you would be arriving. Barton, here, will take your things. I'm Applewood, my Lord. If you'll just follow me?"

The Marquis pulled off his gloves and handed them, along with his whip and hat, to Barton, another footman with a battered face. As the footman retreated with the items to a nearby table and rack, the Marquis made a careful inspection of the butler, but saw no signs of injury on that man's visage.

Applewood led the Marquis to a pair of wide doors set back to the right of the entry hall. The butler opened the doors and announced, "The Marquis of Edmonton to see you, my Lord."

The Marquis entered a spacious room that took up the ground floor of one of the manor's side wings. The room obviously served as an office, library and men's gathering place. Bookcases lined the back wall to the left behind a large desk. Along the front wall to the right were a series of French doors on either side of a large bow window. A fireplace at the far end of the room, also framed by French doors, stood empty, waiting for cooler weather. Groups of chairs were arranged throughout the space for visiting. The Earl stood up with a welcoming smile and moved from behind his desk to greet the Marquis with a firm handshake.

"Welcome, Monton. Have a seat. Would you care for something to drink? I've no doubt it was a hot ride over here despite still being morning." He ushered the Marquis to a seating area near a pair of large French doors where four comfortable chairs were grouped around a small table.

"Thank you, Chadwick. I should very much like whatever you have that's cool."

The Earl turned toward the butler. "Applewood, bring us some of that fresh lemonade Mrs. Mavis just made, and a few macaroons or whatever else is available."

The Marquis lowered himself into a chair with a pleased sigh. "Thank you, that sounds like an excellent proposition. I noticed the conservatory as I rode in. I take it you've imported some lemon trees?"

"And some other tropical fruits," the Earl nodded. "Brought most of 'em back from my Grand Tour nearly thirty years ago, before Napoleon all but destroyed the Continent. Took a year, saw most of the major cities of Europe, but I spent most of my time in southern Europe and northern Africa."

"My Grand Tour was much more abbreviated," the Marquis said. "But I've had the pleasure of visiting many of the countries around the Mediterranean. I developed a taste for Turkish coffee in the mornings, and have a standing order with a London shipping firm to keep me in supply."

"I too prefer tea or coffee in the morning," the Earl said. "I'm not much of a believer in ale for breakfast, as most folks are hereabouts. And it was pretty obvious yesterday you're not used to ale for breakfast, either." This last was said with a humorous glint to the Earl's eyes.

The Marquis laughed. "Lord, no, and I'm sure I made quite the fool of myself yesterday. Hadn't had much for dinner the night before, and nothing to eat all morning.

Half the pantry had to be tossed because of a mouse invasion."

"Yes, heavy rains this spring caused a lot of early grass growth and an explosion of mice in the fields. Now it's hot and dry, we have mice everywhere, but no rain. The crops are drying up and the mice have moved indoors looking for food."

He paused as the butler re-entered, carrying a tray laden with a pitcher of iced lemonade, two glasses, and plates of macaroons and meat pasties.

"Excellent, Applewood, thank you," the Earl nodded. "Help yourself, Monton. I don't stand on ceremony when the women aren't around."

"Women?" the Marquis asked, as he helped himself to a glass of lemonade and a few pasties. "I know you have at least one daughter; my mother mentioned a daughter who raises dogs. I believe I met her this morning on my way here."

"Yes, I heard. That was Elisabeth, my middle child," the Earl said. "I have three children, all grown – two daughters and one son. Elisabeth still lives at home; my son and younger daughter are married and running their own establishments. But right now my mother's sister is visiting us. And when Aunt Lister is around, all ceremony must be observed."

"Ah, yes, my mother mentioned a friend of hers was staying here. Which puts me in mind of why I came by today. M'mother plans to throw a house party. I am tasked with inviting you and your family to attend some of the events as day guests, and with finding out whom else in the neighborhood she must invite to avoid slights." The Marquis pulled out the sealed invitation and handed it to his host.

"Good gad, I ain't the person to ask whom to invite," the Earl said in horrified accents as he accepted the envelope. "For that we'll need to talk with my aunt and daughter." His shoulders seemed to slump. "Ah, well, I probably should bring you to Aunt Lister's attention before you leave anyway. Pity. I generally try to avoid her until dinnertime."

The Earl finished his lemonade, stood, and walked to the library's doors. He opened them and called for Applewood.

A different male servant appeared instead, explaining in formal tones that the butler had been called to deal with a few small matters in the kitchens.

"No doubt," the Earl replied drily, "the small matters come with whiskers and beady eyes."

When the servant ventured no comment, the Earl sighed briefly, and then got back to business.

"Dorn, see if Lady Burton and my daughter are available to receive a visit from the Marquis of Edmonton. We need their assistance with a matter for the Dowager Marchioness of Edmonton."

As the servant trotted up the stairs to the ladies' morning room, the Earl turned back to the Marquis with a smile. "That was Dorn, the underbutler. Good man, but a little too humorless and much too aware of his recent promotion."

"I noticed your butler has the same last name as my man," the Marquis commented.

"Yes, they're brothers," the Earl nodded. "There's a third Applewood brother who serves as a butler at another estate in the neighborhood. I'm told there's a fourth Applewood butler serving somewhere in Town. All from a local family."

A moment later the underbutler returned with the message that the Dowager Countess of Cwmhaven and Lady Elisabeth would be pleased to welcome the Marquis.

"Excellent," the Earl replied heartily. He promptly spoiled his show of enthusiasm by turning to his guest and saying, "Well, let's get this over with, shall we?"

The three men, with Dorn in the lead, walked up the center flight of stairs that led from the main entry to the second story. They turned to a room to the right, immediately above the Earl's study.

As they entered, the Marquis noted it was laid out in a similar fashion to the room below, with a fireplace at the far end of the room across from the doorway, French doors on either side of the fireplace that opened onto a balcony, bookshelves and a desk along the left wall, and sitting areas to the right by a large bow window flanked by more windows along the front side of the wing. But the décor was entirely feminine and light – pale creams and peaches, with light-colored wood furniture. Nothing fussy, but a room that clearly was the domain of the women of the house.

Dorn announced them with a slight flourish, then exited the room, closing the doors behind him. The Earl noticed the older of the two women nodded approvingly at this small display of pretension. Yes, this would be someone his mother would call a friend.

The Earl strode forward to make the introductions. "Aunt Lister, may I make you known to Lord Loveland, the Marquis of Edmonton," the Earl said formally. "My

Lord, this is my aunt, Lady Burton, the Dowager Countess of Cwmhaven." As the Marquis bowed over the Dowager's hand, he caught a coldly appraising expression pass through her pale eyes before she returned a small nod.

"And you've already made the acquaintance of my daughter, Lady Elisabeth," the Earl said. He stepped back to stand slightly behind and to the side of the Marquis.

"But not formally," the Marquis smiled. "How do you do, Lady Elisabeth? I almost didn't recognize you without your hounds." He bowed over her hand. He briefly admired the gown she'd changed into after her walk. In the pale yellow dress with white trimmings she looked like a bright summer day, he thought.

She acknowledged him with a cool nod. "I'm so glad you were able to find your way here," she said.

The Dowager raised her eyebrows at her great-niece's tone. Elisabeth shot her great-aunt a mulish glance, knowing she would be in for a trimming after their guest departed. She returned her attention to the Marquis, and was quite sure she saw him biting back a grin.

"We understand you have a request for us on behalf of your mother?" Elisabeth asked.

"Yes, my ladies. My mother has asked me to extend an invitation to the three of you to a series of events she will be hosting at a house party. She also asked that I inquire of you the names of other families in the neighborhood who should be invited to join the festivities."

The Dowager smiled, a rather frightening look on her harsh face. "A house party. Excellent! It will be a welcome change after Lord Loveland's hermitlike behavior for so many years." She turned to her nephew.

"Robert, why have you never thought to do such a thing? It would be just the way to introduce your daughter to a wider range of acquaintances!"

A small woman the Marquis hadn't noticed before, from her place in a chair set slightly back from the others, shuffled her feet and silently clapped her hands, beaming in delight.

"I am quite happy with my current set of acquaintances," Elisabeth said in a low voice, two spots of color pinking her cheeks.

"Nonsense," her great-aunt said briskly. "The fact that you are still unmarried at twenty-four is proof enough that you need to meet more people. And since you refuse to go to London, a house party is just the thing to bring London to you."

The Marquis tilted a particularly wicked smile at Elisabeth, who was now bright pink from a combination of rage and embarrassment. "I can assure you there will be several eligible men coming from London for you to add to your list of acquaintances, Lady Elisabeth."

She glared at him and would have stood and stalked out of the room if her great-aunt had not clamped a viselike claw around her wrist. She dearly wanted to tug free, but refused to grant the Marquis the pleasure of such a spectacle. Instead, she opted to return the insult.

"Eligible?" she asked. "But aren't they friends of yours?"

The Dowager gasped.

"Yes, they're friends," he replied, slipping under her thrust, "but I think they might like you all the same."

The Marquis heard the Earl make a choking sound, but kept his attention fixed on the bad-tempered beauty who gave every indication of wanting to kill him. Or possibly she wanted to murder her great-aunt. Or both.

The Dowager rushed in before her great-niece could get out whatever next horrible insult she obviously intended to toss at their guest. "You said you wanted to know about the local gentry."

"Yes," the Marquis said politely, moving his gaze from Elisabeth to Lady Burton. "My mother is eager to ensure no one is slighted by being inadvertently left off the guest list."

"Well," the Dowager sat up straighter. "I think the best approach is for me to meet with your mother. But offhand I know she will want to invite Lady Downs to a dinner or two, and of course Squire Mills. He may be a mere squire, but he is a close relative of Baron Wiltshire."

Both the Earl and his daughter tensed at the Squire's name. Bad blood there of some kind, the Marquis thought, remembering the Earl's coldness to the Squire at The Red Clown.

"There are Vicar and Mrs. Smithers," Elisabeth added.

"Yes, of course," the Dowager nodded. She turned to the Marquis. "Please let your mother know I will visit her tomorrow afternoon if convenient. I collect there are several local gentry she will want to invite to her larger doings. I shall discuss it today with Elisabeth and bring a list."

She smoothed her skirts and signaled to her companion to ring for a second cup of tea. "And now," she said, addressing herself to their guest, "why don't you join us for a spell and share the latest titbits from London?"

The Marquis and Earl both seated themselves. The Marquis launched into a discussion of topics he thought might be of interest to the Dowager, as fresh tea and biscuits were brought in and passed around.

The visit was painful. The Marquis talked and the Dowager interjected with questions, but they might have been the only two in the room. Lady Elisabeth sat mute, glaring at their guest, while her father leaned back in his chair and watched the others with a faint smile. The Marquis wondered how long it would be before he could politely extricate himself from this dreadful social call.

After half an hour had passed, the Earl suddenly rose to his feet and offered their suffering guest an escape route. "Well, my dears," he said, "I need to attend to some business with one of the tenant farmers, and I daresay Monton has similar calls to make. If you will excuse us?"

The Dowager nodded regally, once again clamping her hand around her great-niece's wrist. "It has been a pleasure," she said. "I shall look forward to seeing your mother tomorrow afternoon."

The Marquis bowed and the Earl gave a brief salute as they left the room. Once on the stairs, both men simultaneously took a deep breath and released a gusty sigh.

The Marquis retrieved his items from Applewood, who had finished dealing with the "small matters" in the kitchen, and politely took his leave, heading toward the stables. Applewood closed the doors behind the visitor and turned to the Earl.

"All in all, not so bad," the Earl answered the butler's unspoken question. "At least none of them came to blows."

The butler nodded politely. "As you say, m'Lord."

Elisabeth did not encounter the irritating Marquis for the next two weeks, although his presence was inescapable. Everywhere she went in the village the talk was about the fact that the Marquis and Dowager were visiting their West Country estate for the first time in more years than anyone could recall.

"Isn't it a wonder?" Mrs. Marks, the butcher's wife, said gleefully as Elisabeth made a selection of cuts to be delivered to the manor. "Mrs. Milgard saw him just t'other day and he smiled at her. Actually smiled!"

Elisabeth nodded politely, making her escape as quickly as possible, only to hear similar comments at each shop she visited. The miller's wife, the local seamstress, the blacksmith's wife – all were agog at the kind condescension of their noble neighbor, singing his praises and sharing stories of sightings. Elisabeth didn't suppose they had been treated to his cutting comments the way she had, she thought darkly, ignoring the fact she had delivered her own share of snide remarks to him.

And then, as if all the comments and thoughts about the Marquis had at last conjured the man himself, there he was.

She bristled as he approached. She was driving her gig, and although her horse was a charming little grey with excellent lines, she would rather have encountered him while riding Shadow and wearing her new riding habit. But no, she thought with irritation, here she was driving a cart with supplies from town, while he appeared to advantage on that magnificent beast of his.

The Marquis swept her a practiced bow from the saddle, his laughing eyes accurately assessing her mood. "Well met, Lady Elisabeth. Out running errands, I see. But where is your pack?"

"I have just the one today, Lord Loveland." She gestured toward the back of the gig, where a large gray head now raised itself and gazed placidly at him over the edge of the cart.

"My God, Monton, what is that creature?" said a shocked male voice.

Elisabeth jerked her head to the right, where she saw a second rider holding his horse at a stand. She was stunned. She had been so focused on the Marquis that she hadn't noticed his companion. She glanced back at the Marquis, awaiting an introduction.

He raised his eyebrows at her mockingly and held her gaze as he spoke to his friend. "That, Rodney, is a Scottish deerhound. A fierce beast, as you can see." This was said just as Charles yawned and settled back into the gig. Elisabeth felt a blush rise to her face at her dog's lack of concern.

The Marquis's polite smile widened to a grin. "And allow me to make you known to my companion, Lady Elisabeth. This is Sir Rodney Clapham, one of my friends." He stressed the last word pointedly, then added, "from London. Rodney, this is Lady Elisabeth Chadwick, the Earl of Chadwick's daughter. The Chadwick lands run along Loveland's eastern border."

"Charmed," Sir Clapham said sincerely, making almost as elegant a bow from his saddle as the Marquis had done earlier. He was a pleasant-looking young man with curly, sandy-colored hair and the ruddy cheeks of someone who spent most of his time outdoors. His casual handling of the large, restive bay he rode bespoke a man who was a good rider and comfortable around horses.

His lively hazel eyes appraised the beauty with interest. "I believe I know your brother, Lady Elisabeth. Lord Robert Chadwick, yes?"

"Yes," she said warmly. "You must be a hunting man, my lord." She smiled at him without reservation, a radiant look that momentarily stunned the cheerful Sir Clapham. Even the Marquis, just an onlooker to that smile, was somewhat staggered. Good God, he thought, if she ever came to Town she would take London by storm.

Rodney took a deep breath and managed to recover his senses. "Yes," he said, "we have hunted together. Front of the field, Robert. Excellent seat."

"Yes, Robbie has ridden since he was a toddler," she smiled. "We both have."

"Nice mare you've got there," Rodney offered as a tribute. He knew better than to compliment her appearance on first acquaintance, but judged he could slip in a nicety about her horse as a sideways accolade.

"Thank you," she beamed. "Shadow is a delightful goer. Light and fearless. It's a shame to use her for something so dowdy as this gig, but I knew she could use the exercise and I had no time to ride today."

"And your dog needed the exercise as well?" Sir Clapham asked with a smile.

"Oh, Charles had his romp this morning," she said affably. "He just likes to go for rides. He thinks of himself as a carriage dog."

"You'd need a well-sprung carriage for that creature, I dare say. Thought he was a wolf at first."

She laughed. "Wolves are long gone from these parts, Sir Clapham. Now, if you gentlemen will excuse me, I need to be returning home with these supplies." Without waiting for their response, she lightly snicked the reins and her mare moved forward at a jaunty clip. Elisabeth nodded politely to the two riders as she passed.

The men watched her disappear down the road, then Sir Clapham turned to the Marquis with a delighted smile. "Well! I daresay you were going to tell me any day now that the most beautiful girl in England lives next door?"

"Don't worry, Rodney, she'll be receiving an invitation to some of m'mother's gatherings," the Marquis said drily. "But be warned, beneath that lovely face is a shrewish temper."

"No, really? I saw no sign of it. What makes you say that?"

"I've had the pleasure of being treated to her waspish tongue, that's what," the Marquis replied.

"Really? An unmarried chit who don't toss her handkerchief in your path? How refreshing." Sir Clapham grinned, "Perhaps you're losing your touch, Monton."

The Marquis grunted irritably. "As though I want to be noticed by that little hornet. Let's ride, shall we? The rest of the guests begin arriving tomorrow, and this may be the last peaceful day we have."

Lady Sophia Loveland, the Dowager Marchioness of Edmonton, was in her element as the out-of-town house party guests began arriving. She loved playing hostess. She hadn't been to her late brother-in-law's estate in the southwest of England for many years, and had forgotten what a charming property it was. If only it weren't so unseasonably warm and dry. But perhaps the weather would lend itself to some al fresco meals under tents, she thought hopefully. And the manor's large windows and many trees ensured pleasant cross-breezes whenever a bit of wind stirred.

Her son's good friend Sir Rodney Clapham had arrived several days earlier, and yesterday afternoon the Benson-Smythes and their daughter Margaret had made an appearance. Grace Benson-Smythe had been a good friend of the Dowager's since childhood, and was one of the few women who lacked the social ambitions of most of the Dowager's set.

The daughter of a Viscount, Grace had turned down several favorable offers from titled young men to accept the hand of plain Mr. Benson-Smythe. Although he might be incredibly wealthy and was known to be kind-hearted, the Dowager had never understood why someone would willingly marry down.

But Mr. Benson-Smythe's wealth and political connections had meant that Grace and the Dowager had remained in the same circle of Tonnish acquaintances and had been able to continue to see and host each other at parties. Although the Dowager might never admit it to herself, she would have missed Grace's friendship had their social positions diverged.

Grace's daughter Margaret was much like her mother – petite, with light brown hair and pale blue eyes, and possessing a sweet temperament. Both tended to plumpness, but not in an unpleasing way. Indeed, the Dowager had thought over the years, it was unfair of Grace to be able to so easily maintain a pleasingly rounded shape, while the Dowager was forced to starve herself regularly to avoid having to let out the seams on her clothes.

Shortly after the Benson-Smythes had arrived, the Childers were announced. The Dowager greeted Lord and Lady Childer and their two single daughters of marriageable age, Violet and Rose – and what had possessed Daphne Childer to name all her children after flowers, the Dowager wondered, not for the first time. Following on their heels came the Dowager's special friend, Sir Horace Mendam.

"Still seeing old Horace, are you?" her son had asked with a knowing smile when he'd franked the invitations.

"He's quite charming," she'd defended herself. "And he makes a very practical escort. Besides," she'd added irritably, "Alicia Wildwood told me that Millicent Cambridge was making a dead set at Horace and I certainly didn't want to leave him available to her clutches."

Sir Horace Mendam, a widower a few years older than the Dowager, was still possessed of a full head of silver-white hair, had not run to fat, and had all his teeth – all rarities in his age bracket. He also enjoyed a sizable income from a lifetime of shrewd investments. He was much in demand as an escort among the older widows.

"Ah," the Marquis had grinned. "Would this be the real reason for the house party? To get Sir Mendam out of London?"

"Of course not!" She'd given him a veiled glance that he didn't miss. No, he thought, the real reason would be his mother's desire to find him a wife now that the overly cheerful Lady Marybell Wister had failed to achieve his mother's goal of becoming the next Marchioness of Edmonton. He didn't think it would be politic to mention the fact that he'd been instrumental in introducing Lady Marybell to her future husband.

He had no doubt the young women who would spend the next few weeks at his estate were cut in one of two molds – either empty-headed peahens or full of self-consequence. But either way, all would be desirous of advancing their social status, and interested mainly in gossip and parties. Not the kinds of young ladies who interested him, but exactly the kinds his mother kept putting in his path.

No, he thought, he wanted a wife who liked the country, who liked him more than his title, and who was interested in more than fashion and gossip. An image of green eyes lit in laughter rose in his mind, but he determinedly dismissed it. No, he didn't want a beautiful shrew upsetting his life.

He already was going to have enough upsets in his life, now that the house would be filled with company when all he had wanted was a quiet retreat. He looked up as Rodney entered the room, followed by Lord Richard Ringwood.

"Look who've I've just found,'"" Sir Clapham said jovially. "Rescued him from that poker-faced butler of yours, what's his name again?"

"Applewood," the Marquis said, standing. "Apparently every butler in this part of the country is named Applewood. Richard! Glad to see you've made it! Now, if Wentworth can just make it on time for a change, we'll have a fourth for a few card games. Care for a refreshment?" He gestured to a side cabinet where a tray and some tumblers offered a variety of beverage options.

"Thanks, Monton. It was a hotter ride down here than I expected. I've been up in Yorkshire visiting m'sister. Glad to receive your invitation. Good excuse to escape the brats."

The Marquis grinned. "How many now, Richard? She up to an even dozen yet?"

His friend shuddered, his dark blond hair falling onto his forehead. He swept it back with an impatient hand. "I think she has enough for a cricket team," he said in some awe. "Don't know how she keeps track of 'em all."

The men sat in the Marquis's study for a few minutes, chatting of inconsequentials, until the butler knocked on the door requesting the host's presence. "New arrivals, m'Lord. Your mother thought you might like to join her in greeting them."

"Did she, now? That can only mean there's an unattached female in the group."

"I believe it's the Griegsons," the butler said woodenly. "Two daughters and a son."

The Marquis sighed and rose from his chair, motioning for his friends to stay seated. "Enjoy yourselves. I'll be back soon."

He walked into the back hallway, then toward the front of the house. Unlike Chadwick Manor, this home had been built with the study and library toward the back of the main floor. Immediately across from it was a game room with a billiard table and several card tables. Toward the front of the main floor were the visiting rooms – one off each side of the hall.

In the entry he found his mother gaily welcoming Lord and Lady Griegson and their three offspring. Lady Alma was the older of the two daughters, a quiet, too-slender young woman with a pleasant but somewhat vague face. The younger sister, Lady Cora, was pleasingly plump and buxom, and extremely pretty, with a heart-shaped face and full, pouting lips. She pinked up and batted her long eyelashes at the Marquis as he greeted her.

Both young ladies possessed very fine large, brown eyes framed by thick lashes, which the younger sister, at least, used to great advantage. The older sister gazed rather blankly about her, barely acknowledging the Marquis's presence. Their younger brother, young Lord Thomas, with similar eyes that would no doubt one day charm a number of young misses, was just shy of twelve and showing spots on his face. He was both excited and a bit nervous to be at the house party, and was trying very hard to display a bored, worldly air.

"Griegson, welcome," the Marquis said, shaking the other's hand. He'd never cared much for the man, thinking him too rigid in his opinions, but then he didn't care for many of his mother's friends. So much for a quiet, peaceful summer in the countryside, he thought.

"Care to join a few of us in the study? You're welcome too, Thomas." Lord Griegson nodded in relief at the offer while his son tried not to look thrilled at being invited to join the men.

"Applewood, please show them to my study, and then see if the other men would care to join us until tea. And," he said in a lower voice, "bring in some lemonade for our youngest gentleman, if you would." The Marquis had made a special request for fresh lemonade from his housekeeper after returning from Chadwick Manor and confirming that Loveland Manor also boasted some lemon trees in its conservatory.

The butler nodded, clearly understanding that the male guests would be in need of a restful retreat from the noisy greetings among the women. The Marquis, meanwhile, returned to the entry hall to let his mother know he was hosting the men for the remainder of the day.

"Thank you, dear. I'll look forward to seeing everyone together for tea later. I believe everyone should be here by then," she said, referring to the out-of-town guests. The local gentry would make their appearance at tea two days hence.

The Marquis nodded and retraced his steps to the back study. He wondered if he could remodel the lower floor along the lines of Chadwick; he'd rather liked the long, airy study the Earl enjoyed. But then, he thought, it would be unlikely he'd be back to this part of England very often. This being one of his minor estates, he had been thinking of handing it off to his younger brother Patrick whenever he married. For some reason, the thought now rather depressed him.

Eleven

By teatime all the London guests had indeed arrived except for the perpetually tardy Lord William Wentworth. The Dowager Marchioness had treated herself to her favorite card companions — Sir Horace Mendam, Lady Clara Griegson, and Lady Daphne Childer. The Dowager was assured of a nice foursome to indulge her love of whist.

The eligible crop of young ladies was provided by the Griegsons and their daughters Alma and Cora; the Benson-Smythes and their daughter Margaret; the Childers and their two daughters of the floral names; and Lady Georgina Dunbarton. Lady Georgina, long considered the reigning beauty of London, was unaccompanied by her father, who rarely left London. Instead, she had traveled with her companion, a tall, crusty-looking woman who went by the name of Mrs. Breden and spoke with a Prussian accent, and who appeared at times to be acting more in the line of a jailer than a servant.

The Marquis considered the group. Six young ladies and four gentlemen, assuming Wentworth ever put in an appearance. His three friends would provide partners for the young ladies without also offering undue competition for their interest. He was quite certain his mother had made the selections with just that thought in mind.

He wondered if he ought to invite his cousin Charles Ravenwood to stir the pot a little. Nothing like a handsome, unattached Duke to draw feminine attentions. And didn't Charles have a younger brother about Thomas's age? Yes, he thought with a smile, he'd have a rider carry an invitation this very day. He knew Charles was visiting one of his estates less than a day's ride away and would take nothing amiss in a last-minute invitation.

Six young ladies and five gentlemen, one of them an unattached Duke. Better, safer odds, he thought. He looked around the main salon where two servants were pouring tea and serving an assortment of baked treats. The guests mingled, shared gossip, complained about the weather, and discussed plans for the house party.

The Marquis moved among the company, stopping every few feet to chat briefly before moving on, playing the polite host and not giving anyone – especially an eligible young lady – the opportunity to snare him for a private chat. As a result, the gathering's conversations held a fractured quality for him.

"I wasn't aware you owned an estate in this corner of England," Lady Griegson was saying to his mother.

"And then the damn thing bit me," complained Sir Mendam to Lord Childer.

"Well, I knew right away it was the same blue dress," said one of the floral-named daughters to the other, "regardless of the new lace trim."

"Damn fine race," Lord Ringwood said to Lord Griegson.

"I'm certain he's interested in her," said a female voice.

"A ruby in his teeth, I swear," said Sir Clapham. Hmm, thought the Marquis, he'd have to come back to that conversation.

"Hogs! Can you imagine?"

"It was the most beautiful ballroom I've ever seen."

"And from there we went to Italy."

"Excuse me, is there a pond on this property?"

The Marquis would have continued his polite and unseeing amble, but a hand was laid on his arm. "Sir? Is there a pond?"

The Marquis looked down in surprise at the hand, which was quickly withdrawn by a diffident Thomas Griegson. Edmonton smiled at the lad, who was looking up at him a bit uncertainly.

"Lord Thomas," the Marquis said. "As a matter of fact, yes, we have not only a pond, but a stream that runs for a ways along the property line. Why do you ask? Are you interested in fishing?"

"Is it a big pond?"

"Well, it's a small lake, really. Not as big as it was earlier this spring, but big enough to be able to take out a small raft and enjoy some time on the water. My brothers and I spent a lot of time swimming and rafting when we visited this property as children. Here, let me show you." He led the boy through the guests to the French doors and from there onto the terrace. Luckily this side of the house was in the shade during the afternoon, away from the relentless summer heat.

"There," the Marquis pointed. "See down that slope where the trees part? The pond lies just beyond there. If you follow it along to the right, you'll reach the border stream."

"Jolly!" said Thomas, then remembered his manners. "I mean, thank you, Lord Loveland."

"Why the interest in a pond?"

Thomas shifted about, and then peeked up at the Marquis, looking much younger than his nearly twelve years. "I just like ponds and creeks, my Lord."

"I see. And what might you like about ponds and creeks?"

"Who's talking about ponds and creeks?" asked Sir Clapham cheerfully, following them onto the terrace.

The boy made as if to move back into the parlor, but the Marquis stayed him with a light hand on his shoulder. "Thomas and I were just discussing the estate."

Rodney eyed Thomas knowingly. "Want to catch some fish, do you?"

The boy blushed. "Frogs, actually. I won't keep them or hurt them, I promise."

"I wouldn't mind catching some fish, myself," Rodney said. "What say we go down to the stream first thing in the morning? I'll catch fish, you chase frogs."

"Really, sir?" Thomas said in delight. "D'you mean it?"

"'Course I mean it. I'll want to leave early, though. Can you be ready by six?"

"Oh, yes! That would be above all great! Thank you, Sir. I'll just tell my papa!"

The Marquis and Sir Clapham watched as Thomas darted back inside and hurried toward his father.

"I'm glad as least one of my guests is assured of having a pleasant visit," the Marquis remarked.

"Two," said Sir Clapham with a grin. "That is, if you've got any good trout in that stream."

"That I wouldn't know, not having been here in nearly thirty years. But it will be a cool, pleasant spot to spend a morning." He motioned for Rodney to precede him back into the house. He needed to stay on the move if he wanted to avoid being trapped into conversation by any mothers and their free daughters. "I'll have the cook make up a breakfast for the two of you. You and Thomas can pick it up on your way out the kitchen door."

"Excellent! And just to show you how grateful I am, I'll head off Lady Childer and her daughters before they can corner you." And with an insouciant grin, Sir Clapham turned to halt the three women with a greeting as the Marquis once again began slipping through the guests on his unending circuit.

Twelve

The next morning Elisabeth once again slipped out shortly after sunrise to enjoy a long walk on the estate's grounds. As she circled back toward the manor, her hounds approached the stream at a leisurely pace. She looked about, refusing to acknowledge the small pang of disappointment she felt at not seeing the Marquis riding nearby. No, she silently admonished herself, she didn't like him. Why on earth would she want to run into him?

Just then, she was startled to see two of her dogs suddenly break ranks and leap ahead into the mist over the water. "Monk! Spotter! Stop! Come back here!" But for once they didn't obey her. They vanished in mere seconds, their long legs stretched out in a full run. She heard them splash across the stream toward some unknown quarry.

"Help! Help! Sir Rodney, help!" cried a young boy's voice almost directly across from her on the other side of the creek.

A man cursed from several yards upstream and called to the boy not to move.

Elisabeth picked up her skirts and ran as fast as she could through the mist, fearing what she might find. The rest of her hounds paced her as she ran down the bank, their ears pricked forward, waiting for instructions as they stayed by her side.

She dashed through the water, soaking her feet and ankles, yelling at the two dogs as she ran. "Monk! Spotter! Stay! Sit!"

Abruptly she cleared the mist and emerged onto a frozen tableau. A young boy was standing with his back to a tree, his hands raised above his head as he held something as far above the ground as he could manage. His eyes were dilated in terror as the two dogs stood at attention on either side of him. Sir Clapham, whom she recognized as the man she had met the other day when he was out riding with the Marquis, had paused in midstride, obviously on his way to save the lad. He now stood with his head swiveled toward her and his mouth agape.

"Bad dogs," she yelled. "Sit! Sit now! Drop!" The dogs turned to look at her, clearly understanding she was furious, but not sure why.

"You will sit!" she shouted again. This time they complied, realizing they were in deep trouble. "Drop!" she yelled, steel in her voice. The dogs flattened themselves to the ground, now looking thoroughly miserable.

"Bad dogs! You should be ashamed of yourselves!" Elisabeth turned to where Sir Clapham stood, still staring at her. She watched as he blinked himself out of his frozen state and automatically began to make a bow.

"Lady Elisabeth," said Sir Clapham politely. "Is it safe to – Good Gad, there are more of them!" He stared in astonishment as his gaze traveled to the rest of the pack.

She nodded briefly to Sir Clapham, but otherwise ignored him as she walked toward the still-frightened boy. "Hello, I'm Lady Elisabeth Chadwick, from the estate on the other side of this creek," she said kindly. "These are my dogs, and I'm so terribly sorry they have treated you rudely." She held out her hand in greeting. "They're usually quite gentle and well-behaved. I hope you weren't too alarmed." She knew better than to suggest to a boy of his years that he might have been frightened.

"What are they?" he asked, with just the barest hint of a quaver in his voice.

"Scottish deerhounds. I raise them." She continued to hold out her hand toward him.

He looked up at his clasped hands and at her outstretched palm, clearly at a loss as to how to respond. Slowly he lowered his hands to his chest level. "I've got a frog here," he said. "It's a rana temporaria."

"Is it now?" Elisabeth asked. "May I see?" She leaned forward to peer between his fingers as he spread them apart slightly. "Very nice. I quite see why you cannot shake my hand. Don't worry, my dogs won't try to eat the frog. I expect they think maybe you have a sandwich or something."

"I have a piece of roasted chicken in my pocket," he said, still clutching his hands around the frog.

"Well that's it, then. They probably smell the chicken." She turned her attention once again to the abashed Monk and Spotter, and said in a deeply angry tone of voice, "Bad dogs. Apologize!"

To the amazement of both Thomas and Sir Clapham, the two dogs sat up and each laid a paw over its snout and dipped its head slightly.

"There," she said, "that's better. No more tricks from the two of you or no more walks. Do you understand?"

The other dogs all watched her, waiting for instructions. She turned to the circle of dogs, still a little angry. "Sit!" They sat. They were not anxious to join Monk and Spotter in her bad graces.

She glanced with chagrin at the boy and Sir Clapham. "They won't bother you again, I promise. I do apologize. They're really very gentle dogs. And they won't chase your frog if you want to put him down," she reassured the boy.

"Thank you," he said, walking closer to the water and releasing his prize. The three humans and thirteen dogs watched with interest as the frog bobbled for a moment on the gravelly shore and then hopped into the water, appearing again several feet downstream, happy to have regained its freedom.

"I'm Lord Thomas Griegson," the boy said politely to Elisabeth, after watching the frog disappear. He took a deep breath and released it with a gusty exhale.

"Well, that was quite the adventure," said Sir Clapham, daring to move at last. He walked over to pick up his fishing pole from where he had flung it on his way to rescue Thomas. He brushed it off and leaned it against a tree before turning back to Elisabeth.

"A pleasure to see you again, Lady Elisabeth," he said once this task was done. "Now, if you would please forgive me while I quietly succumb to a heart attack." He pulled out a handkerchief and drew it across his brow.

"A heart attack?" Thomas asked a little fearfully.

"Well, it wouldn't be very manly to succumb to a fit of the vapors now, would it?" he winked. "Although I certainly am tempted."

"Alas, I have no camphor to place under your nose to awaken you," Elisabeth laughed.

"Thank God for that," Sir Clapham replied.

The boy walked over to the stream to rinse his hands, then pulled out the chicken leg he'd been about to unwrap before he'd spied the frog. He took a bite and smiled at Elisabeth. "You raise these dogs?"

"Yes, would you like to pet one of them?"

He hesitated a moment, then nodded. He hastily finished off the chicken leg, put the remains in a hamper, and wiped his hands on his pants. As he stepped toward her, Elisabeth saw that his hands were now clenched to his sides.

"Come," she said. "I'll introduce you to Charles. He's not very brave around strangers, so you'll need to be gentle."

"Not brave?" asked Sir Clapham. "That monster?"

She sent him a speaking glance. "He is timid, nonetheless. He came from a bad home." She turned to her dogs and called Charles.

The deerhound stood up and approached Elisabeth a little nervously, obviously uncertain about whether he was in trouble. Just to be safe, he sat as soon as he reached Elisabeth's side, put his paw to his nose, and dipped his head.

She laughed and stroked his neck. "No, sweetheart, you're a good dog. Nothing to apologize for this morning. This young gentleman would like to make your acquaintance."

"So would this older gentleman," Sir Clapham said, moving forward. "I reckon this is the brute who was riding in your cart t'other day. I recognize the scar on his nose. Never had a proper introduction." He held out his hand to Charles, who raised a paw and placed it in Sir Clapham's palm.

"Well, I'll be dashed," Sir Clapham said admiringly. "He has more manners than some people I know."

Thomas next reached out a hand and accepted the dog's paw. And with that, the ice was broken. The boy promptly made the rounds of all the dogs, shaking hands with them and rubbing their necks and ears. He finally sat on the ground between Monk and Spotter, one hand draped across each dog's lower back, chatting them up as Sir Clapham and Elisabeth watched in amusement.

"Well that was a fast recovery," Sir Clapham smiled. "He'll have quite a bit to talk about when we return to the house for lunch."

"The best adventures are those that begin perilously and end happily," she said, returning his smile.

"And I understand you and some of the other neighbors will be joining us for tea tomorrow afternoon."

"Yes, and one or two other events," she nodded. "I look forward to it."

"So you're not unsociable, you have passable looks, and you don't have a stutter. Perhaps you have bad table manners?"

She raised her eyebrows in surprise. "I beg your pardon?"

"Well something must keep you from coming to Town," he grinned. "Perhaps you slurp your soup?"

She laughed up at him, her green eyes sparkling in pleasure. He once again found himself momentarily stunned by her beauty.

"I visit London a few times each year," she said, "just not for the Season. I am the bane of my great-aunt's existence. She desperately wants to see me married off."

"Troublesome chit, are you? Wants you out of her hair?"

She laughed again. "I am a sad case, I'm told. I have a great many flaws – thirteen of them to be exact." She looked around at the dogs, most of whom had made themselves comfortable in a group around Thomas.

"It would be difficult to take them to balls and rout parties, I expect," Sir Clapham smiled.

"It has been difficult to teach them to dance," she agreed soberly, then giggled at his startled expression.

"Do they…? No, you're not serious?" He glanced at the dogs and back at her, and caught her biting her lip to keep from smiling.

"I am beginning to feel some sympathy for your great-aunt," he said.

Thirteen

That evening after dinner, the house party guests adjourned to one of the front salons to enjoy the various entertainments provided by the young ladies. The Dowager Marchioness had quizzed the various matrons about their daughters' accomplishments, and had arranged an impromptu agenda of entertainment.

First up, the Dowager had announced, would be Lady Cora Griegson, displaying her musical skills on a harp that had been carried into the room by two footmen. Lady Cora had angled to be first, knowing that once she was done she would be free to mingle with the guests. She had every intention of attaching herself to the Marquis this evening.

She also knew she wasn't a very good harpist, which the guests also quickly discovered. However, she made such a pretty and graceful picture as she strummed the instrument that most of the men quickly forgot her lack of musical ability. The Marquis found himself amazed that a harp could sound so badly, and equally amazed that no one else seemed to be bothered by the discordant pluckings.

He glanced about the room and met the quietly amused eyes of the beautiful Lady Georgina Dunbarton. As she held his gaze, her lush, uptilted lips tilted a bit higher and she lifted her eyebrows slightly. He quickly turned away, choking back a laugh.

Lady Cora finished her piece – really, the Marquis thought, it was nearly impossible to tell what the intended song had been – and the guests clapped politely. The young lady dipped a graceful curtsy and gave the audience a charming smile. She walked over to her parents, and then continued past them, ostensibly heading toward a servant who was standing near the beverage table at the back of the room.

"Thank you, Lady Cora," the Dowager smiled as that young lady's parents beamed proudly. "And now, we will hear a song from Lady Violet Childer, accompanied on the pianoforte by Lady Rose Childer.

The guests disposed themselves about the room, changing seats and conversational companions. The Marquis, standing near the fireplace, prepared to bear up under another onslaught of poor musical abilities.

But he was pleasantly surprised. The two sisters gave a creditable performance. Lady Violet possessed a sweet, light voice with a surprisingly good range, and her younger sister, Lady Rose, was well trained enough to play at a tempo and volume that did not overpower her sister. This time, when the performance ended, the applause was more sincere.

"Were they not delightful, my Lord?" asked a sweet little voice at his shoulder. He looked down to see the lovely heart-shaped face of Lady Cora smiling up at him. She placed a light hand on his arm. "I do so admire those with true talent." She peeked up at him through her long eyelashes.

Ah, he thought with an inner grin, she's fully aware that she possesses little playing ability. At least she wasn't seeking accolades or compliments. So he gave her one.

"Yes, but I do admire everyone who is willing to perform before an audience, perhaps more so if they are not among the best," he said, smiling down at her and placing his free hand on hers.

She twinkled up at him as he neatly fell into her trap. "It is unnerving to play before others, but it is expected, yes? As is dancing."

"The perils of polite society," he agreed.

She waited for him to continue, but his attention returned to the front of the room where his mother was announcing Lady Alma Griegson as the next performer.

She wanted to tap one of her dainty little feet. Really, he was supposed to ask her if she liked to dance. That would lead to a discussion of dancing, and she had plans for where that conversation could lead.

"Do you like to dance, my Lord?" she asked.

"Yes, but let's be quiet now and listen to your sister." He patted her hand like an uncle would, she thought, quietly fuming. She was well aware of the muscular arm underneath his jacket sleeve. He was excessively desirable, both as a man and as a husband. She wanted him to be equally aware of her attractions. But instead he was focused on her sister.

Lady Alma Griegson, unlike her younger sister Lady Cora, not only had an ear for music, but liked to practice.

The song she played was a haunting Irish ballad about love, loss, and redemption. The Marquis noticed she played with her eyes closed. Her entire being seemed focused on the melody.

He shrugged off Lady Cora's hand to applaud warmly for her older sister's performance. He glanced down at his charming companion to see a flash of irritation cross Lady Cora's lovely face as her sister curtseyed to the group. Not so charitable toward every talented young lady, he thought.

"Excuse me," he said to her. He walked over to where Lady Alma now stood with her parents, and took her hand.

"That was charming," he said sincerely. "I've always enjoyed ballads. Do you often play them?"

She looked up at him, flustered to be the focus of his attention. "I prefer ballads to country songs. They have so much depth, I think."

"Alma," her mother hurriedly interrupted. "I'm sure the Marquis does not seek a discussion of music. My Lord, why do you not join us on the sofa?"

"Thank you, Lady Griegson, but I prefer to stand," he said. "Would you like something to drink?" he asked Lady Alma.

She glanced uncertainly at her mother, then nodded. "Thank you, my Lord." He led Lady Alma toward the beverage table just as Lady Cora arrived at her mother's side. The younger sister's pursuit of her quarry was unintentionally blocked by her father, who captured her hand to tell her how lovely she had looked at the harp. Forced to pause, she sat with her parents as Lady

Georgina Dunbarton took her turn at entertaining the group.

One never wanted to follow Lady Georgina at a musicale. That lady's skills as a harpist and singer were almost unmatched in London. Lady Cora's face flamed as Lady Georgina took several minutes to tune the harp. It was a subtle, but effective, method of insulting Lady Cora's musical abilities.

From the back of the room near the beverage table, the Marquis and Lady Alma stood in comfortable silence, both sipping tea and enjoying the performance. From his occasional glances down, he was certain his companion's enjoyment was sincere. When she set down her cup to offer hearty applause at the end of the piece, he was certain of it.

He caught Lady Georgina's eye and raised his cup to her in a toast. "She is a superb talent," he said to Lady Alma.

"She is amazing," that young lady enthused. "I look forward to every opportunity to hear her perform."

"And do you enjoy performing?" he asked.

She thought about that for a moment. "I enjoy playing," she said at last.

"I noticed you kept your eyes closed while you were playing," he commented.

"It helps me concentrate on the music better."

"I thought it might be something like that," he said. "I hope you will play for us again while you are here."

"Thank you, my Lord."

He escorted her back to her parents, then walked over to where Lady Georgina was standing with his mother and Sir Mendam, both of whom were congratulating her on her performance.

"Lady Georgina," he said, bowing over her hand. "Magnificent, as usual."

"John," his mother said. "Why do you and Lady Georgina not sing for us? You have a beautiful baritone, and I would so enjoy hearing the two of you perform a duet."

I'll just bet you would, he thought. "We have not practiced anything," he said aloud. "But we shall discuss the possibility." He turned his attention to Lady Georgina. "Shall we take a walk about the room?"

"Certainly," she agreed, resting her hand on his arm. As they strolled away from his mother, the Dowager heaved a deep sigh of desire.

"Now she," the Dowager whispered to Sir Mendam, "is exactly the right person to become John's Marchioness."

"She would certainly shine as his hostess in London," he agreed.

The Marquis and Lady Georgina were both fully aware of how many eyes were following them about the room. And both knew just as well that they were not in the least attracted to each other. But the Marquis needed to spread his attentions among his female guests, and Lady Georgina was happy enough to be seen with one of the Town's most desired matrimonial prizes.

By midafternoon the next day, Elisabeth was regretting her plans to attend the afternoon tea. Her great-aunt had been fussing over her since shortly after breakfast, insisting on rearranging her hair, choosing her gown and accessories, and barraging her with instructions on deportment.

Her preferred loose style of wearing her hair had been disparaged as being unredeemably provincial. No, she must wear it swept up, with little tendrils curling down the sides of her face and back. And it must be threaded through with a beaded ribbon.

The tendrils of hair tickled her face and neck, and she impatiently brushed them back.

"Stop that!" the Dowager demanded for the fourth time. "Keep your hands away from your face! Do not fidget so!"

"But I don't like these strands of hair falling about me. They make me want to sneeze."

"Don't you dare!" snapped the Dowager. "You will not shame me, do you hear?"

"I would shame you by sneezing?" Elisabeth asked innocently.

She was rewarded with a gimlet stare. "You will behave as you know you ought, missy. You will not disgrace your family by pulling any of your tricks."

"Yes, ma'am," Elisabeth said meekly as her dark blue gown was pulled off and replaced with an ivory-colored dress with a pale green underslip and matching ribbons.

"But I like that gown," she protested. "And it's new. What's wrong with it?"

"Hush," her great-aunt said. "You will trust my judgment."

Once in the new dress and with her hair done up, Elisabeth glanced at herself in the mirror, and recognized with disinterest that she appeared to great advantage. But really, was it worth all this effort to impress a roomful of strangers she'd likely never see again?

"I supposed this pale green will have to do," the Dowager grumbled, as the maid brought out kid slippers to match the underslip and ribbons. "Why have you never bothered to acquire a green to match your eyes?"

"I think this is a very pretty color, ma'am."

"Hmph," was the encouraging response. "Every other young woman in England knows enough to purchase ribbons to match her eyes. Why cannot you? This is undoubtedly your father's fault."

As if on cue, that personage made himself known with a bellow from the top of the stairs leading down to the entry hall.

"Is anyone planning to actually leave the house in time to get to this accursed tea?" Lord Chadwick yelled in irritation.

"Do not shout!" the Dowager yelled back. "We're just on our way down." She gave Elisabeth a shove and propelled the reluctant miss out the door toward the main staircase.

"I trust you at will least remember the manners I know you were taught well enough to scrape by this afternoon," the Dowager muttered. "If you cannot think of what to say or do, you will nod and smile. The impression you make with her Ladyship's guests is the reputation that will precede you to London."

Precede? Elisabeth didn't like the implications of that word.

"But I do know at least two of the guests," Elisabeth reassured her great-aunt as they reached her father, who was pacing about impatiently.

"Oh?" he asked, as he escorted them down the stairs to where Applewood was waiting. "Just whom do you know at that house, Elsbet?"

"I met Sir Rodney Clapham on the road a few days ago and he said he is a good friend of Robbie's," Elisabeth smiled at her father.

"You met a man on the road?!" the Dowager nearly shrieked. "Are you telling me you introduced yourself to a total stranger?"

"Yes, ma'am," Elisabeth replied politely. "It is quite my custom to approach strange men and make myself known to them."

Elisabeth watched for a moment as her great-aunt goggled at her in shocked outrage, her face rapidly purpling. She heard her father make a choking sound behind her.

"Of course I don't do that," Elisabeth relented, before her great-aunt was carried off by a stroke. "The Marquis introduced us. They were out for a ride. I was returning from the village."

The Dowager, still angry, gasped a few times as she regained her breath. "And was there a chaperone in evidence?" she demanded.

"Charles was there." Elisabeth pulled on her gloves as she smiled serenely at her great-aunt.

The Dowager sniffed, reluctantly ceding ground, obviously thinking Charles was a groom. The Earl smiled faintly.

"And the second guest?" he prodded.

"Lord Thomas Griegson," she said.

At the questioning looks from her companions, she added, "He's a young boy. He likes to collect frogs."

"Well," Lord Chadwick smiled as Applewood opened the door for them, "if the party gets too boring perhaps he will take me out for a little frog collecting."

The Dowager glared at both of them as she marched ahead to the carriage.

Fifteen

As the house party's female guests gathered in one of the manor's two large salons before tea, the matrons formed a circle around their hostess. The six single misses directed the servants to pull several chairs together into a circle nearby, where they could hear the older women's discussion and still be free to conduct their separate conversation. But the same topic was foremost in all their minds. They were engaged in the very important task of ascertaining the antecedents of the neighborhood gentry who were joining the party for tea.

Vicar Smithers and his wife were quickly dealt with and dismissed by the matrons, it being understood that the couple were expected to stay much in the background and be accorded the basic level of courtesy reserved for the local clergy.

The Squire received a bit more attention when Lady Childer mentioned he was a third cousin of the Wiltshires and therefore could claim a Baron in the family. However, the Squire eventually was dismissed as lacking in sufficient connections or wealth – "only a comfortable competence suitable for country living," according to Lady Griegson, whose intimate knowledge of the peerage was legendary – to be of interest to the unmarried daughters at the party.

"I also am expecting Lady Downs," the Dowager Marchioness commented to the group of ladies around her. "She lives nearby on one of her brother's lesser estates."

"Good gracious, Sophia!" Mrs. Benson-Smythe exclaimed. "You don't mean to tell me she is still alive? I had no idea. Lord, she terrorized the other debs and me during our come-outs."

"What do you mean, Grace?" Lady Griegson asked, always alert for some amusing gossip.

"Very strict with her notions of manners," Mrs. Benson-Smythe replied. "She was one of the leaders of the Ton for years, you recall. Well, as the daughter and then the sister and now the aunt of a Duke you would expect no less. But, really, she must be ninety if she's a day. I'm surprised she still gets out."

The Dowager Marchioness shrugged uncertainly. "I have no recollection of meeting her, but she said in her reply that she was delighted to accept my invitation, and she is, of course, one of the highest placed of the local gentry."

"Lord, I hope she doesn't remember me," said Mrs. Benson-Smythe, brushing the skirts of her dress nervously. "She was forever criticizing the way I sat and spoke."

The ladies laughed, but not unkindly. All of them well-remembered the fears they'd experienced during their come-outs that they might commit some sort of social faux pas, or worse, not take.

"Stop that," she grumbled at them, but with a small smile. "It was dreadful. I think I may hide in the corner while she is here."

"Nonsense, Mother," her daughter Margaret said stoutly from the group of young ladies seated nearby. "If she is as old as you say, no doubt her eyes and ears are weakened with time and you will be safe from her notice."

Margaret Benson-Smythe, a petite brunette a bit on the plump side, turned back to the other young ladies with a sweet, confiding smile. "Although I would give a great deal to know what my mother did to merit such displeasure. She always assures me she was perfection itself, and that I in no way measure up to her!"

Lady Georgina Dunbarton smiled indulgently as the other girls giggled. A few years older than most of the other young ladies, and traveling with only a companion rather than her family, she was an object of some curiosity to the others. At twenty-three, she was on her fourth Season, but it was widely assumed it was by choice. As an acclaimed beauty and the daughter of Lord Nigel Dunbarton, who served as a close adviser to the Prince Regent, she was thought to hold higher standards than any of her suitors had so far achieved.

Her looks were striking. Her hair, a charcoal color with silver streaks, framed her pale oval face and highlighted her flawless skin. Long black lashes set off her dark grey eyes, which had been lauded by more than one poetically minded suitor as looking like deep pools of still water under a cloudy sky. She wasn't particularly sure she liked that comparison, nor that she enjoyed having men enshrine her in badly written verses. Full, rosy lips, which naturally curved upward, gave her the appearance of perpetually smiling at some delightful little secret. Many poems had mentioned that trait as well.

Indeed, Lady Alma Griegson had wondered aloud to her younger sister Lady Cora shortly after their arrival, what it was that had attracted that lady to this particular party.

"For she must have her choice of many invitations," Lady Alma said.

"The Marquis, you goose," Lady Cora had replied with a roll of her fine brown eyes. "He has everything she could want in a husband. He certainly is everything I would like. And with Marybell Wister choosing Lord Carrington over Lord Loveland, he must be searching for a new Marchioness. Mama says he's never been present at one of his mother's house parties before."

Lady Alma's equally lovely brown eyes widened in comprehension. "How silly of me. Of course you're right. Well, we can take comfort in the knowledge that we were invited, I suppose."

"I intend to do more than that," said the self-confident Lady Cora with an alarming display of conceit. "I think I shall have the Marquis."

"He may have some say in that," Lady Alma said drily.

"I shall give him no say," Lady Cora said, smiling at her reflection in the mirror. "I think I should very much like to live at an estate as grand as Edmonton Castle. If he wanted to marry Lady Georgina, he could have proposed any time these past four years. No, I think I shall have him."

Now, as the young ladies chatted and surreptitiously listened to their mothers talk with the Dowager Marchioness, they heard the next guests on the list being discussed.

"And did I hear you say over breakfast that the Earl of Chadwick and his family will be here?" Lady Childer was asking their hostess. "I have met him at several of the larger parties in town, but he doesn't seem to care for society overmuch."

"Yes," the Dowager nodded. "He will be bringing his aunt, Lady Burton, the Dowager Countess of Cwmhaven, and his daughter, Lady Elisabeth."

"Oh dear," Mrs. Benson-Smythe groaned. "Another persecutor to torment me."

The Dowager laughed. "Good heavens, Grace, do you mean Lister? What on earth did she ever do to you? She's spent most of her years in Scotland! Indeed, I first met her there when I was visiting friends as a girl. She is several years older, but we have much in common."

Grace Benson-Smythe hunched a pettish shoulder. "Sophia Loveland, don't you dare tease me," she grumbled to the Dowager Marchioness. "I shall have a megrim, I warn you."

"But, really, Grace," you must tell us the tale behind these comments," Lady Childer said. "All these years I thought you were a pattern card of perfection."

"Well, if so, you will be able to meet two of the women who cut the pattern," that aggrieved lady said. "Sophia, you really should have warned me you meant to reintroduce me to those two dragons. I think I feel a headache coming on right now, in fact."

The Dowager laughed. "My dear, you shall not make up an excuse to spend your afternoon in your room eating bonbons! You will stay – if for no other reason than so I can watch you hide behind a potted plant."

Mrs. Benson-Smythe looked around the room for a large plant as if giving the notion serious consideration. The others laughed at her discomfort.

"Do you plan on having any dancing one of these evenings?" Lady Childer asked their hostess, changing the subject. "I daresay the young people would enjoy some dancing."

"I plan on two dance parties," the Dowager Marchioness smiled, thinking of the opportunity for her son to dance with the young ladies at the party. "I have arranged for a quartet to play for us."

"And did I understand you to say that the Earl has an unmarried daughter?" asked Lady Griegson with a sideways glance at the single misses clustered nearby. She was disappointed that her older daughter Alma hadn't yet taken, but she had hopes for Cora, who had done very well during her first Season.

"Yes," the Dowager Marchioness said. "She's the Earl's second child. Her older brother is Lord Robert Chadwick, who recently married Caroline Masters, and her younger sister also is married, but I don't know the details."

All of the women automatically turned to Lady Griegson, who promptly obliged them with the information. "Her name is Anne. She married Baron Conners. They reside at his primary estate in Scotland, although he has a lesser estate in this part of England."

"And this other daughter?" Lady Childer asked.

"I don't believe this daughter has ever had a Season," the Dowager Marchioness replied. "I'm told she likes to stay in the country and raise pugs."

"She's a spinster named Elisabeth," Lady Griegson said indulgently. "I've told my daughters to be all that is polite to her, and not to laugh at any little gaffes she may make."

The young misses had picked up on these comments, with the help of Margaret Benson-Smythe's sharp ears.

"A spinster," Lady Alma Griegson echoed. She hated that word. As the second oldest unmarried lady at the party after Lady Georgina Dunbarton, she had rapidly joined that lady as one of the group's two unofficial leaders. But without possessing the beauty enjoyed by Lady Georgina, Lady Alma was all too conscious that she herself, after a third unsuccessful Season, was in danger of being labeled a spinster.

"Did I just overhear that these Chadwicks are related to Lord Robert Chadwick?" Lady Rose Childer asked, speaking up for the first time. "I went to finishing school with his wife. She was two years ahead of me."

"Oh, yes, I remember Caroline Masters," Lady Violet Childer nodded at her sister. "She was one year ahead of me. She married Lord Chadwick just last year."

"Yes, Robert is the Earl's son," Lady Georgina nodded. Her brow crinkled into an uncharacteristic frown for a moment before she remembered herself. She hoped her expression hadn't been noticed by Mrs. Breden, her companion. That woman was sitting quietly to the side where she could remain largely unnoticed while maintaining a watchful eye over her charge. "Do you know anything about this unmarried sister of his?"

"What is there to know?" Lady Cora Griegson asked cheerfully. She admired her delicate hands as she spoke, not bothering to look at the other girls. "She is unwed and lives in the country. She sounds like a bit of an oddity. Thomas said he and Sir Clapham met her tramping through the stream with some hounds yesterday morning. I'm not sure, but I think she might have been fishing. Or maybe it was something to do with frogs."

"Frogs!" squealed Lady Violet Childer, shuddering dramatically. "Oh dear, you cannot be serious!"

"Well," Lady Cora said, "I cannot be sure. I wasn't listening to him that closely. Something about frogs and dogs and fishing in the stream."

"Did he say anything else about her?" Lady Georgina asked. "What she looks like, perhaps? Lord Robert and Lady Anne are both well-favored. One would expect the same of their sister." She kept her voice carefully bland, as always, so as not to draw her companion's notice.

"No, he just said she was a 'right one,' whatever that means to an eleven-year-old boy," Lady Cora shrugged. Her attention had been distracted by the darling little spangles on the hem of her dress.

"I do hope she doesn't come in smelling of the fields," Lady Violet sniffed.

Lady Georgina turned away from the group and caught the eye of Sir Rodney Clapham, who had just entered the room with a few of the other male guests as tea time neared.

He excused himself from the other gentlemen and came over as she signaled him with one gracefully raised hand.

"Sir Clapham," she asked, "you've met the Earl of Chadwick's daughter, have you not?" she asked. The other ladies looked at him expectantly. Sir Clapham, the son of a Baronet, was relatively well-to-do, boyishly handsome, but apparently determinedly single. A good catch, if someone could snag his interest. He was an excellent dancer, knowledgeable about ladies' fashions, and could be counted on to know all the latest gossip.

"Yes, I've met Lady Elisabeth," he smiled. "So have Monton and young Thomas."

"Is it true she loathes society and prefers to stay home raising pugs?" Lady Cora giggled. She batted her long eyelashes at Sir Clapham, then pouted briefly as he ignored her and kept his focus on the beautiful Lady Georgina.

"Well, I've met her," he said, "but I haven't interrogated her. She does raise dogs, although I wouldn't exactly call them pugs."

"Oh my," Lady Violet smiled. "What is she like? How old is she?"

"She's very nice. Was quite kind to Thomas when her dogs scared him. She's sister to Lord Robert Chadwick, you know."

This fact, already being known, was received without interest by the six young ladies. Realizing he was no longer needed because he had nothing else to add, Sir Clapham essayed a brief bow and lounged away to join the Marquis.

"I hope she'll have something to talk about besides dogs," Lady Cora said, turning back to the others.

"Remember Melody Wingworth and those atrocious hounds she always had with her?" Lady Violet asked, giving another theatrical shudder. The young ladies' delighted laughter drew admiring glances from some of the men in the room.

Sir Clapham wore a slight grin as he strolled over to where the Marquis was talking with Lord Richard Ringwood.

At that moment the butler announced the arrival of the very guests who had been the subject of the girls' chatter. Sir Clapham turned to the Marquis and his grin widened. "This ought to be interesting."

"What's that?" Lord Ringwood asked. Then, as the butler stepped aside following his announcement of the first guests, Lord Ringwood's mouth dropped open in amazement as the Earl of Chadwick led his daughter and aunt into the room.

Sixteen

"I say," a man's voice said from behind Sir Clapham, "what an astonishingly beautiful girl."

If Elisabeth heard the comment, she gave no sign of it. Instead, she serenely followed her father and great-aunt as they made their way to Lady Loveland.

"Thank you for the kind invitation," the Earl bowed over the Dowager Marchioness's hand. "It's rare to have such an engaging social opportunity in the neighborhood. I am delighted you have chosen to visit us and to host this entertainment."

The Dowager Marchioness nearly simpered. "Lord Chadwick, so nice to see you again. And Lister, my dear, what a delight to have you staying here at the same time. It's been far too long."

The two Dowagers leaned forward and lightly touched each other's powdered cheeks, then stepped apart.

"And allow me to introduce my daughter," the Earl continued. "Lady Loveland, this is my daughter, Lady Elisabeth."

Elisabeth lowered herself into a graceful curtsey, aware all eyes were on her, watching for any sign of a bobble. Fortunately, she'd learned her curtseys and fan-play at the hands of a formidable teacher at the finishing school she and her sister had attended. Despite her great-aunt's worries, Elisabeth knew she would not disgrace her family at this or any other social function.

As she rose from her curtsey, she saw that Sir Rodney Clapham and the Marquis had made their way over, accompanied by a third gentleman who was staring at her with his mouth agape. He looked a bit like a landed fish. Her earlier moment of confidence in her manners was dealt a brief blow as she wondered if his stare meant she'd committed some sort of faux pas. But no, she decided, looking more closely at him, it appeared he might be a trifle simple.

She smiled as Sir Clapham was introduced to her great-aunt. He said all that was proper and showed just the right amount of deference to please the demanding Dowager.

"So you are Percival's son," she commented in a tone that hinted at a reprimand.

"I do have that honor, ma'am," he nodded. "Not that I would anticipate you have much good to say about the connection."

"Wastes his time in the woods," she said, "as did your grandfather. Grown men should not collect butterflies. I expect you know my great-nephew, Robert Chadwick."

"I do have the honor of being a friend of Robert's," Sir Clapham nodded.

"Do you. Well, no harm can come of that, I suppose."

Elisabeth raised her eyebrows. Coming from her great-aunt, that was high praise indeed. Sir Clapham seemed to realize it, and smiled as he bowed once more and backed away to allow the Marquis to move forward.

Sir Clapham then moved to Elisabeth's side, where he thought to introduce her to the other man who had walked up with him.

"Lady Elisabeth, allow me to introduce you to Lord Richard Ringwood. He is a longtime friend. Knows your brother, too."

Elisabeth smiled kindly at Lord Ringwood as he was introduced. He managed to close his gaping mouth as he bowed awkwardly over her hand. He stood up, removed his hand from hers and ran it through his mop of dark blond hair as he opened his mouth again. He emitted a few bleats, then abruptly turned and nearly ran to the other side of the room.

She raised her eyebrows at Sir Clapham.

"Don't do too well around beauties," he said in explanation.

She laughed outright at that. "Then this gathering must surely confound him!"

Sir Clapham glanced at the avid faces watching the group around the new guests and winked at her. "Ah, well, he knows these beauties, so he's more or less accustomed. You, however, present a new and dangerous threat – a bright and shining sun that casts every other girl here in the shade. He may never say another intelligible syllable until we leave the West Country."

"And you, Sir Clapham, are a bit of a rogue, I think. You must now walk me about the room and introduce me to your friends, before I begin to think we are all performing on the stage. Or is it all the rage in London to rudely stare at people when they enter a room?"

"Gad, you sound like Lady Burton," he said meekly. "You bid, and I obey. Let us make the rounds."

Seventeen

Sir Clapham first led Elisabeth to the group of matrons who had stepped aside to allow their hostess to greet the new arrivals. As the Vicar and his wife were announced at that moment, the Marquis and Dowager Marchioness, along with the Earl and Dowager Countess, were taken up with welcoming these latest guests, leaving Sir Clapham and Elisabeth on their own.

As they stopped before the matrons, Elisabeth was well aware of the speculation and assessments taking place behind their polite, social faces. And her great-aunt wondered why she didn't want to go to London for the Season, she thought ironically.

"Ladies," Sir Clapham bowed, "allow me to make known to you Lady Elisabeth Chadwick, daughter of the Earl of Chadwick. Her family's estate borders Loveland to the east."

Elisabeth smiled and curtseyed again as Sir Clapham introduced each woman in the circle. Her courtesies were received with a welcoming smile by Mrs. Benson-Smythe and cool nods from the other two ladies.

"Lady Elisabeth," said Lady Griegson, "I have met your father numerous times in London, but he has never mentioned you. Why is that, do you suppose?"

"You must needs ask him yourself," Elisabeth replied pleasantly. "I do know that, in general, he is rather reticent about discussing his family with outsiders."

Glances were exchanged at that veiled insult, the ladies not sure whether it had been deliberate or inadvertent.

"But one would assume he would want to introduce an eligible young daughter to society," said Lady Griegson, "unless there is some reason not to bring you out?"

"I daresay one of these days I shall visit London during the Season," Elisabeth said coolly, "unless something more interesting intervenes."

"More interesting?!" trilled Lady Childer in astonishment. "How amusing that you find country life more interesting than all that London offers. Quite charmingly provincial of you."

"Thank you," Elisabeth smiled again, stifling an urge to level a kick at the woman's shins. All of their shins, for that matter. Elisabeth visited London a few times each year for such errands as purchasing clothes or books, but she'd resisted all her great-aunt's persuasions to participate in a Season. And if these women were examples of the society she would encounter, she'd continue resisting.

At the sounds of a slight commotion at the entry to the room, she glanced back and saw that yet another guest had arrived, the ancient Lady Downs. As usual, she was being escorted by one of the tall, handsome footmen she invariably chose over the more traditional maidservants. As Elisabeth returned her attention to the matrons, she caught a start of dismay on the face of Mrs. Benson-Smythe, who also had looked at the doorway.

Elisabeth turned to her own escort, saying lightly, "Sir Clapham, I fear you and I may be preventing the other arrivals from mingling with the party. Perhaps we should allow these ladies the opportunity to meet the other local guests." Smiling all the while, she surreptitiously pinched his arm for emphasis.

"Ow-oh, yes, of course," he replied instantly. He sketched a brief bow. "Ladies, if you will excuse us."

"Of course, Sir Clapham," said Mrs. Benson-Smythe. Sir Clapham nodded and led Lady Elisabeth to the next group of guests, continuing their counter-clockwise circuit about the room. Ignoring Elisabeth as her escort led her away, the ladies immediately bent their heads together. Elisabeth was almost certain she heard the word "pert" whispered behind her as she moved away.

The next small group of guests was much more hospitable, being the four older men of the house party.

"My dear Lady Elisabeth," said Mr. Benson-Smythe. As she rose from yet another curtsey, he took her right hand and pumped it enthusiastically. "A pleasure to meet you at last. Your father always speaks so highly of you."

"Yes, but his description didn't do you justice," said Lord Childer. "What did he call her, Thomas, a pretty little thing, wasn't it? Never said what a lovely gal you were."

"No, he didn't," Lord Griegson agreed.

"Thank you," she said politely. "But knowing my father, are you sure he wasn't talking about one of his horses?" They stared at her a moment, uncertain how to respond. Then she winked.

They broke into laughter, drawing the glances of everyone in the room. The Marquis, just freed from welcoming Squire Mills, the last of the local guests to arrive, bethought himself of a need to speak with Sir Mendam, and began making his way toward the jovial group.

"So you are young Thomas's father," Elisabeth said to Lord Griegson. "I had the pleasure of meeting him yesterday morning at the border stream."

"Yes, I certainly heard about that," Lord Griegson replied. He turned to the other men in the group. "Do you know this young lady raises Scottish deerhounds? Huge dogs. But I could not credit Thomas telling me you had a dozen with you!"

"No," she said demurely, "not a dozen."

"Well, I didn't think that could be possible!"

"Actually, I had all thirteen with me."

The group broke into laughter again, and Sir Clapham took the opportunity to lead Lady Elisabeth away. He had been about to steer her toward the young ladies, when she lightly tugged his arm in a different direction. He looked toward where she was pulling him and saw young Lord Thomas Griegson shyly hanging back, watching their progress. He escorted Lady Elisabeth up to the lad, circling slightly around Thomas so that he and Lady Elisabeth could face the room while they chatted with the boy. It was always good to keep an eye out for interesting gossip.

"Lord Thomas," she said, smiling unaffectedly. "How are you doing after yesterday morning's encounter?"

He took the greeting as an invitation to step closer, and when she offered him a small curtsey, he executed a worthy bow for such a young man.

"I wasn't sure you would want to speak with me," he admitted, as he straightened from his bow.

"Why on earth not?!" she asked, astonished. "I would never ignore a friend."

He blushed a bright red at the compliment, "Well, m'sisters would ignore me."

"Yes, but that's nothing to the point," she said. "I likely would ignore my brother if I saw him, too. That's what brothers and sisters do."

"Lord, yes," Sir Clapham agreed. "Everyone knows I try my best to avoid acknowledging that any of my sisters even exist." He glanced about the room, noticing how many faces were turned their way.

"Now," he said, bending closer to Thomas, "speaking of sisters, I was just about to take Lady Elisabeth over to meet yours. Anything I should know?"

"Well," Thomas said seriously, "I don't think they like you. I heard Alma telling that short lady there," he said, nodding to Margaret Benson-Smythe, "not to bother with you because you're a hardened case, whatever that means."

Elisabeth tried to stifle a laugh, but the sight of Lord Clapham rolling a wild eye at her was too much to bear. She choked, burst into giggles, and then dissolved into a deliciously throaty laugh, her green eyes alight with mischief.

And that's when the Duke of Ravenwood and his younger brother were announced.

The Duke glanced toward the sound of her laughter, met her twinkling eyes, and promptly lost his much-touted sang froid. In fact, his mouth simply fell open.

Eighteen

The Duke's wasn't the only slack jaw in the room. Every single woman stared at him in amazement.

He recovered his wits and closed his mouth. He dragged his eyes away from the laughing beauty and found his host, who was standing with a group of older men. He advanced toward the Marquis with an outstretched hand.

"John, sorry to arrive so late," he said cordially. His gaze swept the room. He wondered why on earth the Marquis's mother was frowning so horribly at him. As was the older woman by her side.

"You know my brother Peter," he said, introducing the twelve-year-old miniature version of himself who tagged along at his side. "We would have been here earlier, but we stopped at the local inn to freshen up so as not arrive in all our travel dirt."

"A pleasure to have you at any time, Charles," the Marquis said. "I'm delighted you were able to arrive so promptly. Peter, you are shooting up like a weed." The Marquis glanced at his mother's face and bit back a grin.

"Come, let me introduce you and Peter to Thomas Griegson. The lads can enjoy getting to know each other."

He turned toward where Thomas stood with Sir Clapham and Lady Elisabeth, and stopped dead as he realized his gaffe. The Duke nearly bumped into him, feeling like a bit of a fool in front of all the watching eyes.

"Something wrong, John?" he asked.

"No, no," the Marquis muttered, moving forward again. He'd completely forgotten his manners. Instead of taking his cousins to the Dowager Marchioness for an introduction, he'd behaved like a bee heading to a flower, and had found an excuse to make a straight line toward Lady Elisabeth.

He also realized he was not at all pleased to be making Lady Elisabeth known to the handsome Duke of Ravenwood. He'd meant Charles to serve as a distraction to the unmarried ladies here, but he found the idea of Lady Elisabeth being distracted by his cousin an unwelcome thought.

As the Marquis reached Sir Clapham, Lady Elisabeth and Thomas, the silence in the room suddenly broke into waves of excited conversation. The Duke gave Sir Clapham a friendly thwack on the shoulder as the two shook hands.

"Ravenwood, well met," Sir Clapham said. "Monton told me he was inviting you. Glad to have you here. We're sadly outnumbered by the female contingent. God knows when, if ever, Wentworth will make it."

"Lady Elisabeth Chadwick, the Duke of Ravenwood," the Marquis interrupted curtly. The Duke looked at him in surprise, and then watched appreciatively as Lady

Elisabeth sank into a low curtsey. He took her hand as she rose and bowed over it, inhaling the sweet apple-and-cream scent of her skin.

He stepped back, waiting while the Marquis introduced Thomas and Peter. The two boys acknowledged each other uncertainly.

"Thomas," the Marquis suggested, "why don't you show our newest guest the game room? I'll arrange for your beverages and cakes to be served in there."

"Jolly!" Thomas exclaimed. He turned to the other boy. "You'll like the game room. Thank you, Sir."

The two boys trotted off, still taking each other's measure, but happy to vacate the realm of the adults. The Marquis signaled one of the footmen and gave him instructions to serve the two boys an outsized set of snacks with their tea and milk.

"So," the Duke turned to Lady Elisabeth with a smile, "Tell me truly what you think of old Rodney, here. Are you quite under his spell, or might it be possible for another interested party to gain your attention?"

Elisabeth sent a teasing glance toward her escort, before answering. "Oh, I think Sir Clapham is quite the hardened case. He merely seeks me out for protection."

"And I am happy to return the favor," Rodney bowed.

The Marquis raised one eyebrow. "I should think a pack of hounds provides you more than adequate protection, Lady Elisabeth."

"But as they were not invited to this gathering, I must make do with Sir Clapham," she said.

"I am known to be well housetrained," Rodney said modestly.

"And obedient to commands," the Marquis retorted.

"Which makes our relationship so much easier," Elisabeth shot back.

"A good thing for his visage," the Marquis agreed. "I've seen your footmen, remember."

"I find that daily beatings help keep the servants motivated," she said sweetly.

By this time both the Duke and Sir Clapham were staring at the two of them in confusion. And, she noticed, the Duke also looked highly amused. Wonderful, yet another Londoner to appraise her and find her lacking.

"Our two footmen recently took exception to the fact that they were both seeing the same maidservant," she explained to them. "One from your estate," she said to the Marquis.

"Hah!" Sir Clapham laughed. "Playing them off against each other. Wonder where she got that idea?"

"Been giving lessons to your staff?" the Duke asked.

The Marquis shot his cousin a nasty look, and then offered his arm to Elisabeth. "May I take over from Rodney and continue the introductions to our other guests, my lady?"

"No, thank you," Elisabeth said coolly. "I shall let Sir Clapham continue as my escort. You no doubt have other guests to entertain." And with that she once again placed her hand on Sir Clapham's arm and nipped him with a quick pinch. Rodney flashed the Marquis an unrepentant grin and walked off with his prize. He led her toward the group of young ladies who had been rather obviously straining to hear the foursome's conversation.

The Duke turned to his host with a wide grin. "Not the usual empty-headed lovely, is she? And apparently entirely impervious to your charms, John. What is her story? I collect she's Robert Chadwick's sister? I bought a pair of bays off him just t'other week."

The Marquis scowled at his cousin. He had been rocked by her refusal of his escort. He was so used to unmarried ladies trying to gain his attention that he couldn't remember the last time he'd been rebuffed.

"Yes, the Chadwick estate is next door," he said at last. "As to her story, Charles, that I couldn't tell you, except that her great beauty is matched only by her waspish tongue. And she appears to prefer the country. She likes to tramp about the fields with a pack of dogs."

"Sounds like someone else I know," the Duke chuckled. "Good-looking, nasty-tempered, impatient of social protocols and Town life, prefers to seclude himself in the wilds of the countryside. You ought to offer for her."

"Are you out of your mind?!" the Marquis exclaimed. Several heads turned in their direction. The Marquis lowered his voice. "I came here to get away from the ladies, Charles, not to seek a wife."

"Well, one wouldn't know it by this collection of guests," the Duke laughed. "I've never known you to invite a passel of husband hunters to your home before. What gives?"

"My mother gives, that's what," the Marquis grumbled. "She is so disappointed at Marybell Wister's defection that she would have it my heart is broken and must be quickly mended by finding another future Marchioness as soon as possible."

"Then I can offer you some balm for your tormented soul," the Duke said with a malicious smile. "The little

Wister has ended her engagement. She is once more free to pursue you with your mother's good will."

"What?!" This time the Marquis's shout momentarily stopped all conversation. He stared at the Duke in horror. "You cannot be serious!"

"Saw the notice in the paper just yesterday," the Duke affirmed. "Think I'll go say hello to my hostess now. Wouldn't be the thing to ignore her. Can't think why your manners are so lacking as to not take Peter and me to your mother directly upon my arrival. Perhaps you were distracted? But not to worry, I shall win her forgiveness for not greeting her by sharing the latest news from Town. I'll make my apologies for Peter, too." He grinned as he walked away from the horrified Marquis.

Nineteen

The Dowager Marchioness and the Dowager Countess had watched the Duke's arrival and conversation with equal parts astonishment and anger. They had so far forgotten their social duties as to simply stand and stare at the Duke's progress. But, as his arrival had had a similar effect on most of the women in the room, their lapse wasn't noticed.

"How did he come to be invited?" the Dowager Marchioness demanded of her older friend. "Depend upon it, my son is to blame. Ravenwood will draw all the girls' attentions. Drat it!"

"What is Elisabeth thinking, to be so forward in her conversation!" the Dowager Countess demanded back. "I know that expression – she is mocking her host!"

"This has upset all my table arrangements!" the Marquis's mother added in frustration.

"If she were younger, I would spank her!" Elisabeth's great-aunt agreed.

"All the girls are staring at him!"

"She just rejected his arm!"

"Oh, dear. He's coming this way."

"Why in heaven's name does she prefer a mere Baronet's son?"

They stopped talking as the Duke came within earshot. He bowed over the Dowager Marchioness's hand and thanked her for her kind invitation to join the party. This was said with such a knowing twinkle in his eye that she longed to smack him with her fan. Where was her fan, anyway, she wondered distractedly. In her agitation she began patting about her person, seeking to feel her fan.

The Dowager Countess poked her with an elbow. She recovered herself as the Duke turned toward her friend, awaiting an introduction.

"Lister, allow me to introduce the Duke of Ravenwood. He is one of John's cousins through my maternal grandmother, and a close friend of my son," she said through gritted teeth. "Charles, may I present Lady Burton, the Dowager Countess of Cwmhaven and the Earl of Chadwick's maternal aunt."

"Indeed," the Dowager Countess said freezingly, as the Duke bowed over her hand. She essayed a brief curtsey, clearly showing him she wasn't impressed by his rank.

"It is an honor to make your acquaintance," he said humbly. He returned his attention to his hostess. "Am I the last of the guests to arrive? I do apologize for barging in just as tea is about to be served. We were late setting out on the road this morning."

"No," his hostess said grimly. "We are still awaiting Lord Wentworth."

"Ah, let us hope he manages to make it before the end of the party. But is not Lady Marybell Wister coming?"

"Her?" the Dowager Marchioness asked in surprise. "Why would she be attending?"

"Yes, I fear I am being insensitive," he replied solemnly. "No doubt it is her preference to retreat from society for a while, now that she has broken her engagement to Carrington."

"What?!" the Dowager Marchioness shrieked.

"What on earth is Ravenwood saying to everyone to get them in such a pother?" Sir Clapham asked Lady Elisabeth. "I swear, there are more cries of alarm following him about than one hears at a fire."

"He does appear to be a rather startling conversationalist," Elisabeth said uncertainly. "He seemed so charming."

"He must be carrying some rather exciting news from Town," her escort decided. "Apologies, m'dear, but I'd be remiss in my duties as one of the Ton's leading gossips if I didn't unearth the tale." And with that he suddenly left her and made a beeline to the Marquis, who still stood like a statue where the Duke had left him.

Elisabeth stared in outrage at Sir Clapham's departing back. He'd just introduced her to these six young ladies, who looked eager to tear her to shreds, and now he was leaving! Her hands balled into fists as she made herself accept their offer of a seat with a smile as sweetly false as the ones with which they were gifting her.

"That handsome rogue certainly likes to stir the pot," the Dowager Countess of Cwmhaven said irritably to her hostess after the Duke had left them to greet the other guests.

"Yes, but is it true?" the Dowager Marchioness asked fretfully. "Can it be possible that Marybell's engagement to Lord Carrington has ended? What on earth do you suppose happened?"

"Sophia, I don't doubt for one moment that Carrington is the one who ended it," the Dowager Countess snapped, "regardless of what is being put about publicly. There is no way in this world that Mary Wister would let her daughter walk away from a title."

"But how cruel! Marybell must be devastated. Perhaps I should invite her family to join us?"

The Dowager Countess came as near to rolling her eyes as good manners would permit. "Don't even think it, Sophia. If that girl could so easily be distracted from your son's side as to become engaged to one of his friends, and then lose her fiancé in a fortnight, she is a worthless widgeon. She doesn't have the good sense needed to become the next Marchioness."

Elisabeth, meanwhile, abandoned by Sir Clapham, prepared to be subjected to a round of interrogation by the six young ladies. She wasn't disappointed.

"Do you come to London much?" asked Lady Cora Griegson politely, although everyone already knew the answer. She lowered her lush eyelashes over her fine brown eyes as she raised her chin slightly, giving the impression of looking down her nose at Elisabeth. "I don't recall having seen you before."

"I prefer the country," Elisabeth responded. She forced back the desire to raise her chin in return.

"But it is so hot here," Lady Cora's older sister, Lady Alma, complained. "Is it always thus?"

"This is an unusually warm summer," Elisabeth conceded, "but in general the West Country is very mild and pleasant."

"And do you have hobbies with which to stay occupied?" asked the young and lovely, but haughty, Lady Cora. She managed to place an insinuating emphasis on the word "hobbies." Yes, Elisabeth wanted to respond, I like to take hatchets to rude visitors from London.

"I raise dogs," Elisabeth replied instead. "And of course I am active in shire life. I imagine it is much like any country setting."

"Dogs," Lady Georgina Dunbarton said. The word hung in the air. The others looked from Elisabeth to Lady Georgina and back to Elisabeth.

"Yes, I raise Scottish deerhounds," Elisabeth replied.

"Are they not rather large dogs?" Miss Margaret Benson-Smythe asked. She appeared to be looking at Elisabeth with sincere interest.

"Yes, they are," Elisabeth said. "As their name implies, they were bred to hunt deer. But they are not aggressive creatures. They generally are quite mellow companions."

"Well, if one wants a large, hairy companion," Lady Violet Childer shuddered. Lady Cora tittered at the comment.

"I believe I know your sister-in-law," Lady Rose Childer interrupted, impatient of her older sister's sensibilities. "She went to the same finishing school as Violet and I."

"Oh, do you know Caroline?" Elisabeth asked with genuine enthusiasm. "She is a delightful girl."

"Much younger than you, is she not?" Lady Georgina asked.

"I am twenty-four, if that is your question," Elisabeth replied. "How old are you?"

The youngest members of the group – Lady Cora Griegson and Lady Rose Childer, both just eighteen and with one Season each – gasped.

"Not as old as you," Lady Georgina replied coldly.

"Ah, and I thought those were a few white hairs I saw," Elisabeth smiled.

Lady Georgina's face flushed as all the girls reflexively turned to look at her hair. She prided herself on her dark, charcoal-colored locks, but she also knew herself to be prematurely graying. And she wasn't used to other women challenging her title as the Ton's reigning beauty, as this new arrival surely did. She tried to cover her anger with an ironic smile.

"I am told your brother has chosen to live with his bride in Town," she said. "I would have expected him to bring her to live on your family's estate. Is there some difficulty attached to his living here at home?"

Elisabeth smiled again. Her face was beginning to hurt. "Just the difficulty any pair of newlyweds would experience at giving up their privacy. As I'm sure you'll learn if you marry."

More gasps greeted this comment.

"As is true of all of us," Margaret Benson-Smythe hurriedly interjected into the breach. "Oh, look," she added rather desperately, "here's tea."

Twenty

The double doors to the salon had opened as the tea service made its appearance. Servants bustled about setting the massive teapot and tray on the room's serving sideboard, followed by platters of cakes, scones, sweetbreads, and fruits. Maids moved about the room taking requests as the butler poured from the heavy silver teapot.

Elisabeth itched to be gone from this stifling environment, where she was forced to fence with sharp-tongued harpies. She knew she should watch her every word and expression more closely, but she wasn't about to just allow herself to be insulted. Really, what did people enjoy so much about these types of social gatherings?

She glanced to where Vicar and Mrs. Smithers sat in embarrassed isolation in one of the upholstered window seats, ignored by the other guests. She used the interruption of a servant offering her tea to stand and make her excuses to her tormentors.

"Just some cream, no sugar," she requested. "I'll be over there." And with that she left the group and joined the Vicar and his wife.

The Marquis, meanwhile, had emptied his budget to Sir Clapham.

"I swear, Rodney, if that female takes after me again, I'll flee to the Continent. I barely escaped her and my mother's snares last time."

"Yes, odds at White's were running in her favor," Sir Clapham agreed. "You were singularly lucky to have Carrington appear on the scene."

"And what's up with that?" the Marquis demanded. "He cannot hold onto his fiancée more than a few paltry weeks? I'll take good care to find someone more anxious to be wed the next time I need to offload a determined female."

"Hah! Knew you had something to do with that," Sir Clapham said. "Told Wentworth it was just too coincidental that Carrington came down to London to have a look at one of your stallions just as Merry Marybell was closing in. First girl he meets, and suddenly he's engaged to her? I expect his mother descended on him like a typhoon the moment he wrote. She's behind the end of that engagement, mark my words. You ever met Carrington's mother?"

"No," the Marquis grumbled. "But what man would bow like that to his mother's wishes?"

"You almost did."

"I did no such thing!"

"Hmm. Well, maybe not, but you certainly didn't lay down the law to her, either, did you? Just tried to play least in sight whenever Lady Marybell was in the vicinity."

"Well, what do we think of her?" Lady Cora Griegson asked the group. Her lovely face was lit with anticipation. "Did you not think she was the rudest creature you ever met?"

Lady Georgina Dunbarton gave a sniff, but forbore to comment. She was seething with anger at being bested both in looks and verbal fencing by a country nobody. She was also well aware of the watching Mrs. Breden, who would report every lapse of manners back to her father.

Lady Violet Childer was happy to take up the slack. "Such odd manners. I can certainly believe she spends all her time with dogs."

Miss Margaret Benson-Smythe sat silent as the others discussed Lady Elisabeth. Margaret had rather liked seeing someone face down Lady Georgina, who was known to be rather cutting to the younger misses on the social scene.

As a petite, slightly plump, brunette, Margaret was attractive, but by no means a beauty. She herself had been subjected to Lady Georgina's subtle barbs more than once. Unlike the many young women who admired Lady Georgina and considered her a leader of the Ton, Margaret had no love for the dark-haired – and graying, she thought with quiet delight – beauty. She wondered what was going on behind Lady Georgina's composed façade as she looked across at her.

"You're being very quiet, Alma," Lady Cora said to her older sister, who was gazing somewhat distractedly into space. "What did you think?"

"I have not spoken with her long enough to make up my mind," Lady Alma said. She hadn't disliked Lady Elisabeth, but she was deeply jealous of that lady's beauty. She had so wanted to not be the only plain spinster in the room.

Lady Alma turned toward her younger sister, but Lady Cora had lost interest in the conversation. Instead, Lady Cora was following the Duke's progress about the room with avaricious eyes.

"I found her nice enough," Lady Violet Childer said, "but I could not abide being surrounded by dogs and frogs. It seems so odd."

Her younger sister, Lady Rose, wrinkled her nose. "Honestly, Violet, must you be so squeamish about everything? Frogs, of course, I can understand, but what is there to find fault with in raising dogs?"

"I intend to follow Pansy's lead when I marry," retorted Violet, referring to their older sister. "She informed Alfred that she would have nothing to do with his hunting dogs. He keeps their hounds in the country and locked in the kennels when he is not exercising them or hunting. Dogs do nothing but drool and shed."

"Well, they do worse than that," Lady Georgina said caustically, to the others' laughter.

Elisabeth, having directed a servant to place a chair near the window seat occupied by Vicar and Mrs. Smithers, heard the laughter behind her and was certain she was its object.

"They seem quite a lively group of young ladies," said Mrs. Smithers kindly. "I expect you must miss the company of your sister, now that she's set up her own establishment."

Unlike the barbs she'd received from the London guests, Elisabeth knew this comment was meant kindly.

"Yes, indeed, I do miss Anne. We used to have such comfortable cozes. She writes that she is quite happy, and they plan to visit this autumn, but letters are not the same as being able to sit together in the evenings and discuss the day."

"I know just how you feel, with my Melody now a married woman and living two counties over. I am sure I am glad she is happy, but I do miss her."

"But we are delighted in the news we receive of our grandson," the Vicar smiled. "He is growing up so quickly! We are very proud grandparents."

"Indeed we are," Mrs. Smithers agreed. "And I've no doubt that soon either Robert or Anne will give your father that pleasure as well."

Elisabeth smiled in return, but felt for the first time a pang of disquiet at her circumstances. Her father, a grandfather. And she, an aunt. A maiden aunt.

Twenty-One

"The afternoon was a great success, I think," the Dowager Marchioness said to her son with satisfaction. "Despite Grace's determination to hide behind the plants."

They were sharing a few moments of peace in the sitting room that made up part of his suite on the east side of the manor. The Marquis, ignoring polite convention, had pulled off his boots and now sat with his long legs and stockinged feet resting on a large ottoman, slouched down in a cushioned chair in a pose of extreme relaxation. His mother, never one to succumb to casual posture, sat bolt upright on a delicate chair that had been carried in behind her by one of the footmen.

"Yes, what was up with that?" the Marquis asked. "Every time I glanced in her direction she appeared to be bending her knees to crouch behind someone, or she was peering out from behind those bushes you insist on keeping in the salon."

"Those are not bushes!" the Dowager defended herself. "They are lovely flowering ferns that I had the servants bring in from the hothouse for the party."

"Ferns don't flower, Mother."

"Must you forever take me up on everything I say?" she said in frustration. "They are plants, they have flowers. And ferns or not, I think they look nice in the salon."

"And so, apparently, does Mrs. Benson-Smythe. She was forever inspecting them. Or using them as a refuge. I am beginning to wonder if she is a bit dotty."

"She is not dotty," the Dowager said. "She was merely hiding from Lady Downs."

"Lady Downs? The antiquarian with the towering footman? What on earth for?"

The Dowager gave her son an irritated sigh. " 'Tis none of your business, John. Don't tease me about it."

"Very well, then, what shall I tease you about?" he smiled.

"You've already done that with the arrival of our unexpected new guest," she said with a minatory glance.

"Charles wasn't unexpected," the Marquis said. "I invited him and Peter. I thought it would be nice for Thomas to have someone here his age."

"Did you. So unusually thoughtful. And where, may I ask, are you putting them? I thought we were full up. There are just sixteen bedrooms here, you know. Not nearly as large as Edmonton Castle. You should have held your house party there."

"I gave them Wentworth's room," he said, ignoring his mother's suggestion that this party had been his idea. "If he ever deigns to arrive he can bunk with Rodney."

"Your friends Sir Clapham and Lord Ringwood are already sharing a room."

"Fine, then he can share with both Rodney and Richard."

"You have upset all my plans!" she cried, standing up in agitation.

"What, you don't want me to have a third bed brought into Rodney and Richard's room?"

She rose and began to pace about the room, touching various objets d'art on the shelves and tables. "You know what I mean! This party was to help you meet a nice girl, one who could take on the role of your Marchioness after the loss of your fiancée!"

"Lady Marybell was not my fiancée," the Marquis said. "Please do not go about saying so."

"And now you have gone and invited that devilishly handsome Charles Ravenwood here!"

"Well, handsome as Charles is, Mother, he can only take one woman to wife. That still leaves six other women here who might be willing to settle for –" He broke off as he realized what he'd just said.

His mother also was fully capable of doing math. "Six other women?" she asked, picking up yet another figurine on her path around the room. "But I only invited six eligible girls. Who –" She stared at him. "You're including Lady Elisabeth?"

He sighed again. "Well, she is one of the guests, isn't she?"

She paused in her pacing to consider the matter. "The Chadwicks are a very good family. Perhaps I should include her in more of the entertainments."

He watched her warily as she started moving around the room again. Her mood seemed to be picking up.

"Yes," she said decisively. "I'll invite her to the picnic a few days hence. John, I am so glad you are showing an interest in someone at last!"

"Wait," he said. "I didn't say that. I said —"

"All our problems may be over!" she said cheerily, heading toward the door, still clutching a figurine in one hand. "I'd best start changing for supper."

Well, he thought to himself as she shut the door behind her, not all of their problems were over. He'd distinctly seen a small, dark shape scurry behind his mother out the door of the sitting room into the hall.

Yes, he grinned a moment later as a shriek rent the air from the hall, his mother had more unwanted guests than just one wealthy, handsome, and unattached Duke.

Twenty-Two

"Well, that was quite an eventful gathering," Mrs. Benson-Smythe said to her husband as they relaxed in their suite before dinner. She was lounging on a chaise near the balcony, enjoying the fitful breeze that occasionally made its way into the room through the open French doors.

Mr. Benson-Smythe gave his wife a fond smile. Really, he thought yet again, he was incredibly lucky to have met her all those years ago. "You are referring to the advent of the new beauty, I assume? Rather put a few noses out of joint, I should say."

He tugged at the afternoon neck cloth he'd worn to the tea, and finally succeeded in loosening the knot enough to pull it off. "Dratted thing," he muttered. "I must talk with Waller about how tight he knots these cloths. Felt as though I was near to strangulation all afternoon. Could barely get a bite past this noose. Are you bribing him to tie these things so tight that I can't eat?"

His lady giggled, sounding delightfully girlish. "As though I need to worry about you overindulging. I never met such a picky eater. Why, I was amazed when you actually ate an entire scone today. And what did you think of Lady Elisabeth Chadwick?"

"Undoubtedly a pearl beyond perfection," he said as he tossed the neck cloth onto a chair near the wardrobe. "Can't think why Robert hasn't brought her to London for a Season. Could have any of the eligibles for the lifting of a finger."

"Clara Griegson looked as though she had just tasted the most bitter nut meat you can imagine when the Chadwicks walked in. Little hope for Cora to snare any of the titled gentlemen with competition such as Lady Georgina and Lady Elisabeth both at Loveland!"

"You don't seem too concerned about Margie, my dear. Most unmotherlike of you."

"Margie will be fine," she said, twitching her skirts a bit to make herself more comfortable. "She has no need to marry anywhere but where she will, and I hope I have raised her to look beyond title and fortune and face."

Mr. Benson-Smythe didn't answer for a moment as he focused on wrestling himself out of his afternoon jacket. "Why couldn't that cursed Brummell have set a style for baggy clothes?" he complained as he finally got free of the offending article of clothing. "Not enough that everything must be black as though we were all perpetually in mourning, no it all must be skintight, too. Dratted man."

"Yes, dear," his wife agreed absently, her thoughts elsewhere. "But tell me what you thought of Lady

Elisabeth. She seemed to much amuse the group you were in. What is your opinion?"

"I found her quite charming and witty. Not your usual society miss. Nothing out of line, mind you, but more amusing than I'd normally expect to find in a deb. She don't trade on her beauty, I'll say that in her favor. No simpering. Can't stand simpering."

"Oh dear," his wife laughed. "No simpering! She will have nothing in common with any of the other young ladies here."

"Nonsense," he said, walking across the room to the bed, where he sat and began pulling at a boot. "Margie don't simper. One of the things I like best about our girl. Might be shy, but no false airs. I'm very proud of the way you've raised her, my dear."

Mrs. Benson-Smythe smiled in gratification at this compliment. For many years, she had feared never to have a child. But then, as she was nearing forty, she had been delighted to discover she was pregnant. And never once after Margie was born had her wonderful husband given her to believe he would have preferred a son.

Their little Margie showed every sign of growing into a kind and thoughtful young woman. But Mrs. Benson-Smythe was far more interested in gossip at the moment than in discussing her daughter's upbringing.

"And what do you make of that dragon who follows Lady Georgina's every move?" she asked. "Odd that her father didn't accompany her here, don't you think?"

"Nigel Dunbarton has a high opinion of his importance to Whitehall," Mr. Benson-Smythe said with a snort. He tossed the boot in the general direction of his neck cloth and jacket, and began yanking at his other boot. "Thinks the government might fall if he so much as sets foot outside of London. Don't think he's been to his family's holdings for years. His daughter has no choice but to travel without him if she's ever to see anything beyond the limits of Town."

"She's quite beautiful herself," Mrs. Benson-Smythe said. "She always seems so remarkably poised, and she is acknowledged to be an excellent political hostess. But Margie says she is not particularly kind to the unmarried girls."

"No, I daresay she may have the late Lady Dunbarton's looks, but I expect she is cut from the same mold as her father. He's an ambitious, prideful man. It's no surprise to me she's still unwed; none of the royal dukes is available, and I expect she won't settle for much less than that."

"What about Ravenwood?" his wife asked

Mr. Benson-Smythe barked out a laugh. "Charles, saddle himself with a well-bred marble statue? No, she'll grow cold at that gambit." He fell back on the bed as he finally succeeded in tugging off the second boot.

"Well, he certainly seemed taken by Lady Elisabeth," his wife commented. "Perhaps we might see a match there?"

"Possibly. He's a bit of a rascal, and no doubt would like someone with a lively spirit. But, really, my dear, must you seek to matchmake for others? Here's your poor old husband, finally freed from his coat and boots, and sprawled out most comfortably on the bed, and you're ignoring him. Come join me, my dear."

"Well," she smiled roguishly as she rose from the chaise, "there is nothing like a nap after tea."

"Nap?" he said in mock offense. "I'm not that old!"

"Well, good, I'm glad you don't want to nap, because you snore so dreadfully," she giggled as she climbed onto the bed and he pulled her down beside him.

Twenty-Three

"The afternoon went rather well," the Dowager Countess said to her nephew and great-niece that evening at supper. "Elisabeth, you comported yourself quite appropriately."

"Thank you," Elisabeth said, irritated that the issue should even be in question.

"For a change," her great-aunt added.

Elisabeth stifled a retort and glanced to where her father was making inroads into a slice of beef. "And thank you, Father, for your efforts. I did notice them."

"What efforts were those?" the Dowager asked, looking at her nephew. "I thought you spent most of your time visiting with the men."

The Earl glanced briefly at his aunt, then returned his attention to his plate and replied carefully, "I spent a good amount of time introducing Squire Mills to the other guests, to keep him occupied."

"And why should you care about keeping Squire Mills happy?" the Dowager asked Elisabeth suspiciously.

"Because I'd rather he not be happy with me," Elisabeth said bluntly.

"Happy with you? What is that supposed to mean?"

The Earl put down his knife and fork with a clang. "The Squire seems to have taken a fancy to Elsbet, despite my clearly informing him that his suit would not be welcome. I did not want him paying his attentions to her at the tea. I am sure you would agree that he is not a suitable husband for my daughter?"

"Of course not!" the Dowager gasped. "What a ridiculous notion!"

"And yet he persists in it," Elisabeth frowned. "I assure you I have never given him the least indication I would welcome his interest."

"Of course not!" the Dowager said again. "But you are a lovely girl with a generous dowry. It is yet another reason for you to go to London. I am sure you would take, even with your odd manners. You simply must have the opportunity to meet an eligible parti."

Elisabeth wasn't sure if she had been complimented or insulted. She looked at her father, who was watching her carefully.

"Perhaps I should send you away for a while," he said. "Not," he hastened to add before she could interrupt, "necessarily to London next Season, but perhaps to visit Robbie or Anne. Givens is well able to take care of your dogs for a few weeks," he said, referring to the estate's head groom.

"Sending her to Robbie is a good idea," the Dowager said to her nephew. "He lives in London, and he and Caroline enjoy an active social life. It is a place where Elisabeth can meet people. Anne is another matter. She lives far from society. A visit there would be no better than staying here."

"Am I at some point to have a say in this plan?" Elisabeth asked.

"Not if your only intent is to resist," her great-aunt stated. "Besides, there is no need to leave in the immediate future. There are several eligible men at Loveland Manor right now. You would do well to consider one of them."

"Good idea," Elisabeth nodded. "I shall go over tomorrow and inspect their teeth and hairlines."

"Elisabeth Chadwick!" the Dowager stormed, "Do not persist in making these outlandish remarks! This is exactly the sort of behavior that will give gentlemen a disgust of you. Robert, do something about your daughter!"

"I am doing something," he said mildly. "I am keeping the Squire away from her and agreeing that she needs to experience a wider field of acquaintances." He smiled at his daughter. "Elsbet is her own woman, Aunt Lister, and I intend to allow her to make her own choices about her future."

He picked up his knife and fork, and returned his attention to his dinner, signaling the conversation was over.

Twenty-Four

"What do you say to a morning shooting party?" the Duke asked his companions that evening as the company settled into after-dinner groups. He was sharing a card table with the Marquis, Sir Clapham, and Lord Ringwood.

"I would," the Duke continued, "normally await an invitation from my host, but my host seems disinclined to do his duty by his guests."

"Sod off, Charles," the Marquis said pleasantly.

"I say, a hunting party sounds just the thing," Lord Ringwood said, loquacious now that none of the single ladies was nearby. "Walk the woods, scare up some game. We can pack some lunch, get back in time for tea." He brushed his dark blond hair back from his face, a habitual gesture the Marquis suddenly found intensely annoying.

"Richard, are you ever going to get that horsemane cut?" the Marquis demanded.

"Well, you're a charmer tonight, Monton," Sir Clapham said, playing a ten of hearts. "Matter of fact, you've been on the surly side since tea."

"Since the Chadwick chit rebuffed your advances, actually," the Duke grinned. He laid down a trump card over Rodney's.

"Deuce take it, Rodney," the Marquis complained. "What possessed you to lead with that card?"

"Well how was I to know Ravenwood was out of hearts?"

"Possibly by paying attention to his plays?" the Marquis asked sarcastically. "I should have known better than to sit across from you."

"Hah! As if I'm enjoying having a surly bear like you for a partner! I could always switch with Ringwood, here. Serve you right."

"Hey," Richard protested. "I'm not that bad at cards."

"Yes you are," the other three said.

"You know it's either Rodney or Richard," the Duke commented to their irritable host. "If you and I teamed up against this pair of idiots, they'd have to figure out how to keep negative scores."

"Can't do that," said Richard. "Not possible."

"I assure you, it would be," the Duke laughed. "Never saw such a pair of ignoramuses where cards were concerned. My brother Peter could best the both of you."

" 'Tis why I don't enter the play at White's," Sir Clapham acknowledged. "Much rather watch."

"And listen," Lord Ringwood said with a knowing look.

"You'd be amazed at what one can learn from a group of card players in their cups," Sir Clapham agreed. "Why, did you know that old Sturbridge is near bankrupt? Looking to sell either his horses or his daughters. Needs funds badly."

"His horses have better teeth," the Marquis commented as he played a card he could afford to lose against the Duke's trump.

"So, what about Ravenwood's idea of a tramp through the woods in the morning?" Lord RIngwood asked. He played a card, finishing the round.

The Duke gave an exasperated sigh. "Really, Richard? You found it appropriate to play a higher club? I'd already taken that trick."

"Oh, sorry. I never can remember when an ace is a high card or a low card. Don't see why they can't just pick one and make it the same for every game."

"You must be great fun at vingt-et-un," the Duke said. "Remind me to play you sometime. I'll make a fortune."

"Never play for stakes," Lord Ringwood said. "Wagering on horses, that's another matter."

"And marriages," Sir Clapham said, tossing down a card at random. The Marquis groaned at the sight of another low heart and felt a strong desire to clutch at his hair. "I saw your stake against La Wister's ability to legshackle Monton."

"Thank you for your support," the Marquis said to Lord Ringwood.

"Yes, well, he's a stubborn sort, y'know?" Lord Ringwood said to Sir Clapham. "If he don't want to marry, I don't see anyone dragging him to the altar."

The Duke tossed down another trump card. The Marquis, forced to follow suit, threw down a king of hearts that was now wasted against the Duke's trump. Richard reached for a card.

"Richard," said the Duke in freezing accents, "if you dare to play a higher club than mine I shall give serious consideration tomorrow morning to accidentally shooting you. No one will blame me."

Lord Ringwood let go of the card he'd been about to play. He scrunched his face into a look of painful concentration. At last he pulled out the lowest card in his hand. It was a three of hearts.

"Dammit, Richard," the Duke complained. "You reneged last time, you imbecile. If you had a heart you should have played it, and not trumped my trump!" He threw down his cards in frustration. "This game is hash."

"Anyone for billiards?" the Marquis asked, tossing down his cards as well. "We can discuss plans for the morning. If you're all set on beating the bushes, I'll let Applewood know to make sure the guns are cleaned and ready."

"Think I'll wander around and watch some of the other tables," Sir Clapham said. "I'll let the others know we're planning a hunting party," he said, nodding at the men seated around the room, "see if anyone wants to join us."

"I need to send some letters," Lord Ringwood said. "Mind if I use your study?"

"Not at all," the Marquis said. "The pens should be freshly shaved."

"Appreciate it," Lord Ringwood said, rising from the table. "I need to send my man of business news of m'sister's latest little cricket team member. I've promised to settle a thousand pounds on each of her offspring."

"Well that's no way to stop her from breeding," the Duke commented. "No wonder you can't afford to lose at cards."

Sir Clapham stood as well, looked around the room for a moment, then decided on his quarry. The Marquis and Duke watched appreciatively as Sir Clapham wended his way past the table of older gentlemen, tarrying just long enough to be polite, before apparently ending at random near the matrons.

"Good information source there," the Duke approved. "It's amazing the ondits that get about in the female world."

The Marquis and Duke finally rose and strolled into the game room. They selected their sticks, then flipped a coin to determine who would rack the balls and take the first shot. Both expert players, they soon were immersed in the game, not realizing they had drawn an audience. When they finally looked up, it was to see most of the other men in the party quietly exchanging bets on the outcome of the match.

The ladies of the party had wearied of cards, and now were arranged in small groups in the next room, chattering among themselves. Sir Horace Mendam and Sir Rodney Clapham had remained with the women, and were enjoying the attentions of the females of their respective generations.

"No, no, no," Rodney was saying in accents of extreme loathing, "How can you say any gown looks good with more than six flounces? I don't care how popular it is, the look is far too fussy."

He gazed earnestly at the young ladies clustered around him – the four youngest at the party, the Ladies Cora, Rose, and Violet, and Miss Margaret – intent on making his case. They gazed back, taking his opinion seriously. Sir Clapham was known to escort only the most dashing females, and to be an arbiter of all things fashionable.

From a settee a few feet away, the Ladies Alma and Georgina listened with amusement, but took no part in the discussion. Seated behind Lady Georgina, as usual, was the dour Mrs. Breden.

"But did you not think Penelope Greenwood's gown at the Martons' ball was simply gorgeous?" Margaret asked Sir Clapham. "It had fully twelve flounces!"

Rodney shook his head firmly at the small brunette. "The gown must suit the woman wearing it, Miss Benson-Smythe. Miss Greenwood has quite favorable looks, but the gown was simply out of proportion. To carry off a dozen flounces a lady must needs be nine feet tall!"

"You are saying the shorter the lady, the fewer the flounces?" Lady Rose asked.

"Most definitely. A petite lady," he said, studiously avoiding eye contact with Margaret, the shortest among the group, "would be advised to wear no more than two flounces at the most, and those only very small."

"But I love the motion that flounces make as one walks," Lady Cora protested. She smiled down at the six flounces adorning her gown. "Why, based on your judgment, I would be limited to merely three or four flounces. I would look positively provincial!"

"Perhaps," Lady Violet said, "but I have long thought too many flounces do nothing more than capture the dust and dirt of the street."

"Oh, honestly, Violet, there is such a thing as being too fastidious, you know," her sister Rose complained.

"No," Violet retorted, "I don't know that. I like things to be neat and clean. There is nothing wrong with choosing not to expose myself to dirt and debris."

Margaret blushed as the debate continued. She thought of the wardrobe her mama had arranged for her to bring to this house party. She wondered if her maid could remove some of the excess flounces that cluttered her dresses. Sir Clapham was known to have an excellent eye for fashion.

A short time later the Dowager Marchioness signaled it was time for the ladies to retire. The mamas gathered their flock of daughters, and the gentlemen briefly stepped out of the game room to bid the ladies goodnight.

Then, left to their own devices, the men promptly exited the game room, trooped toward the back of the house to the gun room off the kitchens, and began selecting their weapons for the morrow's walk.

Twenty-Five

Just before dawn the next morning, all the men of the party set off on foot through the fields. Four servants led the way, beating the bushes to scare up game and carrying satchels to bag any birds or hares that might run afoul of the hunters.

As they progressed through the fields, the men soon split into two groups, with the older generation preferring to take a more leisurely pace, and deciding to veer along the easier terrain to the northwest side of the estate. The Marquis, Duke, Sir Clapham, and Lord Ringwood headed more directly north, following the edge of the woods that ran between the estate's fields and the border stream.

An occasional shot rang out as pheasants burst forth from bushes or hares darted across the path, but for the most part the men were simply enjoying a good early morning hack through the woods.

"I say, Monton," Lord Ringwood commented as he reloaded after missing a shot, "I was surprised to see Lady Georgina Dunbarton among your guests. Didn't know she ever left the salons of London. She a good friend of the family?"

"She'd certainly like to be," the Duke laughed. "Particularly after four years on the Town without a match."

The Marquis glowered at the two men. "She is on my mother's short list of choices for my future wife. But now that Charles is here, I have hopes the prospect of acquiring a Duchess's coronet might take her eyes off me as a potential prize."

"Thank you so much for that word of warning," the Duke said with a snort. "I'll take care to spread my charms widely."

"Not a fan of hers," Lord Ringwood said. "She don't have the time of day for anyone less than an Earl." As the second son of an Earl, Richard had been given an estate and sufficient funds to maintain it, but was not considered one of the most eligible bachelors among ladies seeking titles. He was well used to being snubbed by the more acquisitive mothers of the Ton.

A nearby gunshot sent a bullet whizzing past the Duke's head. He spun around furiously, to see Sir Clapham pointing a rifle in their general direction. "Rodney, you blithering idiot!" he shouted. "What the hell do you mean by shooting at me?!"

"I wasn't," Sir Clapham said apologetically. "At least I didn't intend to," he amended. "I was following the bird."

"Well you damn well don't follow the path of a bird up over your head and back toward your party, do you?" the Duke snarled.

"Terribly sorry, Ravenwood," Sir Clapham said sincerely. "Lost my head. Was a beautiful bird."

"Well I've a beautiful head, too," the Duke said angrily, "and I'd prefer not to have it blown to smithereens by a fool like you!"

"Yes, yes," Sir Clapham said snidely. "We all know what an Adonis you are. Not a single lady could be bothered to look my way from the moment you made your dramatic arrival yesterday."

"Oh?" the Marquis inquired with raised eyebrows. "Was there anyone in particular you wanted to look your way?"

Sir Clapham gazed briefly at the other three men, all of whom were staring at him curiously, then uttered an oath under his breath and took off ahead of them.

The Duke and Marquis exchanged interested glances. Lord Ringwood nodded to himself. "Thought so," he said.

"Thought what?" the Marquis asked. "You aren't seriously telling us that Rodney is thinking of taking up matrimony?"

"Happened to notice something, that's all," Lord Ringwood said mildly.

Up ahead there was another shot, followed by a curse. The three men hurried to catch up to where Rodney was accepting a reloaded rifle from one of the two servants who had stayed with their foursome.

"Missed again," Sir Clapham muttered.

"There's a broad barn up ahead," the Marquis commented. "You could try your aim at that."

"Let's walk abreast for a while," the Duke said. "I'd feel safer if I knew where Rodney was."

"Good idea, Charles," the Marquis agreed. "Not because of Rodney," he quickly added, seeing that man drawing in an angry breath. "I expect we'll have a better chance of flushing game if we spread out through those low bushes ahead."

The four men fanned out, followed by the two servants.

Another half hour saw two pheasants added to the satchel being carried by one of the servants. Sir Clapham, who'd succeeded in bagging one of the birds, was considerably mollified by his companions' congratulations.

Ahead of them a movement in one of the bushes caught the Duke's eye. He raised his rifle just as a large bird burst into flight. Suddenly a female voice shouted from the woods. "Charles, no! Get down!"

The Duke froze for a moment, then flung himself to the ground. The others looked around in surprise, trying to find the source of the voice.

After several long moments of silence, the Duke cautiously rose to his hands and knees. He'd just regained his feet when the voice yelled again. "No! I said get down! Charles, do as I say!"

The Duke, thinking he must be in the line of fire from another hunter, dropped to the ground again, hugging it while he waited to hear the sound of a rifle shot. The Marquis and Richard had hunkered down as well, and were turned toward the woods trying to see the source of the warnings.

What the hell was going on, the Duke wondered, beginning to grow angry. He got to his hands and knees.

"Charles, sit!"

He sat. Or rather he rolled backwards in an ungainly heap. He sprawled there in confusion, leaning back on his hands, his legs splayed out in front of him. He waited, still expecting to hear gunfire. But what he unmistakably heard instead was the sound of Sir Clapham suddenly bursting into loud laughter.

Then the Duke saw Sir Clapham point at something in the woods. The Marquis stood, looked in the direction Sir Clapham was indicating, and promptly joined Sir Clapham in laughter. From his position on the ground the Duke stared up at them in mounting anger, while Lord Ringwood looked on in confusion.

"What is so amusing?" Lady Elisabeth asked Sir Clapham and the Marquis as she emerged from the woods with a large dog at her side.

The Duke scrambled to his feet, deeply embarrassed to be found covered with grass and leaves and soil from his encounters with the ground. He brushed himself off as Sir Clapham tried in vain to answer her through his laughter. The damned fool was laughing so hard his face was streaming with tears, the Duke noted, and the Marquis wasn't in much better shape.

"Yes, what is so blasted funny?" he demanded irritably.

"Allow me," the Marquis said to Sir Clapham. He turned to the Duke and gasped for breath as he tried to master his laughter. "I believe you know Lady Elisabeth Chadwick."

"Of course I know her. You introduced us yesterday afternoon," the Duke said in a tone that clearly implied his cousin was a chucklehead.

"Yes, but you haven't met her favorite hound. She takes him almost everywhere. His name is Charles."

At which point he and Sir Clapham once again dissolved into laughter, this time joined by Lord Ringwood.

Twenty-Six

Elisabeth watched in confusion as the three men clutched their sides and howled with amusement while the Duke stood there red-faced. Her eyes were drawn more than she would have liked to the sight of the Marquis, his face alight with laughter. She never would have thought to see him enjoy himself so freely. If she had thought him handsome before, he now seemed even more so, with his formal manners given over to such high humor.

Finally, as the three men's laughter began to dwindle to chuckles, interspersed with occasional upbursts of renewed hilarity, the Duke's scowl gradually gave way to a rueful grin. He was, she saw, regaining his normal color as his embarrassment slowly lessened. Then, as most of the guffaws were at last dying away, he stepped forward and essayed a brief bow.

"Allow me to introduce myself to you once again," he said to Elisabeth with an ironic smile. "I am the Eighth Duke of Ravenwood. My full name is Charles Winston William Ravenwood. My friends call me Charles, and I have been very successfully obeying all your recent commands to get down, sit, and stay. That is why I'm covered in dirt."

Elisabeth began giggling. "I am so sorry, your Grace! Charles is not always as well-behaved as one could wish."

"That's true enough," the Marquis said with a look at the Duke. He and Sir Clapham promptly burst into renewed laughter.

"Put a cork in it," the Duke demanded.

"Gad, I cannot wait to tell this story," Sir Clapham grinned.

"Don't you dare," the Duke growled.

"I can see it now," the unrepentant Sir Clapham enthused, his eyes taking on a distant look. "It would make a wonderful Cruickshank cartoon, with you laid out at Lady Elisabeth's feet, and Charles ... er, the other Charles ... lifting a leg over you in salute. The caption could read, 'Good boy, Charles.' "

"Rodney," the Duke said menacingly, as Lady Elisabeth giggled some more.

She tried to cover her amusement with a hand raised to her face, knowing perfectly well she shouldn't be acknowledging she had even heard this male banter, let alone that she found it funny.

The Marquis gave her a curious look. "You are not offended, my Lady?"

She blushed, but said frankly, "Yes, I know I should be, but it is amusing. Not the cartoon, but what must have been happening here." She shot an apologetic look at the Duke, taking in his disheveled appearance with a smile. "I certainly meant no offense, Your Grace. At any rate, it is best that I return home. I am interrupting your morning, and a hunt isn't the safest place for Char – my dog – to be."

She glanced about for the hound and saw that he had discovered the game sack that had been left nearby when the two servants had discreetly moved away at her arrival. "Charles!" she said sternly, "Get your nose out of that!"

The Duke reflexively jerked back his head, then turned beet red as his three companions once again fell about laughing.

"No," Sir Clapham managed to say to Elisabeth as she prepared to depart. "Please stay. I've never been more amused in my life!"

She smiled at that, but shook her head. "I do apologize again, Your Grace," she said to the mortified Duke. "I shall try to keep Charles safely on our land while you are visiting."

She turned and walked quickly away, nearly as pink with embarrassment as the Duke. Fortunately Charles followed docilely at her side and she had no need to issue any more commands.

As the four men watched her depart, the two servants silently reappeared and picked up the game sack. The Duke groaned inwardly. The servants might have had the good sense to remove themselves from the immediate vicinity during the encounter with Lady Elisabeth, but he was certain they had heard every word. There wasn't a snowball's chance in hell of this story not getting about.

"Really, Charles, I never thought to see you come to heel so easily," the Marquis said with a grin.

"Don't hound him, Monton," Sir Clapham laughed. "He's had a rough morning."

The Duke uttered a mild obscenity and glared at his amused companions. "I'm for the house," he said. "I've had enough of hunting."

"Yes," Lord Ringwood chimed in. "You do look dog-tired."

The Duke spun on his heels and stalked off toward the manor, a string of furious oaths trailing in his wake.

Twenty-Seven

That afternoon found Elisabeth, her great-aunt, and her great-aunt's companion in the drawing room of Lady Downs. The invitation had been carried early in the morning to the Dowager Countess by another of Lady Downs's broad-shouldered footmen, and the Dowager had been pleased to accept.

"She may reside almost exclusively in the West Country, but she is excellent Ton and very well connected," the Dowager had explained with satisfaction to Elisabeth when she had returned from her morning walk with Charles. "She was an active leader in society for many years, and her opinions still hold great sway. We will be pleased to visit her for tea."

The ancient Lady Downs had accepted them with extreme formality and pomp. She was ensconced in a thronelike chair that offered her a sweeping view of the hilltop estate's sloping grounds down to the main road running through the valley below, in which rested the local village. As Elisabeth followed her great-aunt's example and offered a deep curtsey, she thought she saw the tip of a spyglass peeping out from a basket of colorful ribbons and tatting threads.

"Lady Burton," their hostess said as the Dowager and Elisabeth selected chairs near her, and Mrs. Doty found a seat near the door, "you are looking well. Are you enjoying your stay in these parts?"

"Other than this unrelenting heat, I am pleased to be able to spend time with my nephew and great-niece," the Dowager replied. On the other side of the room, Elisabeth could see Mrs. Doty nodding in happy agreement. "And it is of course an unexpected delight to be able to attend the events at Loveland Manor."

"Indeed," Lady Downs said drily, giving Lady Burton a direct look. "I was vastly entertained at tea the other day." The two women locked gazes for a few seconds before the Dowager lowered her eyes.

Their hostess turned her attention to Elisabeth. "I daresay you may be able to acquire one or two offers if you play your cards right. Certainly you caused enough of a ruckus among the gentlemen. But I wouldn't waste my time on the son of a mere Baronet like Sir Clapham when you've a Duke and Marquis at your disposal."

"Exactly as I have been telling her," the Dowager agreed.

"I find Sir Clapham an entertaining companion," Elisabeth defended herself. "And it is of no matter if I were interested in him; he clearly prefers to remain a bachelor."

"Do you think so?" their hostess asked. "I am not so certain. But be that as it may, I should not like to see you waste this opportunity."

"Ma'am?" Elisabeth asked, trying to pretend she did not understand Lady Downs's meaning, in the vain hope the subject would be dropped.

"Do not think to play your tricks on me, Elisabeth Chadwick," Lady Downs said straitly. "I've known you since you were a grubby toddler. I am well aware of why you prefer not to leave the comforts of the area where you grew up to attend a Season, but do you also prefer to become an old maid?"

That was plain speaking indeed, even for the formidable Lady Downs. The Dowager Countess raised her brows in surprise, looking back and forth between the other two. Near the door, Mrs. Doty raised the back of one hand to her forehead, as if checking for a fever.

Elisabeth had pokered up at the question, but relented as Lady Downs continued to stare at her. "No, of course I do not actually wish to remain unmarried," she admitted. "In fact –." She broke off as the doors to the salon opened and a footman carried in a massive tea service. He was followed by two maids, who helped arrange the service on the table in front of Lady Downs.

Once the servants had departed, their hostess turned to Elisabeth. "You may pour. I take mine with cream, no sugar."

Elisabeth rose and performed the tea ritual, well aware that this was a test. Once she had served their hostess and her great-aunt, she carried a cup to Mrs. Doty, who nodded gratefully at being remembered. Elisabeth then served herself and returned to her chair.

"Well done," Lady Downs commented. She gave a bark of laughter at Elisabeth's exasperated expression. "Yes, the grubby toddler is still there, isn't she? You don't much like being measured, do you? Just as beautiful and willful as ever your mother was. Well, if I am going to help you snare a Duke or a Marquis, I need to be sure you won't disgrace your position."

"I assure you, I have no designs on either gentleman," Elisabeth said.

"More fool you!" her great-aunt said in irritation. "A veritable honeypot falls into your lap and you ignore it."

"I am not ignoring it, I just don't know either gentleman well enough to have an opinion."

"What is there to know?" her great-aunt demanded. "Both are titled, wealthy, intelligent, and handsome."

"Yes, but are they kind?" Elisabeth asked. "Are they men who will care what I think? Who will want to spend time with me rather than at their clubs? Yes, I want a husband, but I do not want one who will make me miserable."

There were several beats of silence in the room after these heartfelt comments. Then Lady Downs spoke, her voice touched by emotion. "Wise girl," she said at last. "Clearly, we must make opportunities for you to discover their characters."

"We are to attend a picnic at Loveland Manor in a few days," Elisabeth volunteered. "And next week we are invited to a dinner and dance."

Their hostess swiveled her head to look at the Dowager Countess. "Perhaps you should host an entertainment yourself. Give the guests an alternative to Lady Loveland's salon."

"Excellent thought," the Dowager agreed. "It will allow Elisabeth the opportunity to display her hostessing skills."

"And," Lady Downs added, "to control the seating arrangements."

"You do realize," Elisabeth said, "that there are other contenders for the gentlemens' attentions. Unless you are proposing I invite only the male guests?"

"Behave yourself, missy!" her great-aunt snapped as Lady Downs gave another bark of laughter.

"You may set your mind at ease," Lady Downs said dismissively. "To you, all of the young ladies at Loveland may seem like experienced socialites from Town, and certainly they have more experience than you in social settings, but your freshness is an advantage."

When Elisabeth looked at her doubtfully, Lady Downs raised her hands and began ticking off their names on her fingers. "You may rule out the older Griegson girl immediately. Lady Alma has had several Seasons, but no offers. Lady Cora could be stiff competition, though. She just finished her first Season, which I understand was quite successful. I am told Viscount Walthers made an offer, but the little Griegson has her heart set on a higher prize."

"Viscount Walthers? Really?!" the Dowager Countess asked, momentarily distracted. "I had not heard."

"You must do a better job of cultivating your correspondents," Lady Downs admonished the Dowager. Elisabeth watched this exchange in surprise, never having seen her great-aunt willingly defer to another living being, yet throughout this interview her great-aunt had been calmly accepting direction and advice. Amazing. She glanced at Mrs. Doty, who was either nodding her head in sober agreement, praying, or nodding off to sleep. Elisabeth couldn't tell.

"I believe you also may rule out the Childer sisters," Lady Downs continued. "None of Daphne Childer's daughters has enough wit or beauty to attract two such leaders of the Ton as Edmonton and Ravenwood." She turned to the Dowager curiously. "I can never keep the Childer brood straight. Which two daughters are here? Pansy and Violet?"

"No," the Dowager said. "I believe these two are Violet and Rose."

"Ah, that's right. Pansy was married a year or two ago. Let's see, the oldest daughter is Lily, isn't she? Then Pansy, then Violet and Rose. And I believe there are two more still in the schoolroom. I dread to know what their names are," she shuddered.

"Is there a son?" Elisabeth couldn't resist asking.

"Thorn," Lady Downs said in accents of extreme loathing.

Elisabeth bit back a giggle. She waited for her hostess to continue her recitation, but Lady Downs waved a dismissive hand. "There is, of course, Lady Georgina Dunbarton. If she is seriously interested in either the Marquis or the Duke, you will have formidable competition. However, I believe she has other interests. In fact, I have long suspected that –" Their hostess stopped speaking as another wave of servants entered to remove the massive tea service.

But when the footmen and maids had completed their task, Lady Downs did not continue on her previous intriguing topic. Instead, she turned her attention to the Dowager Countess and asked for the latest news about some mutual friends in Scotland, and the conversation veered in a different direction. Elisabeth listened politely, but her thoughts stayed with the previous discussion.

There was no doubt that she found the Marquis attractive, more so after seeing him laugh so freely with his friends. But his reputation was that of, if not a complete rake, certainly a man of the Town, who kept mistresses and regularly raised young ladies' hopes before moving on to a new flirt. She wanted a husband who would be faithful, whose interest in her would not wane as she grew old and her beauty faded.

The Duke also was an attractive man, much in the same mold as the Marquis. Indeed, both were tall and carried themselves with the assurance of sportsmen used to physical activity. They both had thick black hair and deep blue eyes. But while she found the Duke very attractive, there was something indefinable that kept drawing her attention back to the Marquis.

But this was nonsense, she resolutely told herself. She had no idea what the two men's interests were, or if they shared any of her values. And it was far too soon for either of them to develop a serious intent toward her. But what was she to do, she wondered, if she did not soon meet someone with whom she could be comfortable? She was rapidly approaching the state of being on the shelf, with none but her dogs to keep her company. She gave a little shiver; she didn't like these new fears about the future that had begun to appear.

The Dowager suddenly stood, signaling to Elisabeth that the visit was at an end. Elisabeth rose and made her goodbyes to Lady Downs.

"It is always a pleasure to see you," Lady Downs said as she extended her hand to Elisabeth. "Give my regards to your father." She then nodded to the Dowager and issued one last piece of advice Elisabeth didn't understand.

"And if you have any large plants in your salon, Lister, please remove them before your party."

Twenty-Eight

That evening, before the dinner bell, the Dowager Marchioness bustled into the library in search of her son, where she found him sitting with the male guests, discussing horses.

The Marquis looked up curiously as his mother paused just inside the library's entryway. "Yes, Mother? May I do something for you?"

She smiled at the other men, and then turned back to the Marquis. "Yes, John. We've received an invitation from the Earl of Chadwick for an evening of dinner and music. That is, he has invited all of us – the entire house party – to an entertainment, to take place a few days after the picnic. What think you?"

"Sounds like a nice diversion," the Marquis nodded.

"Assuming she has her dogs locked away," the Duke said sourly, as a few of the men chuckled. He'd spent a miserable day putting up with his friends telling him to sit, stay, or come. The story had, of course, spread through the ranks of male guests like a wildfire. Even his valet had been smirking at him. If he had to go through much more of this, he'd start challenging people to duels.

The Marquis grinned. "Yes, Mother, do accept the invitation. It will give the servants a well-deserved break, too."

The Dowager gave her son a perplexed look. It baffled her that he was always so concerned with keeping his servants happy. After all, unhappy servants could easily be replaced.

"I shall write an acceptance, then," she said, turning to leave. "Do remember that we ladies shall require your escort to the village the day after tomorrow."

"Yes, Mother," he nodded.

He turned back to his companions as the library doors shut behind her.

"I'm always astonished at the female love of shopping," Sir Mendam commented.

"And, really, what's to be had in the local shops?" Lord RIngwood asked.

"Ribbons," Sir Clapham said decisively.

"My wife could stitch a bridge to the Continent with all the ribbons she's collected over the years," Lord Griegson commented.

The mention of the Continent woke up Lord Childer, who had been dozing off. "Damned Corsican, wrecked half of Europe. No good wine or brandy to be had anymore."

"And what's to be done about all the wounded who've come home?" Mr. Benson-Smythe asked. "Unemployed, injured, hungry. We must find some sort of useful venture for them."

"What do you propose?" the Duke asked.

"Send 'em all to America," Lord Childer said.

"What, along with the widows and orphans?" the Marquis asked. "Just toss 'em out? We owe them more than that."

Lord Childer bridled at the sarcasm in the Marquis's voice. "Might be better off there. New country, jobs to be had building it. Better than taking to highway robbery and muggings."

"Repealing the corn laws would make a deal more sense," the Marquis said. "We already have crowds booing Prinny."

"What, and rob the landowners of the ability to make a living?" Lord Griegson demanded. "This nation needs a healthy aristocracy to maintain order."

"What it needs is a healthy citizenry," Sir Clapham said in one of his rare serious moments. "And starving out the common man isn't the way to maintain order."

"More likely to lead to a revolution," Mr. Benson-Smythe agreed. "We've seen the results of that across the Channel. These crowds booing the Prince could become something more serious."

"No God-fearing Englishman would ever countenance such a thought," Lord Griegson said angrily.

"Then we need to do better by our soldiers," Mr. Benson-Smythe said firmly. "The civil unrest in London is not going to stop until people can find work and feed their families."

"We would do better to make an example of the men in those mobs," Lord Childer said.

The Duke leaned over to the Marquis with an impish grin, whispering so no one else could hear. "I see your way clear of the machinations of the Griegson and

Childer mamas, John. Make a few radical statements to their fathers. You won't be allowed past their doorsteps."

"Don't count on it," the Marquis replied softly. "They would willingly hitch themselves to the Devil himself if he could provide titles for their daughters."

"Well, I think I shall give my idea a try and see if I cannot dissuade them from seeking to make one of their offspring my Duchess." And with that, the Duke said to the room at large, "Perhaps we could pass better laws if every man in England were allowed to vote."

"That's outrageous!" Lord Childer shouted, turning an angry glare on the Duke.

"Ridiculous!" Lord Griegson said, staring at the Duke in profound shock.

"And we could require every landowner to hire unemployed men proportionate to the size of their landholdings," the Duke added. He shot a quick wink at the Marquis, who watched as the two older gentlemen goggled at the Duke, too astonished for a few moments to be able to speak.

"Interesting idea," Mr. Benson-Smythe said seriously.

The Marquis folded his arms across his chest and leaned back, prepared to enjoy the show.

As the argument continued, the group sorted itself into three distinct camps – Lords Griegson and Childer versus Mr. Benson-Smythe, Sir Clapham and the Duke, with the others forming a set of fascinated onlookers. Eventually the increasing volume of the voices drew the attention of the butler, who peeped in and asked the Marquis if any assistance were required.

"Not unless we elevate to bloodshed," the Marquis said hopefully.

"Perhaps I should ask her ladyship if we should delay dinner?"

The Marquis considered this, but decided it would be more fun to pour oil on the flames. "No, Applewood, I suggest you let my mother know that we would like the ladies to join us here before dinner rather than in the salon."

Applewood looked faintly shocked. "Bring the ladies in here, m'Lord?"

"Certainly," the Marquis said. When his butler continued to stand there gaping at him, the Marquis added helpfully, "That's an order, Applewood."

"Yes, m'Lord," Applewood said. He took a deep breath, turned about, and tottered from the room.

The Marquis wasn't quite sure how the butler had done it, but Applewood apparently had somehow conferred upon the Dowager Marchioness the idea that gathering before dinner in the manor's male preserve would be a high treat for the ladies. That was the only explanation the Marquis could find when a quarter of an hour later the room's doors suddenly swung open and the females of the party entered as a group, gaily chatting and giggling.

Their progress halted abruptly as they took in the sight of Lords Griegson and Childer on their feet, their hands balled into fists, facing off against a determined Mr. Benson-Smythe, framed on either side by Sir Clapham and the Duke. The Duke had adopted a posture of casual amusement, which only helped inflame his adversaries' wrath.

The other men in the room rapidly jumped to their feet in automatic deference to the ladies. As the argument suddenly stopped, all of the men stood frozen, uncertain what to do next.

After a few stunned moments, the tableau was broken by Lady Griegson's shocked voice. "Thomas! What are you about?" she asked, moving forward. She hurried over to her husband, who stared at her as though he'd never seen her before in his life.

Lady Childer and Mrs. Benson-Smythe made their way to their respective spouses, laying calming hands on their sleeves. The Dowager Marchioness sent her son a lethal look.

But no social situation had ever proved beyond her skills, and she quickly began moving about the room directing everyone into pairs to begin the procession into the dining room. As the ladies separated their husbands from the fray, their expressions made it clear there would be further explanations required later.

A gentle hand briefly brushed the Marquis's sleeve, and he looked down to see Lady Georgina's Dunbarton's smoky eyes staring up into his.

"No wonder you gentlemen don't allow us in your clubs," she said in her lovely contralto voice. "You don't want us to know how much fun you are having. Let me guess – either politics or horses."

"It would be politics," he said with a genuine smile. She really was quite a lovely creature, he thought. He wasn't certain why she had never really captured his interest. Too cool of a nature, possibly. Certainly he had never seen her be anything other than socially correct.

"And what do you think we should do for the returning soldiers?" he asked abruptly, curious as to whether she would have an opinion.

"I" she laughed lightly. "Why, my Lord, I leave that to the discretion of those who run this country. Surely you gentlemen can make a wiser decision than I about these matters."

"Yes, but what do you think of the soldiers' plight?" he pursued. He noticed the Duke had somehow managed to back up enough to be within earshot.

She gazed up at him soulfully. "My heart always goes out to anyone suffering," she said.

He watched her, waiting for more. She smiled a little sadly and laid her hand on his arm. "Come, my Lord, let us join the others for dinner. You must not allow the seriousness of the world to distract you from your duties as our host."

She lightly tugged him toward the procession of guests moving toward the dining room. The Duke smiled ironically at the Marquis as they passed.

Dinner was a difficult affair. Conversations waxed and waned in fits and starts as the ladies of the party attempted to chatter their way past the war that had suddenly and inexplicably erupted among the male guests.

From her place at the foot of the table the Dowager Marchioness led a conversation about the upcoming shopping excursion, lauding the surprising number of good shops located in the village.

"For it's at the crossroads of several main roads, you know," she said, speaking loudly to be heard down the length of the table. She sounded for all the world as though she were a geography professor, her son thought in amusement. "They have a delightful little bakery, and the baker and his wife are preparing an extra number of treats just for our amusement."

This temporarily lifted Lord Childer's spirits, since his generous girth was due largely to his love of wine and pastries. But then Mr. Benson-Smythe, seated across the table and picking sparingly at his food, made a comment about the importance of supporting commerce in England's villages. This reduced Lord Childer once again to a sulk, and he retreated into his wine, refusing all his wife's attempts to lighten his mood.

He was surrounded by radicals and progressives, he thought darkly, and he'd be damned if he was going to be polite about it when the Duke of Ravenwood – an actual Duke of the realm, by God – had proposed giving every man the right to vote. Preposterous. That would give his servants as much say as his peers in running the empire. And his servants were all idiots.

Lord Griegson spent his time shooting angry glances up the table toward the Duke, who sat near the head of the table, and thinking of scathing things he would like to say to that arrogant peer. Nothing, not even several sharp elbow jabs from his irritated wife, deterred him from this pleasant pastime.

Sir Clapham cheerfully talked about the amazing pheasant he'd bagged that morning, to the excruciating boredom of the Ladies Violet and Rose Childer, who were seated on either side of him. However, their occasional desperate glances at their mother elicited only heavy frowns in return, making it clear she expected them to assume excessive interest in Sir Clapham's boring bird bagging tale. Rose nodded at regular intervals as she thought about ways she might be able to feign a faint and thus be carried from the table in an interesting manner. Violet practiced her shudders.

Lady Georgina, seated across from the Duke, kept her face serene as she watched the bizarre behaviors around the table. She contributed the expected soothing pleasantries to the conversation, as she privately thought she had never seen such a clutch of knuckleheads. Would this ridiculous dinner never end?

She was aware the Duke was surreptitiously watching her, as he had been doing so often these past few months at social events. His scrutiny this past Season was making her uncomfortable. He seemed to be motivated by something other than the warm regard for her beauty and position that drew so many of her would-be suitors.

She looked down the table at the various faces, and saw little Miss Benson-Smythe cast a fleeting glance at Sir Clapham. She wondered idly if the petite Margaret would have any success in snaring the object of her adoration.

Twenty-Nine

The day between the men's argument and the village shopping trip was spent by the men's exasperated spouses soothing their tempers and reclaiming peace. By the day of the excursion, the male guests, if not completely reconciled with each other, were at least maintaining a surface truce.

The occasional hostile glance was quickly suppressed by watchful wives intent on not giving the eligible bachelors a disgust of any of the single ladies' fathers. Thus, the house party's visit to the village was made with minimal fussing and feuding.

The group's trip coincided with one of Elisabeth's regular shopping trips. But she had learned from her earlier experience with the Marquis and Sir Clapham, and had dressed in expectation of meeting one or two of the house party guests.

She hadn't anticipated seeing the entire group, but fortunately she had ridden Shadow today, while one of the footmen had driven the gig. She would have no reason to feel embarrassed on her mount, who was in high spirits and prancing down the village street as though on parade.

Elisabeth couldn't help feeling pleased to be wearing her new riding habit, delivered several weeks ago from London. In expectation of her great-aunt's visit, and knowing that lady's strongly held opinion about clothing colors, Elisabeth had made a quick trip to the metropolis the previous month, where she had selected a shade of green for the jacket and skirt that exactly matched her eyes. A lovely cream bodice laced with matching green ribbons, a cream and green riding hat, cream leather gloves, and matching boots completed the look.

If she'd had any doubt that she appeared to great advantage, it vanished when she saw the sour looks on the faces of several of the party's matrons. Elisabeth smiled inwardly as she pulled up to the dry goods store across from The Red Clown and prepared to dismount.

She arrived as the guests were milling around in the yard of The Red Clown. The gentlemen were assisting the ladies from the carriages and making arrangements for the care of the horses. A slight debate seemed to be under way as to the merits of the tea and pastry shop versus the inn's ale and bread.

"Allow me," a deep male voice said just behind her and to her left. She turned to see the Marquis standing there ready to assist her.

"I am quite able to dismount unaided," she said, more abruptly than she intended. She found herself unaccountably rattled by the thought of the Marquis placing his hands around her waist.

His smile widened into a grin. "I win," he said.

She looked down at him in confusion. "You win?"

"I bet myself you would be just the sort of prickly woman who would reject any offer of assistance." He extended his arms up toward her.

She gazed at him a moment. She easily could slip down without his help, but rejecting his offer would mean delivering him a public rebuff. And continuing to sit on Shadow and argue with him would only draw attention from the guests and make her look ridiculous. She really had no option other than to accept his offer.

She smiled impishly, and then leaned slightly toward him. She widened her eyes and said in a breathy whisper, "Oh, la, my lord, pray do help me alight from this great and perilous height by placing your strong, manly arms about me. I fear I might otherwise do myself an injury if I attempt to attain the ground without your noble assistance."

"That's better," he approved with a grin as she slid out of the saddle and he caught her about her waist. His next words died in his throat as the sensation of holding her suddenly overwhelmed all of his senses.

He stood there unmoving, stunned by what he was feeling. Time slowed to a standstill as the sights and sounds around them disappeared. His hands seemed to be on fire, a fire that shot rapidly through his entire body. Her delicate cream and apple scent filled his nostrils, and an errant strand of her golden hair brushed against his cheek. Her hands, lightly resting on his shoulders, sent waves of heat through him. Her bright green eyes gazed back at him in equal shock.

Elisabeth couldn't breathe. She felt suspended in space and time. His hands burned against her where they encircled her waist. His shoulders, where her hands rested, seemed to be equally aflame, the muscles bunched and straining against his jacket as he held her a few inches off the ground. Her senses filled with the scent of sandalwood and musk as she stared into his blue eyes.

A sudden burst of laughter from several of the guests in the inn's yard broke the spell. She glanced toward the sound and met the Duke's speculative glance. She blushed fiercely, her face suddenly as hot as the Marquis's touch. She moved slightly, impatient to be set down, all too aware of how this must look.

The Marquis came out of his trance and pulled her slightly closer. "I always appreciate the opportunity to show off my manly strength," he grinned. "Perhaps I should just carry you about the village? No need to set you on your feet at all and risk you turning an ankle or getting your hem a little muddy." He kept his hands tight about her waist, dangling her just slightly above the ground.

Her eyes rapidly narrowed to angry slits. "First of all, if you can find a speck of mud in this dry-as-dust countryside, I assure you I shall most happily dance a jig in it. And second of all, if you don't put me down immediately I shall kick you in the shins. These riding boots have metal tips, you know."

He laughed as he lowered her to the ground and stepped back. "We are intending to visit the little bakery down the street and would be delighted to have you join us. May I give you my escort? And, yes, I am quite sure you are able to walk about unaided."

She started to decline, but Sir Clapham chose that moment to separate from the group by the inn. He crossed the road toward them and added his entreaty to his host's. "Yes, Lady Elisabeth, please do join us. What an unexpected pleasure to encounter you. May I hope Charles is with you?"

He sent an amused glance toward the Duke, who had turned away from them and was helping Lady Cora down from a carriage. That young lady stepped lightly to the ground, then swayed against the Duke, peeking up at him through her long lashes. He responded with a heavy-lidded wolfish smile that brought a blush to Lady Cora's cheeks.

Elisabeth smiled at Sir Clapham. "No, unfortunately, I left Charles at home with the rest of the pack. You will be forced to find some other way to torture your friend today."

"Oh, I think that's already taken care of," the Marquis said with an ironic tone as he watched the Duke fending off the attentions of the Ladies Cora and Rose, who were attempting to prevent the Duke from assisting Lady Georgina down from her coach.

Elisabeth followed his gaze, then slanted her eyes up at the Marquis. Although her lips curved in a smile, her tone was solemn. "When my footmen were fighting over your maid, I found that dowsing them with a pitcher of cold water was quite effective."

The Marquis wondered if she knew the power of that roguish glance. He replied, equally seriously, "Yes, but where to find a pitcher to hand in the midst of the road? Although giving them a good dowsing might also result in getting enough water on the ground to see just how skillful you are at performing a jig."

"I am quite good at a jig," she said, "but would it not be more to the point if you would distract one or two of the ladies with your manly presence?"

Sir Clapham, who was following this conversation with an amazed expression, sprang into action. "Yes, that's a capital idea, Monton. You go rescue Ravenwood while I escort Lady Elisabeth here into the bakery."

"Thank you, Sir Clapham" she smiled, taking his proffered arm. She turned another roguish look on the now-irritated Marquis. "And I promise you, kind lord, I shall do my best not to turn an ankle, despite being forced to walk on my own two feet."

"Well, if Rodney here is not sufficient protection from a fall," he replied, "I will be happy to lift you off the ground, despite the heavy weight that you are."

She giggled at that and turned to walk away with Sir Clapham. She resolutely ignored her still-burning waist and the sensations the Marquis had provoked.

The Marquis grinned with appreciation as she strolled off on Sir Clapham's arm. She was like no other woman he had ever met, he thought. And his hands were still tingling.

Sir Clapham, meanwhile, was astonished that she had found the comment about her weight amusing rather than insulting. Those two had the oddest conversations.

The Marquis was still watching them with a slight smile when the Duke, having at last freed himself of all the female attentions, strolled over.

"Fine filly, don't you think?" he asked the Marquis.

The Marquis turned on him in a spurt of anger. "What kind of insult is that, Charles? I find her delightful."

"As do I, if you're referring to Lady Elisabeth," the Duke said in amusement. "I was talking about her horse. That, surely, is why you're standing here looking pole-axed. You no doubt are admiring her mare. Arabian lines, I think. Or is it the rider who has you so flummoxed? If so, I admit to surprise. Rodney told me you had called her a termagant. Surely you don't find termagants delightful, do you?"

"Rodney is an ass," the frustrated Marquis snapped. He turned on his heel and walked back to the inn yard, where he offered his escort to the two floral sisters. Damn, he could never remember their names.

The Duke, after watching his host's departure thoughtfully, sought out his younger brother Peter and young Thomas Griegson, where they were standing looking at the pastries for sale in the bakery window. The Duke had just thought of the most amusing project. All he needed was to send a rider with a letter to his man of business and make a few arrangements.

After having ensured their cooperation and secrecy with the bribe of two very large plates of pastries, he found seating for the boys in the bakery and looked about for another source of amusement. Yes, he thought, that would do quite nicely. After a quick glance to where Sir Clapham and Elisabeth were seated at a corner table with Lady Georgina, the Duke walked over to the table where Mrs. Benson-Smythe and her petite daughter were enjoying a plate of sweets, and pulled up a chair to join them. He bent his full charm on Miss Margaret, to that young lady's amazement and her mother's gratification.

The Duke was one of the four male guests who had joined the ladies in the bakery. He, Sir Clapham, the Marquis, and Sir Mendam had been abandoned by the other four men, who – despite their political differences – had preferred the sanctuary of the village inn, where hearty ales and a lack of feminine conversation were more to their liking.

The Marquis had escorted the Ladies Violet and Rose Childer to a large table, where the trio promptly had been joined by Ladies Alma and Cora Griegson. Lady Cora made a great fuss about handbags, parasols, and chairs, ensuring she received the full measure of the Marquis's attention as she arranged herself to her satisfaction.

Sir Mendam had seated himself with the Dowager Marchioness and the Ladies Griegson and Childer, who both positioned themselves to keep an eye on the

Marquis's table. The Dowager Marchioness beamed at her son's attentions to his four female tablemates.

The coast was clear for the Duke to monopolize the attention of the two Benson-Smythe ladies.

As he kept them entertained with stories from Town, Elisabeth watched as Sir Clapham began sending the occasional glance, and then the frequent glance, toward the table where the trio sat laughing.

"I have not had too much opportunity to speak with her, but Miss Benson-Smythe seems to be a pleasant young lady," Elisabeth commented to her two companions. "It appears the Duke shares my opinion."

Lady Georgina exchanged a small smile with Elisabeth, then both ladies turned to look at Sir Clapham.

"Well, you should have the opportunity," he said, standing abruptly. She looked up at him in surprise. He held out one arm for her and raised his other arm to signal one of the girls behind the counter. Elisabeth stood up and took his arm as Mary Louise, the baker's oldest daughter, came in response to Sir Clapham's wave.

"M'Lord?"

"We're moving to that table," he said curtly, nodding to where the Duke and the two Benson-Smythe ladies sat. "Please be so good as to bring our food over there."

"Aye, m'Lord," Mary Louise bobbed. She gave Sir Clapham a worried look.

"Thank you," Elisabeth smiled. "We appreciate the service. Sir Clapham wishes to introduce me to his friends."

The girl bobbed again and hurried to bring their plates and glasses to the new table. She moved quickly to keep up with them as Sir Clapham practically force-marched Elisabeth across the room.

Elisabeth was horrified that they had just left Lady Georgina seated alone. She glanced back to see a steely glare marring that lady's usually smooth countenance.

"Sir Clapham!" she hissed. "You mustn't abandon Lady Georgina!"

"What? Nonsense. She'll be fine," he said with unaccustomed ruthlessness.

The Duke looked up and started to rise as they reached the table.

"No," Sir Clapham said with a nasty smile. "Sit, Charles. Stay. We're joining you."

Eyebrows all around the table rose at this lapse of manners. Elisabeth, certain now that Rodney harbored a tendre for Miss Benson-Smythe, glanced briefly at the Duke. His eyes met hers with an answering gleam of awareness.

"Yes, sit, Your Grace," she said. "Stay." The Duke acknowledged her hit with a grin. He turned to Sir Clapham. "So, Rodney, what brings you over here?"

"Thought I'd give Lady Elisabeth a chance to get to know Miss Benson-Smythe better," Rodney said as he pulled up a chair for Elisabeth. He nodded to Margaret. "Lady Elisabeth was just expressing the opinion that she hadn't had much opportunity to speak with you."

"Your Grace," Elisabeth said to the Duke, "don't you think we should invite Lady Georgina to join us? She's all alone at her table."

The Duke glanced over at the seething beauty. "No she's not. I see that Lady Alma is about to join her."

Elisabeth turned to look and saw that Lady Alma was, indeed, just moving into a seat next to Lady Georgina. And whatever Lady Alma was saying had brought a genuine smile to Lady Georgina's face. Elisabeth relaxed and turned back to her new table companions.

Margaret smiled at Elisabeth. "I was admiring your riding habit, Lady Elisabeth. That is a lovely color on you."

"Thank you," Elisabeth smiled. "Do you ride, Miss Benson-Smythe?"

"Yes, I have a charming mare at home. She's smaller than yours, but she's a good goer."

"Yours looks to be Arabian," the Duke said to Elisabeth.

"Yes, out of Windracer," she said.

"Really?" four voices replied at once, in varying tones of awe.

Elisabeth looked around in surprise at her table companions. The Benson-Smythe ladies were looking at her with just as much interest as the two men.

"Yes, my father bought her off Lord Halliwell several years ago."

"I thought I recognized Arabian lines," the Duke said. "Rodney here also has a horse out of Windracer, I believe."

Now the Benson-Smythe ladies were looking at Sir Clapham in awe.

"Two, actually," he corrected the Duke. "I bought a pair off Halliwell's stable after the family ran into difficulties. Got a good deal. He's a friend of m'father's."

"Oh my," Miss Margaret Benson-Smythe breathed reverently. "I so envy you, Sir Clapham. And you, Lady

Elisabeth." She blushed at their surprised expressions. "We're a bit of a horse-mad family, I'm afraid." She peeped at Sir Clapham to see his response and turned even pinker when she saw that he was smiling at her.

"Let us all take a closer look at your mare," the Duke said to Elisabeth. He offered his arm to Margaret, enjoying Sir Clapham's pursed lips. Really, he couldn't lose, the Duke thought with an inner smile. Pay attention to the little Benson-Smythe and Rodney would be irritated; chat with the lovely Elisabeth Chadwick and John was certain to get into a pucker. This was turning out to be a most amusing house party.

The group of five walked outside to Elisabeth's horse. She held Shadow's cheek piece as the others walked about the delicate mare, stroking her and discussing her lines.

"Bred her yet?" Sir Clapham asked.

"Not yet, but soon," Lady Elisabeth said. "We're looking for the right stud."

"You might want to talk to John," the Duke said. "He has an excellent stable."

"That he does," Sir Clapham agreed enthusiastically.

"Or my husband," Mrs. Benson-Smythe said, sounding as though she were about to begin a bidding war. "Perhaps my husband and your father could do a spot of business."

The Duke moved to Shadow's head and leaned down to whisper in Elisabeth's ear, "The Benson-Smythes are extremely wealthy, you know."

She turned to look up at him. "And does Sir Clapham need to marry money?"

He bit back a knowing chuckle as he gazed down into her lovely countenance. Brains and beauty. No wonder his cousin was so obviously besotted. "No, he does not need to marry money. But he's never shown an interest in any of the debs placed in his path until now. It is the most amusing thing to watch him falling under a young lady's spell and trying to figure out what to do about it. I do wish she'd make him work a bit harder for it, though."

"Oh, but I have no doubt, Your Grace, that you will do all you can to make him work a bit harder for it," she said sweetly.

He laughed openly at that. "One appreciates something more if winning it presents a challenge, don't you think? I'm just helping ensure a friend will appreciate what he eventually gains."

"You are a rogue," she giggled.

"Yes, he is a rogue," said the Marquis's irritated voice behind them.

The Duke turned around to face the Marquis, managing to step slightly closer to Elisabeth in the process. "Did you want something, John?"

"Well, Charles," the Marquis said, matching his cousin's insolent tone, "when several members of our party rush outside to begin ogling a horse, it tends to make the rest of us curious." The Marquis gestured behind him, where the other members of the house party were exiting the bakery.

Lady Cora walked up to them and lightly took the Marquis's arm. "Yes, we wondered what took all of you outside. What is so special about this horse?"

"This horse," said Sir Clapham, "turns out to be a filly out of Windracer. You can see some of the same markings as on my pair."

"Really?" The Marquis directed an interested look at Elisabeth. "Is she as fast as she is beautiful? Does she win all the local pony cart races?"

"Pony cart races?" said the appalled Duke. "Who would hitch this lovely creature to a pony cart? It's not to be thought of!"

The Marquis directed a look of innocent inquiry at Elisabeth. She returned the look for a moment, then let out a little huff. "Well, I don't do it very often," she said at last.

"Really, Lady Elisabeth," the Duke said softly as Mrs. Benson-Smythe appeared about to hyperventilate, "you do have the most amazing effect on people."

Thirty-One

"Your Grace, I would so love to take a tour of this charming village," Lady Cora simpered up at him. She continued to hold onto the Marquis's arm, however. One way or another, she was determined to have one of these two for an escort.

The Duke smiled at her as he tucked Elisabeth's hand under his arm. "Unfortunately, Lady Elisabeth has already agreed to be my escort," he said, firmly holding her hand against his arm as she tried unobtrusively to tug free. "But John, here, surely is a better escort for you, since he's familiar with this hamlet."

"I would be delighted," the Marquis said through clenched teeth. "Come along, Lady Alma."

"Cora," she gritted. "I'm Cora."

"Oh, so you are. How forgetful of me," the Marquis said blandly. "It's just that, as sisters, you two look so alike, you know."

Lady Cora stood rooted to the spot, nearly steaming with anger. What a stupid thing to say, when everyone knew she was a diamond compared to her plain sister.

"It's your eyes," the Marquis explained. "You both have such beautiful eyes."

Trying hard to contain her temper, Lady Cora managed to summon up a sweet smile somewhat at odds with her tense face. "Yes, thank you. Shall we walk?" She waited for him to move, but found him to be just as rooted to the spot as she had been. He was exchanging a long, level look with the Duke that she couldn't quite understand. They almost looked like combatants.

Then her brow cleared and she laughed lightly. Of course. The Duke had wanted to be her escort, but he already had been claimed by that odd Lady Elisabeth. He was jealous of the Marquis.

Her laugh broke the moment. The Marquis looked down at her and saw her charming heart-shaped face and her delightfully lovely brown eyes, and he returned her smile. He turned and led her back to the walkway that ran along the village street and past the half-dozen or so shops that made up the village's claim to commerce.

"Lord Loveland," came Cora's light voice as they walked toward the shops, "you must tell me about Edmonton Castle. I understand it is in Leicestershire and is most delightful."

"A big old drafty barn a few miles outside Melton Mowbray," the Marquis said cheerfully as they approached the first shop in the row. "Freezing in the winter. Not enough wood in the entire country to heat it. I have to wear several layers of mufflers and shawls all winter long. Most uncomfortable."

She looked up at him uncertainly. Was he jesting with her? She couldn't tell. He gave her a bland look and directed her attention to the first of the shop windows.

As the Marquis and Lady Cora stopped to look at the first store's window display, the Duke glanced down at Elisabeth's face and nearly laughed out loud at the mulish glare she was directing toward him. No false sweetness there!

"I beg your pardon?" she asked frostily.

"Did I just say that out loud?" he asked.

"I did not agree to be your escort."

"John's right, you are a little termagant."

"I'm a what?!" she demanded in tones of outrage. "He called me a what?"

Sir Clapham walked past. He had Miss Margaret Benson-Smythe on one arm and Lady Rose on the other. "He also compared you to a wasp," he said to Elisabeth as the trio walked by.

Elisabeth's mouth opened and closed as she furiously tried to think up words nasty enough to describe such a horrid man. She stared in turns at Sir Clapham's back, the Marquis's back, and the Duke's grinning face. She pulled mightily at the hand he held captive, but couldn't get loose.

"Set you free right now?" he asked, beginning to laugh. "To what end? So you can murder my cousin? I don't think so. Come along, let's follow the others down this little street before everyone thinks you and I are having a wrestling match."

He led her along the walk, still keeping her hand clasped in a rigid grip. They were followed by Lord Ringwood, who escorted the other two young ladies of the party.

Ladies Georgina and Alma had contrived to have Lord Ringwood escort them by the simple expedient of walking into The Red Clown, approaching him from both sides simultaneously, and directing him to serve as their escort. Trapped between the two women, he lapsed into horrified silence, obediently rose from the table, and led them everywhere they directed.

"It's so nice to see the young people enjoying themselves," the Dowager Marchioness commented to Sir Mendam as they followed Ladies Childer and Griegson into the mercer's shop.

"If you say so, my dear," that gentleman replied a little doubtfully. He waited patiently by the door as the three women exclaimed over the surprisingly large array of high-quality ribbons on display.

Sir Mendam watched through the shop's window as Mrs. Benson-Smythe marched across to The Red Clown. A few moments later she dragged her husband outside and led him to Lady Elisabeth's horse, where the two of them appeared to be engaging in a spirited debate.

The young people trudged along the walkway, dutifully admiring the storefronts. At the last shop along the row, Lady Cora stopped with an exclamation of awe.

"Oh, my! I must try on that hat! Look at those exquisite little bows all over it!" Without another thought to her escort, Lady Cora released his arm and entered the shop. The awed shopkeeper hurried to do her bidding and pulled the hat from the window for her inspection.

Freed from his companion, the Marquis looked around for the Duke and Elisabeth, and saw them standing across the road under the shade of a large tree. He was just about to start across to them when the Duke put his hands on her shoulders, gave her a little shake, and left her side. The Marquis watched as his annoying cousin unhurriedly ambled over to him.

"What was that all about?" he asked.

"I made her promise to stay there. I don't think you want to talk to her until she's a little cooler," the Duke said with a wide grin as he reached the Marquis.

"What do you mean?" The Marquis glanced across the street and saw that she was giving him a fulminating stare. Her arms were folded across her chest and one foot was tapping on the ground. She reminded him of an angry governess.

"Well," the Duke said, stroking his chin consideringly, "I believe she might be a trifle upset at finding out you think she's a termagant. Or maybe it was the comparison to a wasp that bothered her. I'm not sure."

The Marquis glared at his tormentor. "And I know whom to thank for telling her that, don't I?"

"I may have inadvertently let the termagant comment slip, but it was Rodney who mentioned the wasp reference. You know, up until now, I rather thought she liked you."

"Charles, I feel a strong desire to plant you a facer and wreck that pretty face of yours."

"Well, if you think you can," the Duke taunted. Everyone knew he was a regular at the Town's most elite boxing salon.

"Oh, look, Your Grace, my Lord, at the pretty little bonnet I found!" Lady Cora danced up to them with the happy glow of a satisfied shopper. She held a bandbox out toward them, dangling it from one gloved hand. From her other arm dangled her parasol and handbag.

"Yes, do show His Grace," the Marquis said with a nasty smile at his cousin. "He particularly delights in admiring ladies' fashions."

The Duke dutifully reached out and took the bandbox so that Lady Cora could open it and part the tissue paper for his inspection.

The Marquis turned about and started to cross the road toward where Elisabeth had been standing, but she had disappeared. He scanned the street. Her horse was still tied to the rail, and she hadn't joined any of the guests strolling along the walkway.

He walked over to the shade tree and saw a path leading from it that ran between two shops the ladies wouldn't be visiting – the butcher and the blacksmith. He quickly glanced in both of those establishments, thinking she might be hiding from him. Not seeing her, he decided to follow the path.

Before he reached the backs of the buildings he heard her voice. He rounded the end of the butcher shop and found her having a heated argument with a man he recognized a moment later as Squire Mills. The Squire was gripping one of her arms with a beefy hand. He glanced up angrily at the sounds of the Marquis's approach.

Elisabeth turned toward the Marquis. He noted the flash of relief on her face as she saw him. She held out an arm to him as she pulled against the Squire's grip. The Squire released her with an angry grunt and she hurried to the Marquis's side.

"We'll continue this conversation another time, my dear," the Squire said to her, "when you're not so bedazzled with our noble visitors."

She ignored him as he walked away from them and continued along the path that ran behind the buildings. The Marquis watched until the Squire entered the back of The Red Clown.

"Are you all right?" he asked her, once the Squire was out of sight.

"I detest that man," she said in a low, hot voice. "And I am tired of men grabbing onto me today and not letting me go."

"Men?" he repeated in surprise.

"Never mind. Just, please, walk me back to my horse. I've had enough of this day and I want to go home." She sounded very near tears.

"Certainly. But, please, first tell me if you're all right."

"I'm fine. And, and…," her voice ran out. She took a ragged breath. "And thank you," she said. "He has made a nuisance of himself ever since his last wife died. But he has never had the impudence to put his hands on me before."

"How did you end up back here with him?" the Marquis asked.

She gave an angry sniffle. "I did not sneak away to be with him, if that's what you're thinking!"

"I am thinking no such thing. I think you sneaked away so you could walk along the backs of the buildings and reach your horse without having to encounter me on your way out of the village."

Elisabeth looked at him in surprise, but didn't deny his guess. "You said nasty things about me to your friends!"

"Yes, I did. I apologize. But you have been rather nasty to me, too, you know." He said the words in a conciliatory manner, holding out his arm for her to take.

"And you may rest assured I will not grab you and refuse to let you go if you allow me to escort you to your mount."

She took a few deep breaths to calm herself. "Very well. You may escort me." She placed her hand on his arm as regally as a queen. Immediately, she found herself suppressing the waves of sensation she felt from the touch. The feelings penetrated her still-hot emotions, confusing her and making her restless.

He felt the same sensations, and wondered at them. In all his years of dalliances, he'd never encountered a woman who had such a marked effect on him. He looked down at her hand on his arm, amazed that such a light touch could generate such a strong feeling.

It was a quiet, reserved couple who appeared back on the village street. Sir Clapham spotted them first, and hailed them as they crossed toward the shops. Miss Margaret Benson-Smythe looked at Elisabeth curiously, but said nothing.

"It has been pleasant seeing all of you again today," Elisabeth said to Margaret, "but I fear I must be heading home."

"We look forward to seeing you at the picnic in a few days, Lady Elisabeth," Sir Clapham said.

"Thank you," Elisabeth replied, wondering if there were some way she could get out of attending.

The Marquis walked her back to her horse and tossed her into the saddle. She looked down at him. "Again, thank you," she said.

She looked around the village for the pony cart that one of the stable hands had driven to carry supplies. It sat outside the butcher's shop, still waiting to be loaded. She paused uncertainly, then looked down at the Marquis.

"Martin accompanied me to the village," she said. "I really should wait to ride back with him. It's… safer."

"You know," he commented idly as he handed her the reins, "I think I'll see who's still in The Red Clown. I haven't been here long enough to recognize all the local mounts. That big roan, for example. I wonder who rides it."

She gave him a speaking look, but said without inflection, "That would be Squire Mills's horse."

"Is it, now. You know, I think it could use a rubdown. I'll just suggest to the ostler that he ought to remove the saddle and blanket, and give that brute some attention. You don't think the Squire would mind the extra time it would take to saddle his horse when he's ready to leave, do you?"

"It takes me twenty minutes to ride home," she said.

"I hope the ostler doesn't misplace the saddle," the Marquis commented.

She firmed her lips against a grin and gave Shadow the signal to trot off. The Marquis saluted her, then turned to walk over to the inn yard. He held a brief conversation with the ostler, who for two gold coins promptly led the horse into the stable and removed the big roan's saddle and blanket.

A few minutes later, as the Marquis strolled back to his friends, the sounds of irate shouting could be heard as the Squire demanded to know what had happened to his horse's saddle. But the ostler was nowhere to be found and the confused stable boy didn't know where the saddle might have been placed.

Thirty-Two

The day of the picnic dawned bright and hot, promising to be yet another searing summer day. Elisabeth and the Dowager Countess were up early, engaged in the important task of preparing for the picnic.

At the moment, Elisabeth was sitting quietly on a settee in her suite, watching with a small smile as her great-aunt found fault with every stitch of clothing in Elisabeth's wardrobe. The Dowager was busy flinging dress after dress to the floor as she loudly complained about each. The maids were going to earn their pay today.

"And look at this stain on the hem!" the Dowager snapped. "And this one has a rip!" She paused in her energetic disarrangement of the room and turned to glare at her great-niece. She angrily shook a gray underdress at Elisabeth. "Are you seriously telling me that you go about the neighborhood dressed like a hoyden? Have you no daydresses that are presentable?" She flung the offending underdress away and spun about, once again reaching into the wardrobe to root among the hangings.

"I regret I have nothing to please you, ma'am," Elisabeth said as another dress was tossed onto the growing pile. The two maids looked at the clothing and exchanged perplexed expressions. "Perhaps I should stay home where my provincial dresses and manners will not offend the great and mighty Londoners," Elisabeth offered.

"Nonsense!" her great-aunt said from inside the wardrobe. She pulled out another dress, glanced at it, started to say something, then paused and took a closer look at the gown. She slowly straightened and turned to face Elisabeth, shooting her great-niece a narrow-eyed frown in sudden awareness. Elisabeth returned her look with politely raised eyebrows.

The Dowager dropped the dress to the floor and put her hands on her hips. She leveled a demanding glare at her great-niece. "Where are they?" she asked flatly.

"Where are what?" Elisabeth asked.

The Dowager turned to the two maids, who each backed up a step. "Where are they?" she asked again. The maids turned to look a question at Elisabeth. When Elisabeth remained silent, only giving her great-aunt a blank look, the Dowager took a deep breath.

"I am perfectly capable of searching every nook and cranny on the grounds if you do not tell me right now where you have hidden your good dresses," the Dowager said with firm intent. "You think I don't recognize this pink and white dress?" She pointed at the last gown she'd pulled from the wardrobe. "It's four years old and I know for a fact you put it in storage in one of the attics last year. Where are they?"

Drat, Elisabeth thought. She tried to face down her great-aunt, but failed. After a few moments, she relented. "They're in the housekeeper's sitting room."

The Dowager gave her great-niece an evil look, and then turned to the two maids. She pointed to the door. "Get them. Now. And I mean now." The maids scurried out the door.

Elisabeth repressed a desire to quail at the anger emanating from her great-aunt.

"Missy, if you do not start behaving yourself immediately, I assure you I will see that you really do have nothing to wear but this mess on the floor." The Dowager firmed her lips against a smile. Really, Elisabeth's trick had been quite creative. If only she would use that creativity to snare a titled husband from among the eligibles staying at Loveland Manor.

The two antagonists remained unmoving until the door burst open and the two maids, followed by one of the footmen, carried in three stacks of dresses and placed them on the bed. The maids quickly began hanging up the clothing while the footman swept up everything on the floor and carried the pile toward the hallway door.

"Now, Elisabeth," the Dowager said, "I think something like this jonquil and white dress would be ideal for a picnic, and would nicely set off the color of your hair." She beckoned to one of the maids to hold the dress for viewing. Elisabeth tried to look dissatisfied, but had to admit to herself that the dress was one of her favorites.

"Now," her great-aunt directed, "you will allow your hair to be dressed. I shall send my dresser to you. I want to see you in something other than a braid, for heaven's sake."

Elisabeth moved obediently to the dressing table. She sat silently for the next hour while her hair was ruthlessly brushed, tugged, twisted, pinned and decorated. She thought she looked like some sort of mad woodland nymph, but apparently the Grecian knot entwined with white pearls and sprigs of pale yellow silk flowers poking out here and there was all the rage. It could be worse, she supposed. At least she wasn't going to have to walk about with feathers sticking out of her head. She'd never understood or admired that fashion, and would rather die before she'd go to a ball decked out like some sort of giant, waltzing bird.

"Very nice," her great-aunt approved when she returned to the room. "Now, let's see you in the dress."

Elisabeth stood like a statue as the dress was carefully lowered over her head and fastened about her. The bodice was of figured silk and lightweight muslin, trimmed with white beads, as were the little puff sleeves. The rest of the dress was made of transparent white muslin to show off the jonquil underdress. Slits rose from the hem to allow the underdress to appear as she moved. Pale yellow ribbons beneath the bodice and matching yellow slippers completed the look.

"You will do," the Dowager said after a lengthy inspection. "Now, you will confine yourself to the downstairs parlor until I am ready. You will not go outside or to the kitchens or to any other of your haunts where you can damage your attire. You will not move. Do you understand me?"

"Is it acceptable for me to breathe?" Elisabeth asked.

"What will be acceptable is for you to curb that tart tongue of yours," the Dowager said. "I do not know where you get that habit." She beckoned to her dresser and exited the room for her own chamber.

Elisabeth spent the next hour and a half practicing the pianoforte. She loved playing, but not even her doting father could bring himself to express admiration for her musical ability. She had no ear for music, but a great deal of enthusiasm. It was an unfortunate combination.

At last her great-aunt descended the stairs, wearing a lovely lavender dress with pale green trim. As usual, she was clad in the height of fashion. Never would she be like so many ladies of the older generation who clung to the styles of their youth. The Dowager Countess was determined to remain current.

As the carriage that bore them to Loveland Manor pulled to halt in front of the entry, the manor's doors swung open and their host, followed by two footmen, walked out to welcome them. The Marquis helped the Dowager to the gravel drive, handed her to a footman to escort her into the manor, then turned back to face the carriage, but made no move toward it.

He studied Elisabeth for a moment. Her challenging stare told him she had recovered from the events in the village a few days earlier. Good. He much preferred the feisty Lady Elisabeth to the somewhat stunned and fearful girl she'd been for a few moments after her encounter with the Squire.

"You'll be fine on your own, won't you?" he asked Elisabeth with a grin.

"Worn out your manly strength, have you?" she asked from where she stood waiting in the carriage door.

"Perhaps you should get more exercise than just tying fancy neck cloths."

"I'm flattered you noticed. I call this one Strangulation on a Theme."

"Very nice. Pity it isn't a bit tighter. But perhaps that is why you don't have the strength to help me down – you can't breathe."

Gazing at her lovely, so-serious face, the Marquis realized that he was, in fact, having some difficulty breathing. He grinned and stepped forward, offering her a hand.

She clasped it, and once again the world fell away. All she could feel and see was the man before her. He appeared equally dazed, staring at her unblinkingly.

The long moment was broken as the carriage horses shifted impatiently. She gave a start and stepped down from the carriage. He released her hand and placed it on his arm as he led her into the house. Neither of them was aware of her great-aunt standing a little to the side, where she had pulled the footman to a halt as she had listened in astonishment to their banter. She watched them walk by with a stunned expression on her normally harsh face.

Inside the manor, the guests were gathering for a planned walk down to the shaded lawn near the small lake, where the servants had spent the previous day setting up several pavilion tents and placing tables and chairs.

As the Marquis guided her into the large salon, Elisabeth realized with some chagrin that she had forgotten to bring a parasol. She wondered if perhaps she really had become too much of a country hoyden. She certainly never gave much thought to her complexion as she roamed the countryside with her dogs.

She noticed the lovely Lady Georgina Dunbarton eying her outfit, and was certain she saw a small smirk on that lady's face as the lack of parasol, fan and reticule were duly noted. That lady obviously was sizing her up and finding her lacking.

Elisabeth raised her chin slightly, thanked the Marquis for his escort, and left his side. She made a beeline to Lady Georgina, who raised her eyebrows in mild surprise as she realized Elisabeth was walking directly toward her.

"Lady Elisabeth," the other beauty said without inflection.

"Lady Georgina," Elisabeth said, with as little inflection as the other young lady. "What a lovely name. Is it a family name?"

Lady Georgina favored Elisabeth with a look that clearly said Elisabeth was a henwit. "No, it is not a family name. She contributed nothing further, but stood there coolly assessing Elisabeth.

Elisabeth tried another gambit. "I understand from my father that your father is in politics, and you frequently serve as his hostess."

"Yes," Lady Georgina replied neutrally, saying nothing more. She glanced around the room as though bored.

Really, Elisabeth thought in irritation, this lady was known to be a talented and charming political hostess. This was a deliberate snubbing, and she wouldn't stand for it. Maybe she could reach this ice queen another way.

"I also understand your mother passed away when you were a young girl," Elisabeth said. "I too lost my mother as a child."

Lady Georgina seemed to draw into herself momentarily, but didn't reply to the topic. "Oh, look," she said lightly, "it appears to be time to begin the picnic. Shall we walk together?"

"Yes, certainly," Elisabeth replied. She noticed Lady Georgina's companion, who stood a few feet away, fall into place behind them as they joined the general exodus onto one of the manor's side terraces.

Thirty-Three

The procession was led by the Dowager Marchioness and Sir Mendam. They walked through the French doors that had been opened by servants, and onto the large stone terrace off the salon. They angled across the terrace and down the wide stone steps that led toward the back lawn of the estate.

They were followed by Lord and Lady Griegson, walking with the Dowager Countess of Cwmhaven, then by Lord and Lady Childer. The Duke was next in line with Miss Margaret Benson-Smythe, followed by the Ladies Georgina and Elisabeth, and Lady Georgina's constant companion, Mrs. Breden.

A frowning Sir Clapham escorted Lady Rose Childer, and Lord Ringwood had been paired with Lady Violet Childer, who was subjecting him to a cheerful monologue about the perils of eating outdoors. That foursome was followed by Mr. and Mrs. Benson-Smythe.

Bringing up the rear were the Marquis and his two companions. He had been angling toward Lady Elisabeth, but his progress across the salon had been interrupted by

Lady Cora Griegson, who had placed herself firmly in his path and taken his arm. Not wanting to appear to be singling her out after having escorted her through the village a few days ago, he had promptly held out his other arm for her sister, Lady Alma.

As the guests followed their hostess and Sir Mendam through the back garden paths and down the sloping lawn that led to the small lake, an array of pavilion tents appeared before them. Flying above the largest tent was a pennant with the Marquisate's coat of arms.

The Marquis briefly raised his eyes skyward at the sight. Leave it to his mother to be so pretentious.

"Oh, how charming!" Lady Cora said. "It is just how I visualized the scene in The Damsel and Duty, when Lady Golden attends the jousting tournament and Sir Strongheart wears her colors!" Up ahead, Lady Violet was shuddering in delight.

"And look," Lady Cora added, "there are boats for rowing about the pond. Oh, my Lord, would you please take me for a boat ride?"

"Perhaps later," he said, as they reached the nearest tent. "Right now I have to perform my duties as a host and see that everyone is comfortable." He guided them toward a grouping of chairs as he released the sisters' arms. Servants bustled about, offering wine and fruit punches to the guests, and arranging the seating as directed.

As the Ladies Georgina and Elisabeth accepted glasses of punch, Elisabeth looked about her curiously. "I do not see Lords Thomas or Peter anywhere," she said. "I would have thought a picnic would have been just such a thing as they would enjoy."

"They are otherwise engaged, I believe," Lady Georgina said. "The Duke has set them up with a project."

Elisabeth sent that lady a sideways glance. She definitely had caught an undertone of something that sounded suspiciously like amusement. Lady Georgina turned to look directly at Elisabeth for a moment, before returning her attention to the view of the water.

"Let us walk over to that smaller tent, away from the serving area," Lady Georgina said, with an unexpectedly pleasant tone of voice. She turned back to her companion. "Mrs. Breden, please arrange for two plates of fruit to be brought to us."

Lady Georgina linked arms with Elisabeth as they walked over to one of the other pavilion tents, where the Duke and Miss Benson-Smythe were presently sitting. "I think this should be an entertaining location," Lady Georgina said, with a bland look at Elisabeth's puzzled expression.

The Duke rose as they arrived, but Lady Georgina waved him away. "We shall sit over here, Your Grace," she said, pointing to a grouping of chairs and a table set slightly apart from the Duke and his companion. He nodded in acknowledgement and returned his attention to Miss Benson-Smythe.

Elisabeth was surprised when Lady Georgina actually initiated a topic. "You said at tea the other day that you raise dogs. Scottish deerhounds, I believe."

"Yes," Elisabeth said with enthusiasm. "Do you have dogs?"

"No," Lady Georgina said. "I live in Town and am rarely at home. I do know several women who have lapdogs, though."

"I like larger dogs," Elisabeth said. "I particularly enjoy riding, and it is fun to take the dogs out with me. That is one of the reasons I prefer the country to London. I dearly enjoy the company of my dogs, and would miss them if I spent much time in Town. And, of course, I enjoy the freedom of the countryside."

"Freedom?" Lady Georgina asked with a touch of disbelief. "Are social conventions so much different here than they are in London?"

"To some degree, yes," Elisabeth said. "Here, I am able to walk about our grounds and visit with our neighbors and the people in the village, without always requiring the attendance of a maid or footman. Of course, I do usually have my dogs with me for protection."

"There are a great many amusements to be had in Town," Lady Georgina said. "You might find they make up for the lack of freedom." She glanced back to the largest of the tents, where Mrs. Breden was waiting behind several of the house party guests to make her way along the serving table.

"Perhaps," Elisabeth said doubtfully. "I visit London occasionally, but I'm comfortable here, where I know everyone. In Town, everyone stares at me." Lord, why had she said that? It was true, even though few people knew it was one of her chief reasons for avoiding society.

Lady Georgina's lips curved up. "But you would have the pleasure of listening to suitors write poetry lauding your eyes, your nose, your hair, your hands, or whatever other feature took their fancy," she said with a touch of dryness.

"So I could, in fact, compile a collection of bad poetry, then," Elisabeth said, and was rewarded with another tiny uptick in her companion's lips. "I had not realized the opportunities for new hobbies."

Their conversation was interrupted by Sir Clapham hailing them as he rapidly approached the tent where they were seated.

"And the entertainment begins," Lady Georgina said softly, just before taking a sip of punch.

"I say," said Sir Clapham, hauling up beside them. "Pleasant little picnic our hosts have set up, isn't it?" He stood in front of them, shuffling his feet and staring at the Duke's table.

"Where is your companion?" Lady Georgina asked politely.

He swung his attention back to Lady Georgina. "Lady Rose? I stuck her – I mean, she has joined her sister in chatting with Richard."

"How pleasant for him. Do join us, Sir Clapham," she invited.

"What? Yes, think I shall." He pulled up a chair to their table and sat facing toward the Duke and Miss Benson-Smythe.

"And how is your mother?" Lady Georgina asked him.

"What?" He swerved his head to look at her. "M'mother? Fine, fine. Mother's fine."

"Do tell us all that she's been up to lately," Lady Georgina pursued with a pleasant smile. "Does she help your father with his butterfly collecting, or does she have her own amusements?" She leaned forward to partially block Sir Clapham's view of the other table.

Really, Elisabeth thought to herself in amusement, perhaps she should revise her opinion of Lady Georgina. No one would ever guess that she was deliberately torturing poor Sir Clapham.

"I... what? M'mother?" He turned to fully look at both of his table companions, and met two perfectly schooled faces, showing nothing more than polite interest.

Sighing, he launched into a distracted series of comments about his mother's sewing, reading, and gardening habits. His eyes kept darting to the table where the Duke sat, leaning in closely to hear what Miss Benson-Smythe was saying.

Sir Clapham's torment was relieved by an unexpected assist in the form of the Marquis. He arrived at their tent with the Ladies Cora and Alma having reclaimed his escort. The trio was trailed by a servant carrying a tray of plates and glasses.

The Marquis released his charges and directed the footman to place their refreshments on the table between the one where the Duke and Miss Margaret sat and the one occupied by the beleaguered Sir Clapham and the Ladies Georgina and Elisabeth. Lady Cora thanked the Marquis for his escort and immediately flitted to the Duke's table to claim his attention. Lady Alma chose to join the Ladies Georgina and Elisabeth.

Sir Clapham used the distraction to jump up and hurry over to speak to Miss Benson-Smythe. She smiled happily up at him and nodded in agreement at whatever he'd said. She rose from her table, making her apologies to the

Duke and Lady Cora, and rested her hand lightly on Sir Clapham's arm as he led her back toward the others.

"Thought I'd escort Miss Benson-Smythe over to look at those rose bushes," he said. "Anyone care to join us?"

Lady Alma, who was just being seated by the Marquis in the chair Sir Clapham had vacated, declined his offer.

The Marquis, with a malicious glance at the Duke, said he'd enjoy joining them to show off his mother's flowers. Sir Clapham scowled at him and extended a hand to Elisabeth. "What about you, Lady Elisabeth? Care to join us?"

She twinkled up at him. "I adore roses, Sir Clapham." She stood just as Mrs. Breden arrived with the fruit plates. The companion set the plates on the table and chose a chair a few feet away. She gave Elisabeth a dark look.

The Duke gave his cousin an equally dark look at the foursome moved away. Lady Alma, oblivious of the undercurrents swirling around her, leaned toward Lady Georgina with a warm smile to discuss the topic of music.

Thirty-Four

Before they could reach the rose garden, Elisabeth's attention was distracted by Mr. and Mrs. Benson-Smythe, who called to her to join them. Their interest was made clear immediately — they wanted to talk about horse breeding.

Elisabeth joined them, smiling politely and answering their questions as best she could. She loved riding, but she was no expert on lineage or breeding. She watched from the corner of her eye as the Marquis also was called away from Sir Clapham and Miss Benson-Smythe, leaving that happy couple to proceed on their own to view the flowers.

The Marquis had been hailed by Elisabeth's great-aunt, who was standing with Lady Griegson at the border of the rose garden. As he approached them, each lady took one of his arms in a firm grip and began vying for his attention.

"You must let me tell you the latest news of Lady Marybell Wister," Lady Griegson exclaimed. "Apparently, Lady Marybell and her family spent but a brief time at the

Carrington family estate before breaking off the engagement. Then, I'm given to understand…."

She began regaling him with what she'd learned in a letter she had just received from a friend.

"Let me tell you about our family," the Dowager Countess demanded. "You perhaps do not know that we are an old Scot family with ties to the first kings of Scotland…." She launched into a report of her family's various estates, business interests, and antecedents.

"…then traveled to another location in the country, but it appears as though Lady Marybell's parents remain there, and have not departed with their daughter…."

"…family horse breeding operations on the original landholding in Scotland…."

"…all most mysterious…."

"…quite celebrated stables…."

The two monologues blended together as the Marquis glanced about at the other guests. He wondered why these two ladies would suppose him to be interested in either topic.

"Now, no one seems to know where Lady Marybell is," Lady Griegson said conspiratorially. "That seems odd, don't you think?"

"And it has proved to be a good location for our stud farm," the Dowager inserted, continuing her recitation of her family's properties. "My nephew just shipped a fine mare there."

"Why would a young girl go to the country without her family?"

"Well, as you know, the country is an excellent place for breeding."

The Marquis burst into laughter.

Thirty-Five

The Dowager Marchioness glanced curiously at her son as he struggled to contain his laughter. Judging from their baffled expressions, the source of his amusement was a mystery to his two companions.

"Come, Horace, let us take a walk to the water," she said, smiling sweetly at her longtime friend and companion.

They rose from their chairs and began slowly wending their way down the lawn to the lake.

Sir Mendam placed her hand on his arm and gazed at her fondly. "I would be delighted, m'dear. This property is quite charming. You should visit it more often."

"It was owned by one of my late husband's brothers," she said as they moved down the sloping lawn toward the water. "We used to visit occasionally when I was first married. I planted these roses, you know, but I haven't been here in quite some time. I was so happy when I arrived to see that Reggie had taken such good care of them."

"The rose garden is charming," Sir Mendam said. "I took a stroll through it the other morning."

"Smoking one of your cigars, I suppose," she teased him.

"The roses didn't mind," he smiled.

"You know," she said, looking around, "I've always liked this estate. I thought I might claim it for my dower house once John marries. Meerson, the steward here, keeps it in good condition."

"I think your son may become a more frequent visitor, now that he's met the neighbors," he smiled.

"I had hoped he would show an interest in Lady Georgina or the older Griegson daughter, but the Earl of Chadwick's daughter might be a suitable match," she agreed, not mistaking his meaning. "And it would be pleasant to be more closely allied with an old friend like Lister."

"There is another old friend who would like to be more closely allied with you, Sophia," he said.

She reached over with her free hand and patted his arm. "You know I shall not marry until John gets buckled. I don't want him thinking I'm so well cared for that he need not worry about my feelings. After Matthew's death he went on that terrible wild spree for so many years. All that wenching," she said, not mincing words with him. "I feared I might have to rely on Patrick to carry on the line. But I think the worst of John's grief is finally past, and he is ready to move on. And I want him to do so before he becomes too comfortable being a bachelor."

"You raised three fine sons, any one of whom would do you proud in carrying on the family line," Sir Mendam said. "But Matthew's death was a great tragedy, so early and unexpected."

"And so needless," the Dowager said, her tone turning bitter. "It is entirely due to his wife that my oldest son lost his life. Fiona was so determined they visit her family in Ireland before heading to Paris for their wedding trip. Nothing would do for her but to demand they sail there right away, despite everyone knowing the sea is especially treacherous that time of year. If they had just gone directly to Paris instead."

This last comment was a familiar plaint, one Sir Mendam had heard her utter many times during the heat of her first grief. He placed his free hand over her hand where it rested on his arm. They had reached the water's edge, and stood gazing out over the small lake, watching a few ducks glide about its surface.

"It is a great pity," he said carefully. He knew after these many years not to attempt to reason with her or turn her thoughts in a different direction. This was a path she took over and over again, and nothing would sway her from completing the well-traveled memories and long-familiar emotions. He stood patiently, looking out over the water, as she once again worked her way through the remnants of her grief.

As he expected, it wasn't long before she had completed the inner journey. She suddenly turned to him and smiled. Her emotions had always been mercurial, easily influenced by events around her, and he knew that as soon as she awoke from her memories she would return to her role as a hostess. She was ever in her element at society gatherings, and loved nothing more than to entertain. He smiled back at her, happy to see order restored.

"Horace, let us return to the party. I must check to see that the servants are properly setting up the dishes for the next courses. And I'm not sure about that cold pheasant they served. It seemed to me to have a bit too much rosemary. I would value your opinion."

Sir Mendam happily assented to this command. He'd already snagged a piece of the pheasant on the way down, and had found it delicious. He'd cheerfully perform another taste test.

Sir Clapham glanced over at the Marquis, whose face was red with laughter, as he escorted Miss Margaret Benson-Smythe out of the rose garden and back toward her parents. She hurried over to them, enthusiastically exclaiming that her parents must take a turn through the paths. "For the colors and scents are wonderful!" she said.

Her father beamed at her, and looked over at his wife. "I think we would enjoy a turn about the garden. We'll leave you three youngsters to enjoy yourselves," he said with a nod that included Elisabeth. He helped his wife to her feet and smiled fondly at his daughter.

"What do you both say to strolling down to look at the ducks?" Sir Clapham asked Elisabeth and Margaret. "I see our hostess and Sir Mendam are enjoying the view."

As the trio headed down the slope, they saw the older couple begin the return route. The two groups stopped and greeted each other.

"You have a lovely rose collection," Miss Benson-Smythe said to their hostess.

"Quite beautiful," Elisabeth agreed.

"Thank you, my dears. Are you three enjoying yourselves?"

"Yes, indeed, ma'am," Sir Clapham said. "You are a most excellent hostess."

"Please let me know if you need anything," the Dowager said graciously.

"We will, ma'am," Sir Clapham answered with a smile as he led his charges toward the water.

"They seem to be on good terms," Elisabeth commented to her companions.

Sir Clapham chuckled. "Sir Mendam has been a most determined suitor for a number of years. He continues to hope she will agree to become his lady, but I, myself, have doubts his suit will prosper."

"Why is that?" Elisabeth asked.

"For the simple reason that she would be demoting herself from a Dowager Marchioness to a mere Baronet's wife. Lady Loveland places much value on social standing, you know."

"I do not think a title should weigh so heavily when choosing a husband," Miss Benson-Smythe spoke up, blushing slightly. "Sir Mendam seems a very nice man who sincerely cares for her, and that should be more important."

"And he has a tidy fortune," added the irrepressible Sir Clapham.

"Well, certainly one must think to the future," Miss

Benson-Smythe agreed, "but that is not entirely dependent on a title."

"Isn't your father also a mere Baronet, Sir Clapham?" Elisabeth said with a twinkle in her eyes.

"That he is, Lady Elisabeth. I wish Sir Horace all the best. We mere Baronet types must stick up for each other."

The trio at last reached the lake, and stood there looking out over the water much as the older couple had done.

"Boring puddle, ain't it?" Sir Clapham said after a while. "Ought to have some chairs down here or a walkway. I heard someone talk about taking a rowboat out on the water. Is there a boathouse about?"

"There's one over to the left," Elisabeth said, pointing west.

"Excellent." He turned to Margaret Benson-Smythe, entirely forgetting his other companion. "Shall we see if it's a bit cooler on the water?"

Margaret smiled shyly up at him. "Yes, that sounds very pleasant."

Elisabeth saw an opportunity to break away from the picnic for a while, as she obviously wasn't invited to be a member of the rowing party. "You two go enjoy yourselves. I'll just take a turn about the grounds."

"You don't mind?" Sir Clapham asked, suddenly reminded of his manners.

"Not at all," Elisabeth smiled. "I've seen this little lake off and on my entire life. 'Tis nothing new to me."

"Right, then, we're off," Sir Clapham replied. He caught the attention of a servant up by the tents and beckoned the man to make his way toward the water.

"Might need some help getting a boat out," he explained to Margaret.

Elisabeth turned east to walk along the shore toward the border woods as the other two headed in the opposite direction toward the boathouse. She would take just a few minutes to walk through the woods and along the stream before returning to the party. Other guests had broken off from the main group under the tents and were strolling about the lawn, so she didn't think she would be missed if she disappeared for a few minutes.

The Marquis had finally disentangled himself from the Dowager Countess and Lady Griegson, and had stopped for a while to speak with Lord and Lady Childer. He looked about to ensure all the guests were being well entertained, but didn't see the one guest who really interested him. He decided it was time to rescue poor Richard.

Lord Ringwood had been standing for nearly half an hour listening to the chatter of the Ladies Violet and Rose Childer. He was the perfect foil for talkative females, since he rarely worked up the nerve to speak in the presence of a woman. The Marquis apologized to the girls for interrupting them as he pulled Richard away.

"Thank God," Lord Ringwood breathed, once they were out of earshot. "That was horrifying." He stopped as he registered the Marquis's serious expression. "What is it, Monton?"

"A few of my guests seem to have gone missing. Have you seen Rodney?"

"Yes, and you would see him too if you looked across your lake. That's him propelling Miss Benson-Smythe about in that little rowboat. Happy little pair of grigs, aren't they?"

The Marquis followed Lord Ringwood's gaze and saw not only Sir Clapham and Miss Benson-Smythe in a rowboat, but also Mr. and Mrs. Benson-Smythe, who were just being pushed away from the dock by a servant. The Marquis looked back at Rodney's boat, confirming it had only the two occupants.

"And Lady Elisabeth?" he asked.

"Last I saw, she was walking down to the water with Rodney and little Miss Benson-Smythe. A match coming there, I think."

The Marquis found that he could not have cared less about Rodney's matrimonial hopes, although at any other time he would have been amazed at the thought of Rodney willingly walking to the altar. He looked about the grounds.

"Maybe she's in the boathouse," Lord Ringwood offered.

"Perhaps. Think I'll check." The Marquis nearly loped off, not caring that he was drawing the attention of some of the guests.

"And another match coming there, I think," Lord Ringwood said to himself before walking over to the refreshment table where the wine was being served.

At the boathouse the Marquis found one of his footmen, who was industriously preparing a third rowboat in the event another was requested.

"Jenson, isn't it?"

"Yes, m'Lord. What can I do for you?"

"I believe Lady Elisabeth was with Sir Clapham and Miss Benson-Smythe. Is she still about?"

"No, m'Lord. She walked the other direction." He pointed along the water's edge toward the border woods.

"Thank you," the Marquis said, turning about. It would have taken Rodney and Jenson nearly a quarter of an hour to open the boathouse and slide the boat into the water, which meant possibly as much as half an hour had gone by since Lady Elisabeth had disappeared. Did she dislike his party that much, he wondered. No, even if she did, she wouldn't so far forget her manners as to simply walk home. He was certain of that much.

He looked toward the border woods, feeling a little foolish in his pursuit of Lady Elisabeth. He found talking with her both exhilarating and exasperating. He liked her spirit. She didn't pander to him, which was refreshing. They'd only met a few times, but he was strongly attracted to her, and despite – or possibly because of – the way she regularly lit into him, he thought it might be mutual. Should he follow her into the woods?

He stood there for a moment, undecided. Oh, hell, why not? He loped off toward the trees.

Lady Cora Griegson had watched as the Marquis had hastened down the lawn. She had seen his brief conversation with the servant. And when he headed toward the woods, she knew why, because she had seen Lady Elisabeth walk that way half an hour earlier.

She glanced at the Duke, her lovely face showing none of the frustration she felt at his almost avuncular friendliness. He had moved them to join the Ladies

Georgina and Alma, which didn't suit her plans for keeping his attentions all to herself. And now here were the Childer sisters approaching, which meant even more females vying for the Duke's attention.

She gazed consideringly at her table companions, assessing her potential competition.

Her sister Alma she discounted immediately. Even had the Duke been interested in Alma for some bizarre reason, Lady Cora knew her older sister lived in her own private little world, where she was always composing music in her head. Alma had no idea how to flirt, or any interest in doing so. She probably wouldn't even recognize a proposal if she received one, Lady Cora thought in disgust.

Then there was the nearly incomparable Lady Georgina, whose beauty even Lady Cora had to acknowledge. But she didn't think the Duke was seriously interested in Lady Georgina. After all, he'd known her for several years and hadn't yet made an offer, at least as far as Lady Cora knew. She had caught him sending the occasional glance Lady Georgina's way, but she had seen no evidence Lady Georgina was casting out lures in return.

And the Childer sisters simply were not lovely or lively enough to attract such a one as the Duke of Ravenwood. No, the real threat, Lady Cora thought, was the new single female on the scene, Lady Elisabeth Chadwick. Who would have anticipated such competition would exist in the country?

Lady Cora and her mother originally had set their sights on Cora becoming a Marchioness until the Duke's unexpected arrival. She had seen how interested both the

Duke and the Marquis were in Lady Elisabeth, and she had wondered how to remove the threat. Now, at the table, she had a brilliant idea.

She needed to make certain that if one of those eligible lords proposed to Lady Elisabeth, it would be the Marquis. That would free the Duke for Lady Cora. And what better way to force a proposal than to catch the Marquis and Lady Elisabeth in an act of indiscretion? For surely, Lady Cora thought smugly, they must have arranged a meeting in the woods.

She turned to her sister and said gaily, "Alma, come let us go for a walk, my dear!"

Her sister looked at her in surprise, but agreed that it would be pleasant to stroll about the grounds. The two young ladies took off at a leisurely pace as Lady Cora tried to determine the most likely route to take to place them in the path of the Marquis and Lady Elisabeth.

Thirty-Seven

So where was she, the Marquis wondered as he hurried along the small lake's shore toward the shaded woods. Perhaps she had fallen asleep? Or fallen and twisted an ankle? No, more likely she was deliberately dawdling. He felt equal parts alarm and irritation as he walked quickly toward the trees. Surely he was overreacting, but he couldn't shake a growing sense of urgency.

He paused as he arrived at the edge of the trees, listening for any sounds of Lady Elisabeth's presence. He decided to enter the woods and walk along the edge of the creek in the direction that led back up the slope toward the manor, thinking she might have made a circuit back to the party. Perhaps she'd already arrived, and he would look like a right idiot for abandoning his guests to follow her.

After a few minutes of walking as quietly as possible, he heard something that was not the sound of the creek. He paused again, listening. It was coming from up ahead. He started forward again, then stopped as he clearly heard the sounds of a man and woman – Lady Elisabeth! –

engaged in a low, heated argument. Had she come here to meet someone? He felt a knife slide into his heart at the thought. He slipped closer and listened.

"But, you must know my intentions are honorable," the man was saying in a low, angry voice. "I have made that clear."

"What you have made clear is that you think it acceptable to accost me when you find me alone," Lady Elisabeth hissed back in equal anger. "You must know that your attentions are unwanted! I have made that clear, and my father has made that clear. I will thank you to leave me alone! I have a party to return to and I have tarried too long."

"Aye, a party. You're hoping to snare a title, I'm sure," the man replied. "Well it's not often I see you without the protection of your hounds, and I intend to make the most of it. See what your London friends think of you after I return you to their party from a tryst in the woods!"

"You would not dare! Stop!"

At the clear sounds of a struggle, the Marquis bolted forward. He broke through the trees into a small clearing where Lady Elisabeth was struggling in the arms of a large, heavyset man. He had her bent backward in a viselike grip, her arms trapped at her sides, while he attempted to plant a kiss on her mouth. She twisted and turned, trying unsuccessfully to hit and kick at him.

The Marquis dove straight forward, tackling the man and taking all three of them to the ground. As the burly man released his grip on Elisabeth and rolled to confront his attacker, the Marquis found himself once again facing Squire Mills.

The Squire gave an angry roar and lunged at the Marquis. He struck the Marquis's jaw with a vicious right hook as they wrestled with each other on the ground. The Marquis's head rocked back as his face exploded in pain. He tucked in his left arm to protect himself from another blow and lashed out with a punishing right to the Squire's cheek followed by a hit to the man's ear.

Elisabeth crawled away from the two men as they scrambled to their feet. They faced off for a moment, then ran at each other. The Marquis's fist connected with the Squire's nose as the Squire slammed his fist into the Marquis's left eye.

Elisabeth looked around for something to assist the Marquis in what she firmly hoped was the murder of the Squire. She started to stand to pick up a tree branch, but fell to the ground as her left ankle gave out beneath her.

She twisted around to see the Squire aim another punch at the Marquis's chin. The Marquis ducked and drove a hard fist into the Squire's stomach followed by a swift kidney jab. The Squire landed a solid blow on the Marquis's chest. In retaliation the Marquis drove the heel of his right hand up under the Squire's chin and jammed his left elbow into the upper inside of the Squire's right arm.

Blood freely flowed from both men's faces as they fought. Elisabeth grabbed a rock near where she sat on the ground, prepared to defend herself if the Squire prevailed. But the Marquis drove home one last powerful blow to the Squire's head, and Elisabeth watched in satisfaction as the Squire fell back on the ground and lay still.

The Marquis dropped to his knees, then toppled backward. He lay sprawled on the ground while he caught his breath. Elisabeth crawled over to him, still clutching the rock. She gazed down into his face and thought she had never seen anything more beautiful than his bloody, battered countenance.

"Did you kill him?" she asked hopefully.

He gave a weary chuckle. "A bit of a bloodthirsty wench, aren't you?" he grinned through painfully split lips. "Unfortunately, he's alive, but not well. Has he forced himself on you before?"

"He has approached me three times before today," she said. "The first time was at a gathering at Lady Downs's home, then once when I was walking the dogs, and then the other day in the village. The encounter in the village was the first time he dared to touch me. He is loathsome. It's one of the reasons I never go out without my dogs or a groom."

"Until today," the Marquis muttered through swollen lips.

"Until today," she agreed.

"How long has this been going on, and why has your father not put a stop to it?"

"The first time was six months ago, shortly after he buried his third wife."

"Third?" the Marquis exclaimed in surprise, starting to sit up. He gave a gasp of pain and fell back.

"Yes, thrice widowed with no children. Papa thought he had stopped it. He spoke with him and made it clear he would never approve the match. After what happened in the village, Papa threatened the Squire with removal of his position as local magistrate if he approached me again."

He gazed at her through eyes that were rapidly swelling shut. "Come," he said. "Help me up."

"I don't know if I can. I sprained my ankle when you bowled us to the ground." At his kindling look she quickly added an appeasement. "That was very well done of you, by the way. Thank you. I don't know what might have happened, and thanks to you I never shall know. I am so very sorry you were injured."

"It was worth it to hear you praise my manly strength," he said. He started to sit up a second time, moving carefully, but was unable to suppress a groan. His chest ached with every breath he took. He wondered if the Squire's blows to his chest had cracked some ribs. He struggled to his feet, using a nearby stump as leverage, then helped Elisabeth stand. "But I don't think I have enough strength left to carry you. Which ankle is it?"

"My left one. I think it must have gotten twisted under the Squire's weight when we fell."

"My apologies for that." He looked more closely at her and gave a sudden frown. "Blast."

"What is it?"

"You're a mess. Your bodice is torn half off, your hem is ripped, your hair has fallen down, and you've got twigs and dirt all over you. We're going to have a devil of a time explaining this."

She looked down at herself and gasped at the amount of skin exposed by her torn bodice. She pulled the fabric together with one hand and began brushing debris off the skirt of her dress with her other hand. "Perhaps we could say it was footpads?"

He chuckled at that and moved to her left side. He put his arm around her so she could lean on him to minimize putting weight on her left ankle. He didn't want to admit that he needed the assistance at least as much as she did.

"We'll try to sneak past the party and into the kitchens," he said as they began hobbling up the path that followed the stream.

They had nearly reached the last tree before the start of the lawn when the Marquis wobbled dangerously. Elisabeth turned to place both arms around him. "You are seriously injured, my Lord. Perhaps I should make my way to the house alone and send servants back to help you."

"No," he gasped. "Neither of us is likely to make it on our own. We must try to slip in together without anyone seeing you in this condition. We are up above the picnic area and not too far from the house. We can do this."

It had been a good plan, the Marquis thought later, but a better plan would have been to try to make it to Chadwick Manor. They had taken only a few steps out of the woods toward the house when a shriek rent the air.

They turned to see the Ladies Cora and Alma staring at them in horror. Lady Alma gave another shriek and ran toward them. Lady Cora turned and hurried back toward the picnic area, her horror-struck expression briefly breaking into a wide smile before she corrected herself. She ran straight to the Duke.

"Oh, my word!" Lady Violet exclaimed as she and her sister arrived on the heels of the Duke. She turned to stare at the Marquis in disgust. "What did you do to her?"

Lady Alma was partially supporting Elisabeth, who was still attempting to help hold the Marquis upright. The Duke ran to his cousin and grabbed him under his arms in time to prevent him from sliding to the ground. He turned to Lady Alma. "Cover her," he said curtly.

Lady Alma pulled her fan from a skirt pocket and opened it in front of Elisabeth. "We must get you inside," Lady Alma said. Elisabeth released her hold on the Marquis and took the fan with one hand while Lady Alma started assisting her toward the manor.

The other guests were now arriving, led by Lady Cora. They stared in shock at the Marquis and Elisabeth. Servants began running toward them to offer assistance. The Duke directed two footmen to help him carry the Marquis to his chambers, while the Dowager Countess and Lady Alma assisted Elisabeth.

Behind them, Elisabeth heard Lady Cora's voice raised in innocent inquiry. "But why is her bodice ripped and why is his face injured?" she asked into the air. "Did they have some sort of fight?" By the time they reached the manor, the Marquis and Elisabeth were surrounded by most of the house party, all clamoring to know what had happened.

The Marquis managed to instruct a servant through swollen lips to run to the Earl's home and let him know his daughter had fallen in the woods and injured her ankle, and had torn and wrecked her clothes. "Have him bring over a new outfit for her. And tell him to await me in the study while I change."

The Duke turned to another hovering servant. "Get the local sawbones here now," he ordered. The servant bowed and ran off toward the stables.

The Marquis was helped to his suite while Elisabeth was directed to his mother's chambers. Baths were ordered, along with brandy for the Marquis and tea for Elisabeth. She heard that last order and found herself wishing ladies were allowed something more substantial than tea in times of trial.

Once in his rooms, the Marquis summoned his steward. He ordered the other servants who surrounded him to step into the hall for a few minutes, then gave Meerson and the Duke a succinct summary of what had occurred. He sent them to find the Squire and make sure the man was removed from his property.

"And Meerson?" the Marquis said, as the men were preparing to exit the room.

"Yes, m'Lord?"

"Explain to the Squire that I shall be giving word to my servants and tenants that if he ever sets foot on my property again they are to shoot him."

"Yes, m'Lord."

"Charles?"

"Yes?"

"Put the fear of God into that man."

The Duke smiled grimly. "It will be my pleasure."

The Marquis then turned himself over to his valet and two other male servants. His torn and bloodied clothes were taken away to be burned while the bathtub was filled with cans of steaming water. He gingerly lowered himself into the tub, feeling the stings against his cuts and bruises, and the pain of his ribs. And somewhere along the line he had managed to wrench one of his knees, he realized.

He should have known he'd end up looking like this after he'd first seen her two bruised and battered footmen, he thought, as he sank into the hot water. That woman was going to make his life a living trial.

Thirty-Eight

The Marquis was sore and wanted time to think. After his bathwater had cooled, he called for his tub to be drained and filled a second time. He was just rising from the water nearly an hour after entering his room when a sharp rap at the door drew one of the servants to see who had knocked. The Marquis hastily lowered himself back into the water as the Dowager Countess of Cwmhaven barged into the room, pushing the startled servant aside.

Both footmen stared at the Marquis, who shrugged his shoulders. "Leave us for a moment, but stay outside the door." He turned to his unexpected guest as soon as the door closed. He cut her off just as she was drawing a breath to begin what he was sure would be a harangue. "Don't worry, I intend to offer for her."

The Dowager stood for a moment looking like a swollen-up puffer fish, then expelled her breath. She folded her arms across her chest. "What happened out there?" she asked baldly. "The two of you looked like you'd been in a carriage accident. Except that bodices generally are not half ripped off by that kind of event. Elisabeth will tell me nothing."

He gave her a frank answer. "The truth of the matter is that your great-niece had slipped into the woods on her way back to the party from the lake, and Squire Mills found her there and attacked her. That, I understand, is his idea of wooing. Fortunately, I was able to dissuade him from his pursuit."

The Dowager had paled at his words, suddenly looking old and fragile. He sought to reassure her. "He had just grabbed her and was attempting to kiss her as I arrived. I overheard enough as I was approaching to be able to confirm that nothing worse had happened. I know for a fact that he has tried this gentlemanly approach before, and she has repelled him."

"But her bodice was nearly ripped off, and she is injured! Are you certain he did not do worse? She will not speak a word!" He heard the frantic note in her voice, and saw her tightly clenched hands. From his experience of Lady Elisabeth, he rather thought she was keeping mum because she wanted them to get their stories straight before she offered an explanation. But her great-aunt deserved better.

"In my effort to stop Squire Mills I knocked him to the ground and she went down with us. That's when she sprained her ankle and wrecked her gown. But you can rest assured she will be fine. She was more angry than scared. She is cut from your mold, Lady Burton. Not even a rogue like the Squire can best her."

The Marquis watched as the Dowager considered all that he'd just said. He bit back a grin. This was a first for him, consoling an elderly lady while sitting naked in his bathwater. Any other woman her age – well, maybe not the redoubtable Lady Downs who liked to surround herself with large, attractive footmen – would have had a spasm at the very thought of being in a room with a naked man.

The Dowager's color slowly returned, and she gave him a piercing stare. "And you are going to offer for her?"

"It will be my pleasure," he nodded.

"Hmph. The question is, will it be her pleasure."

"Oh, I fully expect her to refuse me," he said cordially.

"What?! No, you must marry her or she will be ruined in society's eyes!"

"Rest assured, I don't intend to take no for an answer, Lady Burton, but you must know that your great-niece doesn't give a fig for society or for what constitutes approval or ruination. It's one of the things I most like about her."

She subjected him to a hard glare. "I do not understand either of you, but it is sufficient that you will be married. I am told my nephew has arrived and is awaiting you in the second salon. I'll keep him company until you present yourself." And with that, she whisked herself out of the room and his valet and the two hovering footmen re-entered.

"Well that was the oddest interview I've ever had," the Marquis commented as he finally stepped out of the tub.

"As you say, m'Lord," the valet said. "Shall I send in Dr. Fieldman now? He has been waiting outside to see to you."

"Is that the local sawbones? Yes, do send him in. Then, Gorse you may help me with my toilette."

When the Marquis finally entered his study an hour later, he found the Earl alone. He looked inquiringly around the room.

"I sent Aunt Lister upstairs to tend to Elsbet. She gave me your summary of events. I would have all the details from you, please."

"I need another brandy," the Marquis commented. "Do you care to join me?"

The Earl nodded and waited while the Marquis poured two small glasses of brandy and handed one to the Earl. The Marquis gingerly sat down in a chair across from Elisabeth's father, who was interestedly assessing the various cuts and swellings that were discoloring his host's face.

"You're a sight, Monton. I hope the Squire is in worse shape."

"I hope so, too," the Marquis said in a tight voice. He launched into the tale, sharing every detail he could remember, particularly about Elisabeth's part in the events. The Earl interrupted him only twice – first to confirm that the ripped bodice he'd been told about had occurred when the three of them had tumbled to the ground, and the second time to hear again that Elisabeth had, indeed, intended on defending herself with a large rock if the Squire had bested the Marquis. This last piece of information brought a faint smile to the Earl's lips.

Once the recitation was complete, the two men sat there in silence for a few moments, each lost in his own thoughts. Finally, the Marquis brought himself back to the present and looked over at the older man.

"I greatly admire your daughter," the Marquis said, "and I wish to request her hand in marriage."

The Earl then revealed his kinship with his aunt by subjecting the Marquis to an exacting interview that, when over, had opened the Marquis's life like a book. Once the Earl was assured of the Marquis's character, the conversation moved on to a discussion of dowries, settlements, the disposition of property, and – men being men – possible horse breeding opportunities.

Only when satisfied that the Marquis would make his daughter a suitable husband did the Earl give his blessing. The Marquis actually found himself exhaling a sigh of relief.

Once the interrogation had ended, the Earl returned to the topic of the assault. "How many people actually know what happened?"

"From my lips, you, Lady Burton, Charles, and Meerson. Whom the Squire chooses to tell is another matter."

"Meerson's an oyster, and neither Aunt Lister nor I will spread word of this. The Duke is your friend. Can he be trusted?"

"Absolutely. Charles has a love of absurdity and making mischief, but he can be trusted when it comes to important matters, especially those involving family. However, I should let you know that I told Meerson to give my servants the order to shoot the Squire on sight should he so much as set a toe on my land again."

The Earl laughed, but then said seriously, "Not the most discreet action to take, but perfectly understandable. The cat's out of the bag, then. Fortunately my word will prevail against the Squire in these parts, and your marriage to Elsbet will dampen any further scandal. I believe our dinner party is scheduled a few evenings hence. We'll call it an engagement party. I'll extend the invitation to Lady Downs and Vicar and Mrs. Smithers, and I'll send messengers to Robbie and Anne. Robbie may be able to arrive in time, if he and Caroline are in London at present, but Anne and Marcus live too far to the north, unfortunately. By then your bruises ought to be an attractive shade of purplish yellow."

"Thank you. But I haven't yet proposed, nor been accepted."

"Best get to it then," the Earl said, rising. "I'll speak with her before she comes down. With your permission, I'll ask your Applewood to summon Elsbet to the study."

"Thank you. I don't think I'm quite up to walking across the room at the moment. The fighting I usually engage in is done in a boxing ring with rules. I had forgotten what a real fight entails."

The Earl smiled and left the room.

Elisabeth received the summons with mixed emotions. As she and her great-aunt left the Dowager Marchioness's chambers and followed the butler down the hall, she was surprised to find that they were not led down the stairs to where the Marquis awaited, but to a small room just off the landing at the top of the stairs. As the butler gestured for her to enter, Elisabeth saw her father rising to greet her.

She ran into his arms, uncharacteristically weepy and trembling. This, more than any words could, told her father just how traumatized his daughter had been.

Perhaps the Marquis's shoot-on-sight command was not such a bad idea after all.

The Dowager followed her great-niece into the room. Applewood quietly withdrew, closing the door behind him.

"Oh, Papa!" Elisabeth cried as she clung to the Earl. He held her tight, making soothing sounds and rubbing her back. She sobbed and shook in relief at his reassurances, but after a while calmed down, sniffling and asking for a hankie to blow her nose. However, when he led her to a small settee, she refused to be parted from him and sat holding his hands with her head cradled on his shoulder.

Her great-aunt looked on quietly, showing unexpected compassion and restraint. Any natural desire to point out the consequences of such folly as walking alone in a woods had been thoroughly squelched by the Earl, who in plain language had told the Dowager not to be a fool, and to leave the handling of his daughter to him.

"My dear," the Earl said at last, "I have had the whole story from Monton. I am immensely grateful for his timely intervention, and thank God you were not seriously injured."

"Yes, Papa," she said quietly. "I was so very angry at the time, but now I realize how frightened I was, too." She paused, and then took her courage in her hands. "Please, Papa, you will not make me marry Squire Mills, will you? I would rather die first."

"Marry Squire Mills? Don't be ridiculous. I'd murder him before I'd let him touch you again. You know that. No, it's not the Squire you were seen with as you emerged from the woods."

"Oh," she said quietly, looking down at her hands, which were still held in her father's reassuring clasp. Then, "Oh!" She turned amazed eyes toward her father. "Must I marry Lord Loveland, Papa?" If her two companions heard the rather hopeful tone underlying that question, they were wise enough to hide their amusement. Her father simply gazed at her.

She looked back down at their entwined hands. "I must marry someone, mustn't I? Either that, or stay here and never marry anyone."

"I am afraid those are your choices, yes," he agreed, shooting his aunt a minatory glance as she looked about to object to there being any choice whatsoever. "Of course, there might be a man eventually, perhaps one who visits the village, who might offer for you. But you were seen emerging from the woods with the Marquis after disappearing for half an hour, and I am told it was plain to all there had been some sort of attack upon your person."

"Yes, but he saved me from that attack. And he was attacked, too, which everyone could see. There was blood everywhere. Could we not tell the truth – that he arrived in the nick of time, and I wasn't harmed?"

"We could, but not everyone will believe you were unharmed. Some will say you were trysting with a lover and the Marquis caught you. Some will say the Marquis attacked you."

"But that is so unfair!"

"Yes, it is unfair."

Elisabeth raised her head from her father's shoulder and looked across the room at her great-aunt. "Ma'am, what do you think I should do?"

The Dowager glanced at her nephew, and then bent a look of unusual tenderness on Elisabeth. "You said to Lady Downs and me when we visited her for tea that you believed it was important to marry a good man, a kind man. I think the Marquis is both of those things."

"But he has such a reputation. Wild."

The Dowager nodded. "There were reasons he behaved in such a manner. I do not excuse it, but I know from his mother that when his older brother died, it hit him terribly hard."

"Older brother?" Elisabeth asked in surprise. "So the Marquis was second in line?"

"Yes, his older brother Matthew had been married for only a few days when both he and his bride perished in a sailing accident. I think the present Marquis went a little mad. He hadn't expected to ascend to the title, and I think he didn't want to step into his brother's role."

"So he lost his brother?" Elisabeth asked. "I know so little about him. Does he have other brothers and sisters?"

"There is a younger brother named Patrick," the Dowager said.

Elisabeth sat silently for a moment, before looking at her father. "Papa, what do you think of him?"

The Earl smiled. "I like him. And he did an admirable job just now of withstanding a grilling about his fortune, plans, prospects, and politics. And, oh yes, his thoughts on marriage. I would approve an offer from him regardless of the circumstances that led to it."

"We don't love each other," Elisabeth said.

"I think that may come in time," the Dowager said unexpectedly. "I think the both of you may be partway there already."

The Earl and Elisabeth both looked at her in surprise.

The Dowager returned her nephew's look. "I heard the oddest conversation between the two of them when we arrived here today." She turned her gaze back to Elisabeth. "If the two of you have been having conversations like that, there is mutual attraction and likemindedness already. It is a good start."

"Lord Loveland is downstairs waiting for you," the Earl told Elisabeth.

Elisabeth sat without moving for a moment, then nodded to herself. She released her father's hands. "I will go down now. Would the two of you please wait here?"

"We'll wait," her father nodded.

He watched her as she left the room and shut the door behind her. He turned and smiled at his aunt. "My girl is about to become a bride."

"If she can mind her tongue long enough to accept his offer," his aunt commented.

The Marquis's welcome wasn't quite what Elisabeth had expected. Of course, not having received a serious offer of marriage before, since she couldn't count the proposal she'd received at the age of seven from the crofter's eight-year-old son or the recent mauling from the Squire, she wasn't sure what would happen. But she had a vague notion that she might find him down on one knee.

Instead, she found the Marquis sprawled out on a large, cushioned chair, holding an empty brandy glass in one dangling hand. His legs were stretched across a small table, and his face displayed an interesting collection of reds and purples. His eyelids were swollen nearly shut, and his lips were puffed and cracked. A bandage was taped rakishly above his left eye, another along his right cheek, and small sticking plasters littered his face and neck. He turned his head slightly to look at her, but made no motion to rise.

"Well?" he said, after Applewood had closed the door behind her.

"Well what?"

"Are you going to marry me?"

"Of course I'm going to marry you," she said in irritation. "I have no choice."

"Thank God. I don't think I could handle having to fight off another suitor. I'm near done in. Do you know that idiot actually tried to bite me?"

"Did he really?"

"Yes, and if you intend to make a habit of leading men on to the point of insanity after we're married, you can just deal with your rejected cicisbeos yourself."

Elisabeth had not yet moved from where she stood just inside the door. She put her hands on her hips and frowned at him. "Aren't you supposed to kneel down on one knee or something?"

He gave her an astonished look. "You must be joking. In my condition?"

"Not as fit as you thought?" she asked nastily.

"Not at all," he agreed. "Get me another brandy, would you?"

"I shall do no such thing!"

"Fine, then ring for Applewood."

She spun around and tugged at the bell pull by the door. The butler appeared a little too quickly. She eyed the keyhole with suspicion. "Applewood, his Godliness the Marquis would like another brandy."

"And that casket you brought down earlier," the Marquis said from his chair. He directed a look at Elisabeth. "Please," he said, waving one arm toward the chair her father had recently vacated, "do sit down, my dear. We have much to discuss."

Not willing to make a scene in front of Applewood, Elisabeth stalked over to the chair and made a production of sinking gracefully down onto it. The butler refilled the Marquis's glass, and handed a second one to Elisabeth.

"Oh, thank you!" she smiled, as she realized she'd been handed brandy. "I've always wanted to try this!" She took a careful sip of the amber liquid and felt its heat spread throughout her body. "Oh, that's wonderful."

"A tippler, are you?" the Marquis asked. "That's good to know. I'll make sure to hide the liquor cabinet keys from you once we're wed."

Applewood went to the desk and retrieved a small wooden chest covered with scrolled iron. The Marquis waved at the table, and the butler carefully placed the container between the Marquis's feet.

"Excellent, Applewood. That will be all. She'll ring if we need you."

"Fine, m'Lord. Will you be joining the others for tea?"

"Not by a long shot," the Marquis said with a shudder.

"Applewood," Elisabeth said before the butler could leave the room, "would you please send a tea tray up to my father and great-aunt? They're waiting in that small room at the top of the stairs."

"Yes, m'Lady," the butler nodded as he left the room.

"Packed them in a closet, have you?" the Marquis asked.

"Yes, it's where I pack everyone who displeases me," she said, looking pointedly at his feet on the table in front of her.

"Oh for heaven's sake," he groused, removing his feet and planting them on the floor. "You'd best get used to them, girl; they go with me everywhere."

"And take up quite a lot of room, I see."

"And speaking of feet, how is it you haven't a bit of your limp left?" he asked with a trace of suspicion.

"Your housekeeper wrapped my ankle in cold compresses and then bandaged it quite tightly. It still aches, but I can move about just fine," Elisabeth said. "And, of course, I am quite physically fit. I no doubt get much more exercise in the country than you do in your Town clubs, sitting about all day drinking and playing cards."

"Yes, I'm a sot and a gambler, and I pay no attention to my lands. Quite a wastrel, in fact. Your father thinks I'm just the person to take you in hand."

"He did not say such a thing!"

"Oh, he's quite relieved to be rid of you. Offered to double your dowry if I'd whisk you and your gargantuan hounds away as quickly as possible."

"I'm glad you realize they'll be traveling with us," she smiled sweetly. "They go with me everywhere."

He laughed at that and waved at the table between them where Applewood had placed the small casket. "Open the box."

She leaned forward and set her glass on the table next to the wood and metal chest. She opened the container and couldn't help giving an awed gasp. "How beautiful!"

"M'mother always insists on traveling with some of our family's baubles," he said. He leaned forward to place his own glass on the table. He groaned at the movement, and Elisabeth realized he was in more pain than she had imagined. His face looked a mess, and his hands were scraped and bruised, but despite all the evidence, she hadn't made the connection that he really had taken a bad beating. It was just that he seemed so strong and invincible to her.

He turned serious. "These will be yours someday, but more importantly, I would like you to look through them and see if you find a betrothal ring to your liking. I want you to have something that suits your preferences. And I was afraid if I picked something you didn't like, you might throw it at me."

She smiled at that, and began the important task of rooting around among the tangle of necklaces, earbobs, brooches, bracelets, rings, and other pieces. At last she found a large rectangular emerald surrounded by diamonds and set in yellow gold. Elisabeth peeked up at the Marquis a little shyly. "My great-aunt is forever telling me I must wear things that match my eyes. May I have this one?"

"You may have anything in there that strikes your fancy. I believe there are some matching pieces as well," he said. "Go ahead and take them if you find them. Little though you care, you're about to become an extremely wealthy woman, so don't feel as though you need to be frugal."

Eventually Elisabeth selected a matching hair ornament and bracelet. She placed all three pieces on the table. The set sparkled in the late afternoon sun's rays streaming through the windows. She carefully placed all the other pieces she'd exhumed back in the travel case and carried it to the desk. As she passed the Marquis on her return to her chair, he stopped her with a hand on her arm. She looked down questioningly.

He gave her a lopsided grin. "I may not be able to kneel on the floor, but I do claim the honor of placing your betrothal ring on your finger." He reached for the ring, repressing another groan at his sore ribs. She knelt down beside his chair and held out her left hand. He slid the ring onto her finger, then reached down and kissed the back of her hand. Magic, she thought, his touch was magic.

"There," he said, sitting back. "It's official. Now, do you mind if I take a nap?"

Which is when Elisabeth finally decanted him a brandy. Except that she missed his glass and poured it all over his head.

The Earl and Dowager Countess looked up in anticipation when the door to the small sitting room opened. But rather than the happy couple they expected to see, in marched an irate young lady.

Elisabeth was fuming. Take a nap! On her engagement day! How dare he! She didn't care how tired and sore he was. Well, maybe she did, but she wasn't going to admit it. But really, was that the best he could do?

"He didn't even kiss me!" she exclaimed as she stormed into the room. "And I was the one who had to kneel!"

"What?" her confused relatives asked.

She flashed her engagement ring at them. "Isn't it beautiful?" she asked gleefully, with a lightning change of mood. "And I have two matching pieces. See?" She pulled the hair clip and bracelet out of a pocket to show them.

"Lovely," the Dowager said, looking at her great-niece warily.

"He made you kneel?" the Earl asked.

"Well, he didn't make me. I did it because he couldn't!"

"What?" the Dowager asked again.

"I think I need to go have a talk with him," the Earl said, starting to rise.

"You can't! He's fallen asleep!" Elisabeth said, suddenly angry again.

"He fell asleep?" the Earl asked, repressing an urge to laugh. "Well, he did have a rather trying day, my dear."

"And he didn't like it when I had a sip of brandy! He called me a tippler!"

"You celebrated with brandy?" her great-aunt asked, feeling as though she had somehow lost the ability to understand the English language.

"Well, he clearly won't be joining us up here for a private chat, so perhaps we'd best look in on him," the Earl said. "I'd like all of us to have some time to talk before we join the other guests in the main salon."

His daughter surprised him by blushing rosily. "You might want to wait until Applewood dries him off and changes his clothes."

"Dries him off?" the Dowager asked. "Is he bleeding again?"

"No, I dowsed him with his best brandy," Elisabeth said. "Oh, my, isn't this ring stunning?"

Forty-One

The house party guests were abuzz with excitement. They clustered in small groups throughout the main salon, each discussing the day's events and speculating on what might be happening behind the doors of the second salon just across the hall. They certainly knew what the social strictures held in store for Lady Elisabeth and the Marquis. None of them knew precisely what had happened between the two in the woods, but the result was a foregone conclusion.

"We can leave aside any hopes of either of you snaring the Marquis," Lady Griegson said to her two daughters, Ladies Alma and Cora. "He will have no choice but to offer for Lady Elisabeth after what we all saw today."

"I'm not interested in the Marquis anyway," Lady Cora said. She glanced about the salon, but the Duke had disappeared right after all the excitement. She wondered where he was.

"I do think you may be able to capture Ravenwood's interest, with a little more time," her doting mother said.

"No," her father said flatly. "Any friend of Monton is not to be considered. "Giving every man the right to vote! It would be anarchy! Preposterous! I won't have a revolutionary in my family!"

His younger daughter exchanged a meaningful glance with her mother. Lady Griegson pursed her lips. Really, sometimes her husband could be so thick-headed.

She made soothing sounds to Lord Griegson, whose face was turning an alarming shade of puce. Bad enough he'd gotten into a fight with the Duke of Ravenwood, but now he was hurting his daughters' futures. She was determined her daughters would marry titles, and a Duke on the premises was not to be lightly dismissed.

"We can talk about this later," she said to her husband. "I would not like to see Cora throw away the chance to become a Duchess." Her husband began to sputter again, so she changed the topic. "But we also must consider Alma's future. Perhaps we should visit your sister Charlotte on the way home. She may have some connections through her husband."

"Aye, Rutherford is related to half of England," he agreed. "Good riddance to Monton anyway. Can't trust a man whose friends are all a pack of radicals."

"Then it's agreed," his wife said. "We'll visit Charlotte. She likely will know some older widowers for Alma."

At this, Lady Alma's attention abruptly snapped back to the present from the ballad she had been composing in her head. She looked at her mother beseechingly. That lady entirely misinterpreted the meaning of her older daughter's gaze.

"No need to worry, my dear. We will ensure you do not spend one more Season without a ring."

"Mama!"

"Yes, I think that is a good plan," Lady Griegson said. "A mature, older man whose children are grown and who would welcome a wife who has gained some London polish, but is still relatively young."

Alma shut her eyes in horror and concentrated on playing mental scales.

A similar conversation was taking place among the Childers, as the Ladies Violet and Rose were discussing with their mother whether any of the other male houseguests might be worth pursuing.

"I had really hoped that Lord Wentworth would put in an appearance," Lady Childer said. "He would be such a good catch."

"Yes," her husband agreed. "Good family, good manners, decent estate."

"What about Lord Ringwood?" Lady Rose asked. She'd found his long, dark blond hair to be quite dashing, and loved the way he was forever brushing his locks out of his eyes. And he always listened to her so politely, never interrupting.

"If one can get him to say boo," Lady Violet complained. "And his hair is so unkempt." She gave a small shudder.

"Really, Violet," her impatient sister exclaimed, "if you do not stop those theatrical shudders, people will think you have a palsy."

"I am not theatrical!" her sister shot back. "I am delicate! How dare you compare me to theater people!"

"What about Sir Clapham?" Rose asked, ignoring her sister. "I find him quite amusing."

"Either gentleman would be a good catch," Lady Childer agreed. She glanced across the room toward the French doors that led onto the balcony. The Duke of Ravenwood had finally made an appearance and was in the middle an earnest, rather intense conversation with his younger brother and the Griegson lad. She watched as the two boys nodded and slipped outside. They looked almost furtive.

"There are always the North brothers," her daughter Rose said, recapturing her mother's attention. "We met them at the Maywell ball last month, remember?"

"I will be sure to invite them to a small gathering when we return to Town," Lady Childer nodded. She poked her husband. "What think you of the Norths?"

"Another good family," Lord Childer nodded.

Lady Childer was distracted again when she noticed the butler slip in with a message for the Duke. The Duke followed him into the hall and a footman closed the doors again.

"How much longer, I asked," her husband said, tapping her arm.

"I beg your pardon," Lady Childer said. "I wasn't attending. What was the question?"

"I asked, how much longer do you think we must stay?" Lord Childer said.

"Possess yourself in patience," she replied. "We were invited for the full three weeks of this house party and we shall stay the full three weeks. There's still the Chadwicks' dinner party, and the final dance party isn't scheduled until after that."

"I miss my own bed," he groused.

She gave him a more direct stare than he was used to receiving from his wife. "I don't care what you miss," she stated firmly. "You shall not add to your rudeness by dragging us away early. You already have gotten into an argument with two close friends of your host, and you shall not subject us to a further display of bad manners by leaving early. You will make all of us look ridiculous."

Her daughters stared wide-eyed at the sight of their mother taking the upper hand with their opinionated father. Lady Childer turned, saw their surprise, and turned an equally direct gaze on them. "And you two shall continue to be all that is charming to all the men of the party, including the Marquis. You shall be delighted for Lady Elisabeth, who, if her father has any say in the matter, is in the process of becoming betrothed, and you shall work hard to place yourself in her good graces. She is about to become a well-connected Marchioness who can help you meet eligible gentlemen."

"But, Mother, she raises dogs and likes to walk in the woods," Violet complained. "She is so odd."

Rose shot out a hand and grasped her older sister's shoulder. "If you shudder again, Violet, I swear I will spill my tea on you."

The Benson-Smythes were focused on a slightly different aspect of husband-hunting. Mrs. Benson-Smythe found herself facing a daughter who had suddenly developed a determination to change her entire wardrobe.

"And I mean it, Mother," Margaret was saying. If you do not let me direct Florence to remove the flounces and ruffles on my dinner gowns, I shall do it myself."

Mrs. Benson-Smythe gave an entirely sincere shudder. No governess or hired teacher had ever succeeded in teaching Margaret how to do anything with a needle and thread except stab herself or accidently sew her stitchery projects to her dresses, chairs, or anything else nearby. The potential results of Margaret doing her own wardrobe alterations were too hideous to be imagined.

"But what's wrong with your gowns, Margie?" her father asked. "I think you look delightful in them. Quite like a little princess on a cake."

"Yes, that's exactly the problem, Father. I look like I'm wearing layers of icing. I want something simpler and more elegant."

"But, darling," her mother objected, "flounces are all the style. Why, Lady Barminster wore a dress with fully a dozen flounces to the Carders' party last month."

"I am too short to wear all those ruffles," Margaret said firmly. "I want no more than three flounces on any dress, and I want no flounces at all on the gowns I am wearing to the Chadwicks' dinner party and the Marchioness's dance party. Please, Mother."

"But I don't understand," her beleaguered parent said in frustration.

Mr. Benson-Smythe considered his daughter's current afternoon dress, which sported five flounces, and gave it as his opinion that Margaret should be allowed to have her way. When his wife gave a gasp of concern, he offered a compromise.

"Look at it this way, my dear. We are at a house party far from Town. If the style suits our little girl, and I rather think it might, there will be no harm. If the style don't suit, only a few people will know of it." He returned his gaze to Margaret. "What has caused this sudden desire to alter your gowns, my dear? I thought they were in the kick of style. I know for a fact your mother arranged for them to be made by an excellent modiste."

When his wife raised her eyebrows in surprise at his apparent knowledge of ladies' fashions, he gave her an amused smile. "Well, from the size of the bills I paid, I have to assume you selected only the best modiste and milliner."

Mrs. Benson-Smythe gave a little giggle. She turned to her daughter and nodded reluctantly. "Very well. After tea I shall instruct Florence to do as you've requested. We have only a few days before dinner at the Chadwicks, so we shall work on that gown first. I had thought we would save the white and silver gown for the final dance party, so we must choose which dress you will wear to Chadwick Manor."

"Oh, thank you, Mother!" Margaret exclaimed. She leaned forward and gave her mother a quick hug. Mrs. Benson-Smythe exchanged puzzled glances with her husband. That gentleman shrugged his shoulders unknowingly.

Forty-Two

As the families of the single ladies plotted and planned their daughters' futures, the Dowager Marchioness sat with her friend Sir Mendam. Their plotting was of a different nature. Having been informed by an almost-smiling Applewood that the Marquis was now officially engaged, she was thinking about the wedding to be planned.

"I do hope John will allow me to hold the wedding in London," the Dowager was saying. "Matthew insisted on marrying that Irish woman with a special license, and I so wanted them to hold a formal wedding in Town. It would have been the social event of the year. But no, nothing would do but that he must marry her right away, after knowing her for just a few weeks. And just see what happened."

"I trust John will not be so disobliging," Sir Mendam said reassuringly.

"Will he not?" the Dowager asked fretfully. "You do not know him as I do. He so often seems to suffer from the same lack of regard for his position as Matthew did. I cannot understand it."

"But Matthew loved and respected you, and so does John," Sir Mendam comforted her. "Despite his casual regard for the proprieties, Matthew was a good and responsible man. He kept the estates in good repair, and represented you well, and John is of a like nature. They do you proud."

"I shall need several months to arrange for a wedding," the Dowager said. "It must take place at St. Paul's. I shall need to begin drawing up the guest list tomorrow. Lister will help me with the bride's side. Oh, I cannot wait to begin. I shall love planning this wedding."

"One hopes Lady Elisabeth will not insist on having her dogs in attendance," Sir Mendam laughed. "I understand they are huge."

"Yes, not pugs at all," the Dowager said as though she had been deliberately misled.

"I am sure Lady Burton will ensure all proper etiquette is followed," Sir Mendam said. "There will be no dogs in St. Paul's."

Across the room, Lady Georgina chatted easily with Lord Ringwood and Sir Clapham. They had watched as the Duke had entered the salon and immediately been approached by young Lords Peter and Thomas, and then as the butler had summoned the Duke from the room.

"Something's up there," Sir Clapham commented.

"Oh yes, I expect so," said Lady Georgina with a quiet smile. "And how are you two gentlemen enjoying this warm weather?"

As usual, she thought, it was Sir Clapham who answered while Lord Ringwood stood as if stuffed, not daring to utter a word in her presence. The man had the most amusing fear of women. She gave him a nod before turning her attention to Sir Clapham.

"Deuced hot," he complained. "But it felt a little more humid today than it has since I arrived. Think we may see some rain soon."

"The fields are very dry," she commented, thinking not for the first time that she might die of boredom if she had to conduct many more banal social conversations. This house party definitely was amusing, but she still couldn't understand what had possessed her father to accept this invitation on her behalf.

This was the first of two house parties he'd sent her to this summer. She was dispatched to one or two such events each year, but usually the guests included political allies and foes of higher rank than she'd found here. The Lords Griegson and Childer were small game in her father's world, and none of the other male guests was particularly political.

"I do so worry about the farmers in this weather," she added in her lovely dulcet tones. "Agriculture is one of the backbones of a healthy nation."

She only half listened to Sir Clapham's response as she thought about her dearly disliked father. His interests were focused solely on politics, with no time for purely social events such as this, or even checking on the management of his estates. Everything in his life revolved around currying favor with the King. Even the choice of his wife and the naming of his daughter had been to serve that end.

Surely he couldn't seriously be concerned that the Duke actually might be a dangerous radical, as she had heard Lord Griegson saying? Aside from the Duke's amusing side venture, which would be of no interest to Lord Dunbarton, she had seen no intrigue here beyond the usual matchmaking. However, she would fulfill her role, which was to dutifully report back any events or comments of interest. She smiled politely at her two companions.

"I expect it was nice to be able to get in a row on the lake," she said to Sir Clapham.

He brightened considerably. "That it was!"

"Yes," she said, with nary a twitch giving away the fact that she found Sir Clapham's pursuit of Miss Benson-Smythe most amusing. "Being on the water is always so refreshing."

Sir Clapham then proceeded to rattle on about weather patterns in England while Lady Georgina encouraged him to share his knowledge and kept the conversation moving. Lord Ringwood looked back and forth between the two of them, but contributed nothing to the fascinating topic of weather.

Forty-Three

Across the hall in the second salon, the Duke was finishing his message and sealing it with a wafer. The Marquis franked it for him, and then had the Duke tug the bell pull. When Applewood appeared, he was handed the envelope and requested to send a fast rider to the intended recipient, have the rider await the response, and return with all haste. The Marquis handed the butler a purse with more than enough coins to cover expenses, then leaned back in his chair.

The Duke sat down across from the Marquis and regarded his host with a dispassionate air. "You look like hell, John."

"Thank you, Charles. Engagement will do this to a fellow, I hear."

"Is that so? Something I'd best avoid, then. Wouldn't want to damage my pretty face."

"I noticed you've been keeping an eye on the beauteous Lady Georgina."

"It's not a hardship to observe someone so lovely," the Duke said. "Besides, she intrigues me."

"How so? She seems just another accomplished society belle to me."

"Hmm, maybe. But I don't think she's what she seems."

"Really? How so?"

"Last year, at the Armandsons' rout, she and I were chatting in the hall."

"Really?" the Marquis said in mock horror. "Pretty odd, that."

"Stubble it," the Duke said. "At any rate, I was making the usual compliments about her beauty, how she cast all the other girls into the shade, and all the expected rot, and she was behaving just as she ought – smiling demurely, responding politely, what have you. And then, as we parted, I happened to glance to the side and caught her reflection in a small mirror above the entry table. And she was rolling her eyes and making a face like she was gagging."

The Marquis started to laugh, then clutched his side. "Ow. Perhaps that's the way all the girls react after speaking with you for a few minutes. Wouldn't surprise me in the least."

The Duke threw a pillow at his host.

"Watch it! I'm an invalid, you know."

"You deserve to be, letting a country bully like that do you in," the Duke said. "By the by, Meerson and I were able to roll him onto a drag and lead one of your plow horses across Chadwick's fields to the Squire's land. We roused him enough to deliver your message, then handed him over to one of the stable lads. The boy confirmed the Squire's horse hadn't left the stable, so the man must have walked over to your lands."

"I wouldn't have minded it if you had rolled him into the stream to drown," the Marquis said, not entirely joking.

"I thought about it, but then you'd have too much explaining to do to the local magistrate."

"The Squire is the local magistrate," the Marquis said.

"Hmm, what if he sends someone to arrest you?"

"He won't. As you said, he's a bully. And Chadwick and I can have him removed from his position. In fact, we ought to set that in motion."

A light rap sounded on the door.

"Come!" the Marquis called.

Applewood poked his head in to ask if the Marquis were now ready to see the Earl and his family.

"Yes, Gorse has me dry and freshly changed. Send 'em down."

"Very good, m'Lord." Applewood bowed himself out and closed the door.

"Changed?" the Duke asked.

"Don't let that termagant near the liquor cabinet," the Marquis said in reply.

"So she's a termagant again, is she?"

"Dumped a decanter of brandy on my head after she accepted my offer."

"I like her better and better," the Duke grinned. "Shall I leave?"

"No, stay. I may need someone to defend me. Besides, you're going to stand up with me. You're a party to this now."

A few minutes later the butler opened the door. "The Earl of Chadwick, Dowager Countess of Cwmhaven, and Lady Elisabeth Chadwick, m'Lord."

"Yes, yes, I know who my guests are," the Marquis said testily.

The Duke rose politely, while the Marquis remained stubbornly in his chair.

"I see what your mother means about you," the Dowager Countess said pleasantly to the Marquis as she followed her nephew into the room. "Welcome to the family."

The Earl and his family were followed by a footman pushing a serving trolley. The cart supported several glasses and a bucket of freshly cut ice holding a champagne bottle.

"Shall I invite your mother to join you, my lord?" Applewood asked. "I took the liberty earlier of sharing your good news with her."

"Yes, of course she must be present," the Marquis said gloomily. "Please summon both m'mother and Sir Mendam. You may instruct the servants to begin serving the champagne, and have a few of these chairs moved so we can visit more easily. We'll hold the toasts until m'mother and Sir Mendam join us."

The butler hurried out of the room. Two footmen entered and rearranged several chairs into a small circle, while the servants who had rolled in the serving cart began pouring and distributing glasses of champagne.

The Marquis held out a hand to Elisabeth, who somewhat shyly moved forward and arranged herself in the chair next to him. He reached out and took one of her hands, holding it lightly. She once again felt overwhelmed by the sensation of his touch, but told herself sternly not to act like a ninny. She must learn not to lose her wits every time he touched her.

Her great-aunt took the seat on Elisabeth's other side and leaned over to hiss at her. "What do you think you're doing?" She stared pointedly at their clasped hands. The Dowager did not approve of public displays of affection.

"Not acting like a ninny," said Elisabeth, too rattled by the nearness of the Marquis to understand her great-aunt's meaning.

The Dowager stared at her great-niece. When had the English language started to sound like gibberish?

As the last of the group seated themselves and accepted flutes of champagne, the Dowager Marchioness entered, wreathed in smiles.

"My dears!" she exclaimed in delight. "We have a wedding to plan!"

"No, there's no need for all that, Mother," the Marquis said. "I've already had Charles send for a special license."

The house party guests in the main salon were startled by the sound of loud screams followed by a crash. As they rushed into the hall, they saw the doors to the salon across the hall swing open as servants ran for help.

To their amazement, their hostess lay on the floor of the other salon near an overturned serving cart. She was screaming, clutching at her hair, and drumming her heels, apparently having some sort of fit.

"Well, that was an interesting experience," the Marquis said to his fiancée as his mother was carried up the stairs to her chambers, still shrieking. She was accompanied by a concerned Dowager Countess and a curious Lady Childer, who was more intent on learning what on earth was happening than on rendering any useful assistance.

Elisabeth turned a bewildered face toward the Marquis. "But it seemed at first as though she were happy we were getting married. I don't understand."

"Neither do I, my dear," he sighed, "but I'm sure I'll be subjected to an explanation at some point. Welcome to the family."

The other guests were alternately gaping at the sight of their hostess apparently run mad and the servants scrambling to pick up the mess in the second salon. Four other servants, who had been in the process of rolling two large serving trolleys into the main salon, caused a minor traffic jam when they paused in the hall leading back to the kitchens. The servants leaving the second salon with the damaged cart found themselves blocked from returning the cart to the back of the house.

As the servants to'ed and fro'ed to make way for each other, the house party guests thronged the hallway just outside the main salon's doorway, causing their own traffic jam when the servants with the two fresh serving trolleys tried to enter the salon. Not knowing quite how to proceed against this human blockade, but determined to do their duty, the servants began offering glasses of champagne to the guests in the doorway.

The guests jostled with each other for a good view, a glass of champagne, and space to breathe. Lord Childer took the opportunity to jab Sir Clapham with a sharp elbow. Mr. Benson-Smythe saw the dirty deed and drove the heel of his shoe into Lord Childer's foot. His shriek startled Lady Griegson, who spilled her champagne on her younger daughter, Lady Cora.

Lord Griegson retaliated by aiming a punch at Mr. Benson-Smythe, but that man turned at the same moment to look for his wife in the scuffle, and Lord Griegson overbalanced. He fell into Lady Violet, who careened into Lady Georgina. And then, as the group in the second salon watched in stunned disbelief, the entire collection of house party guests toppled like a line of human dominoes.

The Duke turned an amazed face to the Marquis. "I have to attend more engagement parties. I had no idea they could be so entertaining."

"Go offer some assistance," the Marquis said irritably.

"I shall preside over the servants," the Duke grinned. "Come along, Chadwick." The Earl shook off his shock and followed the Duke into the hall, where a chain of footmen was lifting each guest and passing him or her onto the next servant.

"Like watching a water brigade, isn't it?" the Marquis asked Lady Elisabeth. He turned to look at her, and saw that she was bright red with suppressed laughter. A snort escaped her, and she quickly set down her champagne glass and tugged her other hand away from the Marquis. She buried her face in her hands, trying in vain to cover her whoops of laughter.

The Marquis watched in amusement as his fiancée shook and snorted and howled. She looked as insane as his mother.

"This is by far the best house party I've ever attended," the Duke said that evening as he, Lord RIngwood and Sir Clapham gathered in the Marquis's suite for supper. They were not alone in avoiding the formal dining room. All of the guests had elected to eat in the privacy of their rooms.

The Marquis shot his cousin an evil glance, but forbore to respond. He was too busy concentrating on carefully chewing his meat pie and greens. It was good to have plain, simple fare, even if chewing and swallowing were a little difficult with his sore jaw. His mother always insisted on serving overcooked foods covered with sauces and dips.

"What was up with your mother?" Lord Ringwood asked their host. "Is she prone to fits like that?"

"Not that I'm aware of," the Marquis said around a mouthful of food.

"You don't seem much concerned," Sir Clapham commented.

"Mmph," their host replied.

"Well I, for one, would bring in a physician to have a look at her," Lord Ringwood said.

"Already done," the Marquis said, after washing down a bite of meat pie with a swig of ale. "Fieldman – he's the local sawbones – is having a busy night of it, between dosing her and attending to all the other guests who want his attention. He's quite certain this is a madhouse, but he's making piles of money off me, so I doubt it matters."

"I hope you're going to have him check on you, again," Sir Clapham said. "You look as though you had a falling out with an angry bear. Tell us frankly what happened, or we'll all think your lovely fiancée did this to you, and Richard will never be able to work up the courage to talk to a female."

Lord Ringwood threw a biscuit at Sir Clapham.

The Marquis swore them to secrecy, and then proceeded to tell the story. The Duke picked up the tale where his role began and provided the finish.

"The Squire is a damned rotter," Lord Ringwood said.

"Fellow should be horsewhipped," Sir Clapham agreed. He looked at their host. "How is Lady Elisabeth doing? I didn't have a chance to talk with her after the fracas."

Fracas, the Marquis thought sourly. The first house party he'd thrown, and the one during which he'd become engaged, and it would be known far and wide as a fracas. His mother having a fit, guests brawling, everyone hiding out in their rooms, doctors required. Gad. Only one thing to do.

"Cards after dinner?" he asked.

"Cards after dinner?" the Dowager Countess asked as the butler directed the serving of dessert.

"Yes, that sounds like a desirable bit of normalcy after the day we've all had," the Earl agreed. "Elsbet?"

"I'll watch," she said. "I don't think I can concentrate yet. What on earth is wrong with Lady Loveland? Does insanity run in the family?"

"No, it does not," her great-aunt snapped. "I don't know what is wrong with Sophia, but she is not mad."

The trio had been mostly silent on the ride back to the manor and during dinner, each absorbing the events of the day, but Elisabeth's question had opened the door.

"Well, I for one, have never seen anything like it," the Earl chuckled. "Screaming and flinging herself into the serving cart! It looked for all the world like a two-year-old's temper tantrum. And then the guests! I thought I was watching lawn bowling."

Elisabeth burst into laughter. "It was so funny! Please don't tell me that's what I've been missing by avoiding London parties."

"Of course not," the Dowager said. "I've never seen such a parcel of idiots. Although, there was the Wynminsters' party. Do you remember that, Robert?"

"Yes, but what can you expect when a man's wife and all three of his mistresses decide to visit the dessert table at the same time?"

"Three mistresses?" Elisabeth asked in astonishment. "Is that common?"

"It is not," the Dowager said with a minatory glance at her nephew.

"But what happened?"

The Earl grinned at the memory. "Pastries were flying everywhere. Women were fainting. Men were placing wagers."

"Wagers? On what?"

"Robert!" the Dowager yelped as the Earl started to answer. He suddenly realized the impropriety of talking about wagers on mistresses in front of his daughter.

"Nothing significant," he said, changing course. "Just which women were likely to... er... prevail."

"My," Elisabeth said. "And all this time I had thought society functions were boring."

"Well, for the most part, people are certainly better behaved," the Dowager huffed. "Do you know, I would swear I saw Lord Griegson deliberately try to kick the Duke as he was hauled out of the pile?"

"Frankly, it looked to me as though Griegson was trying to kick everybody," the Earl grinned. "Amazing brawl." He winked at Elisabeth. "Your engagement party will be the talk of England."

"Cards," the Dowager said firmly. "We are going to play cards."

The Dowager and her nephew were both fierce and capable card players. They sat across from each other in the front salon, not speaking as they concentrated on their plays. Off to the side sat Mrs. Doty, who had joined the group after supper. She danced about in her chair, looking as though she were engaged in a seated version of a prizefight.

With every hand the Dowager lost, Mrs. Doty would take a hit and fall back twisting and turning. When the Dowager took a trick, Mrs. Doty bounced up and down, jabbing her hands as though hitting an opponent. Elisabeth didn't need to watch the players to know how the game was turning out; she had only to watch Mrs. Doty. From the amount of jabbing taking place, it appeared her great-aunt was ahead.

An hour later, after thoroughly trouncing her nephew, the Dowager rang for a cordial before bed. Winning at cards had placed her in a mellow mood.

"Elisabeth," she said with a kindly smile. "Despite the rather raucous events of this afternoon, we do have a wedding to plan. I heard the Marquis say he had arranged for a special license. Do you know anything about that?"

"No, Ma'am, he hasn't mentioned anything about that to me."

"Just like a man," the Dowager sniffed.

"Well, to be fair," Elisabeth said, "there wasn't much opportunity to talk after his mother did... had... er...."

"Became indisposed," the Dowager suggested.

Mrs. Doty drooped to her right and briefly dangled over the side of her chair before righting herself.

"Yes, became indisposed," Elisabeth agreed with a small smile. "At any rate, I know nothing of a special license."

"Well," the Earl said, dragging his attention away from his aunt's bizarre companion, "it would appear to mean a wedding within a week or two, since we won't have to wait for the banns. However, I don't want it to take place before your brother and sister can arrive."

"Oh, yes!" Elisabeth exclaimed. "I want Robbie and Anne to be here. We must write them immediately!"

"I've sent messengers for them," the Earl said. "I doubt they'll be here in time for our dinner party, but we will delay the wedding until they arrive."

"Good," the Dowager approved. "We also have the Loveland dance party a few days after our dinner. It would be appropriate to hold the wedding after that, which gives us at least a sennight to prepare."

"I would like to be married in our chapel, as Anne was," Elisabeth said firmly. "And I want Vicar Smithers to conduct the service, as he did for Anne."

"If that's what you want, you shall have it," her father reassured her. He cast a warning glance at his aunt, whom he knew would have preferred something grander. He'd heard no end of complaints that Robbie's and Anne's weddings had been small, private affairs.

The Dowager considered her great-niece for a moment. "You do realize you will be expected to invite all of the Loveland Manor guests, don't you?"

Elisabeth's look of horror caused her father to give a shout of laughter. He smiled at her unhappy face. "Aunt Lister is right, Elsbet. If for no other reason than to serve as witnesses to spread the tale of the happy ending through Town, they must be there. And anyway, I doubt any of them will wish to leave betimes and miss out on the chance to say they were there."

"I shall speak with Mrs. Mavis on the morrow," the Dowager said. "We will get started on making arrangements."

The next morning, Elisabeth was just finishing her breakfast in the upstairs parlor when Applewood poked his head in the doors and announced the Marquis.

She looked up in surprise as the Marquis strode in, his face the colors of a dark rainbow. Deep purple bruises marked his jaw and left cheek, red scratches covered his forehead and right cheek, and his eyes and lips were swollen and discolored. "You look awful!" she said without thinking.

"Thank you," he said. "Gorse had the devil of a time shaving me this morning. But the best part," he said, sitting gingerly across the table from her, "is that Fieldman confirmed I have some bruised ribs. He doesn't think they're cracked, but they're wonderfully painful."

"I am so dreadfully sorry that the Squire hurt you so badly, and that in saving me you are now being forced to marry me."

"I'm not," he surprised both of them by saying.

"You're not sorry?"

"Well, I'm sorry I couldn't knock the scoundrel out in one punch, but I'm not sorry to be marrying you."

"Really?" she couldn't help looking just a little pleased.

"Really. I love dogs. And your mare will make a delightful stable mate for Crosspurposes."

"And I love this ring," she retorted, gazing at the large diamond-encircled emerald on her left hand.

"So we both have what we want. Excellent, then."

"Is that why you're here? To gloat about my dogs and horse?"

"Actually, I was hoping for a morning coffee, but I see you haven't the manners to offer me one."

"I was just about to leave when you so rudely barged in on me. Did you want some coffee? Your servants don't serve morning coffee and tea at Loveland Manor, then? I wonder at your guests staying so long with such poor treatment."

"No hope of getting rid of them now, not with a wedding in the offing," he said as she belatedly poured him a cup of coffee. He took a sip and grimaced. "Mmm, tepid. Just the way I like it."

"I shall remember that," she smiled.

"Yes, I'm sure you will," he said, putting down the cup. "Come, let's take a walk where we can have some privacy."

She pointedly looked about the room. "We are private here, if you haven't noticed."

"Yes, but not for long, I expect. Do you give it more than a few minutes before your redoubtable great-aunt receives word I am here and hotfoots it into the room to batter us with wedding plans?"

Elisabeth dabbed her lips with her serviette and quickly stood. "We'll take the back stairs."

Once outside the manor, the pair slowly made their way to the kennels. Elisabeth's ankle was aching more today, and the Marquis's chest hurt with every movement. As they approached the building where the dogs lived, excited whines and thumps could be heard. Elisabeth gave the Marquis a concerned glance. "Are you brave enough to meet all thirteen at once?"

"I survived the Squire; I expect I can manage your unruly hounds."

"They are not unruly! Well," she amended, "most of them are not. But some of the newer ones still need to learn their manners."

"Newer ones? Do you mean the puppies?"

"No, I mean the recent arrivals. The ones my father has purchased and brought back with him from his trips."

"For breeding?"

"For rescuing, mostly," she said. "It's not something we set out to do, but I cannot stand the thought of one of these noble beasts suffering. Our original four dogs were a gift to an ancestor from the King, and our family has bred Scottish deerhounds for many generations. But we also protect the breed, and if my father sees one being mistreated, he finds a way to purchase it and bring it here."

They had reached the kennels by that time, and she paused with one hand on the wooden door. "You truly do not mind my dogs? I am concerned they may hurt you if they jump on you."

"I am looking forward to meeting them," he smiled. The battering his face had taken made the expression more frightening than reassuring. She raised the heavy latch and pushed open the door. Thirteen large, eager dogs surged forward, expecting to be let out for a walk.

"No, not yet," she said firmly. She pressed forward as the Marquis followed. He closed the door behind them and they found themselves pressed back against the wooden door as the dogs surrounded them, seeking attention and affection.

The kennel building was organized much like a horse stable, he noted. From where they stood with their backs pressed against the door, he looked down an aisle with small stall-like enclosures off each side. He estimated twenty stalls on each side of the aisle. Sawdust and straw were neatly swept along the aisle and into all of the dogs' stalls. At the far end of the aisle an opening led into a fenced area open to the weather. Immediately to their left was a large supply room, and to their right was an office with a desk, cabinets, bookcases, and a cot. A thick carpet covered that room's floor.

Elisabeth called each dog in turn, naming them for the Marquis as they came forward. A few he could easily tell apart from the others, but it was going to take a while before he would know them all on sight. He suddenly felt both her hands lightly patting his chest. "And this is...," he heard her start to say. She paused and looked up at him, blushing rosily as she realized she didn't know his name.

"John, in case you'd like to know whom you are marrying."

She laughed and turned back to the dogs, still patting his chest. "John," she repeated several times. "This is John."

He took hold of one of her hands and kept it against his chest as he reached out with his other hand and let the dogs sniff him before stroking their ears.

"They like that," she said.

"So do I," he replied. "Feel free to stroke my ears any time. Or any other place that takes your fancy." He moved her captured hand higher up his chest until it rested on his shoulder. With his other hand he circled her waist and turned her toward him.

She stilled as she gazed up into his eyes. He bent down and kissed her. But what he had intended to be a chaste, gentle kiss suddenly ignited into waves of heat. They grappled with each other like two wrestlers, each overcome by unexpected sensations. He banged his elbow against the door, she stepped on his foot, he got his fingers tangled in her hair and poked her in the ear, she squeezed his aching ribs.

The dogs watched the entertainment with interest, wondering what was up with their mistress, but pretty sure she was a willing participant and not under attack. After several nose pokes were ignored, the hounds eventually laid down. A few fell asleep. The others kept watching as the two humans remained locked in an energetic embrace, making odd gasps and groans.

The Marquis eventually pulled back to get a second wind. Elisabeth panted for breath as she reached up and began untying his neck cloth, intent on stripping him naked. Good idea, he thought. He pulled her against his chest so he could reach the buttons at the back of her dress. She found her arms trapped against him and tried to push him away so she could return to tugging off his clothes. His hands caught in her dress buttons as she pushed against him, and a loud ripping sound rent the air.

They both froze, suddenly aware of their surroundings. At least eight sets of canine eyes were staring at them curiously. Gentle snores emanated from the less-interested members of the pack.

The Marquis released her and stepped back. A wad of fabric fell from one of his hands. Elisabeth gasped and tried to reach for the back of her dress.

"Oops," the Marquis said.

Forty-Seven

"What am I going to do?" Elisabeth wailed. Her questing hands had found the gaping hole at the back of her dress between her shoulder blades.

She spun around so the Marquis could take a look. He tried to concentrate on the damage to her dress instead of the creamy skin revealed by the ripped fabric.

Oh, what the hell, he thought. He bent forward and planted a kiss on her upper back between her shoulder blades. She gasped and shivered. He kissed her upper back again.

Elisabeth shuddered in ecstasy. No one had ever told her how good it felt to be kissed on one's back. What else might feel that good? Oh my, he was kissing her there again. Her entire body trembled as he held her tightly, his hands slowly sliding up her sides from her waist.

"Oh, that's wonderful," she moaned.

The Marquis's breath was warm on her back, his hands even warmer as they reached her ribcage. And then they slipped up and lightly cupped her breasts.

"What are you doing?" she managed to squeak out.

"I must need lessons," he laughed softly, moving his mouth up to give the nape of her neck a kiss. "I thought it was pretty obvious."

"Someone will see us. We must stop!" She moaned as she arched herself into his hands.

He couldn't believe what he was hearing, but he certainly didn't want to take her against her will, even if he thought stopping might nearly kill him.

"As you like," he said reluctantly, releasing her.

She stumbled forward as she caught her balance. "Why did you stop?" she demanded, twisting around to look at him.

"Did you not just ask me to stop?"

"Yes, but, but… yes…." She made an uncertain move toward him.

He backed up and leaned against the door, breathing heavily. She was right, they needed to stop. But damn, it was hard. And stopping wasn't the only thing that was hard. He hoped she wouldn't look down and notice the obvious signs of his arousal.

She looked down.

"What's that?" she asked. And then she reached out a hand.

When they finally left the kennel building, the groom who noticed their departure later gave it as his opinion that the two must have been attacked by the dogs. Their clothes were torn and in disarray, they had sawdust and straw all over them, both appeared sore, and the Marquis, in particular, was tottering about like a broken man.

"Those dogs don't never set on no man," one of the other grooms objected.

"Aye, but they jump on one," the first groom said. "And the Marquis bein' new to 'em, they must've given him a tumble."

"Mebbe," said Givens, the head groom, chewing on a piece of straw. He was pretty sure a tumble of a different nature had taken place, but he liked his job and he wasn't about to get in trouble gossipin' about his betters. Besides, it was nearly time for nuncheon.

Elisabeth covered up the rip in the back of her dress by unbraiding her hair and letting it fall down her back. She slipped in the back kitchen door and hurried up the servants' stairs, making it into her rooms without meeting anyone. Once inside her suite, she slipped out of her dress and into a robe, and rang for a bath. After the maids had filled the tub and left, she soaked in the water for an hour, wearing a silly grin on her face. My, she thought, she certainly was going to enjoy being married.

The Marquis retrieved his horse from the stable and led Crosspurposes home on foot. His chest ached, his head was sore where he'd banged it on the edge of the cot, and he had carpet burns on his elbows. He trudged slowly along, through the border woods and across the stream, wearing a silly grin on his face. Damn, he thought, he certainly was going to enjoy being married.

Forty-Eight

The small dancing party that evening, the first of two that had been planned several weeks earlier by the Dowager Marchioness for the entertainment of her London guests, was not the delightful, fun-filled affair she'd had in mind. The quartet of musicians plied their instruments with skill, but the effort was wasted on the company.

Her son rested in a chair, not moving and barely conversing with the guests, his face a lurid pattern of reds and purples. To her every attempt to get him to mingle and behave as a host ought, he responded that he was too sore and too tired. After her third try, he stated flatly that he wasn't going to cooperate until she explained yesterday's behavior.

"I have no need to explain myself," she huffed, before walking across the room to drag the reluctant Lord Ringwood over to request a dance from Lady Cora.

And was that young lady grateful, the irritated Dowager groused to Sir Mendam a few moments later. "No, she must needs twirl about the dance floor staring soulfully at the Duke."

"Well, with John out of the running, she no longer has to divide her attentions between your son and the Duke," Sir Mendam smiled.

"I don't care, Horace. It's unladylike to be so obvious," the Dowager sniffed. "And Sir Clapham has to practically be pried away from Margaret Benson-Smythe. Do today's young men not know their social duties?"

"At least the Benson-Smythes are enjoying dancing," he said soothingly, watching as the couple spun about the floor.

"Oh, who cares about them," she said in vexation, nearly stamping her foot.

As the music ended, she stalked off to mix the dancers again, ensuring each young lady would receive two dances with each of the three available men. She was determined to force everyone to have fun if it killed her.

Lady Georgina, well aware of their hostess's frustration, watched in amusement as the Duke was led to her side to request a dance. Really, he looked for all the world as though he expected the Dowager to pull him by the ear and drag him to the woodshed.

"Why, yes," Lady Georgina said in her melodious voice as she curtseyed, "I would be delighted to accept this dance."

"Thank you," the Duke muttered as the Dowager marched away to commandeer Sir Clapham for Lady Alma.

He took Lady Georgina by the hand and led her over to the end of the room set aside for dancing. "Ah, a waltz. We shall have an opportunity for a private chat."

"Private?" She looked around at the assembled group.

"Well, more private than usually possible," he amended. "Tell me, is this not the most amusing house party you have ever attended?"

"I am sure each house party offers its own unique amusements," she replied graciously.

"Come now. Guests beating up on each other, falling in a heap in the hallway, the hostess having a fit? If this is your normal experience of a house party, you must tell me the homes you visit so I can expand my horizons."

She smiled politely as he led her through the steps, but vouchsafed no reply. He was exceedingly attractive, but she did not dare step out of her carefully crafted society manners. She glanced up at his handsome features again, and decided that perhaps one little step out of bounds might be allowed, if only to poke a bit at his self-consequence.

"So how is your project with your brother and young Lord Thomas faring?" she asked blandly.

The Duke froze in surprise, nearly tumbling the two of them over as she stumbled into him. Her color high from embarrassment, she managed to maintain a neutral expression and ignore the surprised glances of the other guests.

He stared down at her in amazement for a moment, then recovered himself and picked up the steps of the dance again. "What do you know about any project? More to the point, how do you know?"

She gave an enigmatic smile, but didn't answer.

"Does anyone else know?" he asked.

"I do not believe so," she replied quietly. "When do you plan to reveal the plot to the victim?"

He quirked his lips appreciatively. "I thought it would make a nice going-away present when they embark on their wedding trip."

Lady Georgina burst into delighted laughter as the guests stared. She had not been known to be so free with her amusement in anyone's memory. Lady Cora frowned, suddenly wondering if yet another obstacle lay in her way toward acquiring the Duke's coronet.

Forty-Nine

Two days later, the morning of the Chadwicks' dinner party, now a betrothal party for Elisabeth and the Marquis, dawned bright, hot, and humid. As the day progressed, both the humidity and Lady Elisabeth's temper worsened.

She was near the boiling point with her great-aunt's barrage of directives and the bustle of the regular and temporary servants as they prepared the manor for the evening event. Furniture was moved, decorations were hung, supplies delivered, and food prepared. Serving ware had been polished, linens freshly laundered and pressed, and every surface cleaned. She had been forbidden to visit the kennels, but servants uprooted her every time she tried to find a quiet spot in the house. She finally fled to her rooms after nuncheon, only to discover two maids readying a bath and laying out the dress the Dowager Countess had selected.

"If you refuse to take part in planning your own betrothal festivities, you will at least oblige me by preparing yourself," her great-aunt said from the doorway as Elisabeth turned to flee her room. Her great-aunt stood with arms firmly crossed and a fierce frown on her face as she eyed her recalcitrant great-niece.

"And do not give me that mulish look, missy," the Dowager continued, giving Elisabeth her own version of a mulish look. "Everyone is working hard to make this night a great success, and you will do your part."

"Yes, ma'am," Elisabeth finally said. But after the door shut behind her great-aunt, Elisabeth turned and begged the maids to leave her alone for half an hour before returning to begin preparations. She was feeling so tired from the heat and the humidity, and so anxious about the changes that would come with marriage. All she wanted was to lie for a while in peace on her bed.

The servants bowed themselves out, but it seemed no more than a blink of an eye before they were back. Elisabeth was placed in a tub of cool rose-scented water while one maid poured another pitcher of fragrant water over her head and set about washing and then rinsing Elisabeth's hair.

Once out of the tub, Elisabeth wrapped herself in a large towel and sat in a window embrasure, where she submitted to having her hair brushed out by one maid while the other servant tided up the bathing area. But unlike any day during the past month, her hair was not drying quickly in the humid air. The increasing humidity made Elisabeth feel as though she were still in her bath.

"Apparently I will attend my betrothal party with wet hair," she commented to the maids. "Perhaps I shall set a new trend."

"You will be lovely," one of them commented. "But 'tis a shame the weather is turning. Finally coming on to rain, methinks. Likely to storm as not, and soon."

Wonderful, Elisabeth thought, hoping this was not an omen for the party.

When the Dowager checked in on Elisabeth an hour before the guests were due to arrive, she found the maids just finishing winding Elisabeth's hair into a soft braid interwoven with a strand of pearls. The style gave the appearance of a golden halo when Elisabeth turned to face her great-aunt.

"Hmph," the Dowager snorted. "You look nearly saintly. Never have I seen you wear a more inapt hairdo."

"I am hungry and fighting a headache," Elisabeth said by way of thanks.

The Dowager glared at Elisabeth. "I'll have something brought up to you. It won't do for you to take that frowning face down to your party." She left the room, slamming the door behind her.

Elisabeth winced at the sound and wondered why her great-aunt was forever angry. Then, following her maids' directions, she moved to the center of the room where the two servants carefully helped her into her dress. By the time a tray with several small sandwiches and a glass of wine was delivered, Elisabeth thought her head would burst. She quickly drank the wine and ate two of the sandwiches. After a few moments she began to feel better.

A gentle rap at her door heralded her father, who looked at her with concern. "Aunt Lister said you weren't feeling quite the thing, Elsbet. Is it nerves?"

"It is this oppressive humidity," she said. "And all the bustle. I hate parties."

"You do not," her father laughed. "What you hate is having a fuss made over you. Well, if it will make you feel any better, think of all of this as a favor to me."

"What on earth do you mean?"

"Well, once you're off my hands, Aunt Lister will clear out to torment some other relative, and I can have my house back."

"Papa! You don't mean that!"

"About Aunt Lister, I absolutely mean it. About you, of course I'm not serious. But come with me now, please. I have a surprise for you that you will enjoy. But you must come downstairs with me to see it. And we should hurry," he said, cocking an ear toward the hallway. "I am quite certain I hear carriages arriving."

He held out a hand and she clasped her hand in his, following him out into the hall toward the stairs.

Fifty

The first carriage to stop under the portico of Chadwick Manor contained the Marquis and his mother. As their driver pulled to a halt, the Marquis quickly stepped down, ignoring his various aches and pains. He found himself unexpectedly eager to see his nasty-tempered and surprisingly lusty fiancée.

The Marquis turned to hold out his hand to the Dowager Marchioness. As soon as she had alighted, he hustled her across the packed gravel and up the steps to where the butler was ceremoniously holding open the carved entry door. The Dowager resisted his speed, wanting to wait until the other London guests had joined them.

"John, what are you doing?" she gasped, clutching at her headdress with one hand. "This haste is unseemly. We must wait on the others." She tugged against his grip, twisting and turning like a fish caught on a line.

"Not on your life, Mother," he said bluntly as he dragged her along. "They will take a fortnight to sort themselves out."

They arrived at the open doorway just in time to hear Elisabeth start shrieking like a banshee. The Marquis unceremoniously dropped his grip on his mother, who fell into the butler. Applewood struggled to keep the two of them from falling over while never breaking from his trained, impassive expression.

The Marquis ran toward Elisabeth's cries and found her in the clutches of a man. Or rather, he realized just as he grabbed for the man's collar, intent on flinging him to the floor, the man was in Elisabeth's clutches.

"Erk!" the man said as he was pulled bodily away from Elisabeth and fell into the Earl.

"You beast!" another woman shrieked at the Marquis. "What are you doing?" She promptly began beating the Marquis with her reticule.

The Marquis raised an arm to protect himself from the attack and turned to see Elisabeth hurrying to the aid of the man who'd been in her embrace.

The Dowager Countess grabbed the young woman beating the Marquis and held her away from him while Elisabeth helped the man straighten his collar and recover his breath.

Which is when the Marquis recognized Elisabeth's brother, Lord Robert Chadwick. He felt like a complete idiot.

"You're a complete idiot," Elisabeth confirmed.

He felt the heat of an unaccustomed redness flaming his face. Thank heavens none of the other guests had seen his behavior.

"Do these sorts of freakish starts run in the family?" the Duke asked from behind him, a wide smile evident in his voice. The Marquis wondered how the devil Ravenwood had moved so quickly, but then he knew his cousin's love of a good farce.

The Marquis briefly closed his eyes and ground his teeth before bowing to Lord Robert and his wife. "My apologies, Chadwick, Lady Chadwick. There was precedent for thinking Lady Elisabeth might need my help. I acted too hastily, obviously."

Lord Robert turned a quizzical eye on his sister. "Oh? Been having dustups with some of the local lads, have you? Thought I taught you how to protect yourself." He tapped his knee.

Now it was Elisabeth's turn to blush as her brother's words raised eyebrows around the group.

"Robbie!" came the Dowager Countess's shocked voice. "This is not a suitable topic for mixed company. And you," she turned a gimlet eye on Elisabeth, "have no business understanding what he meant."

"But what did you mean?" the young Lady Chadwick asked her husband.

The Dowager Marchioness pinched her nose in an effort to control herself as the men stifled their laughter.

"Later, Sweetheart," Lord Robert said, taking her arm. "Come now, let's help greet the guests."

The others quickly followed his lead. The Earl and Dowager Countess arrived at the salon's doorway just as Applewood began announcing the rest of the arrivals. The Marquis and Elisabeth moved up to stand next in line, followed by Lord Robert and his wife.

To the Marquis's irritation, the Duke positioned himself on the other side of Elisabeth, between Elisabeth and her brother. At the Marquis's raised eyebrows, the

Duke gave him an innocent look. "What? We're cousins. I'm family."

"You're cousins with half the Ton. I don't see you standing in everyone else's reception lines."

"Well maybe I should," the Duke replied. "It can only add to a hostess's cachet to have me standing beside her, don't you think?"

Between them, Elisabeth muttered something that sounded suspiciously like "infernal ninnies." Then she turned a bright smile toward the arriving guests.

First through the salon's entry were the Dowager Marchioness and Sir Mendam.

"And how is it you got through the doorway without being announced?" the Marquis asked the Duke irritably, as they watched the two Dowagers greet each other as if they'd been apart for months.

"Applewood had his hands full with your mother," the Duke replied. "Literally. But I see that old Horace has pried her loose."

"Must the two of you talk over my head as though I'm a piece of furniture?" Elisabeth grumbled.

"Anyone who would be idiotic enough to use someone as prickly as you for a piece of furniture would end up seriously injured," the Marquis commented, before turning a welcoming smile on the next guest.

Under the portico, as the London guests had sorted themselves out, Sir Clapham had stepped up to the Benson-Smythes to offer his arm to Margaret. That young miss paused a moment before accepting his escort, which gave Sir Clapham the opportunity to notice her evening attire.

"A lovely gown, Miss Benson-Smythe," he said approvingly. "I do admire the clean, simple lines you have chosen. Very elegant."

"Thank you, Sir Clapham," Margaret twinkled up at him.

Behind the couple, Margaret's parents exchanged wide-eyed glances. "At last, all is made clear," Mr. Benson-Smythe leaned over and whispered to his wife. "Do we approve?"

"She is still young," his wife whispered back, "but he is a good man. I have been pleased with his behavior. Do you know much of him from Town?"

"Yes," Mr. Benson-Smythe said softly. "He has a good reputation and is quite an amiable gentleman."

The two nodded to each other, much in accord, and not at all displeased by the possible match in the making.

Next through the receiving line came Lady Georgina, accompanied by Lord Ringwood. Lady Georgina was gracious in her greetings, while Lord Ringwood, mute in her presence, nodded silently to his hosts.

Sir Clapham and the Benson-Smythes passed through the receiving line next, followed by the Griegsons.

Lady Alma Griegson and her parents said all that was proper. Lady Cora, last in the foursome, greeted the Marquis politely, and then leaned in to hug Elisabeth as though they were the best of friends.

"Oh, I am so happy for you," she gushed. "I cannot wait to see you after your wedding trip and hear all about it. You must remember to tell me everything that happens."

Blithely unaware of the Marquis's startled reaction and the Duke's extreme amusement at the thought of what "everything" might include on a honeymoon, Lady Cora then turned a sweetly smiling face up to the Duke as though he were her whole delight. He greeted her coolly and promptly passed her on to Elisabeth's brother and sister-in-law, Lord Robert and Lady Caroline Chadwick.

Following the Griegsons were the Childers. Lady Childer also treated Elisabeth to a warm show of friendliness, stating that Elisabeth and the Marquis must come visit them after their wedding trip. As Elisabeth watched them move on, a puzzled expression on her face, the Duke bent toward her.

"Behold the benefits of your soon-to-be status of Marchioness," he whispered. "More friends than you can possibly support."

Elisabeth stayed in the receiving line until all the invited guests had arrived, including Lady Downs, Vicar and Mrs. Smithers, and several other friends from the neighborhood. Notably absent was Squire Mills.

The Vicar and his wife greeted Lord Robert and Lady Caroline warmly, exchanging family news and catching up on each others' lives. The Dowager Marchioness frowned slightly at such excessive condescension on the part of the Earl's son and daughter-in-law until Sir Mendam drew her attention to some of the treats laid out on the buffet table.

Really, she thought to herself as she accepted a plate with some nut pastries and a piece of roasted chicken covered with a delicious plum sauce, she just did not understand this younger generation. Why must they show such concern for servants and the lower classes?

Three hours later the dinner party was in full swing. The London and neighborhood guests moved about the salon, chatting as they filled themselves with the array of foods laid out for their enjoyment and made deep inroads into the Earl's excellent wine cellar. As the company circled from the buffet table to the groups of small tables and seating arrangements and back again, they were treated to background music provided by the same musicians who had played at the Dowager Marchioness's small dance party two evenings earlier.

She had graciously suggested she cancel the second evening of dancing she'd planned, and had offered to provide the musicians for this event. Given the dreary nature of the first dancing party and the distractions about to be offered by a wedding, even if it were a shabby special-license affair, she didn't think anyone would miss a second evening of dancing.

Elisabeth and the Marquis were seated at a small table enjoying the company of Lord Robert and Lady Caroline Chadwick when Applewood approached the Earl, who was chatting with Sir Mendam, and whispered into the Earl's ear. Elisabeth watched as her father left the room behind the butler and disappeared into the entry hall.

Moments later the Earl returned and collected the Dowager Countess. They moved toward the salon entry and waited as Applewood approached at a stately pace, followed by two extremely fashionable individuals Elisabeth didn't recognize. She waited curiously for Applewood to introduce the new arrivals.

"Lord William Wentworth and –" was as far as he got. Before he could announce the lady accompanying Lord Wentworth, the Dowager Marchioness let out a screech.

The entire company turned to see what new fit the Dowager might be about to offer for their entertainment. She was pointing a shaking arm at the doorway, staring in shock at the new arrivals. She turned her goggling eyes to her son. "Oh my word! John! It's your fiancée!"

The guests' heads swiveled toward the entry, then toward the Marquis. But it was Elisabeth who captured their attention.

She jumped to her feet, staring down in outrage at the stunned Marquis. "Fiancée?! You're already engaged to someone else?!" Her voice rose to a pitch and volume that drowned out even the Dowager Marchioness's continued wails. "You snake!"

She swung around in search of the nearest blunt object and found a wine bottle. The Marquis, knowing his temperamental fiancée fairly well by now, ducked. The missile missed his head by mere inches, smashing on the floor at Lady Downs's feet. Lord Chadwick, Elisabeth's brother, yanked his wife away from the table and out of the range of shattering glass.

Made even more irate by missing her target, Elisabeth grabbed every plate and glass she could reach and hurled them at the Marquis, who had crawled under the table and – much to the surprise of the amazed guests – was laughing. She hauled at the tablecloth, pulling it off the table and sending everything flying that she hadn't already flung at the Marquis. She snatched a candlestick and leaned under the table. The Marquis scrambled away and out the other side, scooting backward on the floor, still laughing like a lunatic.

"Don't you dare laugh at me you… you… rake! And after I trusted you enough to let you take advantage of me in the kennels!" She ran around the table after him, intent on pummeling him with the candlestick when she suddenly remembered her surroundings.

She stopped, looked around, and saw everyone staring at her. Her great-aunt gaped in shock, her father glowered in disapproval, Lady Downs smiled in delight. And on it went around the room – amazement, glee, confusion, horror – all the way back to the Marquis, who sat on the floor grinning hugely.

"I hate you!" she shouted. She ran from the room, brushing past the bewildered Lord Wentworth and his surprised companion.

Which broke the spell. From amazed silence, the room erupted into a babble of noise.

The Marquis looked up from his position on the floor to see the Earl of Chadwick looming over him.

"You and I need to have a talk, young man," the Earl said.

"Here," the Duke said, reaching down to help the Marquis to his feet. "You two go sort this out while I talk to Wentworth and Lady Marybell and find out how it comes about that they're here."

"Well, I damned well didn't invite them," the Earl and Marquis growled in unison.

The Duke gave a chuckle and cut a glance across the room to where Lady Georgina stood with an impassive face belied by the liveliness of her eyes. He winked at her and headed toward the salon entry as the Earl led the Marquis out a pair of doors that connected the salon to another room.

Lord Wentworth, known far and wide for his perpetual tardiness, was equally well known for his exquisite manners whenever he finally did put in an appearance. He now shuffled about in confusion as he tried to sort out his social obligations as a guest of the household, two of whose members had left the room. He gave a sigh of relief as the Duke approached.

"Wentworth," the Duke said cordially. "What the bloody hell are you doing here? And in Lady Marybell's company."

Wentworth raised his eyebrows at such language in front of a lady. "I wasn't convinced it was entirely proper, Ravenwood, but Marybell and I were passing this way and I decided it wouldn't do to be in the area and not tender my regrets to Lady Loveland that I hadn't been able to attend her house party. So we decided to make a brief detour and call upon Lady Loveland and Monton. Then, when we learned the entire party was here –"

"And that it was an engagement party!" Lady Marybell chimed in cheerfully.

"Well, after some discussion, we decided to change out of our traveling clothes and stop by to offer our felicitations to the... er... happy...?" He fumbled to a stop, clearly unsure what he had witnessed.

Lady Marybell looked about the room in delight and gave a tiny wave to Lady Loveland, who moaned and closed her eyes.

"I did have some reservations as to the proper course," Lord Wentworth continued after a glance at his companion, "but upon reflection, we determined that it would be a greater lapse of manners to ignore such an occasion. I did wonder if I oughtn't just write a note and have it sent over, but as we were invited guests of Lady Loveland, Marybell thought the extension of an invitation to tonight's party would have naturally included us, and I wouldn't wish Monton to think I was showing a lack of consideration at such a... er...."

"Oh for God's sake, Wentworth," the Duke said in exasperation. "Wrap it up. I don't care what you're doing here. I want to know what you're doing jauntering around the countryside with Lady Marybell Wister!"

"As to that," Wentworth began, "it so happens that —"

"We're married!" Lady Marybell trilled, holding out her left hand to flash a large ruby set in a gold ring bearing the Wentworth coat of arms.

Across the room, the Dowager Marchioness fainted.

Fifty-Two

⚬❦⚬

"I was never engaged to Marybell Wister," the Marquis said flatly to his host the moment the door to the salon had closed behind them.

"That doesn't seem to be your mother's understanding," the Earl remarked.

"My mother, as you may have realized by now," the Marquis said through gritted teeth, "chooses to understand what it pleases her to understand. I came to the West Country this summer, in fact, to escape my mother's attempts to marry me off to merry Marybell."

"And you have no intent to back out of your marriage contracts with my daughter?"

"Of course not! What kind of dishonorable jackanapes do you take me for?"

"I take you for the kind of dishonorable jackanapes who would anticipate his wedding vows," the Earl said pointedly. "If I understood the meaning of Elsbet's words correctly."

The Marquis shifted uncomfortably. "Yes, you understood correctly. It was unplanned, if that matters. I didn't set out to dishonor her."

The Earl abruptly flung himself into a chair and raked one hand through his hair. "That girl is going to be the death of me. Thank heavens the two of you will be getting buckled soon."

The Marquis looked at his host in surprise, and then sank into a chair opposite the Earl. Both men sat frowning at nothing in particular for a few minutes.

"She takes after her mother," the Earl said at last. "I fell top over tails for Lucy the first time I saw her. Full of light and laughter and mischief. And stubborn? Good Lord, that woman was stubborn. But we had a wonderful marriage. Not a day goes by I don't miss her."

"When did she die?" the Marquis asked.

"When Anne, my youngest, was just seven. The influenza took her." The Earl gazed into space, lost in thought.

Just as the Marquis had realized he wasn't about to face a tongue lashing, Lord Robert burst into the room.

"I want to know what's going on here, Edmonton," he said angrily. "Am I to understand the reason for this betrothal is that you raped my sister?"

The Marquis gave a weary sigh. "Lord save me from your hotheaded offspring, Chadwick."

At which point Lord Robert walked up to the Marquis and punched him in the face. "I demand satisfaction!"

The party guests, Londoners and locals alike, swarmed about the room in high excitement.

"Lady Wentworth!" Lady Griegson said, surging forward with Lady Childer in her wake. "The last I heard, you had broken off your engagement to Lord Carrington! You must tell us all about your sudden nuptials to Lord Wentworth!"

"Yes, you must," said an amused Lady Downs, tottering after the two London guests. One of her giant footmen appeared from wherever he'd been stationed and offered his arm. She leaned on his sleeve, planted herself at Lady Wentworth's side, and prepared to grill her. No more than the other ladies did she want to be behind in her gossip. She planned to begin writing letters the moment she returned home, and she wanted as many details as possible.

"Well," the new Lady Wentworth giggled, "I was never so surprised! It was so romantical!"

"Romantical?" Lady Childer asked.

"Lord Wentworth?" Lady Griegson clarified.

Three sets of skeptical eyebrows rose as the three ladies turned toward Lord Wentworth. He bowed slightly in acknowledgment, before having his attention recaptured by the Duke, who dragged him several feet away to further interrogate him.

"Oh, my, yes," Lady Wentworth simpered, raising her hands over her heart. "I had just arrived at my aunt's home in Harrowood after poor Lord Carrington's accident, when –"

"Wait," Lady Downs held up an imperious hand. "Lord Carrington's accident?"

"Lord Carrington had an accident?" asked Lady Cora Griegson, joining the group. She liked to keep close tabs on all the eligible gentlemen in the Ton. Behind her trailed her sister Alma and the two Childer sisters.

"Well, you know that Lord Carrington and I had reached an understanding," Lady Wentworth said demurely. "His mother came to London to meet me, and at first I wasn't quite sure that she liked me, but then she invited us to return to their estate for a visit to become better acquainted."

"So you traveled to Carrington Abbey," said Lady Downs. She wanted to make sure she had the facts straight.

"Well, we started to," said Lady Wentworth, wide-eyed, "when one of the shafts on Papa's carriage broke. Poor Lord Carrington was thrown to the doorway. And I felt so sorry for him because he'd just joined us in our carriage despite his mother wanting his company."

"Was he seriously injured?" Lady Childer asked.

"Well, we had to stop at the next village so he could be tended to. His shoulder was dislocated, and he was in such pain. I was so terribly affected by it all that I had to lie down."

"And after that you went to Harrowood instead of Carrington Abbey?" asked Lady Griegson.

"No, we stayed overnight while the shaft was repaired, and then left the next morning. But it was the most dreadful thing!"

"What was?" asked Lady Violet with an anticipatory shudder. Her sister elbowed her in the ribs.

"Well, that morning at the breakfast table he must've eaten something that didn't agree with him, because shortly after we left, he became violently ill. And I do think it might have been the eggs, because I thought they smelled a bit off, so I didn't eat any, and he helped himself to mine. Poor man!"

"What a terrible journey," Lady Violet commiserated.

"Yes, it just goes to show that you cannot trust the service you get in inns these days," Lady Wentworth agreed. "Shocking. Serving bad eggs to paying customers."

"I shall never eat in an inn again," declared Lady Violet.

"Nor I," Lady Wentworth said. "And you have no idea how poorly he looked. Not at all as dashing as he'd appeared in Town. It quite made me wonder if I had made the right decision. But Mama was so pleased, you know. The Carringtons are an old family, and so well respected."

"And was there another accident after you arrived at the Abbey?" Lady Downs asked with a wry look.

"Why, yes!" Lady Wentworth exclaimed, with another wide-eyed look. "That very evening. Lord Carrington took a tumble just outside my door. A loose carpet thread, or some such thing. And that's when I decided I just couldn't go through with it."

"I don't wonder," remarked Lady Downs.

"Really, a carpet in such tatty, threadbare shape. There's no excuse for it. And I declare a piece of the pediment fell near where I had taken a walk in the garden before tea. Why, how could I live in such a place!"

"I doubt you could," Lady Downs agreed.

"Well, I was quite atremble at the thought of ending my betrothal and being labeled a jilt, but upon much reflection I thought it would be so much better to let Lord Carrington down early, don't you think, rather than keeping up his hopes and then dashing them? He wasn't at all what I had believed him to be — so sensitive to food, so clumsy, and with that great big house falling down around him. So I talked with Papa, who agreed with me, and then when I strolled with Lord Carrington after dinner I asked if he would mind very much if I thought that we would not suit."

"And how did he take it?" asked Lady Griegson.

"I was quite atremble," Lady Wentworth said, "but I had no need to fret. He was greatly disappointed, but valiant. We approached his mother, and she was so understanding. She even spoke to my mother to assure her it was the best thing for all of us. And she offered to send the note to the paper announcing the end of our betrothal. So very gracious and helpful!"

"But how did Lord Wentworth become involved?" Lady Childer asked in confusion.

"Oh, so delightful!" Lady Wentworth clapped her hands. "Papa said he wanted to stop by my aunt's home in Harrowood on the way home, to inspect the rest of the carriage, and who should arrive shortly after us but Lord Wentworth?"

"Does he know your aunt?" Lady Griegson asked.

"No, but he had dropped in to visit Lord Carrington, and Lady Carrington told him about our broken engagement, and when she mentioned I had left a scarf at their home, Lord Wentworth offered to bring it to me. He has such wonderful manners, you know. Although it turned out not to be mine, but Lord Wentworth was so solicitous, and my mother liked him nearly as well as Lord Carrington, and so – and so –"

"And so you entered into another betrothal," Lady Downs said. "I had no idea Lord Wentworth had decided to marry."

Lady Wentworth gave another giggle. "Well, he didn't plan on marrying! But when Mama found us, well –"

"Yes?" All the ladies leaned in expectantly.

Lady Wentworth ducked her head in embarrassment. "I let him kiss me in the garden."

All the ladies leaned back in disappointment. Really, after the events of the past few days, a kiss in the garden hardly merited a second thought.

"He was consoling me, you know, for my broken engagement, and he said he'd always admired me, and the garden was so pretty, and I just sort of leaned toward him –" She gave a small giggle. "And suddenly there was Mama! I'd had no idea she was nearby."

"Nor, I expect, did Lord Wentworth," Lady Downs said.

"And so you were engaged," Lady Cora breathed. "Just like in a novel."

Lady Griegson turned on her daughter in irritation. "Cora! You know you are not allowed to read novels!"

"Novels are not fit reading for young girls," agreed Lady Childer, who herself possessed a large collection of gothic tales on the shelves of her sitting room.

"Yes, it was most especially like a novel," Lady Wentworth breathed rapturously, holding her hands to her heart. "And William has been so kind, helping me through my disappointment in Lord Carrington, and seeing to my every comfort. He is a true gentleman. And so handsome!"

Across the room, the other female guests tended to the Marquis's mother. However, since Lady Loveland resolutely refused to come around, the women mostly stood in a circle waving feathers and fans in her general direction while listening in on the intriguing conversation taking place around the new Lady Wentworth.

The men had gathered around Lord Wentworth, listening to his side of the tale. Since it involved no near-death experiences and nothing more exciting than a cross-country ride with the wrong scarf and a stolen kiss, they soon tired of the tale and wandered off to the buffet table for more food.

Fifty-Four

Upstairs in her rooms, Elisabeth paced angrily about, stopping every few steps to stamp a foot or hit a pillow. Her first thought had been to dash to the kennels, but she knew she dared not risk the wrath her great-aunt would bring down on her head if she left the house. Instead, she moved from sitting room to dressing room to bedroom and back, over and over.

In fact, she had expected to be chased up the stairs by her father or her great-aunt, but no one had followed. Had she disgusted them so much that they didn't want anything to do with her? Were they too busy soothing the guests and making excuses? Trying to quell the gossip? Where were all of them, and why did no one come to offer her comfort or help her plan how to murder the Marquis?

She knew she never should have agreed to the betrothal. What did she really know about him, anyway? He might be handsome as could be – she stopped for a moment and stared into space with a silly grin – but he was obviously a rake! She punched another cushion.

And to be engaged to one woman while offering for another. That poor woman! She'd come to visit her fiancée and had arrived at a party celebrating his betrothal to another woman. She must be devastated. Elisabeth picked up a pillow and heaved it to the floor.

He might be strong and brave – another pause for a silly grin – but he was just as loutish as the horrible Squire!

Her pacing continued. Where was everyone? Were they all downstairs laughing at her? Enjoying a good joke with the Marquis? Comforting his betrayed fiancée – the real one, the first one? Probably. They certainly weren't up here comforting her, agreeing that she was the wronged one. No, they were all ignoring her. She stomped a foot.

She had just decided she would move to Scotland and become a hermit surrounded by dogs when a loud pair of raps sounded on her sitting room door. She jumped.

"Yes?"

"Open the door," came Lady Downs's firm voice.

Elisabeth moved to the door and cracked it open. Behind Lady Downs stood one of that Lady's big, handsome footmen, obviously the source of the loud knocking. She opened the door farther to admit Lady Downs. The footman turned away from the door and remained on guard in the hall. Lady Downs walked past Elisabeth into the room.

Elisabeth turned from shutting the door and saw Lady Downs carefully positioning herself on one of the room's straight chairs.

"If you think you have a tough row to hoe, it could be worse," the older woman said without preamble. "You could be engaged to Lord Carrington."

"Pardon? Who is Lord Carrington and why should I be engaged to him?"

"You shouldn't," Lady Downs said. "If he ever so much as smiles at a single lady, she should run the other direction. Fast."

"What? I don't understand."

"Never mind, child."

Elisabeth flung herself into a chair opposite her visitor.

Lady Downs looked at Elisabeth consideringly. "Worn out your temper at last, I see. You certainly know how to stir up a hornet's nest. I don't remember a more entertaining summer. Unless it was the year my brother was trying his best not to marry his wife. Lost that battle, more fool he."

"I didn't do the stirring," Elisabeth said mulishly. "The Marquis did that when he got engaged twice!"

"Well, as to that, the woman downstairs is now Lady Wentworth, so any of her previous engagements are null and void, and no longer matter."

"Previous engagements?! How many has she had?"

"At least three, apparently – one to Lord Loveland, although I never heard a word of it, so it must have been quite secret, one to Lord Carrington, which she appears to have been fortunate to survive, and one to Lord Wentworth, to whom she is now married."

"So they had a secret engagement! How dare he?"

"Well, he seems to have become unengaged to her before he met you. And no doubt he thought he was doing the honorable thing by you, child. And he was.

Saving you from disgrace or, worse, a marriage to Squire Mills." Lady Downs actually shuddered. "Contemptible man, putting three wives in the grave and now looking for a fourth."

"He's already been married three times?" Elisabeth gaped.

Lady Downs flared her nostrils in irritation. "Not the Marquis, you nitwit, the Squire. You know that."

"Oh. Yes, of course." Elisabeth suddenly felt deflated. She gave Lady Downs a defeated look.

"I don't know what to do." Elisabeth felt tears well up and begin to spill over. She never cried. And now she was crying over that horrible man. She sat there in stony silence and let the tears flow while Lady Downs watched.

After several minutes the tears eventually stopped and Lady Downs raised her eyebrows. "Ready to listen to reason, child?"

"M-maybe," Elisabeth said, with a pouty expression on her face that made her look for all the world as though she were four instead of twenty-four. Lady Downs gave a soft chuckle.

"Well, then, I expect you to wash your face, straighten your hair and gown, and take yourself over to the upstairs parlor where Lister likes to spend her time. And on your way, you will instruct a servant to find Applewood and have him bring your father and Lord Loveland to you. You will then demand a full accounting from Lord Loveland as to his former relationship with Lady Wentworth. You will then demand an apology, accept his apology, and inform him you expect him to shape up before the wedding, which will go forth as scheduled."

Elisabeth's mouth fell open. "I shall not do any such thing! I never want to see that awful man again!"

Lady Downs just gazed at Elisabeth in silence. They stared at each other for a full minute before Elisabeth glanced away. Her eyes fell to her engagement ring, which for some reason she hadn't thought to remove. She sighed in resignation.

"Really, child, I thought you were braver than this," Lady Downs commented.

"Bravery has nothing to do with it."

"Oh, I think it has everything to do with it. You've a right to be angry, I'll give you that. But to see you panic and run out of the room was another thing. Really, you should have faced down that group of nosy parkers. I think you're afraid of those fine Londoners down there and what everyone is thinking. I think you're afraid of not measuring up to the expectations of the Marquis's circle. And I think you're afraid of leaving the West Country. You've a parcel of fears, you do, and you don't appear to be facing any of them."

Elisabeth gaped at such plain speaking.

"But what if he won't apologize," Elisabeth asked a little plaintively.

"Oh, he'll apologize. He wants to marry you. And I've no doubt your father has been lighting into him something fierce. As he should."

"Is that where Papa is?"

Lady Downs gave Elisabeth an amused look. "Your father dragged Lord Loveland off to have a stern talk, and your brother followed. Lister has her hands full with Lady Loveland."

"She hates me!" Elisabeth cried.

"Who, Lady Loveland? No, Sophia doesn't hate you. Certainly not as much as Lavinia Carrington would," Lady Downs laughed. "No, Sophia is just an overly doting mother with a flair for drama."

"What? Who are these Carringtons you keep mentioning?" Elisabeth wondered if the redoubtable Lady Downs's wits were faltering.

"Never you mind. Just be glad you're engaged to Lord Loveland and not Lord Carrington," Lady Downs said. "Now, I'm going to ring for your maid. You need to wash your face and tidy up. And I need to corner Grace Benson-Smythe, who has been evading me all evening, despite the lack of plants to hide behind."

With that odd comment, Lady Downs walked over to the bell pull, gave it a hard tug, and then opened the door. Her footman promptly offered his arm, then shut the door behind them. Elisabeth heard his firm tread as the pair made their way to the stairs.

Elisabeth's maid arrived in response to the bell pull. Elisabeth then did as Lady Downs had directed, and soon was sitting in the room where the Marquis had been brought the day of his first visit to Chadwick Manor. As she awaited her father and fiancé, Elisabeth found her anxiety growing.

What if he didn't really like her at all? What if he still wanted to marry his other fiancée? Marriages could be annulled, after all. Maybe she should find someone else to marry her. She considered the few eligible men she knew.

No, not Sir Clapham, although he was an amusing companion. He obviously was developing feelings for Miss Benson-Smythe. The Duke was out; he was far too strong-willed. Elisabeth thought he was a trifle dangerous, as well.

Maybe Lord Ringwood? He wouldn't say no, Elisabeth thought with amusement. On the other hand, he might not even be able to work up the courage to say his vows at the altar, which could be a problem.

Maybe her brother or her sister knew of someone pleasant and kind who was in search of a wife. Maybe she should do as her great-aunt had suggested several days ago, and go visit her siblings. Yes, she could visit them in turn, meet their friends, and pick a husband. Surely it couldn't be that difficult. She was from a good family, had a large dowry, and was reasonably well-looking. She just needed to make sure they liked dogs.

Elisabeth had nearly decided on this plan when the parlor doors opened. She looked up quickly, a hopeful smile budding and then faltering. It wasn't the Marquis or her father in the doorway, but the Duke.

"Lady Elisabeth," he bowed. "I'm here on John's behalf. He received your request to attend you, and wanted me to let you know he would be a bit delayed."

"Oh?" she asked, a dangerous glint sparking in her eyes.

His lips quirked. "It seems he has fallen into another contretemps and is in no proper condition at the moment to appear before you. He is in the process of making himself more presentable."

"He was looking perfectly presentable the last I saw of him," she said coolly.

"Yes, but that was before your brother delivered a flush hit to your beloved's chin."

"What?!" She jumped up and started toward the door.

The Duke took hold of her arm to prevent her from leaving. "Robert was defending your honor. Seems to be a lot of that going around lately. Has your life always been so stimulating?"

"Robbie hit John?"

"That he did. You will, I hope, pardon your fiancé for returning the favor. He's been much tried of late, you know. By the time I arrived, the battle was well under way and your father was trying in vain to separate them."

"Oh my God," Elisabeth groaned. She stopped trying to leave the room and put both hands over her face. Would this horrible evening never end?

"Is there any liquid refreshment to be had up here?" the Duke asked, looking around.

Elisabeth took one hand away from her face and gestured vaguely toward a cabinet across the room. The Duke guided her over to a settee, then walked to the liquor cabinet and poured both of them a small glass of brandy.

"Here," he said with a grin. "John said to keep you away from liquor cabinets, but you look like you could use a bracer."

"He said what?"

The Duke chuckled and sat on the opposite side of the settee. "A termagant tippler, in fact. You'll be perfect for him."

"More perfect than his other fiancée?" she asked nastily.

"Ah, she has claws," he grinned. "You needn't worry about merry Marybell."

"Who?" First Lady Downs and now the Duke. Elisabeth was getting tired of hearing about people she didn't know.

"The woman you think was his fiancée, who was, in fact, no such thing, is Lady Marybell Wentworth, nee Wister. Known not entirely affectionately as merry Marybell. She has an unfortunate tendency to giggle." He took a sip of the Earl's excellent brandy, obviously French, but mellow enough that it probably had been casked long before Napoleon had upended the Continent and French goods had been banned.

"How do you know she wasn't engaged to John?" Elisabeth asked suspiciously. "The Dowager Marchioness herself said she was John's fiancée."

"The Dowager Marchioness also devolved into a shrieking madwoman the other evening," he pointed out. "Not the most reliable source of information."

"But why would she think they'd been engaged? Surely she learned it from John."

"No such thing," he said, taking another sip of brandy. "She badly wants John to marry, and had thrown her support behind the Wister chit this past Season, but it didn't take."

"So she favors Marybell. I knew she didn't like me."

"I think she favors any young lady of good Ton who can get her son to the altar," he corrected. "But then again, she did have that freakish fit."

"Yes, she did," Elisabeth said, and began to chuckle.

The Duke grinned. "I've never seen anything like it."

"And all the guests!" Elisabeth laughed.

"What a melee!" the Duke said, as he, too, began to laugh.

#

"I'm glad to find you both so well entertained," said a sour voice from the doorway.

Elisabeth and the Duke looked up from where they sat laughing to see the Marquis standing in the doorway. His yellow and purple face now sported a dark red mark on his chin and a new cut on one cheek. His hair stuck out in odd tufts. His evening clothes were ripped and mussed, and his cravat appeared to have made a trip through a meat grinder. He was as inelegant as she could imagine.

Elisabeth took one horrified look at her fiancé and tried in vain to stop laughing. She choked, snorted, and then gave up the fight. Beside her the Duke fell into another round of laughter.

"What is all this ruckus?" asked another voice behind the Marquis. The Dowager Countess stepped around the battered nobleman and stared in disapproval at the pair on the settee.

"Well you may ask," the Marquis said. "I appear to be a source of high amusement to your great-niece."

The Dowager gave him a disdainful glance. "Well, you should learn to stop acting like an imbecile," she said tartly, setting off another round of laughter from the Duke and Elisabeth.

She marched over to the settee and pointed a finger at the Duke. "And you, young man, will do me the courtesy of rising when I enter a room. Where are your manners?"

The Duke abashedly rose to his feet in apology, which gave the Dowager the opportunity to fasten a hand onto his arm. "And now you will escort me back downstairs."

"Yes, Lady Burton," he said, trying to still his chuckles.

"And you will put down that glass of spirits first!" she said firmly.

"Yes, ma'am," he said, obediently placing the glass on a nearby table. "But dare we leave these two alone?" He cocked an amused eye at Elisabeth.

"Hmph," the Dowager said. "It appears they cannot do worse than they've already done. To think I should live to see such disgraceful behavior from my family, and in a public setting. Come along."

The Marquis carefully shut the doors behind them, and then glanced about the room before making his way to the settee. He lowered himself with a groan and sat next to Elisabeth. He looked at her in silence.

"Well?" she finally asked.

"Well what?"

"Just how many fiancées have you had?"

He appeared to consider the matter for a moment.

"In total?" he asked. "Counting you?"

"Yes, in total." She crossed her arms and tapped a foot impatiently, no longer the least amused.

He glanced at that slippered foot and smiled. "One."

She opened her mouth, then shut it again. She regarded him suspiciously.

"Expecting a different answer, sweetheart?" He settled himself a little more comfortably on the settee, turning to lean closer to her.

"I've never been engaged before I met you," he said, "and given how strenuous engagements seem to be, I'm not sure I could survive more than one. Do you know your brother challenged me to a duel?"

She ignored that distraction. "I want to know why your mother called that woman your fiancée."

"I was never betrothed to Marybell Wister. Really, if you'd stayed around to meet her, you would have discovered what a little fluffhead she is. I would have murdered her before the wedding trip was over."

She stared at him stonily.

He sighed. "Marybell's mother is one of my mother's bosom pals. Between the two of them, they tried their best during the past few months to place Marybell in my path, which only served to reinforce my dislike for the idea of becoming legshackled to her. Each Season my mother selects someone she thinks would make me a suitable wife. Each Season I avoid the proffered young lady."

"How terribly dreadful for you," Elisabeth said snidely.

"And had I not wanted to marry you," he said, equally snidely, "I no doubt could have found a way to avoid becoming engaged to you after your tryst with the Squire."

"You know perfectly well I was not trysting with that horrible man!"

"Do I? Just as you know I've had prior betrothals?"

"Apologize to me," she demanded.

"Apologize? For what?"

"For – for not telling me about yourself and that woman!"

He rolled his eyes. "Fine. I'm sorry for not being interested in Lady Marybell Wister."

"That's not what I meant!"

"Well, I'm finding it a little hard to know what you do mean," he grumbled. "Perhaps because your brother hit me hard enough to nearly knock my wits loose."

"He does have a whisking uppercut, doesn't he," she said warmly, betraying her knowledge of boxing cant.

He eyed her appreciatively. "And do you add mills to your list of interests, sweetheart?"

"Of course I don't watch fights," she said primly. "Although I used to watch Robbie train in the stables with a few of the grooms."

"I've never wanted to wed anyone until I met you," he said seriously. "So can we just get this over with and get married?"

She flung herself into his arms. It was the most romantic thing she'd ever heard.

Fifty-Seven

The weather broke late that night. Torrents of rain drenched the dry fields, rapidly turning dust into mud. Ditches and low spots filled with water. Ponds and creeks began to rise. Mice, previously banished to the outdoors by stalwart servants, now made their way back inside to avoid drowning. Throughout the Marquis's estate could be heard the occasional shrieks of female guests as the tiny invaders ran across rooms and scurried under furniture.

The Marquis lay in bed, a pillow over his head, refusing to get up. Three times Gorse, his valet, had attempted to encourage him to rise, and three times the Marquis had brusquely ordered him out of the room. He hurt everywhere and he wanted nothing to do with his guests. He was certain this would go down in history as the worst house party ever.

Finally, shortly after the noon hour, he heard another light tap at his door. He roused himself out of his pout long enough to tell Gorse to go away, but this time it was Meerson, his steward, who poked his head in.

"Good news, m'Lord," Meerson said. "The rider with the special license has arrived. He's rather sodden, but the document is safe and dry." Meerson waved a piece of paper with a wax seal on it.

The Marquis sat up and grabbed his robe from the bedpost. "Bring it in, Meerson."

The steward let himself into the room and quietly shut the door as the Marquis wrapped himself in his robe and made his way to a lounging chair by the window. He looked out at the dark, dreary sky sheeting with rain. It perfectly matched his mood.

The Marquis took the special license from Meerson and examined it. "Looks all right and tight, doesn't it. Please put this in the safe, and have someone swim over to Chadwick Manor to let the Earl know it's here. Maybe then his son will stop trying to kill me. And have someone bring up some breakfast to me. That will be all. Thank you, Meerson."

Meerson retrieved the document and bowed himself out of the room, leaving the Marquis to his peevish thoughts.

The Loveland Manor kitchen staff, not knowing for certain if the Marquis actually wanted breakfast or a nuncheon, now that it was after noon, sent up four trays of food.

The Marquis stared in surprise at an array of coddled eggs, ham, beef, chicken, nuts, fruits, breads, stew, pastries, and jams on three trays, with a selection of coffee, tea, juices and wines on the fourth tray. He wondered if they expected him to remain in his rooms for a week.

He was just filling his plate when Sir Clapham walked in. "Ho, Monton!"

"Rodney, don't you ever announce yourself?"

"Thought I just did," said the cheerful Sir Clapham. He looked at the food laid out for the Marquis's selection. "Feeling a bit peckish, are you?"

"The servants certainly seem to think so," the Marquis said. "I cannot imagine what possessed them to send up enough food to feed an army. And what is it that's so important you needs must barge into my chambers, Rodney?"

"Couldn't let you hide out here all day," Sir Clapham said, helping himself to a slice of ham. "Not when I have news!"

"Oh?" The Marquis finished filling his plate and sat down, beckoning Sir Clapham to join him.

"Well," said Sir Clapham with a wide grin, "I couldn't let you and Wentworth get all the attention, so I've gone and gotten myself engaged."

"What?" asked the astonished Marquis. "To whom?"

"What do you mean, to whom, you nodcock? To Miss Margaret Benson-Smythe, of course!"

"Well, heaven knows there are a gaggle of unattached females on the premises from which to choose," the Marquis groused. "How was I to know who had snagged you?"

"Didn't snag me," Sir Clapham replied huffily, "I asked. Been quite taken with the little Benson-Smythe since I first clapped eyes on her. Got to know her during the past weeks, and decided I like her very much. And I like her family, and they like me." He sat back with satisfaction, daring the Marquis to disagree with him.

"Huh," the Marquis said. "Congratulations, then. Told anyone else yet?"

"Thought we'd do it in a day or two. I'd like you to stand up with me, by the way, so it would be nice if you and Lady Elisabeth could be there for the announcement."

"Are you sure you want us in the same room together?" the Marquis asked around a mouthful of beef.

Sir Clapham grinned. "Maybe on opposite sides of the room."

The Marquis swallowed and sighed. "How bad is it, Rodney?"

"How bad is what?"

"The talk downstairs. I expect half of London will be hearing about last night."

"Oh, more like all of London," Rodney grinned. "Not a doubt this will make the papers. Cruickshank, even. The two of you were quite a sight."

"Wonderful. I've always wanted to be skewered by that vile illustrator. I hope you're planning on a long engagement. I may want to take an extended wedding trip until no one remembers this cursed house party."

"No hope of that, I expect. You'll just have to brazen it out. What do you care about the Ton's opinion, anyway?"

"I care about how they welcome my wife," the Marquis surprised them both by saying.

"No one's going to shun Lady Elisabeth once they meet her," Sir Clapham said. "And besides, Ravenwood and I will stand buff. And so will Margaret and her parents, and Lady Elisabeth's family. But maybe you should take a long wedding trip so that by the time anyone sees you again you won't be looking like a bloody pugilist."

The Marquis grimaced as he glanced at his hideous reflection in one of the room's mirrors. "I see what you mean. Very well, when do you want to make the announcement? Maybe tomorrow evening? I'll invite the Chadwick clan over for supper."

"Thanks, Monton," Sir Clapham grinned as he stood to leave the room. "Oh, by the way, I should perhaps tell you that the servants have organized themselves into groups and are conducting a mouse hunt through the premises. We've got a betting system going as to which team will be the most successful. Care to enter a wager? I've put my money on the grooms."

The Marquis buried his face in his hands.

Fifty-Eight

The residents of Chadwick Manor received the news of the arrival of the special license and the invitation to supper the following night with mixed emotions.

Lord Chadwick and the Dowager Countess both nodded with satisfaction and some relief. Lord Robert smiled grimly. Lady Caroline began excitedly drawing up plans for decorating the chapel. And Elisabeth bounced back and forth between dread and elation.

After listening for several minutes to Lady Caroline and the Dowager discussing chapel arrangements, Elisabeth excused herself and walked to the back of the house and through the kitchens to the cloak room. She donned an oilskin slicker, hat and walking boots. It had been two days since she'd visited the kennels, and despite the torrents of rain pouring from the sky, she could think of no place she'd rather be than with her dogs.

She slogged her way to the working buildings, finally arriving at the door to the kennels. She stood for a moment outside the door, listening to the excited shufflings and low woofings of the dogs, who'd picked up the sounds of her arrival. She was going to miss them.

Her father had assured her that the Marquis had agreed to build a kennel building on his main estate so she could have the dogs with her. She hoped it wouldn't take too long.

Inside the building, the dogs greeted her joyfully, fully ready for a good romp through the rain. Knowing she had only a few days left until her sister Anne and brother-in-law Marcus arrived and the wedding took place, Elisabeth decided to let them have their fun.

For the next several hours she roamed the estate with the hounds, watching as they gamboled in the mud and rain, darted toward interesting scents, and chased each other across the lawns. By the time she returned to the kennels, the hounds were a mess, and she wasn't in much better shape.

Once inside the building, the dogs shook themselves thoroughly, flinging water and mud all over the walls. They rolled in the sawdust and straw, and jumped on her in thanks. She spent another two hours rubbing them down with blankets and doing her best with a brush and a pail of water to clean the walls.

Just as she was nearly done with her chores, the door to the kennels opened and her brother appeared.

"Robbie! What a shame you didn't get here sooner. You could have helped clean them up."

"Yes, I thought I timed that rather well," he said. "I was watching you from the house while you were out larking about. Figured I'd give you time to get most of the clean-up work done."

He reached for one of the sodden blankets and carried it to the supply room, where he tossed it in a barrel reserved for holding rags and towels that needed cleaning. They worked in silence until the blankets were all picked up, the walls were relatively clean, and the dogs had been given fresh water.

Finally, when Elisabeth was satisfied that she hadn't left too much of a mess for the grooms, she turned to her brother with a knowing smile. "You didn't come down here just to help with the work. What do you really want?"

He smiled in return. "I want to talk without all the ears that are usually about. I need to be certain that this marriage is what you want, that you're not being forced into it."

"I'm not being forced," she said. "Did Papa tell you everything that happened? About Squire Mills, I mean."

"Yes, he did," her brother said with suppressed rage. "Why do you think I kept watch on you from the house while you were out romping with your pack?"

"Oh, Robbie, that wasn't necessary. The Squire tried just the once to approach me when I was with the dogs. And Turk and a couple of the others took great exception to him. The Squire knows better than to bother me when I'm with the dogs."

"How can you be so calm about it? The Squire tried to ravish you," he said. "I apologized to Monton yesterday evening after our set-to. I hadn't realized he'd saved you."

"Well he did, and I'm much grateful."

"So grateful that you feel compelled to marry him?"

"No, I don't feel compelled." She paused a moment and a blush rose to her face. "I actually rather like him, you know. I didn't expect to. But I'm happy to be marrying him."

"You don't seem all that happy to me, m'dear. You seem rather scared."

"Well of course I'm scared, you dolt! I'm leaving home and moving to a part of England I've never visited. I'm going to have to learn a new way of life, and I don't know what to expect. It's daunting to suddenly have everything change."

He stared at her a moment. "You know, Caroline said much the same thing to me right before we were wed. I didn't pay as much heed to it as I should have, I think. I couldn't imagine why she was so worried that she might not fit in with our family."

"And she didn't have the added stress of having her future mother-in-law fall into a screaming fit right after the announcement," Elisabeth laughed.

"Yes, I heard about that from Father, but I couldn't credit it. She really had a fit?"

"Indeed. Had to be carried kicking and screaming upstairs to her rooms. One moment she was happy and congratulating us, the next she was drumming her heels on the floor."

"Sounds a bit knockers to me."

"Well that's what I thought, but Great-Aunt Lister said it's no such thing. She assured me there would turn out to be some sort of reasonable explanation eventually."

"I certainly hope so!" he laughed. "You don't want to have her falling into distempered freaks whenever she visits."

"I'll just sic the dogs on her," Elisabeth said with a grin. "Come, let's go back to the house. I'm famished."

"No wonder. It's well past noon."

Since neither of them had removed their raingear while working in the kennels, it was a simple matter to exit the building, shut the door behind them, and splash their way back to the manor house.

After stripping off their outer gear in the manor's cloak room, the two made it only as far as the kitchens, where they promptly set to work on plates of breads and meats left over from nuncheon.

In the company of her beloved older brother, Elisabeth felt her fears and doubts slipping away.

Fifty-Nine

The following evening saw the residents of Chadwick Manor arriving for dinner at Loveland Manor in response to the Marquis's invitation. Elisabeth was actually looking forward to the visit, glad for the respite from a day's worth of dress fittings and wedding preparations.

As the carriages pulled up to the entrance, servants ran out with umbrellas to protect the arriving guests from the third day of pelting rain. The Earl stepped down from the first carriage and turned to assist the Dowager. Lord Robert exited the second carriage, and held out his hands to assist first his wife, then his sister.

The Marquis and his mother awaited the guests in the entry hall, welcoming them as other servants helped relieve them of coats, hats and gloves. The Marquis bowed over his fiancée's hand and gave her a warm smile. "Welcome to Loveland Manor, my dear."

"At Chadwick Manor, we have a covered entrance for our guests," she said in reply.

To everyone's surprise, he laughed at this piece of rudeness and tucked her arm in his. "Come, let us join the others and find some more people for you to insult."

"Why, do they expose their guests to the weather as well?"

"You must know that Londoners expect their guests to consider the honor of an invitation to outweigh the minor inconvenience of possibly drowning between carriage and door," he replied conversationally.

The Marquis escorted Elisabeth into the main salon as her brother and father exchanged looks. This, their silent exchange said, was going to be the perfect husband for Elisabeth.

The evening went more smoothly for Elisabeth than she had anticipated. Perhaps it was the fact that she was more familiar with the others now, and actually had one or two people with whom she felt comfortable talking. Once she realized that no one was going to approach her about the events at the dinner party, she actually found herself enjoying the evening.

When the guests were called to supper, she found herself occupying the position of honor to the right of the Marquis. Of course, she silently chided herself, she should have expected this. She was going to have to get used to her new circumstances.

She glanced down the long dining table to where the Dowager Marchioness sat at the far end, realizing that soon that would be her position when she and the Marquis hosted guests. She hoped it would be a while before this many people dined with them, because she would barely be able to see John at the opposite end of the table.

Across from her the Duke was chatting easily with Lady Georgina, who had been placed next to him. For her part, Lady Georgina seemed to float above her surroundings, replying in bland generalities to the Duke's remarks. Their entire conversation appeared to be about mutual acquaintances in London.

Next to Georgina sat Lord Wentworth and his bride. The two of them were enveloped in the private world that so often belonged to newlyweds. Heads bent together, they had no eyes and no conversation for anyone else. Whatever Lord Wentworth was saying to the new Lady Wentworth appeared to be vastly amusing, since she emitted little giggles every few seconds.

Around the table it went, as all the guests enjoyed the excellent food and wine while they talked in pairs or small groups. Then her gaze ended at the man seated silently next to her, Lord Ringwood. He had not vouchsafed one word all evening, which left Elisabeth with no one to converse with but the Marquis. She was sure this was deliberate.

"Are you enjoying yourself, my dear?" the Marquis said softly as he leaned toward her.

"You have a wonderful chef," she said politely, as the servants began clearing away the last course before dessert. "Does he travel with you? I am certain old Lord Loveland never ate so well."

"M'mother had him brought here once she decided to throw a house party. He usually resides at our London house. I am glad you are pleased with him."

"I am. And," she said rather shyly, "I am enjoying myself. Thank you."

"Good," he said, pleased by her words. "I hope you also will enjoy the surprise announcement I am about to make."

She raised her eyebrows as the Marquis pushed back his chair and stood. Conversation gradually stopped as everyone turned to look at him.

He smiled at the group. "As we are receiving dessert, you will see that the servants are bringing in some champagne."

The guests looked around and realized that champagne glasses were, indeed, replacing the wine glasses at the table. As servants began pouring champagne and delivering the dessert plates, the guests returned their attention to their host.

The Marquis lifted his champagne glass and smiled again. "Rodney, would you please stand?"

Sir Clapham pushed back his chair and rose from the table.

The Marquis continued, "I am pleased to be able to share with all of you that my dear friend Sir Rodney Clapham has become betrothed to Miss Margaret Benson-Smythe."

Rodney reached down to Margaret, who had been seated next to him, as everyone erupted into applause and shouts of congratulations. Margaret rose and stood next to Sir Clapham. She blushed rosily as her fiancé pulled his signet ring off and slid it onto her ring finger. She curled her hand to keep it from falling off, and beamed up at him in adoration.

"As soon as I get home I'll get you a real betrothal ring," he grinned, "but for now this at least is something to show."

Then Margaret, with a complete lack of regard for decorum, reached up and pulled Sir Clapham's face down for a quick kiss.

After dinner, as the females adjourned into the second salon, Margaret found herself the center of attention. Fortunately, her mother was there to deflect some of the less kind comments directed her way. A few of the women seemed to think the engagement was the result of a clandestine plot.

"You certainly have been keeping this romance under wraps," was Lady Griegson's opening salvo, as she approached Margaret. "Were you afraid your parents might not approve of Sir Clapham as a suitor?"

"Her parents like Sir Clapham just fine," Mrs. Benson-Smythe said with a cool smile, as she moved to her daughter's side. "We are delighted to have him joining the family."

"He is reasonably well off," said Lady Childer. "But that cannot matter much to you, I expect."

"Not at all," Mrs. Benson-Smythe agreed, still forcing herself to smile. "Margaret may marry to whom she will without regard for financial resources. What is important is that Sir Clapham is of good family and is a gentleman. He will make Margaret a good husband."

"And we share many interests," Margaret chimed in, determined to defend her intended. "We have a solid foundation for a good marriage."

"Do you not think this was rather a short amount of time to make such a decision?" Lady Violet asked. "I am not certain I could act so hastily."

"I am confident in him," Margaret said calmly.

"As he is confident in you," said Lady Georgina, unexpectedly coming to Margaret's aid. "I have seen how much delight he takes in your presence, and you in his. I am happy for the both of you."

Margaret stared in surprise at Lady Georgina for a few moments, then remembered her manners. "Thank you, Lady Georgina."

"Yes, best wishes," said Lady Alma. "I think you make a delightful couple. You are both fortunate to have found each other."

"Well," Lady Griegson commented softly in an aside to Lady Childer, "certainly he is fortunate to have found her fortune."

"I wonder how she will like living at their country home with a father-in-law who collects bugs or flowers or whatever it is," Lady Childer replied in equally low tones.

Margaret's sharp hearing heard these comments, but she just smiled. She would adore living in the country with Rodney, taking morning horse rides and tending to a garden in the afternoons. It was exactly the kind of life she'd always wanted, away from the noise and bustle of London.

"I expect you will enjoy country life," Lady Georgina said. "It can be a refreshing change of pace from Town life." She also had excellent hearing.

"I know I shall," Margaret replied.

"Where exactly is Sir Clapham's home?" Lady Rose asked.

"In Lincolnshire," Mrs. Benson-Smythe replied. "Near enough to us that we shall not entirely miss seeing our dear Margie regularly." This time her smile was sincere.

By the time the gentlemen had left the table and joined the ladies, the Dowager Marchioness had been successful in organizing some musical entertainment. The men entered the salon to find the Ladies Alma and Georgina laughingly engaged in attempting an impromptu piano and harp duet.

The Duke paused as he entered, watching Lady Georgina with appreciation. She really was an extremely lovely young woman. He realized he rarely saw her so openly enjoying herself.

The ballad the two ladies had chosen was familiar to Lady Alma, but less so to Lady Georgina, who was relying on Lady Alma's lead. Despite several mishaps with pacing and chords, the result was so pleasant that the guests enthusiastically asked for more. The two ladies proceeded to make their way through two other pieces before politely refusing requests for a fourth tune.

The evening eventually wound to a close, and the Chadwick Manor guests departed for home. The Marquis escorted Elisabeth to her carriage with a promise to visit the following afternoon.

"For more of that tepid tea, you understand," he explained. "I find the servants here like to serve it hot for some unaccountable reason."

"As you like," she laughed, before allowing him to help her into the carriage.

Elisabeth spent the following morning gazing out the window at the rain while her great-aunt and sister-in-law laid out their ideas for decorating the chapel. There appeared to be an inordinate amount of twined flowers involved, which Mrs. Doty was dutifully air-braiding.

Elisabeth nodded in vague agreement at every suggestion, while wishing the weather would clear. It had been too long since she had taken a bracing ride on Shadow, with the dogs loping alongside.

"Good news," her father said, entering the room briskly, Robbie at his side.

All four women looked up expectantly.

"Squire Mills has left the area for an indefinite tour of Ireland," the Earl pronounced with pleasure.

"I think he's hunting for another wife," Robbie added. "A wholesome Irish lass, this time."

"Good riddance to bad cess," the Dowager said curtly. Mrs. Doty nodded firmly, before returning to air-braiding flowers.

Lady Caroline beckoned to her husband. He approached and leaned down so she could whisper to him. "Is she playing pantomimes?" she asked, nodding her head toward the Dowager's companion.

"She's Mrs. Doty, my dear," he whispered back. "Just enjoy the show."

After nuncheon, Elisabeth resumed gazing out the window, but no longer filled with thoughts of riding Shadow. Now, she found herself waiting impatiently for the arrival of her fiancé.

Her father and brother had joined the female members of the household in the Dowager's preferred upstairs parlor. The men were discussing politics while the women continued planning the wedding ceremony.

When Elisabeth's ears finally picked up the sound of an approaching carriage, she leapt from her chair and ran to the window to look up the drive. But it wasn't the Marquis arriving.

"It's Anne!" she exclaimed, jumping up and down a few times before running out of the room and down the stairs to the entry hall. Her sister had finally arrived.

She ran outside under the portico, and was quickly joined by the rest of the family. As Baron Conners tried to step down first before assisting his wife, he was outmaneuvered by Anne, who tumbled out of the carriage in a flurry of gown, coat and petticoat.

"Marcus, let me by! I'm home!" She laughed in delight as she jumped down from the carriage. She ran straight to her father and enveloped him in a tight hug, then turned to Elisabeth and gave her an equally tight embrace.

"I rather thought Falstone Abbey was your home, m'dear," Lord Conners said mildly as he stepped to the gravel.

"Oh, you know what I mean," she said, sending him a teasing glance over her shoulder as she turned to hug her brother and then Caroline. With a little more restraint, she hurried to the Dowager and gave her a gentle peck on one powdered cheek.

She stepped away from her great-aunt and clapped her hands. "Oh, I'm so happy to be back! You have no idea how much I've missed all of you!"

She spun around and danced back to Elisabeth. "And you're getting married! We came as soon as we heard, as fast as we could!"

"Faster, actually," her husband replied.

"Oh, not fast enough!" Anne said.

"True," Lord Conners agreed. "It could never be fast enough when one is dealing with a perpetually bouncing traveling companion seated next to one all the way from Perthshire. It's a wonder the springs survived."

He turned to Lord Chadwick and greeted him with a small smile, then made his way to each of the others, his calm and contained demeanor in marked contrast to Anne's high exuberance.

The group made its way inside, leaving the two servants from the second carriage to help the Chadwick staff offload and sort the luggage. Applewood oversaw the proceedings for a few minutes before handing off the duty to Dorn, the underbutler, and making his way upstairs to ensure proper care was being taken of the family.

"The Squire did what?!" Anne shrieked when Elisabeth had reached that part of the tale. She clasped her sister's hand. "How horrible! And how could he ever think you would want to marry someone who treated you that way?"

"Well, it wasn't the first time I've had to rebuff him," Elisabeth said.

"What?!"

"It's true," Elisabeth said, and launched into a digression of her earlier encounters with the Squire.

Even the mellow Lord Conners frowned at the telling. "Not good Ton," he commented.

"But then?" Anne prompted, waiting for Elisabeth to continue her story. When Elisabeth began describing the fight, Anne halted her with an upraised hand. "No, I must know every detail. Do not think to fob me off with 'and they fought for several minutes.' It won't do."

"I agree," Lord Robert joined in, dragging over a footstool to be closer to his sisters. "Let's hear it blow by blow."

"Yes," Anne agreed.

Lord Conners watched in amusement as his lovely, bubbly, and entirely feminine wife displayed a heretofore unknown side of her personality and a decidedly thorough knowledge of boxing cant.

Lady Caroline listened in confusion, not understanding most of the terms, but knowing that they must be important details. She glanced at the Dowager, whose fierce expression made clear her disapproval of the discussion. The Earl and Lord Conners were both smiling, however, so the topic appeared to amuse them. She decided to pull aside Elisabeth and Anne sometime during the next few days to get pointers on all these male terms.

"So the two of you ended up walking back to the house with the entire party following?" Lord Robert asked, starting to laugh.

"It wasn't funny!" Elisabeth said, reaching out to swat him on the shoulder.

"Oh, that part is decidedly funny. Quite like a parade. What a picture it must have made."

"Oh, you haven't heard the best part," the Earl interjected. "There's a much funnier picture coming up."

"You mean when I poured John's brandy on his head?" Elisabeth asked.

"No, when all the guests fell over like bowling pins."

"What?!" Anne shrieked. "What has been going on here?"

The Dowager closed her eyes and pinched the bridge of her nose. "If you must needs go over that entire fiasco again, I am going to my room." She rose and swept out of the parlor, followed by Mrs. Doty bobbing in her wake.

The rest of the group settled in for the remainder of the story.

Sixty-One

When the Marquis's carriage pulled up an hour later, Applewood informed him that the rest of the family had arrived and were upstairs visiting in the parlor.

"Perhaps I should wait until tomorrow, then. I wouldn't wish to interrupt a family reunion."

Applewood looked up as another shriek floated down the stairs. "I would just suggest, m'Lord, that as you, too, are nearly family, your visit would be entirely welcome."

"Very well, then, take me up," the Marquis said, hearing a burst of hilarity from upstairs.

He entered the room to see Elisabeth's face lit up in laughter, and for a moment lost his purpose as he stood on the threshold. Her beauty nearly took his breath away. And then he saw a second vision of loveliness seated next to her, obviously the younger sister.

"John!" Elisabeth waved gaily. "You must come in and add to the story."

The other men rose as he made his way to his fiancée and bowed over her hand.

"Monton," Lord Conners said, stepping forward as the Marquis straightened from greeting Elisabeth. "Congratulations on your engagement."

"Thank you, Conners. I'm pleased to see you have arrived."

"I imagine you are," the Baron said with a small smile. "I understand we're almost the last of the wedding guests to arrive."

The Marquis then greeted Lady Caroline and turned to Anne, awaiting an introduction.

"Anne," her husband said, "allow me to present Lord Loveland, Marquis of Edmonton. Monton, this lady is my wife, Lady Anne Conners, Lady Elisabeth's sister."

As the Marquis started to bow, Anne cut him off. "None of that! You are now family!" She jumped up from the settee and gave him a hug. "We have been hearing all about how you met. Well done with Squire Mills! I wish I had been there to see it."

The Marquis glanced at Elisabeth and grinned. "I see bloodthirstiness runs in the family."

"It's the Scot in us," Elisabeth grinned back. "Would you like some tea? I can have it prepared just the way you prefer."

"Tea would be nice, thank you, but I think I'll take it the way most everyone else likes it, if you wouldn't mind."

Elisabeth's grin widened. She walked to the bell pull and gave it a tug, requesting the servant who entered to bring a fresh pot of hot tea and a plate of food.

She turned back to find Anne had vacated her spot on the settee, and that it was now occupied by the Marquis.

She sat down next to him, feeling somewhat shy about being this close to him in a group.

"Now," Anne said firmly from where she now sat beside her husband, "I want to know what happened to Squire Mills. Elisabeth only knows that you 'took care of him,' and since Papa says he's off on a visit to Ireland, I want to know if you sent him there."

The Marquis looked to his future father-in-law for confirmation. The Earl nodded. "Got word of it early this morning. I think Elsbet was his last hope for a bride in these parts, so now he's gone off visiting some distant relatives. Hope that's the last we'll see of him."

"I pity the poor girl he makes his wife," Anne said. She prodded the Marquis again, "So, did you order him to leave?"

"No," the Marquis said somewhat apologetically. At her disappointed look, he gave the Earl another questioning glance.

"Go ahead," he sighed. "We've already had all the details of the fight, so feel free to tell her everything."

The Marquis obliged, but as the Duke's and steward's actions were relatively tame compared to everything else the group had been regaled with for the past hour, Anne was rather disappointed.

"Oh, too bad. I was hoping you'd had him lashed. But I like the part about issuing a shoot-on-sight order. Perhaps that's what finally chased him out of England. Well done."

"Thank you," the Marquis said humbly.

The Dowager and Mrs. Doty reappeared as tea was served, and the conversation turned to wedding plans.

"We can have the chapel prepared over the next two days, and Elisabeth's gown finished in that same time," the Dowager said. "The wedding can take place three days hence. No sense in putting it off now that nearly everyone's here. I think we shall have a mid-morning wedding, so that we may have a nuncheon directly after, then the newlyweds may leave for their bridal trip in the early afternoon."

She looked at her nephew. "Robert, you will inform Vicar Smithers. And you," she turned to the Marquis, "will inform your guests."

"Yes, ma'am," both men agreed. The Marquis knew better by now than to attempt to negotiate with the Dowager. He hadn't even thought about a wedding trip, and wondered how far they could reasonably expect to travel in four or five hours. He glanced over at Elisabeth, who was looking at him a little warily.

"How do you feel about initially going to Edmonton Castle, my main estate," he said. "It is in Leicestershire, a few days' ride if we take it in easy stages. I think you will like it. It is very comfortable. Once you've had a little time to get acclimated, we can determine where you would like to visit on the Continent."

She let out a little pent-up breath. "That sounds lovely, thank you."

"Oh, you must see Paris!" Anne exclaimed.

"Might be hot there this time of year," her husband cautioned.

"Well, it's summer, of course it will be hot," Anne laughed. "But perhaps you could wait until early fall. That's when we went." She sent her husband an adoring look.

He smiled back, clearly enchanted with his wife.

After another hour, the Marquis decided it was time to take his leave. Elisabeth offered to walk with him to the entry and wait while his carriage was brought around. Her sister and brother-in-law said their good-byes and headed to their rooms for a welcome rest after a day spent traveling and visiting.

"You have a charming family," the Marquis said as they descended the stairs. "I enjoyed getting to know them better today."

"I'm so glad," Elisabeth said with a rush of relief. "Do you think your brother will like me?"

"Patrick? Yes, I'm sure he will. He's due to arrive tomorrow, although I certainly have no plans to hold up the wedding if he's delayed. I want to be shot of this accursed house party as soon as possible."

"Yes, I suspected that's why you wanted a quick wedding," she laughed.

He realized what he had said and tried to recover his position. "And, of course, I very much want to marry you."

She slanted a twinkling glance up at him. "It's a good thing I'm willing to have you, then. I could, of course, have accepted the Squire's kindly offer."

"Well, if you're so inclined, I'll lend you my fastest horses for a quick flight to Ireland."

"Would you? That would be so kind. However, a bird in the hand, as they say. I think I'll keep you."

"Thank you," he said meekly. "I'll bring my brother around tomorrow to meet you. Perhaps teatime again?"

"Yes, please do. I will look forward to it."

They moved to the doorway at the sounds of his carriage being brought around, and she watched as he jumped in and gave the driver the order to return to Loveland Manor. The carriage moved forward, splashing its way around and back up the drive. She hoped it would stop raining before the wedding.

Sixty-Two

The Dowager Marchioness arrived the next morning right after breakfast. She explained her unexpected visit by saying her son had informed her that wedding preparations were under way and she was hoping to offer her services.

The Dowager Countess gladly accepted her assistance and arranged to take the Marquis's mother to visit the chapel and help with arrangements.

"Oh, thank you, Lister You have no idea how much I would like to help. I've always wanted to plan a wedding for one of my sons."

The two friends left the room, chatting together animatedly about seating arrangements, flowers, clothing, wedding party members, and the after-wedding nuncheon.

Elisabeth, Anne, and Caroline retired to Elisabeth's rooms, where Elisabeth endured the final fittings for her wedding dress. The gown had been fashioned by combining a white satin underdress from one of her party gowns with a pale gold lace overdress from another gown. The result, according to Anne and Caroline, was delightful.

"You will look ravishing!" Anne declared.

"Most becoming," Caroline agreed. "And I have the perfect hairclip." She dashed out of the room and returned with a pearl and gold clip and matching pearl and gold drop earrings. "Do you like them? I would be honored to have you wear them."

"They are perfect," Elisabeth agreed. "I admit I have been fearing I would look like a rustic, with so little time to prepare."

"Nonsense," Anne said stoutly. "You could never look like a rustic. You will put all the other women to shame."

Elisabeth gave Anne a slightly teary smile, and then enveloped her sister in a long hug. "Oh, Anne, I have missed you so much!"

The next matter at hand was to determine what Anne and Caroline would wear to the ceremony, since Elisabeth had decided that both of them would serve as her attendants. Both Anne and Caroline had brought several dress gowns. Now they had to determine which gowns would best match.

The three young women hastened back and forth between Anne's and Caroline's rooms, comparing the available gowns. Anne, who shared Elisabeth's coloring, had brought two gowns with gold lace threaded through them, one a light aqua and gold, and one a pale green and gold. Caroline, a brunette, had brought a different palette of colors, but one dress in particular was deemed just right. It was a dusky teal and white gown, and would work well with Anne's aqua and gold dress, and Elisabeth's white and gold dress.

Satisfied and temporarily exhausted after completing this important task, the three young women returned to Anne's chambers, where they sank into comfortable chairs.

"Now what?" asked Elisabeth. "You've both gone through this. What else do we need to do?"

"Well," said Caroline, leaning forward, "the next thing must do is teach me all about boxing. I didn't understand more than one word in ten about the fight between Lord Loveland and Squire Mills."

Elisabeth and Anne, both well-grounded in the intricacies of fisticuffs by their brother, proceeded not only to tell her, but to show her. By the end of the hour, Caroline was familiar enough with boxing cant to hold her own in any conversation, and Anne was sitting next to her sister holding a cold, wet rag to the black eye she'd given Elisabeth.

"Oh, my God," were the Marquis's first words when he and his younger brother Patrick were announced to the three young women in the upstairs parlor. "What the hell happened now?"

"I did it," Anne said proudly. "Got past her guard with a left jab." She turned to her sister. "I told you your arm was too low."

"Well how was I to know you'd been practicing," Elisabeth grumbled. "You must have been doing it in secret, too, for I'll wager anything you like that Marcus knew nothing of it."

"Oh, I have my ways," Anne said airily.

"It was quite the stunner," Caroline contributed.

The Marquis rolled his eyes as his brother broke out laughing.

Lord Patrick turned to his older brother. "Which one of these battling beauties is yours, John?"

"The one who can't guard herself against a left jab," the Marquis sighed. "At least we'll be a matched set at the ceremony."

Elisabeth regarded his face. "Not quite. You've left most of the reds behind and have moved on to yellows and purples."

Lord Patrick gave her a considering look. "I don't know. The wedding's the day after tomorrow. Your eye should turn to purple pretty soon. You two may still match."

Elisabeth grinned at her future brother-in-law. She liked him already.

"Ladies," the Marquis said, finally remembering his manners, "Allow me to present my brother, Lord Patrick Loveland. Patrick, the blonde with the black eye is my fiancée, Lady Elisabeth Chadwick. The young lady with the punishing left is Lady Anne Conners, wife of Baron Conners, and my intended's younger sister. And the third young lady is Lady Caroline Chadwick. She's married to Lady Elisabeth's brother."

Patrick nodded to each young woman. The two men accepted Elisabeth's invitation to be seated as Anne bounced up and rang for refreshments.

"Both Anne and Caroline will be my attendants at the ceremony," Elisabeth informed the Marquis.

"And has the redoubtable Lady Burton signed off on that?" he asked.

"She will when I tell her," Elisabeth said. "Surely I am to have some say in the matter."

"Speaking of having a say, I hope m'mother isn't causing any trouble. I understand she fled the house at first light to land on your doorstep with the intention of helping your great-aunt plan the event."

"Yes, they've been at the chapel all day," Elisabeth said. "As I understand it, they plan to strip half the flower bushes from the West Country for the ceremony."

"A hot, dry summer followed by a monsoon," the Marquis reflected. "I cannot imagine what shape any remaining blossoms will be in."

"And who will be standing up with you?" Anne asked as the servants brought in the tea tray.

"I shall have my cousin Charles and my brother," the Marquis said. "Pending your great-aunt's approval of course."

Anne gave the Marquis a pert smile. "Great-Aunt Lister is quite manageable, if one knows how. Elsbet has never learned the secret, unfortunately."

"You must tell me later what it is," Caroline said. "I fear she means to – that is, I understand she may honor us with a visit after she leaves here."

Anne and Elisabeth burst out laughing. Caroline blushed rosily and busied herself with pouring tea.

Sixty-Three

The day before the wedding, Elisabeth woke to see a watery blue early morning sky through her windows and no rain. She took it as a sign and hurriedly donned her riding habit before running through the kitchens, where she grabbed some bread and cheese and then left for the stables. At the last minute, just in case the Squire really hadn't hared off to Ireland, she retrieved a pistol from the gun room.

As soon as Shadow was saddled, Elisabeth mounted the mare and signaled for a groom to open the door to the kennels. Thirteen joyous dogs bounded out of the building and danced around the horse. Shadow, inured to these great brutes of dogs after all this time, ignored them and paid attention only to her mistress's commands.

Elisabeth snicked the mare's reins, and they were off.

For the next several hours, Elisabeth and the dogs roamed the estate, enjoying the freedom of a day free of both heat and rain. As she was turning toward the stables, she saw a figure riding toward her. Her initial start of alarm flowed away as she recognized the Marquis cantering in her direction on Crosspurposes.

"Well met," he hailed her with an admiring smile. "That's quite a sight, you with your hounds." His greeting was interrupted by Crosspurposes, who began shying nervously as the dogs approached. Elisabeth watched as the Marquis held the stallion in an iron grip and spoke in a voice that was at once both commanding and reassuring.

While not entirely convinced of the harmless intentions of the dogs, the horse did have enough confidence in his master to stand still and not lash out. His occasional snorts and mane tosses gave the lie to his outward calm, but the Marquis appeared satisfied.

"I dropped by to visit and heard you were out riding," the Marquis said to Elisabeth. "I wanted to speak to you privately."

Elisabeth's sudden wariness transmitted to Shadow, who moved restlessly. "About what?"

"Our engagement came about so suddenly that we have not had the time one would have in a normal courtship to learn about each other. It is important to me that we talk about where we shall live."

"Where we shall live?" she repeated blankly. "I assumed we would reside at Edmonton Castle. Is that not your home?"

"That is my primary estate, yes. There is also Loveland Manor, my townhouse in London, and three other estates. I spend most of my time at the Castle, but I do like to visit London for a few weeks each Season and it is my obligation to check on my other holdings once or twice a year. Oh, and there is the hunting lodge."

"I see," she said, feeling a little overwhelmed. "I had not thought about it. I was expecting we would reside at Edmonton Castle, which is where Papa said you had agreed to have a kennel building constructed for me."

"Certainly I would prefer that to be our chief residence. It is where I grew up and it is where I want to raise our family," he said. "I enjoy Town life to a degree, but I much prefer country life, and I believe you do as well. But I also spend time at my other properties. Will you want to travel with me to the other holdings? I would prefer that you do so, but perhaps you do not enjoy traveling?"

"Oh," she said, enlightenment dawning. "You are concerned because I so rarely leave the West Country?"

"Yes," he said. "And I would not like us to lead separate lives, but I do have a responsibility to my properties and dependents."

"Thank you," she said, giving him a shy smile.

"For what?"

"For caring enough to ask. I confess I have been nervous about what lies before me. You have not spoken much of your home or the life you lead. I don't even know if you have other family members in addition to your mother and brother."

"I shall bore you to tears talking about my estates and my many cousins on our wedding trip," he smiled back. "And you must not worry that any of them will be living with us at the Castle. Mother has stated her intention of claiming Loveland Manor as her dower house, and Patrick divides his time between the London establishment and our hunting box. But you have not answered my question."

"What question?" she asked, still distracted by the thought of so many houses to manage.

"Do you object to traveling with me? Shall I have to find a mistress to keep me company?"

"What?!" she said in outrage, before catching the teasing glint in his eyes. Huffing out a breath, she recovered. "If you take a mistress, I shall select a handsome groom to keep me company."

"All the grooms on my estates are old, ugly, and riddled with pox," he said promptly.

"Then I shall invite Lady Downs and her handsome footmen to visit."

"No you will not. You will travel with me if I have to tie you up and toss you in the luggage boot."

"A charming prospect."

"Good, I'm glad that's settled."

She suddenly gave him the unrestrained smile that always knocked him back. "Of course I should like to travel with you. I should like to see as much of England and the world as you would show me. I have been thinking about all the sights I should like to see on our wedding trip, in fact."

The tension left his shoulders and he gave her a gentle smile. "I have fallen head over heels in love with you, you know."

She suddenly felt as though her entire body was fizzing like champagne. "Even with my black eye?"

"Oh, most especially with your black eye. I've always wanted a sharp-tongued wife who boxes. It was at the top of my list, but I despaired of ever finding such a paragon."

She found herself giggling, and reached a hand toward him. He maneuvered his horse around until they could walk their mounts side by side, holding hands all the way back to the stables.

As he helped her dismount, she leaned toward him and whispered, "I think I love you, too, John. And now I must spend some time bidding farewell to my four-footed friends. I shall see you tomorrow." And then she spun about and ran toward the kennels, the dogs gamboling behind her.

He smiled as he watched her race away. He was quite possibly the luckiest man on the planet.

Sixty-four

Elisabeth flung open the door to the kennels and stood aside as the dogs trotted past her. They frisked about the large central aisle of the building, stopping occasionally to lap up water and roll around in the straw. Elisabeth shut the door behind her and pulled a low stool into the middle of the aisle. She watched as they finally settled down, sitting or lying around her.

"I'm going to be going away for a while," she said to the thirteen pairs of curious eyes. "But I'll return, so don't fret." Even though she knew they couldn't understand her, she needed to say goodbye and reassure them, or maybe just reassure herself.

"And when I come back, I'll be taking you on a journey to a brand new home, where you'll have just as much room to run and play as you do now. You're all good dogs, and I'll miss you."

They perked up at the words "good dogs," but since no treats seemed to be forthcoming, they settled back down. She turned to each dog, saying its name, and reaching out to stroke its ears.

"Turk, you're the biggest one here, and it's your job to protect the others. Spotter and Monk, you behave yourselves, you hear? No stealing rabbits from the gamesmen."

She turned to the next dogs in the circle. "Ruadh, sweetheart, you're so pretty. You eat well and keep that red coat nice and glossy. Mab and Gwyn, you help keep these boys in line."

The dogs stared at her solemnly as she continued. "Kenneth and Ailsa, I know what's been going on with you two, and I know you'll be doting parents. And I'll be back in time to help you whelp your puppies. And Bonny and Brid, you keep being so nice and well-mannered."

Last, she turned to the trio of dogs who had developed a friendship born of adversity, the three rescued hounds. "Cork, Mary and Charles," she said. "You mustn't think you're being abandoned. I promise you you're not." She reached out and gave each of them a quick hug.

"Now," she said briskly, rubbing her moist eyes, "it's time for me to leave for a while. Everyone go to your places." She stood up and clapped her hands three times.

Understanding the command, each of the dogs stood and moseyed toward its individual stall. She made one last pass by each dog, petting and cooing, making sure it knew it was loved.

Her final stop was at Charles's stall, where the newest member of the pack was regarding her with worried eyes. She gave him an extra-long hug. "Have faith, Charles. You'll see me again, I promise."

And then, before she broke down completely, she rushed out of the kennels, closing the door behind her, and heading to the house.

Sixty-Five

The Chadwick chapel had been constructed a century earlier on a far corner of the estate by the first Earl of Chadwick. That scholarly gentleman had believed it was good for the spirit to travel to services rather than to make no more effort than to cross through a doorway and enter a chapel that was simply another part of one's house.

The custom of maintaining a private clergyman had long since been abandoned, and the family these days was in the habit of attending services at the nearby village church. The family chapel, however, still served as the site of important family occasions such as weddings, baptisms, and funerals.

The old stone building rested on a small rise next to the family cemetery, protected by a grove of apple trees. Built to seat up to sixty guests, it provided a spacious and welcoming location for the wedding.

The guests began arriving shortly after ten for the ten-thirty ceremony. The morning had dawned clear and crisp, with the promise of a pleasant summer day, putting everyone in a festive mood.

As each group arrived, they were greeted by young Lords Thomas and Peter, who had been pressed into duty as ushers. Following the strict instructions given to them by the rather fearsome Lady Burton, the boys directed each group of guests to their appropriate pews.

The chapel was decorated with streamers fashioned of knotted ribbons intertwined with silk flowers and ivy. Pots of real flowers, robbed from the greenhouses of every estate in the neighborhood, stood at either side of the altar and along the chapel's side walls. The sun itself added to the colorful display by streaming through the large multi-colored leaded-glass windows that rose from floor to ceiling on either side of the east-facing entry.

As they were guided to their seats, even the most jaded of the Londoners found themselves delighted with the setting.

Nestling into her pew, Lady Griegson prodded her husband's shoulder with her index finger and hissed, "I want one of these."

"What? Your own private church building?" he hissed back in astonishment.

"Yes. I have every expectation that this style of wedding will become all the kick, once word gets back to Town. It will quite set us up to be first with the trend. Just think, we could hold weddings at our estate for all our relatives."

"I don't want anything to do with most of our relatives," the much-tried Lord Griegson said. "Who wants that passel of ninnies descending on us every time they have some sort of special do? And I expect they'd want me to foot the bill, as well."

"You can afford it," Lady Griegson whispered.

"Not for long at the rate you want to go on," he groused.

Their older daughter, Lady Alma, who had been listening in astonishment to her mother's idea, finally recommended her parents to hush. They both shot her affronted glances, but at least they ceased their argument. Lady Alma turned to look at her sister with raised eyebrows. Lady Cora replied with a roll of her eyes.

At last all the guests, Londoners and neighbors alike, were seated. The quartet of musicians from the earlier two musical evenings began plying their instruments. Which is when the guests distinctly heard the Duke's loud laughter coming from the room behind the altar.

"Oh, my God," he gasped between waves of guffaws as he got his first sight of the bride-to-be, "what the hell happened now?"

"That's exactly what John said," Elisabeth replied in embarrassment. "I look a fright, don't I?"

"What on earth did you do?" He bent closer to get a better look at the nicely purpled skin around her eye.

"She apparently dropped her guard while boxing with her sister," the Marquis said.

The Duke swung around in astonishment at the ultra-feminine Lady Anne. "You did this?"

"A flush hit," she acknowledged proudly.

The Duke turned to gape at the groom-to-be, and then broke into a fresh round of laughter.

When the Marquis, followed by the Duke and Lord Patrick, finally entered the nave from the door behind the altar, it was obvious to the guests that the Duke was manfully trying to contain his amusement. The Marquis glowered at his cousin, which only seemed to make it worse.

Elisabeth and her two attendants made their way by a side corridor to the back of the church, where Lord Chadwick waited to escort Elisabeth up the aisle. He gave her a light kiss on her forehead before lowering the heavy veil over her face.

As the guests rose for the bridal procession up the aisle, those in the pew closest to the Duke thought they heard him mutter something that sounded suspiciously like, "thank God for veils," before the Marquis elbowed him in the ribs.

The ceremony proceeded smoothly until Elisabeth, her back still to the guests, handed her posy to Lady Anne and lifted her veil. The vicar gave a start of surprise and jerked back a step. He looked to the Marquis, who shrugged his shoulders, and made some sort of gesture the guests couldn't see.

The vicar then swung his head to the bride's attendants, both of whom also appeared to be making hand signals. Lady Anne nodded her head vigorously. The vicar's brows rose nearly to his hairline, and he looked past Elisabeth to her father, seated in the first pew behind her. The Earl nodded once.

Shaking his head in obvious bewilderment, the vicar crossed himself, took a deep breath and proceeded with the service. It was when Elisabeth and the Marquis at last turned to face the audience after being pronounced husband and wife that everyone in the chapel clearly saw her right eye.

The guests gasped. The musicians faltered on their opening chords, then gamely began playing the recessional music as the bruised and battered Marquis and Marchioness of Edmonton happily walked down the aisle.

The Duke held out his hand to Lady Anne, but instead of placing her hand on his arm, he clasped her hand in his. As they followed the newlyweds down the aisle, the Duke held up their joined hands like a referee announcing the winner in a boxing match. Behind them, Lord Patrick and Lady Caroline burst into laughter. It was the strangest wedding recessional anyone had ever seen.

Sixty-Six

The guests followed the wedding party outside the chapel to where an open carriage decked in ribbons and silk flowers awaited the newlyweds. The Marquis helped his new Marchioness into the vehicle, and then watched as she retrieved her posy from her sister and tossed it into the milling crowd.

There was a brief commotion as the posy's arc was deflected by Lady Cora's outstretched fingers, slanted off Margaret's shoulder, and ended up being held by a surprised Lady Georgina, who'd simply been trying to avoid being hit in the face by the flying flowers.

"Oh my," Lady Georgina said, looking down at the posy in her hand.

Elisabeth turned from where she stood in the carriage and smiled down at her husband. The Marquis took his bride's hand and pulled her onto the seat next to him.

He gave the coachman orders to drive on to Loveland Manor, where the wedding feast was being held. As the carriage moved away, the guests were treated to the sight of the Marquis pulling his bride into a fierce and passionate embrace.

No one noticed the many small, whiskered creatures hiding in the grass that bordered the lane. The mice watched curiously as the carriage drove away. Then, glad the weather had at last returned to normal, they all turned and scurried back into the fields where they belonged.

The Marquis and Marchioness of Edmonton had to be reminded to get out of the carriage when it finally pulled up to Loveland Manor. Lost in the sensations of each other, they might have stayed clasped together for hours. But a few throat clearings from their driver, and the sound of their carriage door being opened finally made them aware of their surroundings.

"Shall we go inside and freshen up, my dear?" the Marquis asked Elisabeth. "We will want to look our best to greet our guests."

They made their way into the house, where the Marquis retired to his rooms and Elisabeth was led to the Dowager Marchioness's suite. There, she found not only her maid, but the Dowager Marchioness's dresser and the Dowager Countess's personal maid waiting to help smooth her gown and recomb her hair.

As she glanced around the room, she saw her traveling clothes laid out on the bed. The sight of the travel outfit hit her with a jolt. The clothes, more so than anything else that had happened today, were a tangible reminder that her old life was about to significantly change. She would be leaving the place she had spent most of her twenty-four years, and departing for a new life that, despite her enthusiasm and willingness to enter, still represented the unknown.

Elisabeth stood silently as the three servants fussed over her, straightening her wrinkled dress, removing some dirt smudges here and there, and tidying up her hairdo. Creams were applied sparingly to her hands and face, and a light misting of her favorite scent was spritzed on her hair. At last, the servants stepped back, satisfied with their work.

"There," the Dowager Marchioness's dresser said. "Please follow me, m'Lady. I am to take you to his Lordship."

Elisabeth thanked all of them before being guided to the same small upstairs sitting room where she had met with her father and great-aunt after the picnic. The Marquis was standing in the middle of the room waiting for her. A wide smile spread across his face as she entered. The dresser shut the door behind her, and they were alone.

She walked to him, arms outstretched. He took her hands in his and gazed at her in appreciation. "You are a beautiful bride, my dear, and I would kiss you again, but my valet has told me that, upon pain of death, I must not rewrinkle my clothes before we go down to greet our guests."

"Yes," she laughed. "I hope they arrive soon, because I feel quite like a mannequin who has been dressed up and must now stand unmoving in a store window."

"Well, we two mannequins shall stand here admiring each other while we wait." He gave her a rueful smile. "I am so sorry you had to sport such a shiner on your wedding day. I cannot imagine what the guests thought."

"Probably that we were the oddest bride and groom they had ever seen," said Elisabeth. "Perhaps we should both wear veils on our trip to your home so that the innkeepers do not turn us away."

"It is your home now, too, Elisabeth."

"Oh, yes," she said. "There will be so much to get used to."

"And we won't be staying at any inns, so you don't have to worry about that."

"We won't? But I thought it was a three-day ride to Edmonton Castle."

"It is, but I have sent riders ahead to make arrangements for us to stay at homes of friends on our way. You shall, literally, have all the comforts of home on our journey."

"Oh, dear. Who are these friends? We shall be guests in their homes?" The thought rather dismayed her.

He smiled. "Charles has a minor estate is less than a day away. We shall arrive there in the evening, but all will be in readiness for us."

"Charles?" she said in confusion, thinking of her dog.

"The Duke of Ravenwood," he clarified, "my cousin, who so ably obeyed your instructions to get down, sit, and stay."

She giggled. "Oh! Of course."

"And he shall not be joining us, never fear. He has sent instructions ahead to the staff there to put us up for a day or two. After that we shall stay at the home of a friend of mine you haven't met, but who has agreed to make his home available as well. He is in London at present, so once again we shall have the place to ourselves. Along with his army of servants, of course."

"Of course," she repeated, adjusting her thoughts about what the trip would entail. She much preferred his plans to the series of inns she had envisioned.

"And then we shall arrive at our home," he said. "I thought we would stay there a week or two so you could become familiar with the estate and the servants. Too, you will want to take some time to consider how you will want to redecorate your rooms and the private sitting room that connects our suites. And, of course, you'll want to decide where to build the dog kennels."

"And then?"

"And then it is up to you, my dear Marchioness. You must tell me where you would like to go on our wedding trip and I will begin making the arrangements."

She took a step forward to give him an impulsive hug before remembering they must not muss their clothes. It wouldn't do to give the guests the wrong idea about what they'd been doing since the wedding. She gave him a frustrated look.

He laughed. "It won't be much longer. They are arriving now."

The newlyweds listened to the sounds of the guests entering the house. A quarter of an hour later there was a knock at the door of the sitting room.

"Enter," said the Marquis.

The door opened to admit Applewood. He bowed. "They are ready for you now, m'Lord, m'Lady. Please follow me, if you would."

The butler led them down the stairs. They waited outside the main salon until Applewood nodded to the two footmen standing outside the doors. The footmen flung open the doors with a flourish as the butler loudly announced, "The Marquis and Marchioness of Edmonton!"

The throng of guests all turned toward the doorway and applauded as the newlyweds entered the room. Servants began distributing champagne as everyone surged forth to make their congratulations and engage the couple in conversation.

Elisabeth found herself separated from her husband as the female guests swarmed around her, complimenting her on her gown, commenting on the delightful wedding chapel decorations, and asking her about her honeymoon plans. She was surprised at first that no one mentioned her black eye, but learned through a quick whisper from Caroline that Anne and the Duke had explained everything back at the chapel.

"They were much shocked at first," Caroline said softly, "but the Duke convinced them that the two of you are originals who will set your own fashion."

"Well I sincerely doubt we will be setting a fashion for bruised faces," Elisabeth giggled.

As Lady Griegson, with her daughters Alma and Cora in tow, approached, Caroline moved aside to allow the three to offer their felicitations.

"My dear Marchioness," Lady Griegson crooned. "I am so delighted to have been a part of today's events. You must call upon us when next you visit London."

"Yes, do," Lady Alma said sincerely. "I should so like to get to know you better."

"I understand you'll be spending much of your time at Edmonton Castle," Lady Cora said with a bright smile. "Is it as bad as they say?"

Elisabeth smiled, "My husband assures me it is quite comfortable. I am looking forward to seeing it."

Lady Cora's eyes flashed, but she maintained her smile. Her mother quickly tugged her daughters away before her younger daughter could say anything else offensive.

The space vacated by the Griegsons was immediately filled by the new Lady Wentworth, whose congratulations were punctuated by a series of giggles. Despite being prepared to dislike the young woman the Dowager Marchioness had thought to make her daughter-in-law, Elisabeth found Lady Wentworth to be more silly than threatening.

"I know you will enjoy being a bride as much as I do," Lady Wentworth said. "I am so delighted in my marriage. I have ordered so many new gowns."

"Thank you," Elisabeth said uncertainly, listening as Lady Wentworth went on to describe several of the dresses she'd ordered.

She was rescued by the return of Caroline, this time with Anne in tow. Elisabeth turned to her sister, "Anne, did you really admit to everyone that you hit me?"

"Yes, of course," her sister said with a grin. "I am very proud of it. I never was able to land a hit on either you or Robbie in all the time I was growing up."

"But are you not worried about what people will say?" Elisabeth asked in concern.

"Oh, pooh. When have you ever cared what people think about you? And I certainly don't. The Duke has already defended us, and Marcus will stand buff. And if my husband doesn't mind, then I assure you I don't."

Caroline smiled. "It is one of the best things about being married, Elisabeth. There is much more freedom to do and say what you think."

They were interrupted by the graceful approach of Lady Georgina. As Anne and Caroline moved away, Lady Georgina smiled at Elisabeth.

"I have enjoyed meeting you," Lady Georgina said. "This has been a most pleasant few weeks. And you have my sincere best wishes for a happy union."

Elisabeth smiled back. "Thank you. I look forward to attending your upcoming wedding."

At Lady Georgina's startled look, Elisabeth's smile widened. "You did catch the bouquet, remember."

Lady Georgina laughed somewhat ruefully. "A superstition, nothing more, Lady Loveland."

"Oh, my," Elisabeth said, her turn to be startled. "I am not used to my new name."

Lady Georgina gave her a considering look. "You are most unusual. This really does signify very little to you, doesn't it?"

"What do you mean?"

"Most married women I know revel in their new titles. They spend time practicing their new names in front of a mirror before the wedding, just waiting for the moment they will hear them said by others."

Elisabeth thought about it for a moment before replying. "I revel in the man, not the title, Lady Georgina."

"So you do," Lady Georgina said with a sincere smile. "I look forward to seeing you again." She gave a small nod and walked away.

Her place was immediately taken by Lady Childer and her daughters Violet and Rose. All of them encouraged Elisabeth to visit them in London.

"For you know," Lady Childer said, "I should like to introduce you to everyone I know."

As a circus act, Elisabeth suspected, as she politely thanked Lady Childer for the invitation. She glanced across the room and met her husband's gaze. He gave her a warm smile before turning back to talk with Anne's husband. She wished she could make her way to the buffet table, but apparently the guests of honor weren't allowed to eat.

Lady Downs approached next, followed by Sir Mendam and the Dowager Marchioness. All three gave their sincere congratulations and best wishes. Elisabeth was greatly relieved at the Dowager's attitude, and gave her a genuinely warm smile. The Dowager's reaction was to burst into tears.

"Oh, my dear child!" the Dowager cried. "I've waited so long for this day!" She fell forward and flung her arms around Elisabeth, clasping her tightly. Elisabeth desperately tried to avoid toppling backward under the Dowager's weight.

She was saved from that fate by Sir Clapham, who had arrived with Margaret on his arm. He and Sir Mendam each took one of the Dowager's arms and pried her off her new daughter-in-law.

"I am so happy!" the Dowager exclaimed, bursting into a renewed bout of tears as she clung to a surprised Sir Clapham.

Sir Mendam leaned in and whispered to Elisabeth. "You must know, dear girl, that her Ladyship has always liked you."

"She has?" Elisabeth whispered back doubtfully.

Sir Mendam gave a small smile. "You are thinking of that regrettable scene the night you announced your engagement, aren't you?"

Elisabeth nodded.

"Her Ladyship has a great deal of sensibility, as you may have noticed. John's procurement of a special license rattled her. I fear she was a tad disappointed that she wasn't going to have the pleasure of helping you plan a large, formal wedding. That's all it was, I assure you."

Elisabeth nodded again, wondering privately what kind of reaction to expect if ever her new mother-in-law were more than "a tad" disappointed by something.

Sir Mendam patted Elisabeth on the shoulder and turned to pry the sobbing Lady Loveland off of Sir Clapham. As he led her away, Elisabeth could hear Lady Downs making tsking noises at such a display.

Elisabeth turned to Margaret and Sir Clapham, who was now free of Lady Loveland. Margaret leaned forward and gave Elisabeth a hug.

"I am so happy for you," Margaret said, as she stepped back.

"And I am happy for you as well," Elisabeth smiled at the petite brunette. "I think you and Sir Clapham are a fine match."

"Where are you going on your honeymoon?" Lady Downs asked, from Elisabeth's other side.

"The Mar... that is, my husband... says I may choose anywhere I like. Anne thinks it should be Paris."

"Ooh," Margaret breathed. "I have never been to Paris."

Sir Clapham looked down at her with a smile. "Do I take that to mean you might like a wedding trip to the sights of the Continent, my dear?"

"Wait until later," said Lady Downs. "You will like it much better in the fall. And you can have new gowns made there just before the Season."

Elisabeth and Margaret exchanged smiles at this comment, and Elisabeth noticed Margaret's mother hovering a few feet away, but not approaching.

"Mrs. Benson-Smythe," Elisabeth said, acknowledging her. Mrs. Benson-Smythe flinched.

Margaret turned and held out a hand to her mother. "Mother, come say your best wishes to Lady Elisabeth."

"To Lady Loveland," her mother corrected automatically as she moved forward with obvious reluctance.

"Grace," Lady Downs said with a crocodile smile. "I've been hoping to have the opportunity to speak with you anytime these past weeks."

"Lady Downs," Mrs. Benson-Smythe said, looking as though she wished the floor would swallow her. "I haven't seen you since my come out."

"And I should like to catch up," Lady Downs stated. "You may give our new bride your felicitations and then we shall talk."

"Oh dear," Mrs. Benson-Smythe said. She turned to Elisabeth, pulling her attention away from the woman who had tormented her with criticisms of her behavior and manners during her two Seasons.

"My dear Lady Loveland, please accept my best wishes on your marriage," Mrs. Benson-Smythe said, as she dipped a slight curtsey.

"Very good," Lady Downs commented. "Now, you may escort me to that table over there."

Elisabeth watched as the two women departed.

"What was that all about?" Sir Clapham asked Margaret. "Your mother looks like a schoolgirl about to be read a lecture."

"Apparently Lady Downs served as a self-appointed mentor to Mama when she was first on the Town," Margaret said. "I gather she rather terrified Mama."

"Well I know that feeling," Elisabeth said. "Lady Downs and Great-Aunt Lister have both appointed themselves my advisors for years. I am a great source of frustration for them."

Sir Clapham laughed at that, and led Margaret off to find Mr. Benson-Smythe to help rescue Mrs. Benson-Smythe.

Caroline and Anne quickly approached and began talking about possible honeymoon locations. Elisabeth listened politely while her eyes jealously tracked the guests' inroads on the buffet table.

The Marquis was enjoying the congratulations of the male guests, but he was growing impatient to be off. As the men moved away one by one, lured by the foods being offered, the Marquis found himself standing with Lord Marcus Conners, his new brother-in-law.

"Conners," the Marquis began.

"Please, Monton. It's Marcus. We're both married to Chadwicks now."

"And call me John, if you like," the Marquis nodded. "And perhaps you can give me some pointers on how to survive being married to a Chadwick."

"That's easy," the Baron laughed. "You just do whatever they tell you!"

The Marquis returned a grin. "Yes, I'm rapidly coming to that realization. What a lucky pair of men we are." He turned and gave a warm smile to his bride, who stood across the room chatting with her sister and sister-in-law.

The Duke moved up to join the Marquis and Lord Conners. "John, your mother sent me over here to tell you it's time to leave."

"Kicking me out of her dower house already, is she?"

"I expect the rest of us will be kicked out in the next day or so. But she's right. If you're to reach today's destination before nightfall, you'd better change soon. Shall I have the carriages called around for you?"

The Marquis glanced at his pocket watch. "Yes, tell them to be ready in half an hour. I'll go retrieve Elisabeth."

Elisabeth watched with interest as her husband approached her. Perhaps he was about to escort her to the buffet.

Anne and Caroline stepped away as the Marquis bent down to speak softly into Elisabeth's ear. "It's time to get ready to depart, my dear. We should leave within the hour."

"What? No!" she wailed.

He pulled back slightly and looked at her in surprise. She rested a hand on his arm. "I'm hungry! I haven't had a chance to eat!"

He laughed. "I'll have some food brought up to our rooms while we change, how's that?"

"All right then, let's go." The hand on his arm gave a little tug.

"Ah, so eager," he grinned. "Now I know how to motivate you."

"Don't tease me, John. I think I shall faint from lack of food. I didn't eat more than a biscuit and some tea this morning, and two tiny little sandwiches after we arrived here. And now it's well past noon."

He signaled a hovering servant and requested food be brought up to their rooms and a food basket be prepared for the carriage.

"Yes, m'Lord. I'll have food brought up. The carriage baskets are ready, including the special one." The servant turned and hurried away before the Marquis could ask what he'd meant by a special basket. Perhaps one with some special delicacies?

He turned to Elisabeth and allowed her to pull him out of the room. He was quite sure she didn't realize that everyone would mistake her eagerness to leave for a desire for something other than food.

He turned to glance back to the Duke and saw his cousin leaving the room with his younger brother Lord Peter and young Lord Thomas Griegson.

Sixty-Seven

In the Dowager Marchioness's chambers, Elisabeth was making it difficult for the three servants to remove her wedding dress. She kept twisting to reach for the food tray that had arrived while they tried to undo the buttons on her sleeves. Only the promise of ten minutes of unfettered access to the small sandwiches, meat pies and tea after her gown was removed gave her the willpower to wait.

Once the gown was finally off, Elisabeth hurried to the food tray. She sat there in her slip happily stuffing herself while the servants carefully brushed and smoothed her dress before placing it in a tissue box. It would go back to Chadwick Manor for safekeeping, to be stored alongside Anne's wedding dress and their mother's gown.

Her ten minutes stretched to a quarter of an hour before she was sated. She finally stood up, washed her hands and face, and submitted to being placed into her traveling clothes. Her gold and cream outfit was set off by matching cream-colored gloves and a cream-colored hat festooned with a small cluster of gold and green ribbons. The green ribbons exactly matched her eyes.

She looked at the hat with a small smile. It had never sported green ribbons before. Her great-aunt had been busy. She knew the ribbons were the Dowager Countess's way of showing her affection, and the realization brought tears to Elisabeth's eyes.

At last, nearly an hour after leaving the party, she was ready. A message was sent to the Marquis, who presented himself at the doorway to escort her down the stairs.

As they descended the main staircase, they saw the guests thronging the hall, looking up at them with smiles. Their progress to the door was delayed by the embraces, hugs and handshakes bestowed on them by the company. If the happiness displayed by Lords Childer and Griegson had more to do with the anticipation of getting back to their homes than any good wishes for the newlyweds, it went unnoticed.

As she and her new husband walked outside, followed by the guests, Elisabeth found her father and great-aunt waiting for her, along with Lady Downs. She ran to her father, who enveloped her in a long hug.

"Be happy, my child," he said into her ear. "And though I certainly hope you won't need it, you will always have a home here."

He pulled back slightly and fished a small packet out of his pocket. "From your mother," was all he said. Elisabeth opened the wrapping to discover a pearl and diamond necklace with matching earbobs.

"Oh, Papa, I remember her wearing these. Oh, thank you so much. I will treasure them."

He drew her in for another long hug, giving her a kiss on her cheek. "Go on, now."

She moved to her great-aunt, whose fierce expression was belied by misty eyes. Elisabeth reached up and stroked the green ribbons on her traveling hat and smiled at the Dowager Countess. "Ma'am, thank you so much for everything you have worked to teach me for so many years."

"Hmph. Just you make me proud, missy," the Dowager said, and nodded briskly. Not for her the modern act of embracing in public.

Elisabeth moved to Lady Downs, who had no such scruples about giving Elisabeth a brief embrace. "I am glad for you," she said. "I could not have hoped for a better life for you, Elisabeth. You must stay in touch. I depend upon you to write."

"I shall, Lady Downs, I promise," Elisabeth smiled.

She turned to where her husband was attempting to extricate himself from his mother's clinging embrace. He at last succeeded in shifting her onto his brother who, aided by the silent Lord Richard Ringwood, manfully bore up under the Dowager Marchioness's weight.

The Marquis then turned to the Duke, who stood next to the carriage, beaming as only a mischief-maker could.

"Yes, Charles?" the Marquis asked suspiciously. Well he knew his cousin. "Have you managed to somehow booby-trap our carriage?"

"Nothing like," the Duke said innocently. "The boys and I have a small gift for the two of you, that's all."

The Marquis reached out a hand for Elisabeth as Lords Peter and Thomas carried a large woven basket covered by a cloth out from behind the carriage. They carefully set it at the feet of the Marquis and Marchioness. Family members and guests gathered to watch.

As the boys pulled back the cloth cover, a shaggy gray head popped up and gave a small yip.

"Oh, what a little beauty!" Elisabeth exclaimed. She knelt down and hurriedly peeled off one glove to let the Scottish deerhound puppy sniff her hand. She looked up at the Duke. "Where did you ever find him?"

The Duke grinned. "Thought you might like him. The boys here have been working hard to teach him his manners and some basic commands. He knows sit, stay, beg, come, and down, so he arrives ready to behave."

"But surely you couldn't have done all that just since our engagement," Elisabeth protested.

"No, I did that somewhat earlier. Had the idea a wedding gift might be needed after seeing your effect on John, here."

The puppy stood and glanced up at the Duke.

"Yes," the Duke said, reaching down to scratch the puppy behind its ears. "You know your name, don't you boy?"

He glanced at Lords Peter and Thomas. "You did an excellent job training him, lads. I am greatly in your debt."

The boys beamed proudly as Elisabeth added her thanks and told them what a wonderful gift they had arranged.

"What name does he know?" the Marquis asked, an unpleasant suspicion beginning to form.

His cousin smiled at him maliciously. "Sit, John."

The puppy sat.

"He'll be a comfort to you on your trip to Edmonton Castle," the Duke said.

"Oh, no he won't," the Marquis objected at the same time Elisabeth said, "Oh, what a wonderful idea."

Her husband stared at her in disbelief.

She gave him her melting smile.

The Marquis glanced at Lord Conners, who merely raised his eyebrows and shrugged his shoulders. He glanced at Elisabeth's father, who was struggling to contain his amusement. Elisabeth's brother gave him a wide grin. Behind him, he could hear a growing number of chuckles coming from the other men of the party. He gave up.

"Yes," the Marquis said to Elisabeth through gritted teeth. "I cannot imagine anything more delightful than taking a puppy with us on our wedding trip."

"Oh, thank you! It will give you a chance to learn to love the breed as much as I do! He can ride with us in our carriage, for it is much roomier than the servants' carriage." She stood up to give him a quick embrace, and turned to the boys. "And what a nice basket you have provided. He will feel quite safe and secure in it."

"And we have arranged a special basket of food and water for him, as well," Lord Thomas said.

"Oh, you've thought of everything," she said with a warm smile. "I thank you most sincerely. This is above all that is delightful!"

The Marquis gave his cousin an evil glance, "Yes, thank you, Charles, you have thought of everything."

The Duke gave his cousin a hearty slap on his back. "I knew this would be just the thing. Now, let's get little John up in the carriage, shall we?" He signaled to two footmen to help hoist the basket and puppy onto the floor of the carriage.

The Marquis and Marchioness of Edmonton turned once more to the assembled company and gave their farewells before climbing into the carriage. Elisabeth leaned out the window, waving to everyone until the carriage pulled around a curve in the drive and out of sight of the manor.

She leaned back from the window and felt her husband's arm come around her waist. She looked up at him, love and joy shining from her eyes.

"Well," he said, drawing her closer. "We have at least five hours until we reach tonight's destination, and at least an hour or so before our first puppy break. How do you propose we use our time to best advantage?"

He moved toward her, his intent clear in his heated gaze.

She pushed him slightly away, glanced at the puppy, already curled up asleep, and gave her husband a teasing look from under lowered eyelashes.

"I hope you're as well-trained as your namesake," she said to the Marquis.

"Oh?" he asked. "What is it you want me to do?"

She leaned forward, her lips just grazing his mouth. In her sultriest voice, she whispered, "Beg, John."

The End

Next

To find out what happens next, read Georgina and the Duke, Book Two of the House Party Series.

Ann Snyder

About the Author

Ann Snyder has been writing since before she could print the alphabet. Her first stories, scribbled as a toddler, took the form of ink drawings sketched on every piece of paper and cardboard she could find. This sometimes included the papers her mother was grading and her father's legal briefs, to the confusion of her mother's elementary school students and her father's clients.

She first became interested in England's Regency period while at The University of Iowa when she took a course that compared the art, literature, and music of various periods in history. From there, she began to study the customs and social conventions of that era, and began writing Regency-based fiction.

She has worked for more than twenty-five years as a business writer and communications professional. With the release of Elisabeth and the Marquis, Ann has returned to her first love – writing tales of romance, humor and adventure.

Ann Snyder